WE ARE DYING GODS

Wrath of the Gods: Book 2

C. M. Lockhart

MAP OF THE REALM

Scan the QR code to view the map for the book!

Or visit WrittenInMelanin.com/wato_map

OUT OF CONTEXT COMMENTS FOR WE ARE DYING GODS

Ashleigh D.
9:31 AM May 29

Girl! Leave that boi alone. Matter of fact leave them all alone.

Frederick Asamoa…
4:22 PM Apr 3

I'd give Sarah a hug, but she's all vomity.

Frederick Asamoa…
4:30 PM Apr 3

I rescind my hug offer

La Purvis
12:11 PM Apr 8

This opening. Omg. I already have goosebumps.

Ashleigh D.
8:14 AM Jun 10

This is a very clear description. Really, all the realms are well defined. Lovely.

Amanda Ross
Nov 30, 2022

I know that's right! I LOVE Jack

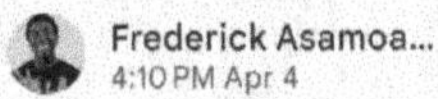

Frederick Asamoa...
4:10 PM Apr 4

Read the room shawty 😂

La Purvis
12:14 PM Apr 8

IN THIS ONE INSTANCE.... I understand, Sarah. The IMAGERY. Fek.

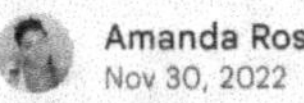

Amanda Ross
Nov 30, 2022

She's so DUMB. Like if she actually stood for something and did something for a change she'd be respected but she's just so goofy

Ashleigh D.
9:57 AM Jun 9

Dark as hell, but not wrong. Dammit.

La Purvis
7:45 PM Jun 17

Cause she eeeeevilllll

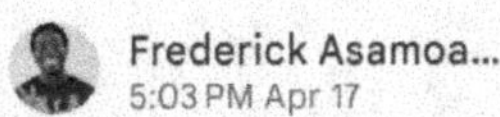

Frederick Asamoa...
5:03 PM Apr 17

Use talk-no-jutsu! I don't want to see them fight! He seems like a fine fellow 😄

La Purvis
2:26 PM Jun 19

Omg I'm so proud of her. Look at this baby grow. YES SARAH!!!!!

For the Black girls who never wanted to be magic.
You — simply existing — are enough.

CHAPTER ONE

In every generation, the goddess shall be more. More than the mortals, more than the gods, more than herself. She will come to embody a wrath that will destroy the realm and create it anew.

— Freya and the Power of Incarnation | Lindl's First Holy Academy

---

FREYA'S DOMAIN — FREYA'S TEMPLE

PRESENT DAY

"What will you do now that you wield the power of the goddess?"

Cedric's soft voice cut through the noise of the battle, demanding Brandi's attention as they stood on the fractured stone steps leading up to what was left of Freya's temple. The tall, white pillars and colorful murals had all fallen into indecipherable mounds of rubble. The smooth stone floors were smashed into jagged pieces and all that was left of Freya's temple — of Brandi's first home — was Freya's throne. Even with the entire temple turned to dust around them, it stood as imposing and unwavering as the goddess herself.

Brandi had to force herself to tear her gaze away from the empty seat and tried to keep her heart from racing at the thought of carrying the mantle that came with the power Freya gifted her. She turned to look at Cedric as he moved to stand next to her. His violet eyes were bright as they bore into hers, searching for some answer within her gaze as if he could read her thoughts with as much ease as the holy texts in Lindl's academies. She held his gaze and shrugged. She didn't have an answer to his question.

In truth, Brandi hadn't even begun processing the fact that Freya had relinquished her power and her title of goddess of the realm — that all the gods had done the same. Brandi felt her blood warming inside her veins, thrumming with a bold new power she'd never felt before, but she didn't feel as if she'd ascended to something greater than what she'd always been. What did it matter that Freya had given up her mantle? Brandi was still a shadow, and right now, all that mattered was the carnage that waited for them on the battlefield.

The clang of weapons against shields and armor echoed throughout the clearing, and Brandi's green eyes couldn't look away from the scene playing out in front of them. A fog of red clung to the air, hovering above the ground and carrying the stench of copper, sweat, and vomit. Mangled bodies littered the ground as the rebels fought against Bert's forces, holding their ground as the shaders Brandi had called forth gathered along the edges of the clearing, waiting for new orders.

They'd retreated to the edges with Lia after they'd devoured Saya, and the battle had escalated far beyond the single shot Brandi had lodged in Bert's shoulder. It was a sight that Brandi had never seen before, and she'd sent more than her fair share of souls back to the gods. As the incarnation of Freya — the goddess of life and the judger of souls — and the queen's blade, Brandi had long since grown immune to the horrors of death. But her targets had always had names and faces, final words whispered on dying breaths. She'd never shied away from watching the light leave their eyes, but watching dozens of souls return to the gods in a single battle was something that stole Brandi's words from her.

The rebels were far more skilled, but most of them were shadows — trained on how to execute their orders without ever being noticed. They weren't trained for large-scale combat, and the soldiers of the queendom outnumbered them three to one. This was a battle they wouldn't win. It was obvious from the screams of dying men and the cries of wounded women, but it was the guttural sound of Sarah retching on the ground behind them, and the sheer stench of it all that turned Brandi's stomach. But it also lit a spark within her.

She wanted to join the battle.

She wanted to feel her blade slicing through the pliant skin of her enemies and claim the life of every soldier who dared to march on Freya's holy ground without invitation. But, more than anything, she wanted to gut the man with hazel eyes who stood on the other side of the battlefield. He clutched his shoulder, blood still seeping through his suit jacket where she'd shot him, but it was clear how at ease he felt standing behind the rear guard.

Two lines of soldiers stood in front of him. The first row bore the crest of the queen on their deep blue uniforms and carried eurithium shields. Second in strength only to the harvested teeth and nails of shaders, the transparent shields were made of minerals mined from beneath the burned sands of the Scorched Desert. Only the queen's personal force carried them, and the fact that they stood in the midst of this battle was telling of how deeply the queen cared for Bert. The second row of soldiers were draped in the deep violet cloaks that signified them as Bert's league of blasphemous researchers. They clutched at the palm-sized spheres that hung around their necks, aiming invisible projectiles at the rebels, no doubt trying to use one of Bert's inventions to even the playing field against those blessed by the gods.

The mere sight of Adam Bertanal flooded Brandi's senses with fresh rage. She took a step forward off the stone steps, ready to launch herself across the battlefield and kick Bert's face in until he had nightmares of her boot in his next life, but Tiki placed one giant paw in her path to stop her.

Brandi's green eyes shot up to its eyeless face, ready to question Tiki on why it would stop her instead of aiding her in crossing the clearing so it could devour Bert itself, but the limp arm dangling from between Tiki's razor-sharp teeth and the pile of mangled corpses piling up at its feet quelled Brandi's rage as realization set in. Tiki had been guarding the entrance to the temple while they'd been meeting with the gods. The rage it felt was no different from her own, but there were times when protecting someone was more important than destroying an enemy. Being able to recognize that moment was a skill that was perfected with time and Brandi struggled to remember that, grasping at the fringes of her patience as she restrained her more reckless impulses.

She had no actual way of knowing how long they'd been away from the battle since time moved slower whenever they were in the presence of the gods. They could have been gone for moments, or it could have been hours. Regardless, the fighting was more than what they'd left it as and the rebels were being pushed back. Attempting to rush across the battlefield now to send Bert to the gods would be little more than a fool's errand — she could admit that. And though she had no real loyalty to the rebels, the only reason they were fighting in the first place was because she'd asked Glenn for their help when Jack had been taken. So, she wouldn't just abandon them, but the only one who was able to truly hold their ground against Bert's forces was Najé.

Holding true to her promise to fight for Brandi's side, she led the charge against the soldiers who'd come to serve as Bert's reinforcements. She was covered in blood and vomit, her sweat tracing rivulets down her brown face as her lithe frame ducked and cut through the mass of soldiers who attempted to attack her all at once. Her long braids bounced against her back as she stopped in her tracks to avoid the wild swing of a soldier's blade before she drew her knee up to ram it into the groin of her next attacker. He doubled over and she dragged her dagger across the nape of his neck, stepping aside to let him fall to the ground as she faced the next two soldiers approaching her.

She was fighting with all her strength, but Brandi could see the exhaustion edging in on her moves. She was sharper than the rest of the rebels, but she was only one woman, and the soldiers were a unit trained on crushing dissent in the queendom. They were patient in waiting for their opportunities to strike, protected in their armor, and practiced on how to destroy an unorganized rebellion. And despite their skill, the rebels all fought as individuals or in clusters of three. They had no leader to command them and no idea how to fight as a cohesive force.

If something didn't change soon, the rebels would fall and Bert would return to the queen's side, lauded as a hero. He would be rewarded for what would be seen as a self-righteous effort to protect his queen and her throne. The simple thought of that made Brandi grind her teeth.

Command us.

The words slipped into her mind as gentle as rain against her skin and Brandi looked over to Tiki, whose black tongue lapped up the blood dripping from its giant maw and felt her heart pound at the words. This battle was hers to fight. And, for once, she wasn't alone in it.

"How you feeling?" Brandi asked, directing her question to Noble and Jack. She could feel her blood warming beneath her skin, throbbing in her veins with every heartbeat. The power she carried now was almost suffocating with how much of it swelled in her chest and she wondered if the others felt the same. "Can you fight?"

"I feel like Rothe just shoved the whole sun down my throat, but," Jack released a deep breath, sparks drifting from his smirking lips as a gold ring circled his brown eyes, "yeah. I can fight."

"I'm always good to go," Noble said as the wind picked up around them. "Just tell me what you need, Green."

"We need to put an end to this," Brandi said. "Najé's drowning," she pointed out, nodding in her direction, "and we need to get the rebels out of the clearing."

"And then what?" Noble questioned. "Bert's not just going to let the rebels run away."

"I'm not going to give him a choice," Brandi said, glaring at the man standing on the other side of the clearing and channeling the heat circulating through her veins into her hands where a green light bloomed beneath her fingertips.

"How long do we have?" Jack asked, glancing down at her.

"Three minutes," she answered. "Both of you need to be behind the tree line before then."

They nodded at her words and moved into action. Noble cut through the battle, gliding through the rebels and soldiers as if he were Carna's wind. He headed straight for where Najé fought in a circle of soldiers that inched closer to her, while Jack stood and worked to control his blessing from Rothe. Like Najé and many of the other devout Rothians who fought with the shadows, he had been blessed by Rothe before he ever met Brandi — gifted with the ability to increase his strength tenfold. But with Rothe's full power residing in him now, Brandi saw the brief moment he struggled to contain it all. It was short-lived, but she didn't miss the burst of flames that spiraled up his arm to his elbow before dissipating into a cloud of smoke, leaving a faint golden light emanating from beneath his brown skin. He cracked his knuckles and strode into battle, smashing through the metal helmets of the soldiers who approached him and gripping the rebels by the nape of their necks before hurling them toward the trees.

"Catch them," Brandi said, giving the order to the shaders who began moving to break their falls.

"What of us?" Cedric inquired, his violet eyes locking onto hers as she turned to meet his gaze. He stood beside Sarah, her long hair in his hand as she kneeled on the ground and she tossed the last of her stomach into the grass next to the stairs.

"Can you fight?"

"I'm a scholar," Cedric said, shaking his head.

"Then take Sarah and get out of here," Brandi said, directing them toward the forest beyond the destroyed temple. The battle was contained in the clearing before them and the silence beyond the trees felt louder than the war cries of the rebels. "Head north until you reach another clearing covered in moss and fallen trees. There will be shaders there," she warned, "but they won't bother the vessels of the gods. You'll be safer than here."

"Alright," Cedric said, his eyes wide and his voice shaking at the mention of shaders. "We'll wait for you there."

"And pray to the gods while you wait," Brandi demanded, Freya's abdication of her throne creating worrying thoughts in her mind. "See if you can reach them. We need to know if we're really alone in all this now."

"Understood."

Cedric nodded and reached down to pull Sarah's arm over his shoulder and help her up from the ground, but he released her when her face turned an unpleasant shade of green at the sudden movement and she lost her stomach again. Both he and Brandi looked down at her with mild disgust as she swiped at the vomit clinging to her bottom lip before staggering to her feet. She wobbled but managed to keep her balance as Cedric stepped forward to help her.

"Make sure she rests up," Brandi told him. "There's going to be a lot of wounded rebels who will need her attention."

Cedric nodded again and Brandi watched as he led Sarah to the edge of the clearing. When they disappeared behind the trees, she turned her attention back to the battle. Najé and Noble were gone from the clearing and only Jack remained, dragging the last of the rebels behind him, their unconscious bodies piling up as he fought to protect them from Bert's encroaching forces. He was the last one remaining and Brandi took a deep breath as she whispered the words that had always lived on the tip of her tongue.

"Bless me," she whispered, hissing as a heat like nothing she'd ever felt surged through her, burning her skin from the inside out, ***"for I am the wrath of the gods."***

As always, her bow formed in the palm of her hand, manifesting in a wave of searing heat. She huffed out a breath of steaming air and worked to keep her hands steady as fire pulsed within her palms. She tried to keep her mind clear, but molten lava dripped down her spine, drying her tongue and tingling her scalp, nearly forcing her onto her knees. She gasped and focused on Jack, who was still fighting in the center of the clearing. She forced her mind to chase after the single desire of protecting him — of ending this battle and having the time to be grateful that Asari had healed him from Bert's torture — as she opened her green eyes wide. Light built behind them until they were bright enough to rival the light of Rothe's sun and she lifted her bow to the sky, releasing a fiery arrow that was wrapped in the same green flames she'd manifested before when she'd entered the clearing.

It exploded into a thousand more and the soldiers in Bert's rear guard that carried the eurithium shields huddled together and raised them to the skies, protecting them from the blazing green fire that rained down on everyone left in the clearing. Jack stood still in the center of the barrage and not a single arrow came close to hitting him or the rebels he'd saved. The high-pitched screams of the soldiers were the only sounds that filled the air until they were replaced by the crackling of flames that licked at the charred flesh and broken bones that were left behind.

Brandi pulled another arrow and pointed it at Bert as she took measured steps into the clearing with Tiki following behind her. The flames on the ground danced at her approach, parting at her feet as Tiki began ripping into the bodies that clung to the last bit of their life. It threw its head back and released a sharp bark that brought forth the other shaders from the trees, hemming in the last of the soldiers as they began following Tiki's lead and cleaning up the remains of the battlefield.

The soldiers protecting Bert shook at the display, their uniformed shield breaking and creating gaps as many of them lost their will to fight and dropped to their knees with looks of horror and despair written on their faces. Brandi held Bert's gaze in an unwavering stare as she moved to stand next to Jack.

"There's no point in running, Bert," Brandi called out, her voice low and even as she spoke to him. "This is where you return to the gods."

"Return me to the gods?" Bert scoffed at Brandi's words and his lip curled as he looked down his nose at her, no doubt feeling secure behind half a dozen soldiers with near-indestructible shields. "You have forgotten your place," he spat. "You dare speak to me with such authority? You're nothing more than —"

Brandi released her arrow, letting it find a home between the brown eyes of a soldier with deep brown skin that had grown ashen in fear. Her head rocked back from the force of the arrow, and her shield clattered to the ground as her body went rigid and crumpled beneath her weight. Blood pooled around her and the remaining soldiers gasped as they clamored to fill the gap her absence created. They stood firm in their positions, but Brandi had made her point.

"You've forgotten who I am," Brandi stated, narrowing her eyes. "Your status means nothing to me. I'll send you to the gods, same as everyone else."

"Brandi," Jack said, her name a gentle whisper as he placed a hand on her wrist. "We have to let him go."

"What?" Brandi questioned, her green eyes darting up to Jack's. His face was set in a hard line and his brown eyes bore into Bert's. "You can't be serious?"

"We're not ready to fight the entire queendom," Jack said, looking down at her. "If we send him now, the entire monarchy is going to press down on us."

"And? I don't care about that."

"Then what was the point of saving any of these people?"

His question wasn't harsh, but it was unexpected. It was rare for Jack to think outside of what was best for them, and them alone, but his words served as a reminder to her that they were surrounded by hundreds of wounded and exhausted rebels. She could feel their eyes on her skin, watching to see what they'd do next. With Glenn gone and Najé exhausted, they were without a leader to guide them and, for better or worse, she and Jack were now filling that role for the time being.

If she sent Bert to the gods now, it would be the same as declaring war on the monarchy. That wasn't much of a problem for her or Jack, but they'd already seen the outcome of what would happen if the rebels went up against the queen's soldiers in an all-out battle. It wouldn't be pretty. And Jack had a point — what was the purpose of saving them from this battle if she was just going to lead them into another?

"I want to send him too, Bee," Jack whispered through clenched teeth. "But now's not the time."

Her entire body pulsed with a burning heat as she held his gaze before returning it to Bert, but she lowered her bow as she watched him. Jack made a valid point, and if he was willing to be patient in sending Bert to the gods, then so could she.

"Leave," she demanded. "This is not the moment I send you to the gods, but once the battlefield is clear, I won't stop them."

Brandi watched as Bert's hazel eyes darted to the shaders surrounding them. Tiki sat to her left and Lia stood on Jack's right, blood dripping from her mouth as she finished off the last of someone's internal organs, leaving the bones for the younger shaders behind her. Less than a dozen corpses remained, and only the smaller shaders still fed on the remains. The rest of them prowled the edges of the trees, low growls rumbling from deep within their chests as they edged closer to where Bert and his soldiers stood.

"Don't think you've won here," Bert warned. "We're not done."

"No," Brandi agreed, "and we won't be until I escort you to the gods myself. So, I suggest you get your affairs in order," Brandi said, letting her bow dissipate. "I'm not a patient woman."

He spared a single moment to glare at Brandi and Jack before he gave the call for a full retreat. The soldiers wasted no time in rushing back to the edge of the clearing where they'd, no doubt, left behind the fleet of pods they would have needed to reach Freya's domain. Only Bert's personal guard retained their composure and kept him surrounded as they withdrew. Once they were gone, Noble strode into the clearing with a barely conscious Najé clinging to his shoulder and wobbling on her feet. She offered Brandi a weak smile and Brandi glared at her before turning to Noble, who wore a questioning look on his face.

"What now, Green?"

"Now, we regroup," she said, turning on her heel and walking back towards the temple in the direction she'd sent Cedric and Sarah in. "Follow me."

The trek through the dense woods of Freya's domain wasn't an easy one. Of the three hundred rebels who'd arrived to support Brandi's efforts to rescue Jack, a little more than two hundred of them had survived the battle, and half of them were wounded and groaning from broken bones and steady-flowing gashes. A third of them had already lost their fight with consciousness and were being dragged by their comrades over the uneven ground. Their dead weight left deep grooves in the moss beneath them and Brandi could sense the unease emanating from the shaders who watched their quiet march from the shadows. Tiki walked in front of them, leading the way alongside Brandi and Jack, and Lia brought up the rear, ensuring that no hungry shaders preyed on the terrified rebels.

It was a necessary precaution, but the shaders wordless anxiety and distrust for the outsiders only served to intensify her own exhaustion. She was already beginning to regret offering her help to the rebels, but it was too late to change her mind now. They'd come to her aid when she'd asked for it, and she wouldn't ignore that to abandon them to their own devices. So, until they were out of Freya's domain, she would be responsible for them. At the very least, she'd stay and allow her presence to protect them from the shaders until they could cross through the barrier into one of the other gods' domains. As long as she was with them, Tiki would keep its pack away from them while the wounded recovered from their injuries.

Brandi would do what she could for now, but she wouldn't deny that she was anxious to get away from the rebels and the hope they carried for her in their eyes. She could feel the weight of their gazes and expectations bearing down on her, and it triggered her desire to escape far more than just the battlefield. She rubbed at the goosebumps rising along her arms as she stepped over one of the thick roots in the ground, and Tiki pushed a gentle hum of concern into her mind. It was a wordless thought, and Brandi placed a hand against its giant leg as they walked.

"I'm fine," she whispered. "Just tired."

That is normal, Tiki hummed. ***You have fought a great battle.***

"I should have sent Bert."

You ended things as no one else could, Tiki reminded her. ***There is great value in that.***

Brandi didn't say anything else and let her conversation with Tiki end there. She wasn't satisfied with the way the battle had ended, but she knew better than to dwell on it. There may have been value in letting Bert return to the queendom — she didn't think Jack was wrong in pointing out how unprepared the rebels were to face the full force of the queen's soldiers — but just the thought of him continuing to exist in the mortal realm was enough to heat her blood with rage. It chased away the chill that was settling over her skin as the thick of Asari's night set in and she tried to push the thought away from her as she led the way for the rebels, weaving through the trunks of the trees and avoiding poisonous thickets until the clearing she remembered came into view.

She doubted anyone other than her and the shaders could see it with how far away it still was, but she let her green eyes dance over the familiar place for a moment, letting the memories she held of quieter times crash over her. The lake to her left flowed out through Lindl and Carna's domains, all the way to the Blind Sea. She'd spent countless days splashing and bathing in the clear waters underneath Rothe's sun with Tiki and Lia. The shore surrounding the lake was rocky and covered in smooth pebbles that gave way to the spongy green moss they stood on now. Looming gray stones were piled on the opposite edge of the lake and several shaders rested on them now, lounging in the bright light of Asari's full moon. They raised their heads as if sensing the presence of the rebels, and Tiki moved toward them.

Your people will stay here for the night, Tiki hummed. ***Inform them not to leave the clearing. I promise them no protection within the depths of the forest.***

Brandi nodded and Tiki melted into the night, making its way over to where the other shaders were. It took another twenty minutes for the rebels to reach the clearing, and before Brandi could sigh in relief that they'd finished the journey, she felt a pair of clammy palms grasping onto her arm. She tilted her head to see who it was, expecting to find some wounded fighter reaching out for help, but instead, she found Cedric. His light brown skin was ashen, and his violet eyes darted between her and the shaders on the other side of the lake, who seemed to be watching them.

"Thank the gods," he whispered. "You're finally here."

"Did you think I would abandon you or something?" Brandi asked, brushing his hands away from her. He looked disheveled and Sarah was sitting on the ground beside him, her knees bent with her forehead resting against them as her long hair acted as a curtain around her face. Brandi couldn't tell if she was awake or not, but she could tell from the subtle lift of her shoulders that she was, at least, still breathing. She didn't look any better than she had when Brandi had sent them off though, and she wondered if Sarah would be up to the task of healing the rebels when the time came. It was something they'd find out soon enough as the last of the rebels staggered up behind them and she directed her attention back to Cedric.

"On an intellectual level, I understood that shaders would be here," Cedric said, licking his lips as his eyes darted once more to where the shaders lounged on the rocks across the lake, "but it's a completely different experience to see them in person."

"But you were literally standing next to Tiki at Freya's temple,"

Brandi pointed out.

"You were there!"

"Dear gods," Brandi sighed, pulling a hand through her hair. Her once neat cornrows were frizzing at the root, and she knew she would have to do something with them soon, but it was a problem she would have to deal with on another day. "I just need to know if you did what I asked. Or did you spend the whole time cowering in fear at the shaders who didn't bother to attack you?"

Cedric froze at those words as his eyes narrowed and Brandi waited for his response. She didn't know what went through his mind as he watched her, but she could tell that her words were sinking in. It was clear that he hadn't allowed himself time to process the facts in front of him and Brandi glanced at the shaders his eyes were locked on.

"I already told you," Brandi said. "You're a vessel of the gods. They wouldn't have hurt you."

"You'll have to forgive me," Cedric whispered. "It appears my fear led to ignorance."

"Did you pray?" Brandi asked, ignoring his request for forgiveness and redirecting the conversation to getting the information she wanted out of him. She didn't fault him for being afraid of shaders — even Jack had been the first time he met Tiki — but she'd have no patience for someone who couldn't follow simple instructions.

"I did."

"Great," Brandi nodded, stepping past him towards the clearing. "We need to discuss that."

The moment she stepped out from behind the trees, the shaders let loose a low growl of excitement. It would have sounded terrifying to anyone who didn't know their thoughts, and she wasn't surprised when Jack's steps faltered behind her. He'd been a few steps behind her the entire way, but he'd been silent the entire way. It was unusual for him, but they hadn't had a moment to talk since Asari had brought him back from the brink of having his final meeting with the gods. As her eyes met his, he offered her a quick smile, and she felt her own lips quirk upward in response as he stopped at the edge of the trees to stand beside Cedric. The other rebels stumbled up next to him but kept their distance as another growl reached them from across the water.

Daughter of Freya, the smallest shader squealed as it rose to its feet. ***I have heard much about you!***

It jumped from the rock it was on and bolted over to Brandi, its body a black blur as it circled around her, sniffing at her clothes and wagging its tail. She could sense the fear radiating from the rebels behind her, each of them holding their breath as if that was the secret to keeping the shaders from feasting on them should they have the desire to. Brandi could almost laugh at the irony it would be for them to have survived the battle at Freya's temple, only to be led deeper into the forest to be eaten by shaders.

"Do you have a name, little one?"

Brandi reached her hand out the young shader as she asked the question in the common tongue, hoping to ease the minds of the rebels gathered behind her. She didn't want them to believe that shaders weren't dangerous — they were, and the rebels were right to be afraid of them — but she wanted them to understand that the creatures were intelligent.

They could be reasoned with.

I am known as Ronka, son of Shika! The shader responded. ***And you are Brandi! Daughter and incarnation of Freya!***

Brandi smiled at the shader, choosing not to correct Ronka on her lineage. There was no reason to explain that she was the daughter of Temari and Ross Freylin. They were already returned to the gods, and she was Freyan — no matter how many generations existed between them, Freya was her mother, just as she was mother to the entire realm. Brandi released a soft laugh as Ronka nuzzled her hand and pushed his soft fur into her body.

"Where is your mother?"

Ronka paused his movements to lift his head toward the rocks he'd descended from. He let loose a brief howl into the night and the other three shaders rose, descending from the rocks with a gentle grace. They moved with measured steps, approaching her with a caution that Ronka didn't think to have. Their giant paws left shallow prints in the moss beneath them, and they stopped a short distance away from Brandi, the two shaders in the back flanking the one in front.

You have asked for me?

"I did," Brandi said, lifting her head to look at the shaders. Ronka was still a child and stood no more than four feet tall. His mother, though, was lean and closer to Lia's height with the same kind of thick, curly fur. Brandi would never describe shaders as beautiful, but there was an elegance about her that Brandi could appreciate. "Are you the one known as Shika?"

I am.

Brandi dipped her head in a show of respect. "It's an honor to meet you."

And I, you, Shika responded, bowing her head in return. *These are my mates, Fiya and Rysan.*

Brandi nodded at them before returning her gaze to Shika. "This clearing is your home?"

Yes. Tiki has allowed us to raise our children in this quiet place. We watch over it.

"I understand. I hate to ask this of you, but would you allow us to rest here for a while?" Brandi waved her hand towards the rebels who had fully gathered behind her. "We have wounded who need to recover before they'll be able to leave Freya's domain."

Has Tiki not already given you permission to be here?

"It has. But this is your home. It seemed right that I ask your permission as well."

And if we were to deny you?

"Would you deny me?"

Brandi stared at the shader, feeling Shika's presence size her up before her enormous frame rumbled and a low-pitched hiss escaped from her in laughter. Her mates sat behind her in silence as Ronka's tail began stirring up a breeze from his seat next to her. His large face swung between the two of them as they conversed, as if he had not been born into darkness.

You may stay, Shika agreed. *But on the third rising of Rothe's sun, depart from here. Fiya is large with child and due to birth soon.*

"Of course," Brandi agreed. "We'll be gone by then. And may Freya bless you with a healthy child who is close to her own heart."

Shika puffed warm air from her nostrils, as Tiki often did when it was happy, before turning to walk back to the rocks they'd descended from. Ronka hung back and Brandi reached down to run her fingers through his soft fur as he let out a soft growl and pushed his head further into her hand.

Can I stay?

"Not tonight," Brandi told him, knowing she wouldn't be able to handle the energy a child like him carried. "But we'll go hunting together before I leave."

Okay! Ronka agreed, hopping around her with excitement. **_It's a promise!_**

With those words, he hurried off to follow behind his mother. With him gone, the clearing was devoid of shaders and Brandi turned to face the rebels. She held her arms out wide toward the quiet space surrounding them as Asari's moon shone down on her from the break between the clouds.

"Settle in," she called. "For the next three days, this is home."

CHAPTER TWO

The plight of mortals do not sway the gods to action, but the prayers of the devout do not fall on deaf ears.

— Of Gods and Mortals | Lindl's Third Holy Academy

FREYA'S DOMAIN — THE CLEARING BY THE LAKE

NIGHT OF DAY 1

The rebels were quick in establishing themselves in the clearing. Without a single word of complaint, they huddled together in small groups of five to collapse under the weight of their exhaustion. Those who could remain on their feet moved under the swift direction of Jack and Najé. The two didn't speak, but they were natural born leaders, organizing the rebels into groups with an efficiency Sarah had never witnessed before. They made no attempts to communicate with each other, but Sarah wasn't surprised by that. It had only been a few hours since Najé gave Jack over to the queendom under the queen's orders — they were working together out of necessity for the moment, but she knew better than to think there was anything other than bad blood between them.

Najé gave orders to the rebels overseeing the wounded. She had those with the most severe wounds and who were unable to walk moved near the crystal waters of the lake — close enough to make it easy enough to bring fresh water to them, but far enough away to keep them from contaminating their only source of water. She assigned runners to retrieve water in whatever vessels they could find to start cleansing the worst of their injuries, while those with basic first aid knowledge began doing what they could. Jack stood on the other side of the clearing, directing the remaining rebels to gather wood for campfires, clean water from the lake to drink, and to use what resources they had on hand to create fishing lines.

Sarah sat on the ground next to where Cedric stood, watching from the edge of the tall trees with wide eyes as they all moved with determination and focus. Within a few moments, the clearing that had seemed chaotic with broken bodies littering the ground was divided into four quadrants with clear walking paths between them and budding campfires in their center. She couldn't stop herself from feeling impressed as she looked out at the clearing full of rebels.

She'd been overwhelmed by the mere sight of battle — the rivulets of blood, vomit, and excrement mingled with the unsettling image of skin and muscle ripped away from bones that were twisted in directions they should never go. It had stolen her ability to do anything but crouch over into the grass and relieve her stomach of everything she'd ever eaten. Even now, as she clung to the tree beside her, trying to drag herself up from the ground, she struggled to keep her legs steady beneath her. Cedric had all but dragged her through the woods, and she struggled now to breathe through the guilt choking her at the sight of people hobbling over to the lake on clearly broken bones. Her body still trembled at the memory of their screams echoing through the trees, and she fought to keep her legs steady beneath her now.

She'd never borne witness to so many people leaving the mortal realm at once, and as she gulped down mouthfuls of air to try and settle her burning stomach, she prayed to Asari that she would never see anything like that again. It was a selfish wish, but as Sarah watched the rebels hold in their own cries of pain as they did what they could to tend to the wounds of those around them, the little pride she'd clung to through her life vanished. She knew that every breath she took was a scoff at the queendom, but that was nothing compared to the uppercut these people had just dealt the monarchy. For the first time in her life, she understood what it meant to resist those in power. It was far more than simply existing because of someone else's sacrifice or holding onto the memory of those who had already returned to the gods. She was her mother's daughter, but she recognized just how worthless being a princess was if all she could carry was the title, and realizing that made her chest feel hollow.

Her thoughts were racing, but there was no way to escape from her own mind. So, instead of trying to parse through every emotion that came with her realization, Sarah turned her attention to Cedric and Brandi. They stood beside her, speaking to each other with quiet words.

"So," Brandi asked, "what's your take on all of this?"

Her green eyes followed Jack around the clearing, watching as he carried firewood and the carcasses of a few deer over to the final quadrant. The shaders had brought them to the edge of the clearing after Brandi spoke with them. Sarah hadn't heard the conversation, but she'd guessed it had been to ask for their help since Brandi made it clear to everyone that none of them were to leave the clearing unless they wanted to be eaten by shaders.

"I'm going to make the request that you be more specific," Cedric replied. "What is it you're asking my opinion of?"

"Everything," Brandi said. "The rebellion. The shaders. The gods."

"It's varied," Cedric said, shrugging his shoulders. "The shaders are a bit terrifying, but it's interesting to see you interact with them. There were no texts within the academy walls to even suggest something like that was possible. So, that intrigues me, as does this rebellion. I'm not much invested in the realm's politics," he admitted, "but I do know there has never been a resistance rise against the authority of the queen. Not of this magnitude."

"It's happened before?" Brandi asked, her eyebrow lifting in curiosity.

"It's why the queen and her consorts have their own soldiers," Cedric explained with a nod. "It's rare that anyone ever tries to contest the validity or outcome of the bid, but it's not unheard of. But each time, it was only a handful of people and they were crushed beneath the unwavering might of the crown. What happened back there?" Cedric shook his head, his eyes gleaming with what Sarah could only guess to be unbridled academic ambition. "That battle will change the course of the realm," he whispered, a smirk pulling at his lips as he glanced over at Brandi. "Assuming it's not destroyed first, of course. But never has there been a force that could truly challenge the might of the queendom."

"You sound excited about that."

"I'm a scholar," Cedric said, laughter tinging his words. "Who wouldn't be excited about witnessing the realm change in real time? Who else will write about it?"

Brandi shrugged at his words, leaving his questions hanging in the air, and Sarah wished she could hear her thoughts. Just as Brandi wanted to know Cedric's thoughts, Sarah wanted to know hers. Their actions would shape the future of the realm and it made Sarah wonder if her existence as a princess would make it into Cedric's rendition of this historic battle. But then again, what was there for her to be remembered for? She'd been dragged away into the forest after puking at the foot of Freya's temple on the fringes of the battle. Her face flushed at the memory, and she decided she'd rather be left out of the story altogether rather than have Cedric immortalize one of her worst moments in a textbook.

"And what's your take on the gods?"

The question tore Sarah away from her embarrassing thoughts as she listened for Cedric's response. She hadn't given much thought to what Asari meant when he'd pulled her away with him after Azinne's departure. Her thoughts had been on healing Jack, knowing that Brandi would never forgive her or the gods if they allowed him to be returned to the gods. But he'd mentioned that she'd become part of a new era of gods. She had no idea what he'd meant, and she waited for an explanation now as Cedric mulled over his words.

"I don't feel their presence anymore," Cedric answered. "And when I tried praying to Lindl, he didn't answer me. So," Cedric shrugged, looking over to Brandi, "for once, I don't know what I think about all this. I don't have enough information to form a conclusion."

"Spoken like a true scholar," Brandi scoffed, shaking her head. "But that's what I needed to know."

"And what are your thoughts on all this?" Cedric asked, leaning forward, his violet eyes boring into Brandi's green ones. "Surely you have some?"

Brandi stared at Cedric for a moment, her eyes giving him a once over as if she were deciding his worth in that moment. Cedric didn't waver under her intense inspection, and Brandi shrugged before shoving her hands into her pockets. She returned her gaze to the rebels, her eyes following Noble as he made his way over to them in long strides.

"I'm not sure," Brandi admitted. "I'm not a fan of the deal Freya made or the gods leaving us to take their place, but I can't do anything about that. All I know," she said, glancing at him, "is that I struggled to contain my blessing when I called on it."

"Meaning?"

"Meaning," Brandi emphasized, "something's changed. You can feel it too, can't you? Like there's fire in your veins and your blessing is growing stronger?"

"I guess you could describe it like that," he said with a nod. "Maybe it's because we're gods now?"

"Maybe," Brandi shrugged. "Just let me know if we need to start praying to ourselves."

"That sounds absolutely blasphemous."

His words were even, lacking any trace of emotion, and Brandi barked out a laugh before shaking her head and walking away, their conversation ending with those words. She began making her way to the opposite end of the clearing where Jack was, and Sarah watched as she passed Noble. He caught her attention and paused to whisper something to her and point in Najé's general direction. Brandi rolled her eyes before continuing on her way. Noble stared after Brandi for a moment before shaking his head and striding over to where she and Cedric stood. His dark eyes were narrowed at them, and Sarah flinched back from his glare as he yelled over to them.

"Are you two planning to stand there all night?"

His words were sharp, carrying no traces of his usual amusement. It made her heart race, and though she hadn't been able to keep her eyes off him as he'd been walking over, his unrelenting glare made her want to look away from him now, but she fought against the urge. His words from *The Unseen Horizon* took root in her mind and she forced her blue eyes to hold his gaze, even as his irritation became palpable as he approached.

Noble wasn't serious about most things. In most every conversation Sarah had with him, he'd been as unbothered as Carna's winds. The only person he truly cared about was Brandi, and he wasn't shy in making that known to everyone around him. His open confession still made her wonder if his feelings for Brandi wouldn't be romantic if Jack weren't around, but she knew he would probably never have an answer for that. He was Carna's vessel, and she knew firsthand what it was like to carry the weight of a god in her soul — for the insatiable desire for the goddess to become almost indiscernible from their own. He felt it just as strongly as she did, and he didn't fight it.

It was an aspect of him that she both respected and hated.

Because, despite how she might feel about it, the fact remained that Brandi was like a tether for their souls — an unbreakable connection they couldn't pull away from. They carried their own will, apart from the gods, but it paled in comparison to their demands and Sarah couldn't deny them any more than Noble, Jack, or Cedric could. She knew that. And she knew that her desire to be close to Brandi — to be needed by her — wasn't purely her own. But she could no longer determine how much of it was her own selfish whims and how much of it was Asari's compulsion. Either way, it wasn't something she could just ignore or separate herself from. Noble was no different. And having to accept that fact irritated her beyond anything she could explain because, no matter what she did, she could never be Noble's favorite.

It made her question why her heart would even bother racing when he looked at her. What she felt for him amounted to nothing more than pointless emotions, but whenever she saw him, they dominated her mind. She wanted him to like her — to notice and want her as a woman. It was irrational but she couldn't push it aside, so she shrugged at Noble's question and finally broke away from his gaze.

"What do you expect us to do?"

"Heal people," he stated. "Or do you plan to just stand around and watch these people return to the gods?"

Sarah flinched at the tone of his words, but what could she say? That she'd been too busy trying to keep her legs steady beneath her and listening in on Brandi's conversation to use her blessing to help anyone? That wasn't an excuse she wanted to give, much less one that Noble would want to hear. So, instead, she pushed away from the tree she'd been using for support and staggered forward, wobbling on her feet and stumbling with her first few steps. Noble watched her with his hands in his pockets as she tipped forward, and he took a slight step backward. Her heart sank at the realization that he was more than willing to let her crash face-first into the ground, but Cedric's hand shot out to catch her before that could happen. His hand around her waist felt much different than Noble's when he'd done the same thing back at the bar in Lindl's domain, and her face flushed at the memories of what his hands on her skin had led to. She forced those thoughts back though and offered a small smile to Cedric as he helped her find her footing.

"Thanks," she said, planting her feet on the ground.

"Take your time," Cedric warned. "You're not going to be much use to anyone if you can't walk."

"You're not much use to anyone just standing around, either," Noble pointed out.

Cedric met Noble's gaze, and for a moment Sarah just stood between them, wondering how things would unfold. Like Brandi, Noble's sharp eyes seemed to be assessing Cedric's worth. He was shorter than Noble, and leaner — softer. He wasn't built like a fighter, but as with Brandi, he didn't falter or flinch back from Noble. Instead, he glanced at the cluster of campfires behind Noble where a group of rebels were preparing to cook a few hunted deer.

"If we're done here," Cedric said, clasping his hands behind his back and stepping around Noble, "I'll go lend my skills elsewhere."

With that, Cedric was gone. He navigated his way through the rebels with sure steps. His back was straight, and he moved with long strides, walking with a confidence Sarah had never felt. For a moment, she was envious of him and the look of approval that slipped across Noble's face before he turned back to her. She wanted to know how Cedric could be so unfazed when moving through a throng of trained shadows and rebels, but before she had time to dwell on the thought, Noble wrapped a firm hand around her elbow and began escorting her through the crowd. She stumbled after him, tripping over her own feet as she struggled to match his pace through the crowd of people. Most of them were unconscious — soft snores drifting up from the rebels who were able to lose themselves in the solace of sleep, and labored breaths rattling through the chests of those who struggled to find it. There were a few people who were wide awake though, and it was their unwavering glares that made Sarah's heart race and her breath catch on the nerves tightening her throat.

"Where are we going?" Sarah asked, doubling her pace to keep up with Noble's long strides.

"To the far edge of the clearing," he said, pointing to where Najé stood. "That's where they moved the rebels who are flirting with the gods. Or could you not be bothered to even listen to what was going on?"

"I heard them," Sarah said, her voice an octave too high to be natural as she tried to defend herself. "I just…"

"Didn't care," Noble finished for her.

"What?" Sarah asked, her cheeks flushing pink for much less pleasant reasons. "Why would you say that? Of course, I care."

"Sure you do, Blondie," Noble snorted. "That's why you weren't healing people the moment they got here."

"I was…" Sarah started, shaking her head. "That's not…" Sarah sighed as she searched for the words she wanted, tears pricking at her eyes as her voice grew thick. "I just didn't want to be in anyone's way," she whispered.

"And it never occurred to you that you were the only one who could help these people? That the reason Brandi sent you away from the battle was so that you could rest and be ready to save as many of their lives as possible?"

"I didn't think about that," she admitted.

"Too busy thinking about yourself, I'm sure."

"But… why didn't someone come get me?" Sarah asked, her question strained and weighed down with regret.

"The first order Najé gave was for the medics to tend to the wounded," Noble snapped. "But even if she hadn't, why should it be someone else's responsibility to stop what they're doing just to tell you what needs to be done? You're not a child."

Noble doubled his pace after that, forcing Sarah to jog next to him in order to keep up and leaving her no time to react to his words. She wouldn't deny that she should've been helping the rebels from the moment they stepped into the clearing, but she also wanted to scream at him that someone could've told her to do something sooner. She knew it was childish to want to shift the blame from herself, especially when it was her own inaction that put others at risk, but she couldn't shake the thought that any one of them could have given her orders. They'd never shied away from bossing her around before and Brandi had been standing right next to her. Why didn't he have an attitude with her?

Sarah already knew the answer to that question, and she drove her teeth into her bottom lip as she tried to keep her mind from spiraling further into those self-loathing thoughts. She and Brandi were nothing alike — there was no point in comparing herself to her. To Noble, Jack and the other shadows, Brandi could do no wrong and she could do nothing right. That was the way of things, and as she glanced around at all the broken people lying on the ground around them, she couldn't find a single decent reason to believe that they were wrong about her.

She chewed on her bottom lip as the thoughts circled her mind, but they disappeared the moment they made it to the far edge of the lake. The injuries she'd seen from a distance were horrific up-close. Her stomach lurched at the sight, and she held her breath to keep from vomiting where she stood. There were rebels lying on the ground with their limbs obliterated — the sharp edges of white bone poking through torn flesh and muscle. Open gashes soaked through makeshift bandages and every inch of skin that she saw was turning some varying shade of black, purple, and blue. It brought her face to face to the reality that while she'd been standing on the sidelines, the people around her were suffering and the guilt that engulfed her made both her heart and legs feel heavy. She wanted nothing more than to spin back the hands of time and make different decisions, but that wasn't a power Asari blessed her with. So instead, she took a deep breath, freed herself from Noble's grasp, and headed over to Najé.

She fell into step behind the tall woman and waited for her to finish giving orders to a rebel who looked to be twice her age. He departed the second she finished speaking, and Najé didn't waste any time moving through the ranks, barking orders at anyone who could still stand.

"Get to C-four," Najé demanded, throwing a quick glance over her shoulder.

"I need you to explain that to me," Sarah said.

"The clearing is a grid," Najé stated with a sigh. "Numbers across, letters down. Starting point is the lake. Start at C-four and make your way across to C-eight. Then move on to D-eight and work your way back. Repeat that through rows E and G. Row F is the path you can use to walk between blocks. Report back when you're done."

Sarah nodded and turned on her heel, trying to make her way to the area Najé pointed out to her, but it wasn't long before she got turned around. She tried to pinpoint the blocks on her own, but the sound of people begging her to put them out of their misery, and the smell of blood and human waste seeping into the wet soil disoriented her. It wasn't until Noble grabbed her upper arm and began leading her through the mass of people that she was able to collect her thoughts.

"Keep it moving, Blondie," he snapped. "If you stop here, they'll think you've come to help."

"I can't find C-four."

"This way," he said, guiding her down the path between groups of people. Sarah nodded and kept pace behind Noble as he released her arm and led the way. She kept her eyes trained on the muscles in his back as he moved through the crowd, but as he veered them off to the right, Sarah looked over to their left.

"What about A-one through C-three?"

"They've already returned to the gods," Noble answered.

Sarah sucked in a sharp breath at that, her blue eyes growing wide. Her hands trembled as she shoved them into the pockets of her jacket. She'd taken it from the stockpile of clothes meant for the rebels when they were still in Lindl's domain, along with a pair of jeans, a white shirt, and a pair of sneakers. She didn't think the black miniskirt and halter top she'd worn to *The Unseen Horizon* was appropriate for heading into Freya's domain, and her instincts had been correct. She was grateful to have at least her skin covered as Noble exposed her flaws as a person, and she struggled to find her voice. When she did, it was tiny and hollow.

"Could they have been saved?"

"Yes."

His answer was short and definitive, and it made her blood run cold as she was faced with the realization that her own insecurities had cost people their lives. She understood now that her abilities were the only reason the others assigned any value to her presence. She'd been avoiding the others, believing that she would only be in the way if she were to try and help. But the truth of the matter was much different than what she'd expected — she was an asset to the others. Had she been healing everyone from the start instead of standing around feeling sorry for herself, she would have been able to save dozens of lives.

Noble had every right to be angry with her.

"I'm sorry," she whispered.

"No one here wants your apology," Noble shot back, "or your tears. Just make yourself useful."

Sarah nodded and swiped at the tears rolling down her cheeks before dropping to her knees beside the first group of rebels in C-four. The first two people she saw were boys — no more than sixteen. One had his right leg twisted off, connected by a weak section of torn muscle and skin, and the other was missing his right arm — everything below his elbow was gone. Both of them were close to bleeding out and unconscious. She took in a shaky breath and rolled her shoulders back, closing her eyes as she pulled at the deep well of power that Asari had blessed her with.

For most of her life, she hadn't understood why Asari had chosen her or known what to do with his power. It had been an overwhelming burden, but she wasn't the same eight-year-old girl who was terrified of the god of the moon anymore. She understood, at the very least, what Asari had meant when he'd told her to serve the goddess and her vessel. He'd meant for her to do much more than simply heal Freya's physical vessel when she required it. The power he'd gifted her wasn't meant to be restricted to one person. She could accept that now. And, much like she had the first time she'd ever called on Asari's power to heal Brandi, she took deep breaths and reached out to the god, her lips moving in quiet prayer.

"Hear me, Asari," she whispered, ***"the plea of your chosen. Light the way for the wounded. Guide them out of their darkest nights."***

Her muscles clenched as the surge of burning heat that bloomed in her fingertips raced up her arms to her chest before cooling into ice in her veins. She hissed as her body tried to adjust to the fluctuating power, cycling through searing heat to bone-chilling ice. She focused on it until she could feel the rhythm of it — until she could control it. She grasped at it, but it felt like sand slipping through her fingers and she ground her teeth as she pressed her hands into the ground. A small ring of light bloomed beneath her fingertips, but it wasn't enough. It brushed against the boy on her left with the broken leg, but it wasn't big enough to reach the boy on the right bleeding out from his missing arm.

She dug deeper into the well of power, shuddering from the heat that singed her bones as she dragged it up from the pit of her stomach, forcing it through her veins until it rose in her chest, and she exhaled crystals of icy mist. Her power had grown since they'd left the temple and she fought to keep control of her mind as it flooded her senses, threatening to drag her beneath the burning pain and trap her there until she screamed out for the gods to release her soul from her body. It surged forward with sharp edges, slicing against her insides until her breaths were shallow and her mind was spinning. Still though, she fought to keep it under her control as she searched for the words to call forth the power she needed to save the boys in front of her — to save every person in that clearing.

She turned her eyes to the moon as heat continued to bloom in her chest and she whispered beneath her breath.

"Do you not hear me?" Sarah called out. *"I'm calling on you Asari. Will you forsake me for the convenience of your own whims? Am I not your beloved daughter who calls upon your name seeking your favor and power? Your mercy, your healing, and your guidance?"*

She waited for a response, and when none came, she dropped her head and funneled her rage into the ground until it grew a few inches wider, but it still wasn't big enough to do what she wanted to do. As she watched the color drain from the boy's faces, the fury she felt with herself ripped from her in an angry scream. Every eye within the clearing was drawn to her, but she didn't care. When these people had needed her most, she'd vanished — hidden herself away on the fringes of their group, praying that no one would find her when she should have been the first one at their sides, offering them aid. She should have been calling on the gods from the start, and she held nothing back as she turned her head up to the moon once more.

"You told me that my eyes carry your moon. That I am the origin of a new era of gods," Sarah yelled into the night. ***"You gifted me your power and sought refuge within my soul. And now you refuse to aid me? Are you as fickle as the stories paint you to be? Will you go back on your word and abandon me here?"***

Sarah waited once again, and when Asari's voice didn't pierce her mind she clenched her teeth, biting back a scream of pain as fire shot down her spine and steam rolled off her skin in thick waves as ice shot across her skin. She closed her eyes against the pain before forcing them open to stare at the moss her fingers were curling into beneath her.

"Shall I call upon Rothe instead? I've never known him to ignore his children, and am I not his daughter as well?"

Tears slipped from beneath Sarah's eyes as silence settled over the clearing. She was out of words to call upon the god any further and as the breathing of the boys in front of her began to fade, she lost the grip she had on her power, and it spiraled out of her control. She threw her head back to the moon and stared at it with unblinking eyes as pale light shone from her eyes, piercing the darkness around them. Her fingers dug into the soft ground as light bloomed beneath her palms, unfolding outwards like pale blue flower petals until every wounded body was encased in it. As she wept, Sarah poured the overwhelming power that had been burning her from the inside out into the circle. Sobs broke free from her chest, but it wasn't enough to drown out the sharp cracking of bones as they were reset or the wet sloshing of torn muscle and skin regrowing. People screamed and rejoiced in equal measure as fatal injuries began mending themselves. She didn't have the power to regrow limbs, but for people like the boy in front of her, she was able to heal what was still attached.

She watched as his leg righted itself and regrew the muscle, bones, and tissue that had been ripped away from him. His labored breathing evened out, and as the last traces of heat left her, she pushed the ice in her veins through the pulsating flower that spread throughout the clearing until it shattered, the petals dissipating into a swirling fog rising from the ground. Its cool touch eased the pain of every person who had been injured, no matter how small the wound was.

When she was done, she pulled her hands from the ground and sat back on her knees, sucking down heaving breaths of the sour air. Her head spun, her teeth chattered, and she wrapped her arms around herself as relief was over at the sight of the boys in front of her cracking their eyes open.

"Thank the gods," she whispered, the words leaving her lips as she doubled over and collapsed to the ground.

Chapter Three

Those who seek forgiveness do not deserve it, for those who deserve it would never have need to seek it.

— Have Mercy on Me Freya, For I Have Loved | Lindl's First Holy Academy

---

FREYA'S DOMAIN — THE CLEARING BY THE LAKE

NIGHT OF DAY 1

"I'm sorry."

Brandi sucked her teeth and rolled her eyes at Najé's apology. She'd been expecting Najé to force one on her, but no matter how heartfelt she tried to make it sound, Brandi had no interest in hearing it. There was nothing Najé could say to her that would change the fact she'd been willing to exchange Jack's life for the sake of the rebellion, and they both knew that.

As far as Brandi was concerned, the only thing left for Najé to do was to stand firm in her choice. It couldn't be undone, and it irritated her that Najé's brown eyes kept drifting back to her. Even as they'd moved around the clearing, helping the rebels to set up camp and ease their suffering, her gaze had been relentless on Brandi's back. And every time their eyes met, Brandi could do nothing more than glare at her before a burning fury erupted inside her and she was forced to look away.

Her original plan had been to avoid Najé until the rebels were able to leave Freya's domain. She figured they'd go back with the rebels to whatever headquarters still remained and Najé would return to the Queen's Tower. They'd decide what to do next from there, but Brandi never had any intention of talking to Najé ever again. Noble had been the one to go out of his way to suggest she give Najé her moment to apologize. It wasn't like him to interject his own opinions into her personal life — it was an unspoken agreement between them that she wouldn't mind his business if he didn't mind hers. But she could admit that his advice was sound. Najé wouldn't allow anyone to ignore her for long and she would be relentless in trying to corner Brandi until she heard what she had to say.

It had been easy enough to avoid Najé — there was more than enough to do around the clearing to keep every pair of hands busy. But once Sarah's healing fog faded away, everyone had been lulled to sleep. Only a few rebels remained conscious, and with no one left to give orders to, Najé had approached her — heart in hand.

Brandi had been sitting next to Jack, her entire body pressed up against his as Cedric roasted some of the meat Tiki and Lia had brought to them over the open fire. Noble had gone to retrieve Sarah and he placed her unconscious body on the ground next to the fire. Brandi had hoped they'd be able to discuss what they'd witnessed in Freya's temple, but they were all exhausted and the conversation had been cut short before it ever started as Najé approached them. Her gaze flicked over to Jack before it settled on Brandi, staring at her with desperation as she made her request for Brandi to hear her out before following her into a dense cluster of trees.

It didn't afford them much privacy, but it was out of earshot of the rebels and Brandi didn't expect them to be there for long. She knew from the way it started out that their conversation was going to be pointless, but she could muster up enough lingering respect for Najé to reject her apology to her face. So, she stood with her arms crossed and her face expressionless as she let Najé's words hang between them. She could hear all of the emotion the two words carried, and she took a deep breath before she responded, working to keep her voice even as the memory of what Najé had done sparked a fresh wave of rage and fire in her blood.

"I reject your apology," Brandi said, holding Najé's gaze. "So, if that's it, I'm leaving."

She didn't wait for Najé to respond before angling her body back toward the clearing. Her mind was already returning to the others and the conversation they'd put on hold. She wanted to get it over and done with so she could disappear with Jack on her own for a while. The rebels weren't allowed to leave the clearing, but Freya's domain was her home and the shaders weren't a threat to her. It would be a simple task to find a place for them to be alone, and all she wanted was a moment to appreciate the fact that Jack was still alive in the mortal realm. But her thoughts of him were cut short as Najé reached out to grab her.

"Wait a second!"

"For what?" Brandi asked, stepping out of Najé's reach as she turned back to face her. "I have nothing else to say to you."

"You can't be serious?"

"You apologized. I rejected it," Brandi pointed out. "There's nothing left to discuss."

"Just," Najé huffed, rubbing at her forehead, "let me explain."

"There's nothing to explain. You tried to have Jack sent to the gods."

"I didn't have a choice!" Najé shouted, staring at Brandi as if holding her gaze would make her understand. "It was a direct order from the queen, and I'm the rising director of her shadows. If I hadn't given the command to send him, I would have been targeted for treason and risked exposing every member of the rebellion." She took a step forward, frustration seeping into her voice and making her sound desperate as she looked at Brandi's unwavering face. "You have to understand that, don't you? It was a direct order," she emphasized. "There was nothing I could do."

"There's always something you could do," Brandi stated.

"No, there's not. Sometimes, you have to take what you've been given."

"If you don't like what you've been given, then take what you want," Brandi stated, taking a step in Najé's direction. "Aren't you the one who taught me that?"

"So, what?" Najé questioned. "You think I should have risked the entire rebellion and everything we've built just to save Jack?"

"You would have for Sal."

The words hung between them as Brandi stared Najé down, knowing she would be unable to refute her words. Sal was Najé's world — just as much as Jack was Brandi's. It was the nature of the way they lived. Either they forged unbreakable bonds they'd destroy the realm for, or they lived like Noble — refusing to commit anything to anyone beyond a single night. For people like them, there was no in between. Najé knew that just as well as she did, and it's why Brandi refused to accept Najé's apology. There was no way that she could.

"The problem here, Najé," Brandi said, working to keep her tone even as her rage stoked the flames within her blood, "is that you're asking me to forgive you for something that I should be sending you to the gods for."

"Brandi…" Najé whispered, shaking her head as her brown eyes began to shine with unshed tears. "I'm sorry. I'm so, so sorry."

"I know you are," Brandi said with a nod of her head. "But I don't care. How you feel now doesn't change what you did."

"But I didn't have a choice," she stressed. "You have to believe me."

"But I don't," Brandi retorted, her words sharp. "You could have just left."

"Everyone can't do that, Green."

"Wow," Brandi scoffed, mild surprise lifting her eyebrows as he stared at Najé. She was amazed that she could still be trying to defend herself against what she'd done, and Brandi shook her head. "You're still full of excuses."

"It's not an excuse, it's the truth!"

"Point out a single person in that clearing who didn't make the choice to leave, and I'll forgive you." When Najé's eyes widened but her mouth remained shut, Brandi raised her finger to point back to where they'd come from. "Name a single rebel who died on the battlefield today who didn't make that same choice."

When Najé still said nothing, Brandi bit back her frustration and tried to ignore the heat pooling in her belly. It roiled in the pit of her stomach like an angry sea of liquid fire, and she tried to ignore it as she held Najé's gaze. Her hands were floundering in the space between them as if she were unsure of whether she wanted to reach out for Brandi or wrap them around herself, and Brandi took a step away from her.

"Everyone has to make a choice at some point," she pointed out. "I made it. Glenn made it. Even Sal has made it," she said, rolling her eyes at how Najé's attention perked up at the mention of his name. "The problem is, you never decided whose side you were on because you're incapable of being loyal to anyone but yourself. You're not loyal to the queendom. You're not loyal to the shadows. And you've proven that you're not loyal to me."

"What about you then?" Najé shot back. "You're not loyal to any of those things either, so which are you? A liar or a hypocrite?"

Brandi narrowed her eyes at those words and fought back the urge to just walk away from the conversation altogether. After she'd been caught playing both sides of the conflict — serving the queendom and the rebellion — Brandi didn't feel like Najé had the right to question her loyalties. If it hadn't been for her actions, the rebels would never have made it away from Freya's domain or had a place to rest for the night. If it had been left up to Najé, the rebels would've been cut down by Bert's soldiers just for the sake of keeping her cover.

"I've always been loyal to the gods," Brandi said. "I only served the queen because I had to."

"And you left when it was convenient for you. How is that loyal?"

"I left when Freya demanded it," Brandi clarified. "I warned you that Freya didn't want Sarah returned to her, but you refused to listen."

"It doesn't matter," Najé huffed. "You made your choice when you left the tower, and I made my choice on the battlefield."

"After I forced you to make one," Brandi scoffed. "A choice is made with freewill, Najé. What you did was survive."

"Then what do you want me to say, huh?" Najé asked, her shoulders drooping under the weight of the conversation. "What can I do to make this right?"

"You can't make this right," Brandi stated. "You have to live with this, and I'm done talking to you about it."

Brandi turned to leave with those words, her mind already thinking of finding Jack and a spot to sleep for the night. The conversation she needed to have with the others about Freya's temple would have to wait until the morning, because the fatigue she'd been fighting off settled over her like a thick blanket in the middle of summer that she couldn't shake off. It warmed her blood until sweat began to collect at her elbows and behind her knees. She thought of sinking into the crystal waters of the lake and groaned when Najé called back out to her.

"Then what about the rebellion?"

Brandi rolled her eyes as she continued walking away and shook her head as she called over her shoulder.

"That has nothing to do with me."

"It has everything to do with you," Najé called back, trying to grab

Brandi's attention. "I don't know what happened in that temple, but Glenn is gone. She just grabbed Patches and left."

"And?" Brandi questioned, spinning on her heel to face Najé.

She knew that Glenn abandoned the rebellion because of the punishment Freya had doled out to her. She would spend the rest of her life traveling the realm, serving others to atone for her disobedience to Rothe. Freya had been clear that there would be no room for grace should she fail to do as she was told, so Brandi didn't blame Glenn for not wasting time. She didn't know if she'd ever see the woman again, but Brandi found that she wasn't too heartbroken about that. She'd spent most of her life without Glenn — her absence was no longer something that Brandi noticed. But the distress on Najé's face told Brandi everything.

Najé would be lost without Glenn. And thinking about it now, it made sense to Brandi that she would feel that way. Najé had always been part of the rebellion, so she'd never been without Glenn. When Brandi had been mourning the loss of her guardian, Najé was still meeting with her. She could almost laugh at the realization now — that all the times Najé had disappeared on missions without a word, she'd likely been meeting up with Glenn to help with the rebellion. It's why the brunt of the work had always fallen onto Brandi's shoulders. And it wasn't lost on her that neither of them ever whispered a word to her about it. She wondered if things would have been different had Glenn chosen to include her in the rebellion the way she'd included Najé, but that was something she would never know.

Glenn had chosen Najé, and she pointed that out to her now.

"Glenn trained you as her successor," Brandi pointed out. "So, go be the leader."

"I can't," Najé said, shaking her head. "But you can."

"No."

"You can take over now that Glenn is gone," Najé continued, ignoring Brandi's refusal.

"You're cracked," Brandi said, shaking her head and stepping further away from her as if her bad ideas were contagious. She had no interest in the rebellion, and even less of a desire to help Najé. As far as she was concerned, preventing the collapse of the realm and defeating Azinne were the first things on priority list. Leading a band of defected shadows against the queendom didn't rank on her scale of importance and she'd already repaid her debt to them by ending the battle and rescuing them from Bert's forces.

"I'm not," Najé said, shaking her head.

"You have to be to even suggest something like that to me."

"Someone has to do it," Najé said. "And I can't."

"Because you're going back to the tower?"

"Don't say it like that," Najé sighed, exhaustion lacing her words. "I told you already, I can't just leave. There are people that I'm responsible for now as the director. And if I don't do damage control with Bert, try and explain all of this away somehow, then everything we've built could fall apart." She shook her head as she looked at Brandi. "You might not get it, but there's a bigger picture here."

Brandi looked at Najé and couldn't hold back the hysterical laugh that broke free from her. It was fueled by too many emotions for Brandi to count, but it made her clutch her stomach and double over. Here she was, tasked with defeating a time being that the gods couldn't touch, housing the entirety of Freya's power, and replacing her as the literal goddess of the realm, and Najé thought she couldn't understand the importance of a tiny rebellion against the crown. It was a hilarious thought and Brandi's sides ached as she looked up at Najé who stood with her arms crossed.

"I don't get what's so funny," she huffed.

"No," Brandi agreed, catching her breath and fighting back another fit of laughter. "You don't. You really don't."

"Please, Green," Najé pleaded, stepping forward and trying to close the distance Brandi had placed between them. "For me. If the two of us are in charge, the monarchy won't stand a chance."

"No."

Brandi's voice was definitive and all the laughter in it from earlier was gone. Najé studied Brandi and she stood in the pale light of the moon and the confusion crossing her face made it obvious to Brandi that she was struggling with what to say next. It was clear that Najé hadn't expected Brandi to reject her offer — she probably hadn't expected Brandi to reject her apology, either. It was poor foresight on her part though if she hadn't because there was no way that Brandi would have accepted either of those things. And the fact that Najé had considered that she might made Brandi wonder what Najé truly thought of her. They'd been tied at the hip since they were children, so maybe Najé thought salvaging their relationship would be easy — that it would take precedence over everything else and that an apology would fix things, resetting everything back to the way it used to be. And had she not left the shadows, Brandi might have at least considered her offer to help with the rebellion.

But she had left.

And an apology wouldn't change what Najé had done.

"Why?" Najé finally asked. "Why won't you help me with this?"

"Because I don't want to," Brandi stated. "And I'm sick of people trying to force me into roles I don't want."

"What are you talking about?"

Brandi opened her mouth to respond, but instead she closed it and said nothing. There was no point. She couldn't tell Najé that she was Freya incarnated — that she'd only left the shadows because Freya had demanded it or that she'd watched Freya make a reckless deal with a time being that placed the fate of the entire realm on Brandi's shoulders. She couldn't tell her that the responsibility had been thrust into her lap and that she'd wanted no parts of it, or that she'd considered letting the realm be destroyed if that meant she wouldn't have to be the one to save it.

Najé would never understand that, and even if she would, Brandi had no desire to entrust that information to her. Brandi's shoulders sagged under that realization because, aside from Jack, Najé had been one of the few people she trusted with just about everything. But if Najé could sacrifice Jack's life, then Brandi couldn't trust her. She would serve the entire realm up on a silver platter to the time beings before she ever let anyone hurt Jack again. Just remembering what Najé had allowed to happen to him lit another spark of rage inside Brandi, and this time, she couldn't hold it back.

She was furious, and it seemed like no one cared about how she felt.

Freya didn't care that what she was asking of her was too great — Glenn didn't care that Brandi had needed her to be more than teacher — Najé didn't care that she'd betrayed her in a way that Brandi would never be able to forgive her for. No one seemed to care that she was beginning to fracture under the weight of all their expectations because they held no reservations about asking her to lead the rebellion, destroy the monarchy, and protect the realm. Everyone wanted something from her and she was exhausted. She was tired of everyone she knew looking to her as if she had the solution to every one of their problems.

"You know what?" Brandi said, shaking her head and swallowing against the flames climbing up her throat and spreading to her limbs. "Don't worry about it. My answer is still no."

"Hold on a second, Green," Najé said, concern settling across her face as her eyes searched Brandi's face. "What's going on with you? Talk to me."

"Why?" Brandi scoffed. "You wouldn't listen. You just want to hear me say I'll lead the rebellion, and I'm not doing that."

"Brandi…"

She saw Najé open her mouth to say something else after she called her name, but Brandi had already checked out of the conversation. All the anger and fury she'd been trying to hold back broke free of her control, and the sharp spike of white-hot pain being shoved down her spine made her scream beneath the weight of Freya's overwhelming power. Molten lava rolled through her veins like burning waves and she scratched at the skin on her arms as her bones felt as if they were crumbling to ash inside of her. She didn't have room to contain all of Freya's power inside of her body and she reached out to Freya — her silent request to the goddess a fervent plea for her to stymie the flow of power she was sending her way.

This is your power. I cannot stop it.

Freya's words, as they always did, felt like an iron spike being hammered through her brain and Brandi whimpered at the pain. Her hands flew up to massage her temples as she staggered back from the sudden pressure of it. She fought back the tears that pricked at her eyes and reached her hand out behind her to brace herself against the nearest tree.

"Green!" Najé called, crossing the last of the space between them and reaching out for Brandi. "Are you okay?"

"Don't ask that like you care," Brandi hissed, slapping her hand away as she fell back into the rough bark of the tree. She couldn't focus on Najé when every attempt she made to slow down the deluge of power flooding her senses was met with an even greater surge that stole her breath and made her weak in the knees. It was like trying to dam a volcanic eruption with twigs, and she let out a guttural screech as the heat raged through her, burning hotter and stronger than the first time she'd met the gods fourteen years ago. She locked her knees, refusing to fall to the ground in front of Najé, but her body convulsed with every wave of power that crashed over her until she was left gripping the tree for support and gasping for air.

"Tiki!"

Her plea wasn't loud, but it was enough. In seconds, she heard the sound of its thundering paws racing through the forest towards her. She spared a glance at Najé and saw her eyes widen and her body swivel as the pounding came closer to them. Before she could make sense of what was approaching though, Jack and Noble came crashing through the trees, no doubt panicked from her screams. In the split second it took for them to take in the situation, a look of unbridled fury, like nothing Brandi had ever seen, descended across Jack's face.

"What did you do to her?"

"Nothi—"

Before Najé could finish her word, Jack was across the small space and had driven his fist toward her jaw. She lifted her forearm to block it, and the sound of the blow shattered the silence of the night and sent Najé flying backward. She screamed as her body slammed into the tree behind her, the force of it shaking free a pile of leaves and sending the small animals near it scurrying away from them. She slumped to the ground cradling her arm as Jack strode toward her, fire circling up his arms as he closed the distance between them. Brandi tried to call out to stop him as Noble rushed to her side, but her throat was on fire and her words died before they ever left her mouth. She shook her head as she used the last of her strength to shove Noble in their direction, and he rushed across the clearing, yanking Jack backwards before he had the chance to drive his boot into Najé's huddled body. Jack shook off his hand and glared at him as Noble shoved him toward Brandi.

"You're dumber than anything the gods should tolerate," Noble snapped. "Go check on Brandi!"

Jack held his glare for a moment before he looked down at Najé.

"I don't care about what you do to me," he said, his voice low. "We've never liked each other much anyway. But if you ever hurt Brandi again," he warned, "the gods will not be enough to save you from me."

His words hung in the air, and he scoffed at Najé trembling on the ground before turning on his heel. Before he could walk a single step back across the clearing though, he stumbled back into Noble and Najé let out another blood-curdling scream.

Asari's moon broke through the clouds and revealed two large shaders stalking into the clearing around them. Low growls resonated from within their chests and their sharp double row of teeth were bared as they stepped out from behind the trees and into the light. The largest one stopped beside Brandi as the other one stepped in front, blocking the others from getting to her and snarling at them in warning.

I have come, Tiki whispered into Brandi's mind, its thoughts cool and soothing as it stepped forward, crouching to catch Brandi on its back as she lost her balance. ***What has happened?***

Brandi shook her head against Tiki's back as she let herself sink into its soft, sweet-smelling fur. She wanted to explain to it that Jack had been protecting her the best way he knew how and that everything was all a wild misunderstanding that rose from her suffering under the weight of her newfound power, but her body felt like it would crumble to dust from the simple vibration of her own voice. So, she said nothing, and Tiki somehow understood.

It gave wordless orders to Lia, and she growled at the others, stomping her feet against the ground until it shook beneath them. Najé took the warning and scrambled to her feet, rushing away from where they stood and sprinting back to the clearing as fast as she could. Even Noble, who had been her sworn protector since she was a child, was forced to back away from them with desperation and worry etched into his face. His dark eyes danced between Brandi and the shaders before he was forced to turn and leave too, entrusting her safety to the shaders who guarded her.

The only one who didn't move was Jack.

Lia pounded on the ground again, but he didn't flinch away from her. His brown eyes were locked onto Brandi, and he didn't budge from where he stood even as Lia rushed up to him, snarling in his face.

"I'm not leaving her."

His words were firm, and Lia studied him, low growls resonating from her chest as he stared back at her, his gaze focused on where her eyes would be had she been born with them. Before she could think to take a snap at him though, Tiki stood from where it had been crouching. Brandi clung to its back and Tiki let out a sharp bark before turning away from the clearing and melting into the night. Lia continued to bare her teeth at Jack before she relented and kneeled just enough to allow him to climb onto her back.

"Thank you," he whispered, accepting her offer and bracing himself as she took off after Tiki and Brandi. Tiki led the way back to the shader's side of the lake where Ronka, Shika, and her mates waited. They'd moved to the furthest edge of the lake, distancing themselves from the clearing and away from the curious eyes of the rebels. They shifted around in their huddle to make room for Tiki and Lia, huffing warm air in their direction before returning their heads to their crossed paws. Lia settled in next to Tiki and rested her large head on its back as Jack scrambled over to Brandi to cradle her in his arms.

"I'm here," he whispered. "I've got you."

Brandi sank into him, and Lia let out a low whine, huffing sweet air over them. And it was her attempt at offering comfort that finally undid Brandi. Her emotions were colliding too fast for her to process anything but the rage that had been building up inside of her. But, surrounded by Tiki, Lia, and Jack, she was able to let out a deep breath and release the pent-up power boiling her veins. And as her blood cooled, she reached out to place her hand against Lia's giant nose. The shader nuzzled it before Brandi let her hand drop away and she turned her face into Jack's chest.

Rest now, Tiki soothed. **You have endured enough.**

CHAPTER FOUR

In the beginning were the gods, and the gods were the beginning of all creation. But before the gods there was the goddess, and with her mind and might alone, she shaped the core of this realm into what it would be.

— Freya, The Beginning and the End | Lindl's First Holy Academy

---

REALM OF THE GODS

When Brandi opened her eyes, she was surprised to find herself back in Rothe's domain. It was the crack of dawn and Rothe's sun was just beginning to chase away Asari's stars. The deep blue sky was tranquil with Asari's moon fading away in the distance as pink rays of light lit the underside of Carna's clouds. The breeze was brisk on the balcony she stood on, but at thirty-two stories above ground, it always was. She loved being at the top of the highest buildings — it was the only way to get an unencumbered view of any domain. So, when she and Jack had moved out of their dorms in the tower to live together, they'd picked an apartment at the top of one of the tallest buildings in fragment 10316.

From their balcony, she could see all the way out to the burning sands in the Scorched Desert. The smoldering flames were a sight to behold first thing in the morning, its warm light casting shadows over the land before the sun took its rightful place in the sky. It was a sight Brandi never got tired of looking at, and she let out a deep sigh as she leaned against the stone railing and looked out at it. This moment, right before dawn, was one she'd be content to live in for the rest of eternity.

Soon though, the sun would crest over the desert and people would begin to wake from their slumbers, stirring the air and ending the early morning quiet she loved to revel in. So, she closed her eyes and let herself believe she was back home. That Jack was sprawled across the bed inside their apartment and in a few hours, she would go with him to meet Najé or Noble for a mission briefing. She'd train a few of the new shadows and have lunch at *Rieta's Bakery* before they set out. It would be business as usual, and the worries of the gods would be the furthest thing from her mind.

For a moment, she let herself believe everything was as it had always been.

It wasn't until she felt a presence moving to stand beside her that she opened her eyes to meet the only other pair of green eyes that matched her own. She didn't greet Freya with a smile as she'd always done in the past, instead choosing to turn her attention back to the sun that was frozen just below the Scorched Desert.

"You're showing up in my dreams now?"

"You speak as if my presence is unwelcome."

Brandi's gaze darted up to Freya at those words, but she rolled her eyes and remained silent. She was surprised to see the goddess sitting on the ledge next to her, her long legs dangling over the edge in the wind as she looked out over the Scorched Desert. After her dramatic exit in her temple, Brandi wasn't convinced that she would ever see any of the gods again. But, with Freya sitting next to her, she couldn't tell if she was relieved or annoyed — the goddess had always been dramatic and never missed an opportunity to be the center of attention, so Brandi should've known that Freya would never give up her throne with such ease.

They sat in silence as they watched the unmoving sunrise. It wasn't until Freya's amused laughter broke through the silence did Brandi tear her gaze away from it.

"You know," Freya said, leaning her elbows on her knees and resting her chin on her palms as she turned to look at Brandi, *"it's amazing that you've seen the entirety of the realm, and this is the place you choose for your inner realm."* Freya chuckled as she shook her head. *"I would have never guessed it."*

"What are you talking about?"

Freya lifted her eyebrows as she looked at Brandi.

"You haven't realized where we are?"

"We're in Rothe's domain," Brandi answered, letting her eyes dart around them. She'd recognized the view immediately — from the king-sized bed and the bright white walls to the sheer curtains that separated them from the inside and the textured stones beneath them. Everything was familiar to her.

"And since when could you go to sleep in my domain and wake up here?"

Brandi blinked at Freya as she processed her words and pushed away from the ledge of the balcony as realization sunk in.

"We're in the god realm."

"We are," Freya nodded with a giggle.

"And I brought us here?"

"You did," Freya said, nodding again. **"I'd hoped you would create my garden, but I guess that was just wishful thinking on my part."**

"What?" Brandi snorted, rolling her eyes. "You thought I would just imitate you?"

"It wouldn't have been the worst thing, would it?"

Brandi didn't say anything to that because she didn't have an answer. Her mind was still exhausted from her conversation with Najé, and she didn't have the capacity to perform all the mental gymnastics it took to converse with Freya. She hadn't processed anything that had happened that day yet and all she wanted was to be alone and have her own thoughts be her only company.

"So," Brandi sighed, "what are you doing here?"

"I came to check on the new goddess of the realm," she said. **"I wanted to make sure you were okay."**

"Checking on the person you shirked your responsibilities onto?" Brandi barked out a laugh. "How kind of you."

"Shirking?" Freya repeated, lifting her head as her eyebrows rose. **"No one is shirking their responsibilities, Brandi. Despite what you may think of me, or any of the gods,"** she added, **"we did not want to place the burden of the realm on your shoulders. If we could carry the weight ourselves, we would."**

"Is that meant to make me feel better?" Brandi asked, crossing her arms as she leaned back against the railing. "To forgive you?"

Freya narrowed her eyes at that, and Brandi couldn't help the sense of satisfaction that snaked through her at getting under Freya's skin. She knew she shouldn't feel that way, but she didn't think it was right that she was the only one getting frustrated with the situation. Everything Freya said was beginning to feel like nothing more than lip service to her. She wanted to check on her? Brandi could almost laugh at that. She'd done nothing but ask for Freya's guidance every time she'd met her, and each time she'd sent her away with vague suggestions and empty encouragement. So, what would Freya do now if she wasn't okay? Because she'd already made it clear that she wouldn't be offering any kind of help. And knowing that was enough to keep Brandi from apologizing as Freya glared at her.

"It was meant to make you understand," Freya said, swinging her legs over the edge of the balcony, putting her back to the horizon in order to face Brandi. ***"As gods, we have always existed outside of time. We bear witness to it, but it is impossible for us to understand the flow of it, to fight against someone who controls it. We have no desire to place the fate of the realm into the hands of mortals, but we had no other option. We are being forced to trust that our children will be able to do what we cannot."***

"And what is it you expect me to do exactly?" Brandi snapped, narrowing her own gaze. "Because in every conversation we have, you seem to avoid telling me that."

"Tone," Freya warned.

"What about it?"

Brandi stared at Freya, anger building in her chest as she studied the goddess. Her long green locs were piled high on top of her head with two of them hanging down to frame either side of her face. Her dark green dress flowed down to her ankles, swaying in the breeze that brushed past them. Her beauty was effortless, and Brandi wondered how much she was allowed to get away with because of it. It made her shake her head as she turned away from her towards the horizon.

"Don't think you can place the entire realm on my shoulders and then treat me like a child," Brandi said, her voice even. "If you're going to tell me what you want me to do, then tell me."

"I cannot."

"And why not?" Brandi asked, grinding her teeth in frustration. "You've been great at it up until now! Send this person to the gods," Brandi said, recounting the orders Freya had given her, "leave the shadows, abandon the queendom, find the vessels, give Terra your code. You've never held back in telling me what to do before," Brandi shouted. "So, what's stopping you now?"

"You have to decide for yourself what happens next," Freya answered, and Brandi threw her hands up in the air as she sucked her teeth and rolled her eyes. Talking to Freya was like talking to a brick wall — she was getting nowhere.

"Fine," Brandi huffed. "Leave me to deal with this by myself. I don't care."

"I'm not leaving you," Freya said, her voice gentle. **"There's just nothing more I can do for you."**

"Have I not been a faithful servant to you?" Brandi asked, the words cutting against her tongue as they tumbled from her lips before she could rethink them — because that was the only reason she could fathom for Freya refusing to help her. "Is that why you aren't helping me with this? Because I haven't been a loyal vessel?"

"Of course, you have," Freya said, her face softening as she looked at Brandi.

"I don't understand, then," Brandi stated, shaking her head as she searched Freya's face for some answers.

She'd always been loyal to Freya — without question. Like Jack, she'd believed the gods could do no wrong. That was the nature of being faithful to them, wasn't it? Praying and worshipping and believing without a single doubt that they were always right. Having faith meant fostering an unwavering trust in the gods and knowing that they had the answers mortals were unable to find. It meant believing in their guidance and remaining obedient to them even when the bigger picture was unclear. That faith was to be rewarded, but she felt like Freya was abandoning her.

"There's not much to understand," Freya said. **"I cannot guide you any further because, as of now, I do not know any more than you do. You know for yourself that we gods have limitations,"** she pointed out, offering a weak shrug. **"We comprehend more than you, better than you do, faster than you do, but we are not all-knowing. We created this realm, and we guide our children through it, but we are not omnipotent. So, I cannot shed light on a situation that has also left me in the dark."**

Freya stepped down from where she sat on the edge of the railing and walked over to Brandi, and she allowed herself to be pulled into a hug. Freya's embrace wasn't as comforting as it had always been in the past, but Brandi still lifted her arms to wrap them around the goddess and Freya squeezed her.

"I am sorry, Brandi," she whispered. ***"I wish there was more I could do for you. But I have gifted you my throne and the support of all those who are faithful to me. I have put the enemy within your reach, and we have given your friends the power they need to support you. That is all that I can do."***

Brandi heaved a deep sigh as Freya's words sunk in. Never had she imagined that the gods would have no answer to her questions — that they had failed in guiding her because they did not know where to lead her. The mere thought of having more knowledge than the gods felt like blasphemy, and she could almost laugh at the idea of knowing more than Lindl. She pushed herself away from Freya, taking a deep breath of the cool air before relaxing her shoulders. She wouldn't allow herself to be intimidated by the looming task in front of her. Like everything in her life, she would face it head on.

And she would destroy it.

"I don't know how I'm supposed to solve a problem that you can't," Brandi admitted. "I don't even know where to start."

With those words, the realm around them pulsed, and both Brandi and Freya tensed. Brandi shoved her hand into her pocket, twisting her fingers through the holes of her favorite knife, ready to drive it into whatever enemy appeared before them, but Freya threw her hand in front of Brandi, using her body to shield her from the growing crack ripping apart the fabric of the god realm. With each pulse, it grew bigger, widening until a bald man with a black suit, dark gray skin, and a starry void in his eyes stepped through with a grin.

"Perhaps I could offer you some assistance."

"What are you doing here?"

Brandi asked the question with a sigh, closing her eyes as she lifted her hand to her head to massage her temples. The conversation with Freya had been more than enough for her first visit to the god realm, and she had already been exhausted when she arrived. But lifting her gaze to the starry eyes staring at her from the opposite side of the balcony, she sighed and accepted the fact that there was still more to come. She leaned back against the balcony and waved her hand to the space between them, giving him the floor as she waited for an answer. But, it was Freya who spoke next, her stony gaze cutting into the side of Brandi's face as she fumed at Brandi's lack of apprehension.

"Brandi!"

Her name was a hiss on Freya's breath, and she let her gaze dart over to the goddess before she shrugged and looked away from her. It never ceased to amaze her how Freya's moods could change in an instant. One minute Freya was soft — comforting her as she struggled beneath the weight of her responsibilities and encouraging her to forge her own path ahead, and the next she was angry — glaring at Brandi for handling things the best way she knew how. It was dizzying and mind-boggling and just thinking about it made her head pound. She'd never doubted Freya before, but as the softness of their previous moment drifted away into memory and Freya seethed next to her, Brandi felt a cold rage settling in her chest. Because whether she was asking for help or handling things on her own, Freya was displeased with her and she had no more patience to cater to Freya's moods.

Her absolute faith in the goddess had been fractured.

She was disillusioned now, and that terrified her. Because who was she without her faith in the gods? Who was she if not the incarnation of Freya? If not the wrath of the gods? Questioning that was enough to spread the cracks forming in the foundation of who she understood herself to be, but they weren't questions she could hope to answer while standing between a time being and a goddess. So, she sighed and pulled a hand through her hair.

"Don't say my name like that," Brandi sighed, looking at Freya. "He's a being of time who has proven he can break into the god's realm whenever he wants. What do you expect us to do if we don't talk to him?"

"That's not the issue here," Freya snapped. **"There's a certain level of decorum you should maintain when you stand before your enemy, and you're being far too casual."**

"Enemy is such a harsh word," a silky voice crooned from the other side of the balcony. "I'd rather you consider me an active observer."

"Those words are contradictory," Brandi pointed out. "And correct me if I'm wrong," she said, quirking an eyebrow as she gazed into the starry void of the eyes watching her, "but, did you not just steal the immortality of the gods and threaten to wipe our entire realm out of existence?"

"I did," Azinne nodded. "But that doesn't inherently make me your enemy, does it?"

"I don't see how it doesn't," Brandi said.

"Well then," he chuckled, "you should try seeing things a little differently."

"Why?" Freya scoffed. **"So that we'll see you as some kind of twisted hero?"**

"I am an observer," he repeated, leveling a cool stare at Freya. "I intervene only when necessary."

"You intervene," Freya stressed the word, rolling her eyes, **"to be amused."**

"And is that such a terrible thing?" Azinne asked, lifting his eyebrows. "I've told you this once already," he said. "All of time is nothing more than a game. And though my job requires certain things of me, I can, at the very least, be entertained."

"And you would destroy an entire realm?" Freya asked, shock and disgust lacing her words as she frowned at him. **"Simply for that?"**

"Yes."

Azinne's answer was short and carried no hesitation with it as he held Freya's gaze. It was a sight Brandi couldn't look away from. No one — not even Rothe — ever dared to stand up to Freya and to be so bold in disagreeing with her. There were times when the gods weren't shy about making their thoughts and opinions known, but there was never a time when any one of them stood in direct opposition to Freya with such confidence. It unnerved Brandi to know she got some pleasure out of seeing someone defy Freya so openly, but that wasn't an emotion she felt the need to unpack in this moment.

Instead, she focused on the hostility brewing between them as they stared each other down. It hadn't been a full day since they'd been standing in Freya's domain, bantering back and forth in front of the other gods. She'd watched Azinne grin as Freya signed the contract that would determine the fate of the realm. It had been simple enough — they would attempt to destroy each other's mortal vessels, and if Azinne won, everything would be destroyed. If the gods won, the time-beings would leave the realm in peace. The winners would have their immortality restored while the losers forfeited their souls.

It was a game with everything on the line, but Freya had been confident in signing her name to the dotted line. But as Brandi watched them now, it was clear that something had changed.

"Fine," Brandi said, breaking their staring contest as they both turned to look at her. "You want to be entertained. Time is infinite and you're bored. I can understand that," she said with a nod.

"Can you?" Azinne asked, chuckling.

"In the figurative sense, yes," Brandi shrugged. "I've only been alive for twenty-one years, and I'm guessing that's not even a blip on your radar."

"No," Azinne laughed, "it's not."

"So, no," she admitted, "I don't fully understand you, but," she emphasized, "I do understand what it is to be put in circumstances beyond your control," she said, glancing over to Freya. "And I understand what it is to be bored out of your mind enough that antagonizing others doesn't sound like such a bad idea. Anything to cure the boredom, right?"

Azinne studied her for a moment before he threw his head back and laughed. It was a big sound that rattled the walls of the building behind them and echoed throughout the realm. It bounced around inside Brandi's head until she felt like the sound was vibrating her bones. It was bigger than life and it filled her mind with images of a thousand different lifetimes. It made her nostalgic for things she didn't understand, and she wondered at Azinne's multitudes.

"There are an infinite number of universes," he explained. "And each one contains a million different realms, just like yours. And I have been watching over them since the beginning of time, until the end of time, outside of time." He shook his head at that as he stared at her. "Can you comprehend that? I exist in the past, the present, the future, and not at all. I am nothing more than a manifested concept of the Galaxiers, born to do the work they find too menial to do themselves." His long fingers curled into tight fists before he relaxed them and sighed. "I am nothing and I wish to be…" his voice trailed off as he hesitated, his eyes searching her face as if he wasn't sure he could entrust her with his next words. "I wish to be something," he finished. "More than a figment of someone else's imagination. But," he shrugged, "that is beyond me. I am incapable of being more than what I am, so I seek to be entertained as I oversee the realms rather than to lose myself by dwelling on the infinite possibilities of things that can never be."

"Is that why it's necessary for you to be here now?" Brandi asked.

"Because trying to destroy our realm is your attempt at detaching yourself from the infinite?"

Azinne grinned at her words but shook his head.

"I am here because your goddess has broken the rules," he said, flicking a glance over to Freya.

"Broken the rules?" Brandi repeated, shaking her head. "What do you mean?"

He studied Brandi as confusion settled on her features and a slow grin spread across his face. He slid his hands into his pockets as he let his gaze dart between the two sets of green eyes that watched him, his shoulders shaking with silent laughter.

"I see your goddess hasn't told you."

"Told me what?" Brandi asked, whipping her head around to look at Freya, who avoided her gaze. "Told me what?" Brandi repeated, pushing away from the balcony towards the goddess.

"It's nothing," she said, brushing the comment away with her hand. **"You shouldn't worry about such —"**

"She bewitched the first time being of this realm," Azinne interrupted. "All in a wasted effort to keep her precious children from being subjected to his jurisdiction."

"What?"

The question was barely a whisper on Brandi's lips, but it brought silence to the rest of the realm as she stared at Freya with open shock. The goddess avoided her gaze, making no effort to deny Azinne's words and Brandi coughed a laugh of disbelief as she shook her head. She braced herself against the balcony behind her, letting the palms of her hands dig into the rough surface as her brain struggled to find the right words.

"Explain," Brandi demanded, her heart pounding in her chest with confusion and anger.

"I don't have to answer to such a disrespectful demand," Freya huffed.

"Disrespectful?"

Brandi's surprise stole the rest of her words and her mind stopped as her pulse jumped into her throat. Her blood rushed in her head, the sound of it drowning out any thought she might have had as her fingers twitched against the cool stone separating her from a thirty-two-story drop. She shoved her hands into her pockets and took a single step forward, her body pulsing with rage.

"You brought this on the realm," Brandi whispered, her voice hoarse from the strain of stringing together words and forcing them out of her mouth through her blinding anger. "You've forced me into this and endangered the life of the only person I care about. You have made it so that all the messes you've made are now my responsibility to clean up, and you have the nerve to fix your mouth and call me disrespectful?"

"Insolent child!" Freya hissed. ***"Who do you think you're talking to?"***

"Apparently someone who's refusing to give me any answers!" Brandi shouted back.

"Would you like me to tell you the story?" Azinne offered.

"You mind your business!" Freya spat at him. ***"This has nothing to do with you."***

"But it has everything to do with her," Azinne replied, his voice smooth as silk. "And if she wants to know, then I will tell her."

"You'll do no such thing!"

"Careful there," Azinne warned, lowering his voice as his grin slipped from his face. "I am not one of your lovers, smitten with your every action. I will happily destroy your realm without giving you a chance to redeem it." Freya sucked in a sharp breath and Azinne's natural grin returned. "Govern your next words accordingly."

"I haven't told her because there is no reason for her to know," Freya said, her words sharp and she glared at Azinne.

"I disagree," he said. "Tell her the truth or I will."

"Fine," Freya snapped, turning to face Brandi after fuming in silence for a moment. **"I'll tell you, but it won't change anything."**

"Stop telling her lies," Azinne hummed, crossing his arms as he leaned against the balcony. "For her," he said, smiling in Brandi's direction, "it will change everything."

CHAPTER FIVE

The goddess needed neither light nor water, nor sky nor moon. Alone, she was complete and brought forth life. Alone, she was the originator of creation. And alone, she brought forth the inception of destruction.

— Freya, The Beginning and the End | Lindl's First Holy Academy

---

REALM OF THE GODS — BEFORE THE BEGINNING OF TIME

The first time Freya ever saw the plain wooden door with the golden knob appear in her garden, she was alone. The other gods were in the mortal realm, setting up barriers and carving out lands for their children to roam in. She'd been lazing on one of Carna's clouds, drifting in and out of her dreams beneath Rothe's warm sun.

At first, she hadn't noticed the door. It was inconspicuous and appeared near the tallest trees on the farthest edge of her realm. In her sleep-laden mind, she hadn't paid much attention to the light glinting off the handle, but the sharp knocks that resonated throughout the realm had startled her.

She bolted upright and turned toward the sound, her eyes wide as the door opened and a man walked through. Like he would be the second time she would meet him, he wore a black monochrome suit. His eyes carried shifting stars she'd never seen within them, and he was nearly as tall as Rothe. He stood with his back straight and his hands clasped behind him. And as he took in all the vivid colors of her garden, she stared at him.

Unlike her own dark melanin skin that shone in the light of Rothe's sun, his gray skin seemed dull, as if it were absorbing the light. He seemed to be a blot of darkness in her bright garden, but — for better or for worse — she couldn't look away from him. And when his dark eyes found hers, neither could he.

He took bold strides over to Freya, his gaze locking her in place as he approached. His dark eyes were nothing like that of the other gods. So, when he reached out his hand to help her down off the clouds, she accepted it. And when he kept her hand in his, she didn't pull away.

"I am Zareal," he said, a smile pulling at the edges of his lips. ***"And you are?"***

"Freya. Goddess of this realm."

"Yes," Zareal nodded, closing his eyes as if he were recalling some information he'd heard long ago. ***"Yes, you are."***

"What are you doing here?"

"Ah," he hummed, his eyes searching her face for an answer to a question she didn't know. ***"I am here to face my downfall, of course."***

"Excuse me?"

He chuckled and released her hand as he took a few steps back to lower himself into a bow. He held it for a moment before rising back to his full height and smiling at the goddess, his white teeth a startling contrast to his gray skin and starry eyes.

"Pardon me if I caused you any confusion. I am Zareal," he repeated. *"I am a being of time and the liaison between this realm and the Galaxiers. It is a pleasure to meet you, Freya, goddess of this realm."*

"And I, you," Freya said, confusion lacing her words as she nodded at him. *"But I'm afraid I don't understand. Who are the Galaxiers?"*

"They are the overseers of the universe. Of all universes. And I am their liaison. I am a being who both controls time and exists outside of it."

"You keep using this word, 'time'," Freya said as she turned to walk towards her gazebo, pausing to glance over her shoulder. Zareal followed behind her, matching her languid pace as she moved through her garden, soaking in the sun's warmth and the gentle breeze that danced across her skin. *"What is it?"* Freya asked, glancing over her shoulder again to meet Zareal's gaze. *"I've never heard of it."*

He laughed before nodding his head in understanding as he considered her question. There were no words to articulate how long he had been doing his work for the Galaxiers — no words for how many universes he had seen — how many realms he'd had the pleasure of starting time for and the burden of ending it. He wished he had a better answer to give her, but for the gods of the realms he visited, the hardest thing for them was always understanding who he was. Because, for them, they were the highest powers in existence.

For them, time was not a concept they could easily comprehend.

They struggled to accept that more existed beyond their boundaries than within it — that what they knew and understood was only a fraction of the greater universe and the multitude of the known universes, and not even significant when it came to the knowledge of the Galaxiers. It was impossible to explain that their creations were mere blips compared to what the Galaxiers were capable of.

The gods created within the rules of their realms, but the Galaxiers were the ones who created the rules they functioned within. It was a concept that he was never able to explain to gods — and it wasn't for a lack of trying. He'd simply learned that it was impossible to explain to a god that they were insignificant in the scheme of things and that time was a form of reality that must exist in their realm, but one they could not create and held no control over. So, instead of trying to tackle that question, Zareal smiled and caught up to Freya's side.

"It would be hard to explain to you," he admitted.

"Try," Freya coaxed. *"Unless you think me dull-witted and incapable of understanding?"*

Zareal laughed. *"You mean to get your way by having me insult you if I refuse? That is a devious level of trickery, Freya, goddess of the realm."*

"Is it?" She asked, her lips tilting upwards. *"I wasn't aware it was trickery. I only meant to discover your true thoughts on the matter."*

"My true thoughts," Zareal said, crouching down to gaze at the

bright green flowers growing around them that gave off the sweetest scent, *"are that it would be hard to explain. There are no words to explain to you a concept that does not yet exist in your realm."*

"Oh. So, this time of yours," Freya said, moving to stand beside him and gaze at the maple flowers she'd planted in her own domain in the mortal realm, *"doesn't exist here?"*

"Not yet, no."

"And you're here to bring it to us?"

"Yes," Zareal said with a nod, straightening back to his full height and turning away from the flowers that danced in the wind. *"You may consider it a gift."*

"A gift? Then it would only be right that I give you something in return."

"That isn't necessary," Zareal said, laughing under his breath at the thought of a god being capable of offering him anything. *"To give you time is my job. My duty. To accept something in return for that would be inappropriate."*

"I disagree," Freya said, stepping into the shade of her gazebo and descending into the seat in the center. *"It is always appropriate to return one kindness with another."*

"And what would you offer a man who carries in him no desires?"

"You have no desires?" Freya asked, her eyebrows shooting upward as she looked at him. *"Not a single one?"*

"I have no need of them."

"Well," she sighed, *"that is where your thinking is flawed.*

Desires aren't necessities. They're wants. Frivolous things that bring us joy when we attain them."

"I've never wanted for anything," Zareal admitted. *"I have all my needs met now."*

"But I'm not asking you about your needs," Freya laughed, gazing up at him with amusement lighting her green eyes. *"I'm asking you what you want."*

"And what should I want?" Zareal questioned.

"I can only tell you what the other gods have desired of me."

"And what was that?"

"Love," she whispered. *"Affection. Children."* She turned to hold Zareal's gaze and lifted her eyebrows in curiosity. *"Would you desire the same things from me?"*

"I'm not sure."

"Well," Freya said, a smirk pulling at her lips, *"anything else would have to be something your own mind created."*

Zareal smiled at that. He'd never met a god like Freya and the thought of him wanting something from her amused him. He'd never wanted for anything — the nature of being a time being under the jurisdiction of the Galaxiers meant that everything he could need since the beginning of time, and after it would end, would be taken care of. And when his every need was met before he could even think to ask for it, he'd never entertained the concept of wanting more. But as Freya looked up at him with her bright green eyes and the sun dancing across her brown skin, the thought crossed his mind that he would want to sit with her — to immerse himself in her world of light and color — even if it was only for a moment.

"Actually," he said, taking a step forward and giving voice to his thoughts, *"I can think of one thing I might enjoy."*

"And what would that be?"

"I would like to sit with you, there," he said, pointing to a cluster of bright orange and red flowers that were blooming a few feet away from the gazebo. *"I think you and I could have a lovely conversation, if you'd allow it."*

"That's all you want? To sit and converse with me?"

"Is that asking too much?"

"Not at all," Freya laughed, returning to her feet. She reached for his hand to pull him along as she guided him toward the flowers he'd pointed towards. *"And maybe while we talk, you can find the words to explain what this 'time' is."*

"Very well," Zareal said, his face brightening at the idea of getting to know her world as she saw it. *"If that is what you wish, then I will do my best."*

Freya turned to smile at him — her face lit with unbridled joy — and it was then that Zareal understood what the Galaxiers had meant when they warned him that should he arrive in this realm unprepared, that it would be his downfall. When they'd issued the warning to him, he hadn't understood. He'd completed every task set before him with immaculate precision and had been confused why they thought a tiny realm that was still on the cusp of creation would be the thing that would ruin him.

But as they sat amongst the flowers and the light from Freya's smile blinded him to the realities of the wider universes, and the warmth from her hand seeped into his, he felt his heart pound for the first time. He gasped at the feeling and lifted his hand to his chest as it sputtered to life inside his ribcage. It continued to beat in a frantic rhythm as Freya leaned into him, the sweet scent of her garden lulling him into a sense of safety and comfort he'd never felt. She'd released his hand, but she pressed her body against his as she told him all about her realm — about the flowers and the shaders, the other gods and their children. And with every word, Zareal's heart beat faster as she painted a realm filled with life and love and color with her words.

Her joy was infectious in a way he'd never felt before. And it was without fully understanding the feeling inside his chest that he told her every secret of the universe that he held. He told her of the realms crafted of endless waves, of airy mountains, of lightless caverns and of nightless deserts. He told her of the Galaxiers and did his best to explain to her what time was — how he existed before it, within it, and outside of it. He was so enraptured by her laughter and her smile, her gentle touch on his arm and the warmth that radiated off her, that he was in no way prepared to deny her when she invited him deeper into her garden like the seductress she was.

It wasn't until she'd shown him the heights of a bliss he'd never imagined and he was lying in her arms, his face pressed into the warmth of her bare skin, that she whispered to him a question that made him realize just how far he'd fallen.

"Do you have to bring time to this realm?"

He lifted his head then to look at her, surprise chasing away the lingering daze of euphoria clouding his mind as he gazed into her green eyes.

"I don't understand the question," he said. *"I am a being of time. So, yes."*

"But you don't have to be," she whispered, placing her hand against his face.

"Then what would I be?"

"Mine," she smiled. *"A god."*

His eyes searched her face as he considered her words. As tempting as they sounded — as much as he wanted to please her and give in to her wishes — he knew that he never could. Some things were absolute, and what she wanted was impossible for him to give her.

"I can't."

"Of course, you can," she giggled. *"All you need to do is stay here with me."*

"And what of your other lovers?"

"What of them?" Freya asked, raising an eyebrow in confusion.

"Would they be content to split their time with you a fifth way?"

"I love them, but," she said with a smile, *"I am still my own. I decide who I spend my time with. They respect that."*

"I wouldn't," Zareal said with a shake of his head.

"And why not?"

"Because I would not want to share you," he said with a smile. *"Knowing your love has made me greedy,"* he said, turning his face into her palm to place a soft kiss against it, *"and I would want every one of my moments to be with you because I know nothing lasts*

forever."

"*Some things do,*" Freya argued.

"*Nothing is eternal,*" Zareal emphasized. "*After everything I've told you, you know that to be the truth, too.*"

"*Then what of my children?*" Freya asked, her eyes welling up with tears. "*Would you not allow them to be eternal?*"

"*No,*" Zareal said softly. "*It is impossible. They will have their moment and you will love them, but then they will leave you. That is the way of things,*" he said, kissing her wrist. "*That is the way of this.*"

"*Of this?*" Freya questioned, pulling her wrist away from his trailing lips. "*You mean to love me and then leave?*"

"*We,*" Zareal whispered, "*are not eternal either, Freya.*"

"*You're saying you won't love me forever?*"

"*I'm saying,*" Zareal said, choosing his words with care, "*that I won't be with you forever. I must return to my duty and you,*" he said, reaching out for her again and dropping his hand when she pulled away from him, "*must return to yours.*"

"*And nothing I say would convince you otherwise?*"

"*No. But,*" he said, his voice lilting upwards with a tiny spark of hope, "*I do not have to go yet.*"

"*I think it would be best if you did,*" Freya said, her voice cold as she rose from the bed of flower petals beneath them to slip into her dress.

"*Freya.*"

Zareal said her name with all the heartbreak he felt growing in his chest. He'd only just learned what it meant to have a beating heart and already he wished he could return to a time where he hadn't known what it meant for it to ache. He rose from the flower bed as well and he looked at her.

"We still have time."

"Do we?" Freya quipped. *"Because I was under the impression that you were about to start it."*

"Will you not forgive me for who I am? For what I am?"

"I won't forgive anyone who brings harm to my children," she answered, her words gentle. *"You are no exception."*

"I've already broken the rules for you," he pointed out. *"I told you of the Galaxiers, of my duty. Simply being here with you is against our policies, and I was warned against it. I'll be punished for that."* Zareal shook his head as he looked at her, hoping she would turn around and face him. *"Would you deepen my wounds by denying me what time I have left with you?"*

"Would you change your decision about allowing time to enter this realm?" Freya asked, her green eyes peeking up at him from over her shoulder with hope.

"I can't do that," he sighed.

"Then neither can I," she said, her shoulders sagging under the weight of her words as she turned away from him again.

"And what of the child that grows within you now?" Zareal asked, his chest tightening as her back straightened in what could only be surprise. *"I see all time, Freya,"* he reminded her. *"I know what will be."*

Freya turned to face him with a defiant smile, and his heart twisted at how beautiful she looked even when he knew her words would cut him deeper than any knife.

"Then you know what will be," she said. **"I suggest you leave before the others return,"** she whispered, walking away back towards the gazebo. **"They need not know what's happened here."**

"I'll have to return," he warned. **"I have to bring time to this realm."**

"Then do so as a stranger."

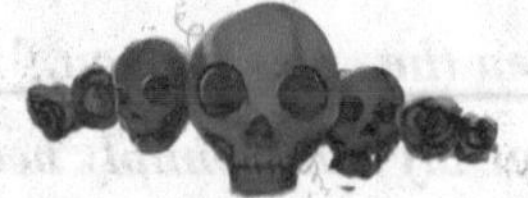

REALM OF THE GODS — PRESENT DAY

"And it is with those words that my predecessor decided to destroy your entire realm," Azinne said, throwing his hands up with a flourish and finishing Freya's story.

"So," Brandi said, dragging out the words as she worked to organize her thoughts. "Zareal is the one who wants to destroy the realm? Not you?"

"Now you're catching up," he said with a chuckle. "It's her vengeful lover who wants to destroy everything," he said, pointing to Freya. "I'm merely an observer, as I said before."

"I still don't believe that," Brandi muttered. "But let's focus on something you seemed to gloss over," she said, turning her head to Freya, who now leaned against the balcony with her back to Brandi and Azinne. "You had a forbidden love child?"

"That's another long story," Freya sighed.

"Well, we've got time," Brandi snorted. "You literally gave birth to it!"

Azinne cracked up at that, his laughter cutting through the tense air around them and the anxiety building in Brandi's gut. Her muscles tightened with every word that left Freya's mouth, but Azinne was managing to be an unexpected reprieve in a sea of uncertainty. She clung to the sliver of peace he offered as she shook her head and glanced between the two of them.

"Who was the child?" Brandi asked. "That may be the vessel that Zareal has chosen."

"It isn't," Freya said, turning around to face them again.

"You can't possibly know that."

"I can, and I do."

"How?" Brandi demanded.

"Will you not trust me on this?"

"We've been over this, Freya," Azinne sang, grinning as Freya shifted in her discomfort. "Tell her, or I will."

"Why can't you just stay out of this?" Freya hissed.

"I will not keep your secrets," Azinne chuckled. "And I have no intention of letting you keep them either."

"You are absolutely rotten," Freya hissed.

"I am honest," Azinne replied, his wide grin still in place. "Apologies, if that disrupts the nature of who you are."

Azinne and Freya returned to their staring contest and Brandi sighed, closing her eyes against their childish behavior, and taking a moment to make sense of her thoughts. She struggled to imagine Freya with anyone other than the other gods, but she couldn't say she was surprised either. Freya had always been open with her love — it's why she had four lovers to begin with, even though Rothe was the only one she viewed as her equal. It was the one aspect of Freya that Brandi had never understood.

Jack was her person.

She loved him too much to ever imagine there being someone else who could be on par with what she felt for him. Just the idea of it was enough to make her head ache. She would never want multiple lovers, so it was hard for her to understand why Freya would allow someone else into her life when she already had the gods. Brandi couldn't make sense of it, and she gave up trying to as she shook her head.

"Will one of you answer my question?" Brandi asked, pulling them back once more from their staring contest. "Who was the child?"

"That would be you," Azinne said, pointing a finger at Brandi.

She stared at him with wide eyes as his words echoed in her ears and seeped into her brain. She felt as if all her senses were being pulled through a river of molasses as she turned to face Freya. Brandi watched as Freya's face morphed from outrage to panic before settling in pity.

"*I'm sorry,*" she whispered.

"No," Brandi whispered, shaking her head. "No."

"You can't reject a truth simply because you dislike it," Azinne said, his words soft as he watched her with the same caution one used when cornering a wild animal. "It's not as simple as that."

"Nothing is simple with you," Freya snapped, glaring at Azinne. **"Why do you feel the need to go out of your way to tell her irrelevant things?"**

"Irrelevant?" Brandi asked, her eyebrows shooting up as she looked at Freya. "You don't think knowing whose daughter I am is relevant?"

"You are my daughter," Freya stressed, pressing a hand to her chest. **"That is what matters. And you have always known that, have you not?"**

"There is a huge difference between being a descendant of your children and your literal daughter!" Brandi pulled her hands through her hair as she stared at the ground.

"It may be difficult to hear, but it's something you must accept," Azinne said, standing up straight. "You are the daughter of Freya, former goddess of this realm, and Zareal, time being for the Galaxiers."

"Azinne!"

"Silence," he whispered, narrowing his starry gaze on Freya as he shocked them both by stealing her voice. "I may not be a god as you are, but I control time. And nothing, not even sound, can travel without it."

"Why would you make it a point to tell me all of this?"

Brandi asked the question as she lifted her head to meet Azinne's gaze. Her mind was reeling, but she didn't want to pass up the opportunity to get answers — real answers — from the only other person who seemed to have them. Her body vibrated with too many emotions for her to name them all, but curiosity dominated her mind. She wanted to know the truth — the absolute truth that she knew she'd never get out of Freya. So, her heart jumped into her throat as Azinne grinned at her.

"Because you are now the goddess of this realm, and the game cannot start unless you agree to play."

Brandi paused, processing his words before she nodded her head. "What are the rules?"

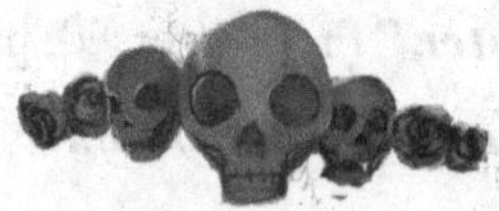

Brandi couldn't tell how long she stood on the balcony listening to Azinne, but her mind was overloaded by the time he finished speaking. Freya, unable to speak, had stormed out of the realm, leaving the two of them standing on opposite ends of the balcony. Azinne had started his story with the beginning of the realm, recounting the story of Zareal's demise from his own perspective and filling in the details that Freya had skipped — like the fact that Zareal had been his mentor or that the punishment he had spoken of to Freya was exile.

"It's the end of time where nothing exists," Azinne explained. "There's no sound, no light. No stars or thoughts or breath. Just infinite... nothingness."

"That sounds miserable."

"It is," Azinne said, nodding. "It is the place from where time beings are created and the place none of us wish to return to. And it is why I suspect that Zareal, for all the love he claimed to have for your goddess, remained duty-bound to the Galaxiers in such a way."

"That seems a strange place to draw the line," Brandi snorted. "Fall in love with the goddess, have a child with her, and destroy the realm, but he still delivers time?"

"I cannot make sense of that for you either," Azinne said, laughing. "I can only tell you the facts and my own thoughts on them. Both his actions and his reasons confuse me."

"You can't understand why he fell in love with Freya."

"No," Azinne agreed. "I do not see the appeal of loving a god."

When Brandi said nothing, he lifted his eyebrows in question, his starry eyes searching her face, and she stared back, narrowing her gaze as he surveyed her.

"What?" Brandi asked.

"You don't think it strange I can't love a god?"

"Why would I?"

"Most goddesses are insistent upon being the exception," he pointed out. "They believe they will be the one to corrupt me."

Brandi let out a burst of laughter at that. She could imagine other worlds with goddesses like Freya — gods who were the creators of love and beauty, hopes and dreams, romance and lust, who couldn't imagine anyone being anything but infatuated with them and their existence. It was a terrifying thought, but if he'd encountered hundreds of gods like that, she could understand how he would be desensitized to their appeal.

"I have no interest in corrupting you," Brandi told him. "I have someone already, and I have no desire to garner any attention that isn't his."

"Fascinating," Azinne muttered, a smile pulling at his lips. "You are absolutely fascinating."

"Let's stay focused," Brandi said, redirecting the conversation. "I understand the rules. And that Zareal broke the first two. But he brought time to the realm," she pointed out. "Would that not be enough to satisfy the Galaxiers?"

"No. They punish all who defy them, regardless of whether or not their intentions were malicious."

"That doesn't seem fair."

"Their expectations of us are clear and unchanging," Azinne shrugged. "I cannot find fault with anyone who treats everyone the same. But they are not ruthless."

"They sound that way."

"No," Azinne said, shaking his head as his eyes darted away from Brandi toward the frozen horizon in thought. "If they were, they would have stripped Zareal of his power and exiled him. But for some reason," Azinne pointed out, returning his gaze to Brandi, "they did not. They allowed him to return to this realm."

"And why would he do that?"

"Because he loves your goddess."

"I don't understand," Brandi said, her eyebrows drawing together. "Didn't he refuse to stay with her?"

"And if you could not stay with your beloved?" Azinne questioned. "If he swore love and loyalty to you only to love others while you were forced to watch over him and the children he sired for three thousand years? Would that not drive you mad?"

"Fair point."

"We may be beings of time, but we are not immune to emotions."

"I wouldn't have guessed," Brandi said, rolling her eyes.

Azinne laughed at that. "We are not meant to intermingle with the gods we watch over. But there are those of us who desire connections."

"And you're not one of them?"

"No," he said with a shake of his bald head. "I have no desire for any kind of romantic connection."

"Is that why you threatened the realm? Because you don't know what it's like to want to protect someone you love?"

"Everyone has someone, Brandi," Azinne said, his voice low. "It may not be romantic, but there are those I care about. And I acted in such a way to force the hand of your goddess."

"Why?"

"Because when your goddess seduced Zareal, I was instructed to take his place. But when I arrived, he had already returned and started time for this realm. Not only that, he'd warned the gods against my arrival and coerced the goddess into a mortal form. I could no longer carry out my orders as the Galaxiers instructed."

"So, what did you do?"

"I reported back to them. And when they told me of Zareal's deeds and of you, I requested permission to test the gods of this realm to see if they were worthy of remaining in existence. The Galaxiers granted my request."

"I don't see why my existence would factor into your decisions."

"Because you are the daughter of Freya and Zareal," Azinne explained. "You are both a genuine god and a being of time."

"How would that even be possible?" Brandi questioned. "I'm not three thousand years old!"

"Unfortunately, even I do not know the answer to that," Azinne admitted. "My best guess is that she gave up her corporeal body to remove herself from even the most minute influences of time and then used your latent powers of time being growing within her to ensure she gave birth to you when she was ready to, and not a moment sooner."

"I hear what you're saying," Brandi said, pulling a hand through her hair, "but it's still hard to believe you."

"Well, answer me this," Azinne said. "Why do you think all the gods were able to bless you? Do the bodies of mortals not suffer under the weight of a single blessing in this realm?"

"Jack didn't."

"Your lover is an exception," Azinne pointed out. "And he flirted with his ultimate end for three days because of it, did he not? How many blessings do you carry?"

"It doesn't matter."

"It's at least four, by my count. You think a mortal could survive that?"

"I'm Freya's vessel," Brandi offered up, shaking her head. "I'm built different."

"And you think that absolves you of natural limitations?" Azinne laughed. "Can you not converse with Freya's creatures of the night?"

"So?"

"Can her other children do that?" Azinne questioned. "How many of her other vessels have those creatures known?"

"I don't know," Brandi shrugged, looking away from him. "Maybe they just never had the opportunity."

"Those creatures live exceptionally long lives," Azinne pointed out. "If they were able, they would have served all the vessels of the goddess as they serve you."

"They don't serve me," Brandi argued. "They're my family."

"And when have they ever acted against your wishes?" When Brandi said nothing, Azinne sighed. "A being who cannot disobey orders is a servant. You must know this."

"I was just told something different," Brandi whispered. "That's all."

"Freya told you whatever she thought you would believe," Azinne said, shrugging his shoulders as he slid his hands into his pockets. "But it's evident your power as a time being is growing. You should have noticed your body reacting to it by now."

"Maybe," Brandi shrugged, thinking back to how she'd collapsed under the sudden swell of power she'd felt while talking to Najé. "But I still don't see how I would be of any use to her in the first place."

"Because time beings are immune to the powers of a god," Azinne explained. "Without you, she would have no way to oppose me."

"I'm not immune to their powers," Brandi pointed out.

"Because half of who you are belongs to the goddess. It is why she could incarnate within you. You are still her child, but you are your father's daughter as well."

"But why would she want me to fight you?" Brandi asked.

"Because her plan has always been to remove time from this realm," Azinne answered. "She heeded Zareal's warning because she knew you would exist and have the power to fight us on your own terms."

"My own terms?"

Azinne nodded. "Should you want to, you could wield your powers against any of us. It is why you are a danger to both the gods and the time beings," he explained. "You are not beholden to the Galaxiers for rescuing you from exile like we are. And should you want to command time for this realm yourself, you could. You could stop the flow of it and give Freya the thing she wants most."

"For her children to be eternal."

"Yes," Azinne nodded. "It is why she has worked so hard to gain your loyalty to her. So that you would never question her and acquiesce to her wishes."

"And what of Zareal?" Brandi asked. "Why would he warn Freya if he was the one who wanted to destroy the realm?"

"That's something you would have to ask him," Azinne answered. "But he saw what would be in this realm. Perhaps he knew she would resist the Galaxiers and that they would punish her and the gods she loved accordingly. His own revenge against Freya and the realm she loved more than him."

"And why haven't the Galaxiers stopped him?" Brandi asked, her anger rising at the thought.

"They wait to see what you will do," Azinne shrugged. "You are a time being, raised a mortal, and ascended to goddess. You are a walking paradox, and they wish to see how you will handle this situation."

"And what of you?" Brandi asked, holding his gaze. "You've explained everyone's motives but your own."

"I told you already," he said. "I came here to test the gods and be entertained."

"And how do you plan to accomplish that now?"

"I'm glad you asked," Azinne grinned. "I want you to sign a new contract with me."

"What about the contract you already made with Freya and the other gods?" Brandi questioned. "You would just renege on that?"

"The moment Freya gifted her position to you, and you became the goddess of this realm, the contract was null and voided," he said, annoyance coating his words. "I'd wanted to force their hand a bit more to see what they would do. My job was to test them after all," he reminded her. "But the moment their immortality came into question, the gods relinquished their power into their vessels and hid within your souls."

"That makes no sense," Brandi said, blinking her eyes as she tried to make sense of Azinne's words. "If that's true, and the contract was voided, then…"

"They had no intention of ever helping you fight me or my vessel," Azinne stated. "It was a loophole, but their immortality, and mine, returned the moment the other gods turned over their power to your friends and Freya made you goddess of this realm."

"So, they ran," Brandi whispered, her voice shaking with disappointment and rage as the realization of everything sunk in. She shook her head as she lifted her head to meet Azinne's gaze.

"Which is why I want a new contract with you," Azinne said, nodding. "The terms are simple. If you destroy the monarchy, I'll help you against Zareal, the one who actually wants to destroy your realm."

"And if I refuse?"

"I'll help Zareal instead and watch you fight against both of us," Azinne said with a grin.

Brandi groaned in frustration, and she threw her head back to look at the dark sky above them. She no longer found the same peace in the scenery she once had and hated Azinne and Freya for ruining such a simple pleasure for her.

"Why do you want to see the monarchy destroyed?" Brandi finally asked, lifting her head to meet his gaze once more. "It's one measly queendom. It can't be that important in the scheme of things."

"It's for my own personal amusement," Azinne shrugged. "I just want to see you do it. But if you can," Azinne smirked, "I'll consider you, the current goddess of this realm, to have passed my test, and I'll advise the Galaxiers that this realm is worthy of existence. How's that sound?"

Brandi glared at him as she considered the options presented to her. If she ignored him, she'd be up against two time beings trying to destroy the realm — one for vengeance, and the other for amusement. If she did sign a new contract, she'd have to destroy the monarchy, but only one of them would be her enemy and the Galaxiers would no longer be a threat to the realm. It didn't seem like much of an option to her as she pushed away from the edge of the balcony, rolling her shoulders back with a sigh.

To say she was overwhelmed would be an understatement — there was too much going on in her mind for her to sort anything out, but she understood two things with an unwavering clarity.

One, she would never trust the gods again. They'd abandoned her and her friends to defend the realm on their own and she'd never forgive them for that. And two, destroying the monarchy that Freya had built and forced her protect, now sounded like fun. And if it would garner her an ally in the process, then all the better — she would destroy the monarchy and deal with everything else after that.

"I have caveats," Brandi said. "Non-negotiable."

"I'll hear them," Azinne said, crossing his arms as another grin pulled at the corner of his lips.

"You can't change your mortal vessel from whoever it is right now," Brandi said. "You cannot bring any harm to Jack. And if I win, I want to meet the Galaxiers."

"I can agree to those demands," Azinne said, dragging out the words and nodding his head. "But if you fail to destroy the monarchy by, let's say…" his words trailed off before he grinned again, "end of summer? Then, I win," he chuckled, "and you have to become my apprentice."

"Why would you want that?" Brandi asked, shock tightening her throat at the idea of being forced to leave the realm.

"If there are prizes for winning involved, I want the chance to win something too. And I told you once already, didn't I?" He laughed, "I find you fascinating. My job would be much less boring if you were with me."

"But Jack…"

"He can come too," Azinne interrupted, waving his hand through the air. "I'd have to bend a few rules, but I'm not a monster. I understand that you two are a package deal."

Brandi paused, weighing the risks of what he wanted against her own desires, but she knew what her decision would be the moment he agreed not to take Jack away from her. She would never be able to shake the terror she felt at seeing him trapped in a pod, suffocating to his last breath. And it didn't matter who she was facing, she would never allow something like that to happen again, whether she was fighting the queendom, the time beings, or the overseers of the universe. She wouldn't risk Jack. As long as Azinne never asked her to do that, she had no reservations about nodding her head in agreement.

"Are there any rules I should know of?" Brandi asked.

"Nope," Azinne said, grinning as she walked over to him.

"Fine," Brandi said, offering her hand to him. "Then you have a deal."

CHAPTER SIX

For without destruction, creation is meaningless.

— Freya, The Beginning and the End | Lindl's First Holy Academy

---

FREYA'S DOMAIN — THE GOD REALM

MORNING OF DAY 2

"I see you've finally decided to join us."

Low growls followed behind the words, and Brandi struggled to force her eyes open. Her body was heavy — as if her bones had been reforged with lead while she slept — and she felt her mind trembling from the exertion of being conscious. She couldn't suppress the groan that escaped her as she coaxed her body into an upright position, and she was surprised to find herself sitting among the rubble at Freya's temple. She had a vague memory of Tiki taking her away after her conversation with Najé, but she doubted that Tiki would take her back to her destroyed home. She winced as she lifted a hand to her forehead and looked around, but she couldn't make sense of why Freya was standing across from her or why Tiki and Lia were standing next to Royal and baring their teeth at the goddess.

"What…?"

Brandi didn't have the chance to finish her question before the world spun around her and she was tilting backwards. She felt as if her head was too heavy for her neck to support and she was bracing herself to crash back into the rock below her, but Lia swung her tail to create a soft pile of black fur beneath her. She gasped in relief as she sank into the sweet-smelling fur, her eyes locked on the gray, colorless, sky above her. She'd thought she'd returned to the mortal realm, but she was wrong. Everything was motionless around her, the same as it was whenever Freya had summoned her soul to her temple in the past.

"Try not to move around too much," Royal warned, glancing over his shoulder at her. "You're still in the god realm and have been for almost two days. Your mind is fragile right now," he told her. "If you try to do too much, it could collapse in on itself."

"But why…?"

"Am I here?" Royal finished for her. "Because once Crown told me of the battle and of the deal she'd made, I had a feeling she would come after you," he said, narrowing his eyes at Freya, who stood on the other side of the rock formation. "I came to warn your shaders, but it seems they didn't need it." He scoffed as he shook his head. "It appears Freya is nothing if not predictable."

"You say that as if I came to hurt her," Freya sighed.

"And you're saying you didn't?" Royal questioned.

"Of course not," Freya huffed. ***"I came back here to try and wake her from the god realm. It was her first time manifesting it***

and," Freya said, pointing to Royal, *"as you just made clear, she'd been in there too long."*

Do not trust her, Tiny Human! Lia growled, stomping her feet against the ground. *She meant to rip your soul from your body!*

"I would never do anything like that," Freya snapped. *"I was trying to keep her from being trapped there forever!"*

Brandi's thoughts were racing through her mind at full speed, and as she sat up once more with the support of Lia's tail behind her, she failed to make sense of what she was seeing. She couldn't understand why Royal was there or where he'd come from. The last time she'd seen him, it was in Lindl's domain. He still wore the same baggy jeans and unzipped hoodie, but his gray eyes were narrowed at the goddess, and she'd never seen Tiki so angry. Its hackles were raised, and low growls rumbled through its chest, vibrating the air. And the moment Freya took a step forward, it snarled and snapped at her, sending her stumbling back to where she was before in shock. Brandi couldn't believe her eyes as Tiki shifted forward, growling at the goddess as it reached out to Brandi.

Are you alright? Tiki asked. *Lia speaks the truth.*

"I'm fine," Brandi whispered, placing a hand to her forehead. "Where's Jack?"

He is still beside you, Tiki answered. *You have not woken yet in the mortal realm. She did not bring him here with you,* it explained.

"She couldn't stop us from coming, though," Royal added. "An unfortunate side effect of us being her first creations. She can't control us as she can her other children."

"You always did assume the worst of me, Shade," Freya said,

rolling her eyes with a sigh.

"Must you call me that?" Royal asked through gritted teeth.

"Shade?" Brandi repeated, her eyebrows drawing together as she looked toward them.

"That is the name I gave him in his first life," Freya said, answering Brandi's unspoken question. ***"He was the first creature I created and the ancestor of every shader you know. Although,"*** she said, turning back to Royal, ***"I don't understand why you insist on rejecting the name I gave you."***

"Because I hate it," Royal stated, his voice empty of any emotion. "And it's been a long time since I've been even remotely fond of you."

"That's harsh," Freya laughed. ***"But I can't say I'm surprised."***

Brandi's green eyes darted between Freya and Royal as they spoke, and similar to how she'd felt with Azinne, it was hard for her to accept that there was someone willing to stand in direct opposition to Freya. It added more pressure to the cracks that were already splintering her faith in the goddess, and she shook her head. She'd known who Royal was for most of her life, but with the way he treated her, she'd always assumed that he and Freya were close. To see him stating his disdain for the goddess to her face confused Brandi more than anything else.

"Wait…" Brandi said, looking toward Royal. "I thought…"

"That we were close?" Royal asked, shaking his head. "We were, once. Just like you are with those two," he said, nodding toward Tiki and Lia, "but that was a long time ago."

"What happened?" Brandi asked, looking between him and Freya. She couldn't imagine Tiki and Lia not being her closest friends and wondered what could have soured their relationship to this extent.

"She wouldn't let me rest in peace," Royal spat, glaring at Freya. "I'm not immortal. Every lifetime I'm born into a family, and around my twelfth birthday, she's born into the mortal realm, and I get back every memory of my previous lives."

"You should be grateful for that, Shade," Freya said, placing her hands on her hips as she stared at him. ***"Do you know how many souls pray to remember their previous lives? For the wisdom that comes with it?"***

"Don't!" Royal shouted, the word sounding more like the growl of a shader than that of a human. "I never asked for this!"

"That's no reason to be ungrateful," she huffed.

"Ungrateful?" Royal laughed. "Every life I have, you steal it away from me! Forcing me to serve you again and again."

"Do you know how many people would love to serve me? To speak with me as often as you do?"

"I don't care!" Royal shouted. "I'm sick of you! I've watched my kin return to you, human and beast alike. And still, you call me back to this realm. Even after I've grown to hate you, you send me back here!"

"Because you were my only friend," Freya whispered. ***"You have always told me what my lovers could not. Without your voice of reason, what was I to do?"***

"You could have befriended one of my children," he snapped. "You could have trained a mortal priest to serve you as the others have. You had a daughter!" Royal shouted, gesturing to Brandi. "Do not make it seem as if you were alone because you didn't have a choice."

"Do not speak as if you understand my actions, Shade," Freya snapped.

"No one could understand your actions because they make no sense!"

Silence settled over the clearing and Brandi's head swam as she looked between the two of them with wide eyes. She'd never seen Royal so much as raise his voice before, and the way his voice boomed made her nerves stand on end. It was like listening to an angry shader's howl and she shook her head, trying to clear it of the sound. Knowing that Royal hated Freya changed everything she knew about him, and her eyebrows drew together as realization dawned on her.

"Is that why," Brandi said, struggling to form her words, "you refuse to see Noble?"

"He's Carna's vessel," Royal said, nodding his head. "He'll know who I am. And I don't want him looking at me like a beast rather than his brother."

"He wouldn't," Brandi whispered, thinking about how much Noble respected his brother. It didn't matter that Royal had left without a word and that he hadn't seen him since he was eleven years old — whenever he spoke of him, there was nothing but warmth in his voice. He'd told her once that he'd thought of going to search for Royal, just to find him and know where he'd been, but his promise to protect her was more important to him. It's why she'd always felt guilty meeting up with Royal, but he'd sworn her to secrecy, so she'd never uttered a word to Noble about his brother. But as she watched his shoulders sag, she wished Royal would have more faith in Noble.

"You don't know that," Royal whispered. "And it shouldn't matter. I shouldn't have to choose between being a good brother and serving a wretched goddess."

"Sharp words, Shade," Freya said, her voice cool as she narrowed her eyes. ***"Choose your next ones carefully."***

"Or what?" Royal coughed out. "You'll destroy my soul? I wish you would!"

"You don't mean that," Freya said, waving her hand through the air.

"I really do," Royal countered, lowering his voice. "And it's why I'm no longer serving you."

"What?" Freya asked, her eyebrows rising as green eyes bore into his. ***"What are you talking about?"***

"I see I've got your attention now," Royal smirked. "You've forgotten something basic, Freya. Your children have free will. We don't have to serve you."

"Why wouldn't they?" Freya questioned. ***"Who else would they serve?"***

"There's a new goddess in this realm," Royal said, crossing his arms. "And she doesn't abide by your will."

Freya's eyes cut over to Brandi and the sharp look sent a chill down her spine as she stared back. She could feel the air shifting around them as Freya focused her attention on her. Brandi wanted nothing more than to disappear, but she didn't avert her gaze. She'd never been on the receiving end of Freya's wrath before, and though she wished she was still naïve to the experience as Freya studied her with a new light in her eyes, Brandi understood that if she wilted under the pressure now, she'd disappoint the ones who were defending her now and she'd never forgive herself. So, she kept her back straight as she looked at Freya who smirked at her before returning her gaze to Royal.

"This will be your goddess?" Freya asked, incredulity coating her words as she gestured to Brandi. ***"This child who can't even keep her soul from being trapped in the god realm on her own?"***

"Yes," Royal stated. "And not just me. Or are you too conceited to realize that the shaders have already severed their loyalties to you?"

Freya's eyes grew wide at Royal's words, and the silence that fell over them was suffocating. It made the air feel thick and Brandi closed her eyes to focus on her breath as Freya fumed in front of them. Her gaze darted to Tiki and Lia, who snarled at her, before she shook her head at Royal with unblinking eyes.

"What have you done?"

"I've done nothing," he said, shrugging his shoulders. "The shaders have decided for themselves who they will serve. And that is no longer you. Their new leader," he said, waving a hand towards Tiki, "has chosen a new master."

"I am the creator," Freya scoffed. ***"They can't just deny me!"***

"Why not?" Royal laughed. "They are not bound to you as I am. You gave them the freedom of choice, assuming they would never choose anyone but you. But you miscalculated," he laughed. "They love Brandi more than they fear you."

"That's absurd."

"Is it? Then why have you been unable to tame another shader,

Freya? Why do you need me to stay by your side?" Freya sucked in a sharp breath at Royal's words, and he stepped forward again. "You can't answer me because you don't actually know anything about your children. You've been consumed with your own desires to the point where you can't even see those who stand before you." He pointed at Brandi. "Despite your best efforts, your daughter is already a better goddess than you."

"Blasphemy."

"Open your eyes!" Royal shouted. "Do you not see the ruler of beasts sitting at her side? Have you not seen how the entire queendom," he jabbed a finger at Freya, "the queendom you created, quakes in fear at the mere idea of her opposing them? Or are you blind to the way every child born under your lover's sun and moon responds to her? They want to serve her!"

"She is not a goddess!"

"Isn't she though?" Royal chuckled. "You did not raise her to be one, but she is one all the same. And that frightens you, doesn't it? The fact that you are not immune to time. To change. You are as beholden to it as the rest of this realm, and you hate that. Because you think gods are meant to be beyond it. And you can't stomach the thought that the child you birthed is not an extension of yourself that you can control, but a completely separate being. And she's more powerful than you can ever be."

"Silence."

The word was even, but the rage in Freya's voice cut through the air and Royal's eyes narrowed as he glared at Freya. Brandi looked between the two of them and recognized that Freya had given an order that mortals couldn't disobey.

"I've listened to enough from you," Freya said. **"I will not continue to allow your disrespect in my own lands."**

"Is it disrespect, though?"

Brandi was surprised to hear the words tumble from her own lips, but as Lia pressed her tail into Brandi's back as encouragement, and Royal nodded at her, Brandi pushed herself to her feet. Her heart pounded in her chest and her legs felt weak beneath her, but she didn't let herself back down from Freya, and made no effort to retract her words. Instead, she took a deep breath and stood before Freya with the same confidence she'd seen in Azinne and Royal.

"Oh? Would you like to air your grievances as well, Brandi?" Freya asked, her voice as light as the wind. **"I imagine you might have a few of them after all that you learned from Azinne."**

"I don't know if you could call what I'm feeling right now a 'grievance'," Brandi said, fighting to keep her voice strong. "I'm feeling a lot of things right now," Brandi admitted, "but mostly, I'm just curious."

"About what?"

"Why you wouldn't tell me the truth." Brandi paused, waiting for Freya to jump in with an explanation, but when she remained silent, Brandi shook her head. "You've lied about every aspect of who I am for my entire life. And I want to know why. So, I'm asking," Brandi said. "Why didn't you raise me as your actual daughter? Why would you let me believe I was mortal this entire time?"

"It's what was best for you."

"Best for me?" Brandi repeated, her mind trying to work its way around such a flimsy answer. "Best for me?"

"Brandi…"

"No," she said, shaking her head, holding up her hand. "I give you a chance to tell me the truth, and that's what you tell me?"

"What else were you hoping I would say?"

"I don't know," Brandi sighed. "But I hoped you would at least take some responsibility for what you've done. But the idea that lying to me about everything was your idea of doing what's best?" Brandi coughed out a laugh and swayed on her feet. "You let me believe I was an orphan, Freya."

"I've always made it known that you were my daughter," Freya said, her voice softening. *"The same as every child who walks this realm. I never lied about that."*

Do not try to downplay this matter, Tiki growled. *You feign ignorance in hopes of dismissing her rightful anger with you. You wish to have her remain complacent in serving you and I will not allow it!*

"You should remain in your place, beast," Freya warned, her glare sharp as she stared at Tiki. *"This conversation does not involve you."*

"Did you think I wouldn't believe you if you told me the truth?" Brandi interrupted, placing her palm against Tiki's side and leaning into it, both for support and to keep it from lunging at Freya. "Did you think I would stop serving you?"

"I did not tell you for the same reason I withheld the full story

of creation from you the first time we called you into our realm. You were too young. Your mind was too fragile to comprehend that you were a true born goddess. That you carried more power than we did." Freya shook her head. *"You would have either denied the truth, shunning your connection to us, or you would have spiraled into madness. And those were risks I refused to take."*

"And what about a week ago?" Brandi said, her voice trembling with disbelief and anger. "You sat across from me in Terra's house and told me I was a descendant of your original people."

"I told you that you shared no lineage with the other gods," Freya pointed out. *"And I told you the history of Freylins. I never said you were one of them. You drew that conclusion on your own."* Freya shrugged as she looked away from Brandi. *"I just never corrected your misassumption."*

Brandi stared at her then. She had no words to respond to Freya and her face fell blank as her mind raced over her thoughts, trying to catalog her memories. She knew that Freya was right, but it didn't change the deception.

"That's the same thing," Brandi scoffed, tears pricking at the corner of her eyes as her chest heaved with a burst of burning rage that threatened to suffocate her. She struggled to suck down deep breaths and regain her composure as Freya watched her. The former goddess was unbothered by Brandi's emotions and stood watching her as if she were a toddler throwing a tantrum over a lost toy. There was pity and amusement resting behind Freya's green gaze — as if she were aware of some truth that Brandi had yet to understand. Freya watched her as if she were being spoiled and petulant — like her complaints didn't even rank on the scale of things that were important. And there was something in the way Freya looked at her that made Brandi shut down.

Her raging emotions fell away, and nothing was left but an empty reality. And for the first time in her life, she felt as if she were seeing the goddess and the realm for what they truly were. She lifted a shaky hand to her frizzy hair and scratched at what was left of her once neat parts.

"This is my fault for having expectations," Brandi muttered to herself.

"Expectations?" Freya asked, taking a step closer and trying to decipher the meaning of Brandi's blank face. ***"What do you mean?"***

"I shouldn't have expected anything from you," Brandi answered. "Not love. Not protection. And certainly not the truth."

"Wait a second —"

"You're selfish," Brandi continued, rambling more to herself than to Freya at this point. "You don't know how to do anything but serve yourself and your own needs. I know that better than anyone, so why did I think I would be any different to you? Because you protected me as a child? Because you're the mother of this realm and Temari was nothing but kind and that was all I had to go off of?" She shook her head as her nails continued to dig at her scalp. "I don't know. It doesn't matter," she murmured. "Everything you've ever done for me was so you could manipulate me. It was never out of love. It was never about me or about saving this realm."

"What are you talking about?" Freya asked, lifting her voice to be heard over Brandi's mumblings.

Brandi's head snapped up, her hand pausing from its infinite scratching.

"You don't care about me," Brandi said, her voice growing in strength with each of her words. "You don't care about me or this realm or anyone in it. You only care about Zareal and getting what you want from him."

"And what is it that you think I want?"

"A life outside of time," Brandi answered without missing a beat. "You're obsessed with removing death from this realm, and he's the only one who can make that happen. And maybe you thought he would bend the rules for you, give up being who he is to become a god at your side. But he wouldn't. And my existence," Brandi said, her voice cracking as her emotions threatened to rise again before she shoved them down with an almost painful force that left her chest aching, "is meant to be a weapon. You gave birth to me so that I could be used against him."

"You truly think I would do that?"

"I don't know what I think anymore," Brandi answered, her voice soft and nearly getting lost in the breeze. "But it's not lost on me that in all this time, you've yet to call Azinne a liar."

When shock danced across Freya's face and she said nothing, Brandi let the last piece of hope she'd been clinging to wither inside her chest.

"I don't know what he hopes to gain by telling me the truth," Brandi admitted, "but, right now, he's given me more reason to trust him than you have."

A stretch of silence blossomed between them before Freya sighed. ***"I'd offer you an apology for making you feel this way, but I don't believe you'd accept it."***

"I wouldn't."

"Then allow me to say this instead," Freya said. ***"I may have kept my secrets, but Azinne is not worthy of your trust."***

Brandi snorted. "You think I don't know that?" She shook her head. "I'm not dumb enough to believe either of you would ever tell me anything that didn't suit your own whims."

"So, what will you do, then?" Freya questioned.

"I don't know yet," Brandi answered. "All I know is that you've manipulated me. You've lied to me. You've forced me into dangerous situations and you've intentionally misled me into believing things so that I would do what you wanted. You've poured all your burdens into my lap and then abandoned me to deal with them on my own. So," Brandi said, sinking further into Tiki's side and shrugging, "I'm done asking for your help. I'm going to do what I want, and I don't care what you, Azinne, or anyone else has to say about it." She scoffed as she shook her head. "I'm done being a tool for everyone else to use."

"Do what you feel you must," Freya said. ***"I've always encouraged you to make your own decisions, and that won't change now. But what of the realm?"*** She asked, lifting an eyebrow. ***"Are you content to just let it fall?"***

"Yes. But I'll see how I feel in the morning."

"And there's nothing I can do to convince you to change your mind?"

"No. And if you try to stop me," Brandi said, locking her eyes onto Freya's, "I'll help Zareal destroy you myself."

"I see," Freya hummed, tapping her fingers to her chin as she nodded her head. ***"Then there's no further point in my being here,***

so I'll take my leave. But Brandi," Freya said, pausing as she searched her face, *"be careful."*

"Please don't feign concern for me now," Brandi scoffed. "You've had every opportunity to explain things to me, and you've chosen not to."

"There are many things that go beyond a simple conversation," Freya said, turning on her heel to walk toward the trees at the opposite edge of the rock formation. *"But regardless, I shall be here when you're ready to speak with me again."*

"Don't wait on it," Brandi warned.

Freya smirked at that before disappearing into the trees, leaving Brandi to sink to the ground between Tiki and Lia. Royal stared after Freya, but turned his head to Brandi as she cradled her head in her hands on the ground. Her heart was pounding in her chest and her head felt like it was ready to split in two. But she refused to slip back into the mortal realm until she got all the answers she wanted from them.

"Did you know?"

The question was vague — broad — but Brandi didn't know what else to ask. Royal had spoken as if he'd always known she was Freya's true born daughter, and neither Tiki or Lia had corrected him. It had been a minor thing during their conversation with Freya, but in the silence of the aftermath, it was something her mind wasn't able to let go of. And as she lifted her head to glance between them, her chest felt heavy.

"Answer me," she whispered, locking her gaze onto Tiki. "Did you know Temari wasn't my mother?"

Yes.

"And you never thought that was something I would want to know?"

Every truth comes in its own time and whether you were god or mortal was of no importance to us. You are ours, same as if you'd been born into the darkness. And we are yours. That is all that has ever mattered to us.

"It would have mattered to me."

Why? Were we not enough for you?

The question made Brandi pause and Tiki sat in silence, waiting for her answer. But what answer could Brandi offer it? She'd always felt as though Tiki were enough. For her, Tiki and Lia had been her first true experiences of having a family. And she would never be able to put into words how grateful she was for them accepting her into their clan. But there was still the reality that she wouldn't have needed to be adopted into their clan if Freya hadn't planned to use her as a tool of vengeance from the beginning. She wouldn't have been forced into the service of the queendom in order to satisfy Freya's own wishes, and she had a hard time accepting that. She could have been so much more than what she'd been allowed to be, and knowing that made her chest ache with an emotion she'd never felt before.

She could've been more than a tool for the queendom — for the goddess.

"I wish you would've told me," Brandi whispered, her voice thick. "I would have wanted to know."

Then we must apologize, Tiki said, stepping forward to nuzzle its giant head into Brandi's side. *We have never meant to cause you harm.*

Lia mimicked Tiki's action on the other side and before she could control them, silent tears slipped down Brandi's cheeks as she held onto them. Royal had the decency to look away, but she hid her face in Lia's fur anyway, clinging to her shaders as she mourned for parents and her childhood in a way she'd never allowed herself to before.

She could barely remember her parents anymore, and she wondered what they had looked like. Her memory of them had long since faded — her mother's image replaced with those of Freya and Glenn, and her father's face was nothing more than a mild blur in her mind. She remembered that she'd loved them and that she'd been inconsolable at their return to the gods, but she didn't remember who they were. She didn't remember her father's laugh or her mother's hug or their warmth anymore, and she hated herself for forgetting. Because how could she forget?

She thought of visiting their memory marker — a stone pillar that had been erected sixteen years ago in a tiny clearing near their house where there was a break in the treetops to allow Rothe's light to shine down. She thought for a moment that it would offer her some closure, but she knew better than to believe that. Their spirits were gone, and their bodies had long since been devoured by shaders, as was the tradition within Freya's domain.

She didn't allow bodies to be buried within her sacred lands, so whenever her children returned to the gods in her domain, their physical bodies were fed to shaders — returning the last of their lifeblood to her original creations. It was one of the highest ways to honor the goddess of life who judged their souls, and Brandi's parents had been no different. Maybe if their bodies had been buried in the Scorched Desert like the

Rothians — or if their likenesses had been painted and preserved like the Lindlians — then maybe she could have sought out the answers she wanted. But what point would there have been in that? She wasn't their daughter. She didn't carry their blood in her veins, and she felt as if she'd been uprooted at the realization that everything she'd known about her childhood had been a fabricated story.

She hadn't lost her mother.

Her father wasn't the man she'd mourned.

She hadn't been forced into the queen's service because she'd lost her family — because her father had denied a position as a consort — because she'd made a deal with Glenn to protect Sarah and repay the debt she owed to her parents. Those things had happened, but they weren't the cause that Brandi had always assumed they were — they were the effect. The ripples of a much larger plan that had been in play for thousands of years.

Brandi had always known that Freya had lived multiple lifetimes — even before Freya explained Zareal's request of the gods, part of her, on an instinctual level, had understood there was a greater purpose for her reincarnations than her own amusement. But she'd never imagined that her entire existence was merely a means to an end. Understanding that made Brandi's chest feel hollow and she clung to Tiki and Lia until her eyes were dry and her exhaustion was becoming too much for her to continue fighting off.

"You alright?" Royal asked as she lifted her face from her shaders and swiped at her eyes.

"Fantastic," Brandi croaked, wincing at the sound of her own voice.

"I'm just tired. I need a nap before I can destroy the queendom."

Then rest, Tiny Human, Lia hummed as Tiki paced around them once before settling its large body behind her, twisting its tail around both of them as Brandi sank into its sweet-smelling fur with a yawn. **We shall be with you when you wake.**

"Hopefully I can actually get some sleep this time," Brandi mumbled, already drifting off. "Before anyone else can think of something they need to tell me."

CHAPTER SEVEN

The goddess does not give her love in equal measure. There are the mortals she birthed, the shaders she created, the gods she loves, and then, there is Rothe.

— Rothe, The First and the Favored | Lindl's Second Holy Academy

---

FREYA'S DOMAIN — THE SHADER'S PRIVATE CLEARING
MORNING OF DAY 2

When Brandi opened her eyes to the pale blue morning sky of the mortal realm, it was in a raging panic, her body paying the heavy price for her time spent in the god realm. Harsh screams ripped from her throat as liquid fire raced through her veins and seeped into her blood. As promised, Tiki and Lia were by her side, and Lia's quick nudge to Brandi's side sent her sprawling to the ground in an ungraceful fashion, but it had saved her from retching all across Tiki's back.

Jack rushed to her side, calling her name as he wrapped an arm around her shoulders, supporting her as her body rejected the contents of her stomach. Shika led Ronka and her mates away, leaving Brandi alone

121

with Tiki, Lia, and Jack. It wasn't until she collapsed back into Jack's arms that he carried her to the edge of the lake, placing her on its edge as he worked to clean her up. He moved in silence around her as every emotion she'd held back during her visit to the god realm wrought havoc on her mind before leaving her numb — as little more than a shell of herself. She barely noticed as he set up a small campfire and removed the *Ciel Noir* from her around her neck, expanding it and grabbing a bar of soap and a pair of toothbrushes from their bags inside.

It wasn't until Jack stripped them down and guided her into the freezing water, dipping them both beneath the icy surface of the lake, that she felt like her mind was coming back to her and beginning to clear. She clung to him as they resurfaced, and he pressed soft kisses to her face and forehead as he lathered them up before dunking them beneath the surface once more. He wrapped himself in a towel before bundling Brandi up in a blanket and handing her a toothbrush. When they were done, he took a few moments to wash their clothes and set them by the fire to dry before carrying her inside the *Ciel Noir*.

He sat her down in his lap and she wrapped her arms around his neck, sinking into the warmth of his bare skin. She felt his heart beating against hers and tightened her grip on him, burying her face in his neck as she fought back a fresh wave of tears. She would never be able to verbalize how grateful she was that he was still with her, and she relaxed into his arms as he tightened his grip on her.

"I thought I was going to lose you," she whispered.

"Sorry," he whispered back, pulling her tighter against him. "I won't let it happen again."

"You better not," she chuckled, her voice thick with tears as she slid her fingers into his hair. "I need you here with me."

"I'm not going anywhere without you, Bee," he said, pressing kisses into her shoulder before pulling back to hold her gaze. "I promise."

Brandi nodded once before leaning forward to kiss him. The blanket she'd been wrapped in fell to the ground, and Jack wasted no time placing her on top of it. They didn't need any more words between them as they melted into each other. It wasn't until the sun was glaring down on them from the center of the sky that they pulled apart. Jack pulled himself into one of the seats and covered himself with his towel before spreading his knees and beckoning Brandi forward.

"Come here," he said, pointing to the floor in front of him. "Let me do your hair."

Brandi crawled forward and sat on the floor between his legs, letting her eyes drift closed as his fingers brushed against her scalp, undoing her braids. His fingers were gentle, and she melted into his touch as he worked to undo the tangles in her hair.

"So," he said, looking down at her, "you ready to tell me what happened? You were out for almost thirty-six hours."

"I didn't realize it had been that long," Brandi hummed, resting her head against his leg. "I guess we should get ready to head back."

"They can wait," Jack said. "Talk to me, first."

Brandi thought about how to tell him everything that had transpired in the god realm. Her thoughts on everything were still muddled, and she didn't know what to think about her conversations with Azinne and Freya, especially now that she knew the truth. She didn't doubt that there were still things that Azinne was keeping from her — Freya too — but she couldn't worry about the things she didn't know. The tasks in front of her were daunting enough as they were. So, instead of trying to make sense of it all on her own, she took a deep breath and released it in a slow exhale as she told Jack everything. From her argument with Najé, to meeting Freya in the god realm, to Azinne's arrival and her subsequent argument with Freya and Royal. She left nothing out, pausing only once to return to the lake and dunk her head in the water so that he could finish detangling her hair. He was parting her hair into sections and weaving them into individual braids before twisting them down into neat knots, and by the time she finished her story, he was done.

"So," he said, his words slow as Brandi moved to sit beside him, "you were able to access the god realm. And you created your own version of it?"

Brandi nodded. "I created our apartment. Tousled sheets and all."

"And you were able to do that because we're gods now?"

"That's what I gathered, yes."

"So," he shook his head as he looked, apprehension crossing his face as his eyebrows pinched together, "do we all have some version of the god realm we can create?"

"I guess so?" Brandi shrugged. "I mean, all the gods had their own version of it, so I don't see why we wouldn't."

"And while you were there, you met Azinne. But he's not the problem anymore," Jack said, lifting his eyebrow as Brandi nodded at him. "Zareal is?"

"Yes."

"And he's also your actual father?"

"Yes."

"And he wants to destroy the realm because Freya is…" his hands searched through the air as if would be able to grab the right words out of them before shrugging his shoulders and dropping them at his sides, "Freya."

"Yes."

"So that makes you half time being, doesn't it?"

"Technically," Brandi said, avoiding his gaze and nodding, "I was a goddess before that whole thing at the temple."

Jack coughed out a laugh at that and rested his elbows on his knees as he stared out through the transparent walls of the pod. His face was still as he thought about her words and she wondered what he was thinking. He hadn't had much more time to process things than she had, and his relationship to the gods was a lot newer than hers. She knew he was strong, but she also knew that enough weight could break anyone. So, she waited with her heart in her throat for his reaction to all this new information, hoping that he was able to take it better than she had.

"You know? Of all the things you've told me, you having always been a goddess doesn't actually surprise me."

"It should," Brandi snorted.

Jack shook his head as he leaned back in his seat. "It was probably blasphemy, but I always loved you more than the gods. So, you being a literal goddess is the one thing you've said that makes sense to me."

"You say that so casually," Brandi said, a chuckle escaping her as she grinned at him.

"I'm nothing if not honest," he said, shrugging as he smiled back at her.

Brandi shook her head at that and leaned into him. He wrapped his arm around her shoulders, and they sat in silence as they each processed what Brandi had shared with him.

"Tell me what you're thinking," Brandi said, trailing her fingers over the muscles in his stomach.

"I'm thinking that if your hand gets any lower, we're going back to the blanket."

Brandi rolled her eyes and removed her hand from him. "Be serious. You're a god now," she pointed out. "Doesn't that, I don't know," she shook her head, "scare you a little?"

"I'm always serious about you," he teased. "But honestly? Being a god isn't really a big deal to me," he said with a shrug. "We're the same people we've always been, right? The gods must have trusted us with these roles for a reason," he said, lowering his voice and letting his eyes drift to his hands. "I have to believe that."

Brandi said nothing in response to that, and she let her head fall against Jack's shoulder. She could guess at the emotions he was trying to process, because she'd been trying to make sense of the same things in the god realm. It was hard to accept the gods' actions when they were a direct contradiction to everything they knew about them. She threaded her fingers through his and he squeezed her hand.

"But you know? Not much has changed. I just want to keep you safe and happy. And everyone else wants way too much from you," he snorted, shaking his head. "But destroying a queendom? Sure, that we can do," he said, "but protecting the entire realm from someone who's been planning its destruction for thousands of years? That's an unreasonable request," he sighed, shaking his head. "And I'm pissed off the gods don't seem to have any problem with placing all their burdens on you like this."

Brandi pulled back to look at Jack and fought back the urge to cry as he pressed another kiss to her forehead. The urge itself irritated her, and she pushed it away, but she couldn't deny that she loved Jack for offering her comfort. Unlike the gods, or the queendom, or even Noble and Najé, Jack never treated her like she was an unbreakable force. He always treated her as if she were fragile in his hands, and there was something about that, that always made her heart skip and her throat tighten.

Because she wasn't invincible.

And it felt glorious when even one person acknowledged that.

"So," Jack sighed, turning to look down into her green eyes, "where do we go from here, Bee? Are we joining the rebels?"

"If that's what you want to do."

"What?" Jack asked, his eyebrows shooting to the top of his head. "What do you mean if that's what I want to do?"

"Exactly what I said," she stated, looking up at him. "I'm tired, Jack. And I don't really care about what the gods want anymore or about what's best for this realm," she said with a quick shake of her head. "I care about you. And only you," she stressed. "So, if you ask me to destroy the queendom and save this realm, I will. But only if you ask me to."

"And if I say I don't?" Jack asked, searching her face for an answer. "Then what?"

"Then we watch it burn together."

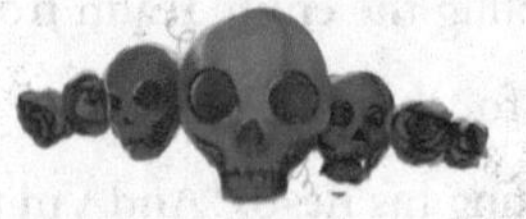

Half an hour later, Jack and Brandi were arriving back at the clearing. They'd returned the *Ciel Noir* to the chain that hung around her neck and the entire clearing fell silent as they broke free of the trees. Tiki and Lia strolled into the clearing behind them and Brandi's green eyes sliced through every person who dared to meet her gaze, sending them shrinking back from her in fear and astonishment. The rebels parted as she walked through them, creating a clear path for them as if she were the queen herself.

"Where's Najé?"

Her question cut through the silence surrounding them, and only one girl managed to gather her senses enough to sprint in the direction of the makeshift sparring ring situated in the center of the clearing. Brandi noticed it the moment she came back and hadn't been surprised to find it there. Shadows never slacked on their training, and trapped in the middle of Freya's domain, there wasn't much else for them to do.

It didn't take long for the girl to come back with Najé and Lia stood to her feet, a low growl rumbling from her chest as Najé's eyes darted between Brandi, Jack, and the giant beasts standing behind her. The girl was quick to make herself scarce and Brandi could feel the eyes of the rebels as they all watched to see what would happen next. Brandi hated being the center of attention, but she held Najé's gaze as she approached — her steps measured, slow and deliberate.

What would you like us to do? Tiki asked. ***We will rid you of her should you ask us to.***

Brandi tore her gaze away from Najé to glance up at Tiki. It sat to her right, its posture alert — unlike Lia who was growling and primed for attack, the dark curly fur on her body standing on edge as she bared her teeth. She appreciated both of them for jumping to her defense, but she shook her head as she turned back to Najé.

"They want to eat you," Brandi stated.

Najé's eyes darted to the two beasts on either side of Brandi before returning to her face.

"Is that what you called me over here for?"

Brandi glanced over Najé once before turning and tossing the *Ciel Noir* to the side, giving it space to expand. When it was done, she turned back to Najé and gestured to it.

"Let's talk."

Brandi led the way inside the pod with Jack and Najé following behind her. It was clear that Najé hadn't expected Jack to be joining them, but she didn't say anything as she sank into the seat across from Brandi and looked around. The pod wasn't huge — just big enough to fit five people — with the controls next to the first seat where Jack sat. She watched Najé flick her brown eyes between her and Jack, waiting for one of them to say something to her.

"You wanted me to take over the rebellion," Brandi said, diving straight into the reason she'd called Najé over to her. "Why?"

Dozens of questions raced through Brandi's mind when it came to Najé, Glenn, and the rebellion, but the reason behind Najé's desire for her to lead was the one she wanted to focus on. She could think of a dozen reasons why Najé would be the better fit to take over Glenn's role, and her mind no longer had the space to try and guess at Najé's motives, so she was there to ask her outright. But if they were going to have even the slightest chance of destroying the monarchy and saving the realm, then taking over the rebellion was their best option. And that meant, at least on the surface, Brandi would have to play the part of forgiving Najé and mending the rift between them.

The idea alone was enough to make Brandi's blood boil, and she felt her shoulders tense. It wasn't until Jack rested his palm on her knee, a simple gesture to remind her that he was still there with her, that she was able to cage her anger and set it aside. She was grateful for his presence, because as much as she wanted to believe that she could handle anything, the last few days had proven to her that she couldn't. She cracked under pressure, just like everyone else, and she wasn't nice enough to care about anyone else's well-being. Even now, sitting across from Najé and preparing to take over the rebellion, she wasn't convinced that trying to save the gods and the entire realm was in her and Jack's best interest. But they'd agreed before returning to the clearing that if Najé was still willing to hand the rebellion over to them, then they should at least try to save the realm.

It's not something Brandi was sure she wanted to do, but Jack had a lot more patience in him than she did — an ability to see a bigger picture when she could only see herself. He anchored her in that way, and she was grateful for him making the decisions that she couldn't. Because, if it weren't for him, she'd have abandoned the realm to whatever the gods could do on their own and spent the last of her time with him and Tiki — hunting, sleeping, and simply existing until the realm collapsed around her. It was a morbid thought, but it came rushing to the forefront of her mind as she held Najé's gaze and waited for her answer.

"I already told you." Najé shrugged. "Someone has to do it and Glenn is nowhere to be found."

"That doesn't answer my question," Brandi pointed out. "Why do you want it to be me who takes over?"

"Because you're the only one who can lead it to where it needs to be," Najé said, her voice growing more serious with each word.

"And what makes you think that?"

"Because anyone else who takes over will try to be like Glenn," she stated. "They'll want to protect the integrity of the crown."

"You say that like it's a bad thing."

"It isn't," Najé said, shaking her head. "But," she leaned forward again, staring at Brandi as if she were willing her to understand, "you don't care about any of that, do you? You care about what's best for the people of this realm. Even if that means destroying the throne and forging a new one."

"And that's where you're wrong," Brandi said, laughter falling out of her at the mere idea that she cared about anyone after the ultimatum Azinne had given her and her conversation with Freya. "I don't care about anyone."

"That's not true."

"It absolutely is," Brandi snapped. "I care about him," Brandi said, pointing to Jack. "This one, singular person," she specified. "Everyone else in this realm could meet the gods and I wouldn't bat an eye to help, even if I could."

"Then why'd you come back to ask me about taking it over?"

"Because I wanted to know," Brandi shrugged.

"And does my reasoning satisfy you?"

"Not really," Brandi said, rolling her eyes. "You seem to be under some impression that I care about changing this realm."

"Because your actions speak louder than your words," Najé said, smirking.

"And what are my actions saying?"

"That you're the woman who can do what everyone else couldn't," Najé stated, as if her words were the absolute law of the realm. "Your actions tell me that you're going to change this realm. That you are going to take us where Glenn couldn't. That you can see a future," she paused to shake her head before correcting herself. "That you will create a future that even the gods couldn't predict."

"Sure," Brandi said, rolling her eyes, knowing that the gods couldn't predict much of anything.

"I'm serious," Najé said. "I only speak on the things I've witnessed for myself. And I've seen how the queendom fears you. How the gods love you and Freya's beasts serve you." Najé leaned forward in her seat, her gaze locked onto Brandi's. "Whether you want to or not, Green, you're going to change this realm, simply because you exist in it."

"You say that as if I'm more than just a tool for the queendom," Brandi scoffed. "A discarded one at that."

"You're not," Najé said, stomping her foot as she lunged forward, anger brimming in her eyes as she glared at Brandi. "I'm a tool," she said, pressing her hand to her chest. "Glenn is a tool. The shadows out there," she said pointing to the rebels who stood watching them from outside the pod, "they are tools. But you? You've never been one."

"Right," Brandi scoffed, thinking back on all the missions she'd completed for the queendom and for Freya. "That's why they call me 'The Queen's Blade'."

"They call you that because you were the best of us," Najé stated. "But the reason they forced you into her servitude is because they knew they wouldn't be able to stop you if you became their enemy."

"You say that like you know it's true."

"Have you forgotten who my father is?" Najé asked, her eyebrow lifting as she looked at Brandi. "I've heard countless conversations between the consorts and the members of the council talking about their wariness of you. Of how they needed to be sure to keep you under their thumb."

"You're lying," Brandi said, denying the words. "I've never been anyone that important to the queendom."

"They never wanted you to know you were that important," Najé corrected. "But how many Freyans do you see serving the crown?" She countered. "How many of them carry the blessing of the goddess? The fortune of the gods?" Brandi had nothing to say to that, and Najé sighed. "I wish you could see yourself the way the rest of us do, Green. You're incredible for far more reasons than what you seem to realize."

"I agree," Jack interjected, and Brandi rolled her eyes at him before refocusing on Najé.

"So, what?" Brandi asked. "You think I can do a better job than you, and that's your reason for not wanting to take over?"

"I don't want to take it over, because I can't be their leader," Najé admitted. "I am a product of this queendom, and my first thought will always go towards the protection of the crown," Najé admitted. "That's been ingrained into me since the day I took my first breath. My role is to serve the queendom, and to serve my father's daughter."

"Riné?" Brandi asked, and Najé nodded.

"She's a princess of the crown," Najé said with a shrug. "And as the rising director of the shadows, I have one of two responsibilities. Serve her as the next queen or send her to the gods as a failed princess."

"Your father would really ask you to do that?"

She laughed. "Of course he would. You know we don't get to pick the targets, Green."

"No," Brandi sighed. "We don't."

"But that's my burden to bear," Najé said with a weak smile. "And I'll handle it accordingly when the time comes. But the point is," Najé said, bringing them back to the matter at hand, "is that you're not like me. You haven't been force fed absolute servitude your entire life like I have, and you didn't join the shadows as a last resort just to survive like everyone else. You've always thought for yourself and that's why the council fears you. They can't control you. The fact that the Rothens girl is still alive is proof enough of that."

Brandi snorted at the mention of Sarah and wished she'd been able to defy Freya's commands. If she'd simply returned Sarah to the gods when the queendom had ordered it, they wouldn't be here now. She wouldn't have abandoned the shadows, and she wouldn't have trekked across the entire realm for the sake of protecting a useless princess, and there would have never been an opportunity for Jack to be taken by the monarchy because they would've still been working for it. Keeping Sarah alive always seemed to be more work than it was worth and now, knowing what she does about Freya, Brandi doubted whether she'd made the right choice. It was a decision that had already been made, so there was no point in dwelling on it, but it still made her shake her head.

"Okay," Brandi said. "I hear you. But are you sure you're good with me taking over? I'm not exactly the best leader in the world."

"Well," Najé smirked, "that's the thing, isn't it? You're a good leader because you're not trying to lead anyone. You're simply walking in your own direction and that alone inspires people to follow you," Najé said, turning to look at Jack. "Right, Mr. Green?"

"Sure," Jack said with a shrug. "I would follow you anywhere. Without question."

"You're in love with me."

"Irrelevant," he stated. "I was following you before I loved you. Or do you not remember me chasing after you in Rothe's domain the first time we met?"

Brandi stared at him for a moment before she let a laugh slip out of her. She shook her head and let her fingers trail the neat parts in her hair as she considered Najé's words. She wasn't surprised that Jack had agreed with her. They didn't like each other, but it was very Rothian of them both to try and strong-arm her into a position she had no interest in. It made her want to laugh again, but instead she swallowed it and met Najé's gaze.

"Fine," she conceded. "I'll take over the rebellion, but I have a few conditions."

"Of course you do," Najé chuckled. "Tell me."

"You don't get to complain about the decisions I make," she said, holding up her fingers.

"Done," Najé agreed. "Not a big deal."

"You have to cut all ties with the queendom."

"I already told you—"

"I'm serious about this," Brandi warned, cutting off her excuses. "I will never forgive you for what you did to Jack, but he's not trying to send you to the gods, so I won't either. But if you want this to work," she said, waving her hand between them, "then you abandon the queendom. Of your own free will," she emphasized. "I'm not making you leave this time. If you go back to them, I won't stop you."

Najé hesitated for just a moment and a thick silence settled around them as her gaze focused on the floor of the *Ciel Noir*.

"I won't go back," she whispered. "I've already learned that lesson. I'm with you, Green. All the way."

"Good," Brandi sighed. "And last thing," she said sitting back in her seat. "I'm sending Bert, the queen, and all of her consorts to the gods." Brandi paused and watched Najé as her words hung in the air.

"All of them, huh?"

"Every last one."

"I don't know if I can agree to that one."

"I wasn't asking for your permission," Brandi stated. "I was letting you know what my conditions are. Do you want me to take over or not?"

"I guess I'll have to deal with that."

"I'm glad we agree," Brandi nodded. "Now, can you get in touch with Sal? I need to ask him for a few favors."

CHAPTER EIGHT

Mortals are interesting in that, even when confronted with absolute facts, if they dislike it, they will find a way to delude themselves — masking the truth, cloaking it in skewed reasoning, twisting it around their own logic, transforming it into something it never was. Something they can accept.

They do this often.

They call it 'hope'.

— A Mortal Fascination | Lindl's Third Holy Academy

FREYA'S DOMAIN — THE CLEARING BY THE LAKE

AFTERNOON OF DAY 2

"Alright, Green," Noble said, leaning back in his seat inside the *Ciel Noir*. "Where do we go from here?"

Sarah's ears perked up at the question and she was glad that Noble had been the one to ask it. She'd been wondering the same thing, but had been at a loss for words ever since Brandi had summoned them to the pod.

Terra had equipped the *Ciel Noir* with a transparent inside and a pitch-black exterior. It allowed them to see outside, but it prevented anyone from seeing them. It was an odd experience to see people watching them and know that they couldn't see them staring back, but Sarah was surprised to find that she wasn't too much bothered by it. She'd spent the majority of her life as the center of someone's attention — for better or for worse — and the rebels hadn't shied away from outright gawking at her. By now, she was accustomed to unwavering stares and was instead grateful for the small bit of privacy afforded to them in this moment.

"Now," Brandi said, her voice empty as she kept her gaze locked on something beyond the clearing, "we destroy the monarchy."

"So, we're really doing that?" Noble asked, crossing his arms with a smirk. "And what brought on this change of heart?"

"It's not a change of heart," she clarified, shifting her eyes to meet his. "It's a deal."

"A deal?" Cedric inquired. "With who?"

"A time being."

"And what do we get in exchange?"

"An ally," Brandi said, leaving her answer at that.

"I don't quite understand," Cedric said, his eyebrows pulling together. "The gods already agreed to some sort of game with a time being, didn't they? How has our priority shifted from finding and eliminating their vessel to destroying our monarchy?"

"A lot's happened between now and then," Brandi shrugged. "Things have changed."

"And we're not going to get an explanation of those things?"

"Do you need one?" Brandi questioned, turning to face Cedric. "You can't just trust me?"

Her voice was still empty, but there was an edge to it that made the hair on the back of Sarah's neck stand on end. She'd grown used to the condescension in her words — the lilt of irritation and impatience and the dip of disappointment and disgust. But her absolute lack of emotion sent ripples of anxiety across Sarah's skin, and she couldn't pull her eyes away from Brandi as she watched Cedric. It wasn't until she caught a glimpse of Noble watching her from the corner of her eye that she averted her gaze, returning them to the rebels who watched them from outside the pod.

"I barely know you," Cedric said, confusion lifting his words. "And asking for blind trust of this magnitude is a somewhat unreasonable request." He paused and glanced around the pod with anxious eyes before honing in on Sarah. "Surely, I'm not the only one who feels this way?"

Sarah's heart hammered against the base of her throat, and she cursed herself for having turned to look at Cedric as he spoke. Heat crept up her neck now as her blue eyes darted around to the others. They all watched her with intense gazes, and she could feel a cold sweat pooling in the creases of her elbows. She pulled at the sleeves of her jacket, trying to alleviate some of the discomfort while doing everything she could to avoid looking at Cedric.

"Why would you look at me when you ask that?"

"You are the only one who might agree with me," he said with a slight shrug. "Or did I misunderstand the relationship you two have with her?"

The question was directed at Noble and Jack and both of them narrowed their eyes. The air in the pod became stifling as their hostile energy snuffed out any doubts lingering in the air, and Cedric tugged at the collar of his shirt as he cleared his throat.

"As I thought," he mumbled.

"Answer him, Sarah," Noble said, turning his dark gaze onto her as she blushed a deep shade of red at his use of her name. "Do you think a bit of blind faith is an 'unreasonable request'?"

Sarah's tongue felt thick in her mouth, her nerves drying out her words. She blinked back anxious tears, knowing they wouldn't help her now, and shook her head. Her blonde braid swished across her back, but she wanted to be clear about whose side she was on, even if her words failed her.

"I…" she coughed once and dug her nails into her palm, trying to get a grip on her racing thoughts. "No." She lifted her gaze to Cedric and shook her head again. "Trusting Brandi isn't unreasonable."

"Are you sure?" Brandi asked, leaning back and resting her elbow on the top ledge of the seat. "I wouldn't blame you if you thought it was."

"I trust you," Sarah said, proud of the strength in her voice. "I wouldn't be here if I didn't."

"Sounds like you're on your own then," Noble pointed out to Cedric.

"I see," he whispered, turning to look at Brandi. They stared at each other for a long moment before Cedric's lips quirked upward. "Well, I am a man of knowledge. But I am also a servant of the gods. I seek Lindl's wisdom in all things, and he has led me to you," he mused. "So, I will trust the judgment of the gods until I can decide for myself whether or not you are worthy of my faith."

"'Worthy' huh?" Brandi rolled her eyes. "As long as you play your part, I don't care if you think I'm 'worthy'."

"And what exactly is my part?"

"You're a man of knowledge, aren't you? So, do your research. Find out the origins of the queendom," she said, planting both feet on the ground. "Study the rules of the bid. Learn about the best ways to transfer power from one leader to the next. Figure out what we should do once we remove Leia from the throne."

"You're serious," he whispered.

"As the god's wrath," Brandi stated, her eyes narrowed. "If we topple the system without a plan, we'll create a mad scramble for power and the queendom will be worse off than it is now, with a false queen on the throne."

"So, you want me to… what? Architect some new structure of power?"

"Exactly that," Brandi said with a nod. "Decide what comes after the monarchy."

"Why me?" Cedric asked, his face paling in the face of Brandi's request. "I'm not…"

"Because none of us have the time," Brandi snapped, the familiar lilt of impatience coloring her words cut through Cedric's insecurities. "Unless you have the capabilities to bid for the throne, behead the queen and her consorts, or lead a band of rebels against the monarchy? If you do, speak up."

Noble and Jack both smothered their laughter when Cedric said nothing, and Sarah hid her tiny smile by looking at the ground. Cedric could only stare at Brandi with wide eyes, his plump lips parted in surprise. Sarah snuck glances around the pod, and for the first time, she began to understand why Noble had found her discomfort so amusing. Cedric wasn't accustomed to Brandi's bluntness — he didn't know that she was the kind of woman who brought solutions to her problems. She didn't waste time second guessing her actions, and she expected the same of those around her. Sarah had already learned that lesson, and she could admit that she was grateful to be on the inside of the joke for once.

"I understand," Cedric said, straightening his shoulders. "I'll return to the First Holy Academy and create a plan."

"No," Brandi said, shaking her head. "You'll go to the Queen's Tower. The library there will have more of the kind of information you'll need."

"And am I meant to just waltz in?" Cedric asked, his eyebrows lifting.

"We have a better plan than that," Brandi said rolling her eyes. Cedric studied her for a moment, his face still as his mind no doubt raced through a dozen questions he probably wanted to ask. But as he tore his gaze from Brandi to glance once more around the pod, he swallowed them and sat back in his seat with a nod.

"Great," Brandi said. "While you're working on that, I'll have Lena look more into the origins of the gods."

"Why?" Cedric asked, his bright violet eyes giving away his curiosity.

"I don't really need to explain that to you," Brandi pointed out.

"Come on, Green," Noble interjected, grinning at her. "Curious minds want to know."

Brandi's eyes shot over to Jack, who had been sitting next to her with his arms crossed. He hadn't said a word the entire time they'd been in the pod, but the way he spread out, his knee was pressed into Brandi's. Sarah didn't miss the way he nudged her and the brief moment her eyes softened on him before her eyes glazed back over to nothingness as she returned her attention to Cedric.

"Fine," she conceded. "I'm sure you've all noticed that you carry a significant amount of the god's power now. Like," she shrugged, "all of it?"

"I think I noticed a slight increase," Noble quipped. "Yeah."

"Well, what do you think happens if we keep all their power?" Brandi questioned.

She waited as silence filled the pod and realizations sunk into everyone around the room. Sarah's blue eyes grew wide as the meaning of Asari's words in Freya's temple slammed into her with full force. Her head whipped up, and she looked to Noble, who had his face set in a firm line as he watched Brandi.

"Wait a second," Sarah whispered, panic exploding like fireworks in the center of her chest, "that means…"

"We are 'the origin of a new era of gods'," Noble finished, repeating the final words the gods had spoken to them at Freya's temple. He sat back in his seat and shook his head as a smirk pulled across his lips. "You're telling us we're actually gods now, Green?"

"More or less."

"But if we keep all their power," Cedric said. "Then that means the realm…"

"Becomes our responsibility," Brandi finished. "And that's why I need Lena to research the origins. If we have to replace the gods, recreate a political structure, and possibly recreate the boundaries within the domains, then we should at least know what they did. How they did it if Lena can figure that out."

"Are you sure you don't want me to do that?" Cedric asked, raising his eyebrows. "That seems a much more involved task than creating a new system of politics."

"And you think you're more capable than she is?"

Brandi's words were sharp and silenced the entirety of the pod. Chills ran up Sarah's arms and she shivered against the briskness in Brandi's question. Cedric froze under her unrelenting gaze, and he immediately began to shake his head and backtrack his words.

"That's not what I meant."

"I think it is," Brandi said. "But let me be clear about something. I trust Lena. But you?" Brandi scoffed and narrowed her eyes. "I barely know you."

Cedric flushed at having his words thrown back in his face, and Sarah looked away from his embarrassment.

"If the political structure fails, we can mitigate the damage," Brandi reasoned. "Fill the inevitable vacuum of power with a figurehead we control until a suitable leader can be found and a legitimate court and process established. But if we fail at being gods? The entire realm will fall back into nothingness. That's not a responsibility I would trust to just anyone," Brandi pointed out. "And why bother putting my faith in a man when I could rely on a woman?"

"That's harsh," Noble said, feigning a wince. "Make us sound like we're useless, why don't you?"

"Your words," Brandi shot back. "Not mine."

"I don't know," Jack sighed, nudging her knee again. "I can think of a few things you need me for."

Brandi paused at that and said nothing as Jack smirked at her. She rolled her eyes at him, but not before letting a smile pull at her own lips and nudging his knee back. It was another small moment, and Sarah glanced over to Noble to see what his reaction was. She remembered him telling her that watching the two of them together got easier, but she wondered if he still felt the uncontrollable pull of jealousy, too. But when she looked at him, his gaze was focused on the rebels just beyond the curved walls of their transport pod.

Several of the rebels sat in neat rows by the lake, meditating, while others huddled around small fires to cook the meat the shaders had brought back for them. Brandi had made it clear that no one was to leave the clearing without her permission unless they wanted the shaders to hunt them for sport, so they'd turned to Najé for guidance while Brandi met with the other vessels inside the *Ciel Noir*. Najé had delegated the responsibilities of the camp with ease and fallen into her role as surrogate leader as if she'd been born to do it.

It made Sarah wonder why she would defer to Brandi's leadership when it was clear that she had the natural qualities for it. But she didn't have much time for the thought to linger before her attention was pulled back to the conversation at hand.

"Let's stay focused," Noble interjected. "We've got Cedric covering politics and your little corpse covering the research of the gods," Noble listed off. "What else do you need for this coup to work?"

"Not much," Brandi answered. "Jack and I will lead the rebels. Najé will realign the shadows to our cause. Sal will destroy the queen's army from the inside. And Sarah will disrupt the monarchy."

"Disrupt the monarchy?" Sarah repeated, her voice pitched two octaves higher than usual. "What does that mean?"

"Weren't you listening earlier?" Brandi asked, quirking an eyebrow. "You're going to place a bid for the throne."

Sarah's face paled in the dying light of the pod and Brandi bit back a huff of annoyance. She'd mentioned bidding for the throne not even fifteen minutes ago, when Cedric had been preparing to ramble off whatever excuses he could find to not do what she'd asked of him. She slammed her back into the seat and shoved her hands back into her pocket, slipping her fingers through the holes in her favorite knife and squeezing. It calmed her down a bit, but Jack's gentle nudge against her knee is what reminded her to keep her cool.

Her emotions had been rampaging since she'd left the god realm, and as much as she hated to admit it, Jack's presence was the only thing allowing her to keep a lid on everything. Because he knew everything and had decided to stay with her. He hadn't run away knowing that she was the furthest thing from being mortal, and he'd decided to save the realm even after she'd offered to let it burn. His love for her and the realm they lived in was enough to assuage every surge of doubt and anger that flared to life within her.

His presence was a constant affirmation that she wasn't doing this for the gods. She was doing this for Jack.

"Breathe, Blondie," Brandi said, taking the deep breath she wanted Sarah to copy. "Don't pass out in here."

Sarah took in two shaky breaths before gripping her hands together in her lap. Brandi noticed the slight tremble in her fingers and tried to find an extra helping of patience as she waited for Sarah to regain some of her composure. Part of her was irritated that neither Cedric nor Sarah had given any thought to what would come next for them, given what the gods had told them. But she knew better than to expect anything of anyone, and her disappointment in them was her own fault.

"You want me to bid for the throne?" Sarah finally squeaked out. "But why?"

"You're the only one who can," Brandi pointed out. "And we need the monarchy focused on something other than what we're doing."

"And what will we be doing?" Noble asked.

"You," Brandi said, pointing to him, "are going with her," she said, pointing back to Sarah. "She'd be returned to the gods without some kind of supervision. And," Brandi smirked, "she needs a Carnian consort."

Noble's face fell at that, and his shoulders sagged as he looked at her. Brandi could almost laugh at the dejected look on his face, but she held back her amusement. This wasn't the time or place to tease him about his desire to sneak off with a princess, but Sarah's deep blush and stolen glances in Noble's direction weren't lost on her. It was clear that she was more than thrilled to think about Noble being her royal consort. But her dreams were crushed before they were able to blossom into anything more than a fleeting hope.

"I'm not doing that, Green," he said with a shake of his head. "And before you get upset," he said, holding up a hand to stop Brandi's rebuttal, "there's nothing you can say to me to change my mind. I draw the line here. I'm not doing it," he said, his voice firm.

"You hate me that much?"

Sarah's tiny voice cut through the pod, and Noble's jaw tightened as he turned to look at her. His normal lightheartedness was gone, and he kept his voice even as he spoke.

"It has nothing to do with you, Blondie. I've already got someone I'm willing to meet the gods for. I don't need anyone else."

Sarah's eyes dropped at that, and Cedric turned away from the conversation. He seemed to wince at the words, and Brandi had to admit that Noble's words could cut deep. It wasn't the first time she'd seen him remind someone that he was with them for a good time and not a long one, but it was the first time she'd ever felt sorry for the person on the receiving end. Sarah was so much like a lost duckling who imprinted on him, it was almost sad to watch.

Almost.

"Are you sure about this?" Brandi asked, turning the conversation away from Sarah and the tears welling in her eyes. "She's going to need four consorts in order to win the bid, and she has no prospects right now.

And you know that Asuna and Cazie won't have any problems finding them. They've been raised to take over the crown," she pointed out. "If Sarah's going to have any kind of fighting chance in this bid, then she needs to enter it with a solid consort or two."

"Are you going to suggest that Jack volunteer?" He shot back, the edge in his voice sharp against Brandi's ears. "She'll need a Rothian consort too, right? So, if he goes, I'll go."

Brandi bolted upright in her seat at his words, and the pod filled with a suffocating heat that sent Sarah and Cedric into fits of coughing. She stared Noble down, rage boiling beneath her skin as she clenched and unclenched her fists at her side. She knew she needed to get her anger in check, but the idea of Jack courting Sarah as a royal consort made her want to lunge at Noble and rip his throat out with her bare hands for ever uttering a thought like that aloud. She gritted her teeth and closed her eyes, forcing back the surge of burning power she hadn't grown accustomed to yet, and glared at Noble in silence before he lifted his hands to her in a show of peace.

"You can send me to the gods if you want," he said, his voice low and unwavering, "but, I'm not doing it, Brandi. Don't ask me again."

"Fine," Brandi conceded. "You don't have to be her consort. But," she said, "you do need to go with her as a bodyguard. I don't trust Leia to respect the rules of the bid. Knowing her, she'll try to dispose of her like she did Venetia."

Sarah stiffened at the sound of her mother's name, and Brandi's attention darted over to her for a moment. Facing her mother's past was something that Sarah would have to adjust to in the castle. The queen's court was a brutal place — one of emotional manipulation and mental warfare. It made field missions with the shadows seem like tea parties with sponge cake and lemonade. No one would cater to her feelings, and if she thought they would spare the name of her mother in order to protect her sensibilities, then she was in for a rude awakening. She would need protection, and Noble was the only person Brandi trusted to keep Sarah alive in her stead.

"Fine," Noble said with a nod. "Anything else?"

"Find out which of the council has made a deal with a time being."

Noble snorted. "Sure. Give me the easy task."

"I know you can handle it," Brandi said, letting the trust she held for Noble seep into her words. She held his gaze for a moment and smirked when his stoicism cracked and gave way to the grin she was used to seeing on his face.

"You're sure they're on the council?"

"It's a hunch," Brandi admitted. "But it's a lead worth following. If I'm wrong, we would have at least crossed some of the most powerful people off our list of possible culprits."

"Fair," Noble nodded. "And what of Sarah's actual consorts?"

"We'll ask Sal about it," Brandi said, deciding as the words left her mouth that it was the perfect solution to the problem. "He can help her navigate the court as a proper princess. And he'll know which potential consorts the other girls haven't sunk their teeth into yet."

"Um," Sarah whispered, her voice cracking on the sound. "Do I not have a say in this?"

"Not really."

"But this is my life," Sarah pointed out. "If I don't win…"

"They'll send you to the gods," Brandi finished. "We're aware."

"And you're fine with that?" Sarah asked, sliding to the edge of her seat with wide eyes. "Does my life mean nothing to you?"

"Do you think you're the only one putting your life on the line?"

"What?"

Sarah's genuine surprise filled Brandi with a burst of hot rage, and she grit her teeth together as she closed her eyes. She rubbed a hand across her forehead, searching the depths of her soul for the last dregs of her patience. She refused to pray to the gods for more of it and instead leaned into Jack, pushing her knee into his and letting his presence calm her as she counted down from ten.

"We're plotting a coup, Sarah," Brandi said, keeping her words slow and even. "Overthrowing the monarchy. Replacing gods. Creating new religions," Brandi stated. "Do you think that we're not all risking a swift meeting with the gods if any one of us screws up?"

"I didn't…"

"You didn't think about that," Brandi sighed. "You never do, but that's not an excuse."

"I'm sorry."

"Don't apologize," Brandi warned, her eyes narrowing. "No one wants apologies. Just stop repeating your mistakes."

Brandi paused to take a breath before leaning forward to hold Sarah's gaze.

"Look," she said, searching Sarah's eyes for any glimmer of doubt or hesitation. "We're about to destroy the entire realm here. We're going to send people to the gods. People you know," she emphasized. "And we're going to do it without a shred of remorse."

Sarah sucked in a sharp breath at that, and Brandi shrugged.

"We're terrible people, Sarah," Brandi said, leaning back in her seat once more. She watched Sarah and let her words hang in the air. The boys seemed a bit confused as their eyes darted between the two of them, but Sarah knew what she was waiting for, and Brandi would wait. She fiddled with the knife in her pocket as Sarah swiped at her shiny eyes and straightened her shoulders before offering a weak smile.

"You're right," she whispered, her voice thick with unshed tears. "So, I guess we'll be terrible people together."

Brandi flashed Sarah a quick smile of approval and she blushed a deep shade of red, but Brandi's mind had already moved on to the next task at hand as she leaned forward with new determination in her eyes.

"Now that we've gotten all that settled, let's get down to business."

CHAPTER NINE

Tell me, have you known love if you have not known betrayal? How could you possibly know what it is to treasure something if you have never feared losing it? For what is love if not an obsession of the heart? What is it if not an incomprehensible craving to carry the entirety of another being within ourselves — if it is not the intermingling of souls until they are indecipherable from one another, no longer separate entities but a single amalgamation of pure, uninhibited emotion?

— Have Mercy on Me Freya, For I Have Loved | Lindl's First Holy Academy

---

FREYA'S DOMAIN — THE CLEARING BY THE LAKE
EVENING OF DAY 2

When Sarah left the *Ciel Noir* with Noble and Cedric, Rothe's sun had already set, and she felt like she was teetering on the edge of a complete breakdown. Her eyes stung from all the tears she'd forced herself to hold back, and her throat was tight. Every breath felt like she was sucking it down through a straw, and she wanted nothing more than to go home. She wanted a warm hug and a soft bed and to be around someone —

anyone — who cared about her.

It was hard enough listening to others talk about her future as if she were nothing more than a pawn on a chess board, but it was suffocating to know that there was nothing she could say to argue with them. She had no real talents — no skills or abilities of which to speak of. And no one knew that better than her. The only thing that made her special was her mother. If she hadn't been born the first daughter of the late princess Venetia, second princess of the crown, then the others wouldn't have even known she existed. That unsettled her, and it made her feel claustrophobic in her own skin. She rubbed at her arms as she tried to push the feeling away, her eyes roaming the clearing for a familiar face. But the moment she found one, her chest felt like a boulder had been shoved into it and she had to fight back a fresh wave of tears.

Noble sat around one of the many campfires with a group of rebels she'd never seen before. They welcomed him into their fold with open arms — both in the literal and figurative sense — and Sarah's breath hitched in her throat as she watched them. She didn't know who the man was, she could only see the back of his shaved head and the one lean arm covered in tattoos that wrapped around Noble's neck, but she knew he was no stranger to Noble when he pulled Noble in for a kiss. Noble didn't fight back in the slightest, pulling the man closer as the rebels around them shouted and whistled at them. Laughter flowed around them as they pulled apart and the lanky man took a close seat next to Noble, their shoulders pressed together as they fell into the conversation with everyone else. It was effortless and Sarah couldn't look away from the way Noble draped his arm around the man and held no reservations about sharing his grin with everyone.

She was too far away to hear what Noble said, but it sent another round of laughter rolling through the group and earned him a light shove from the man he was sitting next to. Even from where she stood, she could tell that it was out of affection rather than irritation, and it made her stomach twist with jealousy. She looked up to the pink sky, as her face flushed to a matching shade and tried to focus on anything other than Noble. She didn't want to remember how cold his eyes had been when he'd looked at her or the way he'd been so vehement in his refusal to be her consort. Just the memory of it brought the prick of fresh tears behind her eyelids and she groaned under her breath as she pressed her hands to her face. All of her energy was so focused on keeping her tears at bay that she almost jumped out of her skin when a gentle hand was placed against her arm.

She squeaked in surprise and jerked away, her eyes widening when her brain recognized the wavy dark hair, light brown skin, and violet eyes. Cedric had yanked his hand away and taken a few steps back from her, watching her with caution as if he were dealing with a feral animal.

"Are you alright?"

His voice was filled with concern and Sarah flushed. She knew she had to look every bit of the emotional wreck she felt and wished she could just hide out in the *Ciel Noir* for the rest of her life. But Jack and Brandi were still inside and hiding would do her no good. Cedric had heard every word of the plan Brandi had set forth — had heard Noble reject even the idea of being with her — and concern lifted his eyebrows as he watched her unraveling at the seams.

"You seem a bit…" he paused as he tried to find the right words, and Sarah didn't miss how his gaze drifted over to Noble before returning to her. "Flustered," he finished, offering her a sympathetic smile.

"I am," Sarah sighed, hating how wet her voice sounded to her own ears. "I'm so flustered and overwhelmed that I could scream and I just," she swiped at her face before dropping her eyes to the ground and letting out a heavy sigh. "I'm tired of crying."

Cedric hummed under his breath before nodding once and leading the way through the clearing back over to the lake. He didn't tell her to follow him, but she did since she had nowhere else to go. Sarah didn't know if the lake was where he felt most comfortable or just the place where the rebels allowed him to sit alone in peace. There weren't any other people around — no campfires to warm the coming night and no meat smoking over an open flame to entice their empty stomachs. Instead, it was cold and damp, but that didn't stop Cedric from resuming his seat on the edge of the lake. He sat with his legs crossed as he looked out over the water.

Sarah didn't wait for an invitation before she flopped down next to him. She pulled her knees to her chest and let her chin rest on top of them. The last of the light from Rothe's setting sun was behind them and the pink hues of the sky were fading to a dark blue. Asari's stars had already begun to make an appearance and the breeze that had been welcome during the day carried a bite to it now that made goosebumps rise along her skin. Even so, the air felt clean, and she took deep breaths of it to ease the tight lump in her throat.

"You don't think I'm weak for wanting to cry?" Sarah asked, her voice shaking as a few tears broke through her defenses and slipped down her cheeks.

"What's wrong with showing your emotions?" Cedric asked.

Sarah coughed out a laugh. "I guess you wouldn't get it."

"No," Cedric argued, "I don't think you get it. The expectation isn't for you to be like the rest of them."

"I know that," Sarah whispered. "But they're strong. And I'm useless. I want to be more like them."

"It's odd that you should believe that."

"And why shouldn't I?" Sarah asked, resting her cheek on her knees so she could look at Cedric. He still looked out over the water that reflected the darkening sky, and it gave her the perfect opportunity to study him. His long hair hung over the right side of his shoulder in a loose ponytail, and Sarah wondered why he kept it so long. It shined in the brightening light of the moon, and his brown skin was flawless. He seemed soft compared to Jack and Noble, but Sarah found that the look suited him. He wasn't a fighter, and he didn't pretend to be one.

She wished she could be as content as he was in his own skin.

"I have nothing of value to offer," she explained. "I can't hunt or cook or even heal people without being told to do it apparently," she scoffed at herself and shook her head. "I'm clumsy. I know pretty much nothing about the realm outside of Asari's domain and I cry too much. No one here likes me."

"All that is true," Cedric agreed, and Sarah winced. Part of her had been hoping he'd refute her words — especially the last part about no one liking her. "But you've yet to tell me how that makes you useless."

"Were you not listening to me? Should I list off more of my flaws for you?"

"Allow me to clarify my meaning," Cedric said, his voice gentle as he tilted his head to meet her gaze. "You've listed off the things that make you who you are. In this moment. You haven't yet told me what makes you useless."

"I don't know what kind of answer you're looking for."

"Then let me rephrase the question," Cedric said, a smile pulling at the corner of his lips. "Do you think Brandi is stupid?"

Sarah's attention spiked and her heart pounded with extra force in her chest as she straightened her back and turned her full focus to Cedric. "Of course not."

"Then you think she's incompetent?" He suggested. "Or that she's a poor leader?"

"What are you saying?" Sarah asked, shaking her head. "No! I don't think any of that!"

"Then why do you insist on insulting her decisions by looking down on yourself? She has already made it apparent to everyone here how much faith she has in you."

Sarah could say nothing in response to Cedric's words, and her mind worked to process what he was saying. She let her knees fall apart, crossing her legs in front of her so that she could rest her elbows on them. She focused on the calming sound of the lake sloshing against the shore and tried to breathe through the headache building behind her eyes. She closed her eyes against the pressure and rubbed her fingers across her forehead, trying to soothe the ache.

"I don't understand," Sarah said. "You think Brandi has faith in me?"

Cedric nodded before returning his gaze to the water in front of them.

"What you've failed to realize is that you have more to offer Brandi than what you give yourself credit for. I don't know you well," he admitted, "but my connection to Brandi is just as strong as yours. However, she has not relied on me yet to do anything other than to assist you," he pointed out. "You though? She's put the lives of her comrades in your hands. She did not carry any doubt that you would agree to help her overthrow the queendom." He shrugged. "There are things that only you can do, and she has faith that you will do them. That speaks volumes about who she believes you to be, despite what you believe about yourself."

"I never thought of it that way."

"I'm sure you didn't," he chuckled. "Brandi is not the most open person I've ever met. But," he said, his voice lowering as he gave a near imperceptible shake of his head, "she is incredible. That's for sure."

"Careful," Sarah teased. "You fall in love with her, and Jack will feed you to her shaders."

Cedric laughed at that but said nothing in return, and it made Sarah wonder what was going on in his mind. He was, without question, brilliant. The fact that he'd secured a spot at Lindl's First Holy Academy was proof enough of that. And if his insight into Brandi and their relationship was accurate, then he was even more impressive than she originally thought. But if she were to believe his words about Brandi's belief in her, then the same would be true for him. Brandi hadn't hesitated to rely on him at Freya's temple, and she hadn't seemed conflicted about asking him to rebuild the queendom after they destroyed it. He might have seen it as a task that was beneath him, but Sarah thought it was incredible that Brandi trusted him with a task that large on his own.

He held the power to reshape everything they knew of the mortal realm and decide on how future generations would come to know the monarchy — if there even was a monarchy at all — and Brandi was trusting him to not screw it up. He might think that Brandi held high expectations for her because there were things that only she could do, but she wasn't being sent to the queendom alone. She was nothing more than a glorified distraction, and all of them knew it. But she decided to not dwell on that. The fact remained that she was a princess of the crown.

She had every right to bid for the throne and she'd decided to follow Brandi, no matter what, when she was eight years old, and she'd renewed that vow just a short while ago inside the *Ciel Noir*. If Brandi needed something of her — asked anything of her — Sarah would give it to her without question.

She couldn't tell how much of that desire was Asari's lingering affection for Freya and how much of it was her own desire to remain close to Brandi as her own person. All she knew was that the desire was real, and that she would put her full effort into satisfying it.

"Do you think her plan will work?"

The question was soft, and Sarah hadn't realized she'd harbored any doubts until the words had left her mouth. Her eyes widened as she looked over the lake, but she felt no desire to try and take them back. She wanted to know Cedric's answer and, with Brandi's plan going into effect first thing in the morning, she didn't know if she would ever have the opportunity to ask him again.

"It's too late to back out of it now," Cedric joked.

"True," Sarah agreed. "But just because we think it might fail doesn't mean we won't see it through."

"Fair point," Cedric said, letting the sounds of the nearby rebels drift over them before he spoke again. "I don't know if it'll work or not," he admitted. "I don't know why we're trying to overthrow the monarchy or what's changed between Freya's temple and now. There are too many missing variables for me to say whether we'll be successful or not."

"Brandi seemed different, didn't she?" Sarah glanced up at Cedric. "From when we were at the temple, I mean."

"I'd like to say yes," Cedric sighed, "but like I said before, I barely know her."

"Does that make you nervous?" Sarah asked, turning to look at him. "About trusting her, I mean."

"No," Cedric said, stretching the word as he mulled over his thoughts. "I'm not nervous about trusting her. It's more so that I'm nervous about the ramifications of following through with her plan."

"You're worried about what will happen to you if we fail."

"I'm worried about what will happen to Lena," he whispered. "I knew from the moment that Lindl chose me as his vessel that my life would no longer be mine. I've accepted that and have no qualms with following blindly behind the goddess. Whatever it is she may want," he clarified. "But I don't want Lena dragged into all of this. She's too gentle for that. Too brilliant."

"Well, aren't you selfless," Sarah sighed. "Thinking about someone else's wellbeing at a time like this."

Cedric laughed. "It's the opposite, in fact. I want Lena all to myself for as long as I can keep her to myself. That's all."

"Smitten," Sarah said under her breath, laughing for what felt like the first time in weeks. "It must be nice to be loved like that. I'm jealous," she said with a sigh, closing her eyes against the light breeze slinking over her skin.

"You have your heart set on Noble."

It wasn't a question, but Sarah blushed and nodded anyway. There was no point in denying the truth, especially one that was obvious enough for everyone to see. She'd been silly to ever think she could outsmart Noble at his own game. Without Russ around to guide her, she was useless, and she had no idea where he was at. But the tears and blushing looks that had worked on Kyle would never work on Noble.

"I'm sorry," he said, giving her elbow an awkward pat. "I do hope that things work out for you."

"There's no need to placate me," Sarah said, forcing a half-hearted smile to her lips. "I know he has no interest in me. He's made that clear as day already."

"Being a royal consort isn't a matter to be taken lightly," Cedric offered. "Maybe there's more to it than what we could see."

"I doubt it," Sarah said. "It would be fun to let myself believe that it wasn't about me, but you heard him. He already has someone he puts before everyone else. How could I ever compete with Brandi?"

"Brandi?" Cedric repeated. "Correct me if I'm wrong," he said, his words slow as his eyebrows raised higher, "but I thought… she and Jack…"

"You thought correctly," Sarah confirmed. "Noble doesn't have that kind of relationship with her, but still," Sarah shrugged. "He's made it no secret that she comes first in his life and always will."

"Odd," Cedric whispered.

"Very odd indeed," Sarah said with a nod. "Especially since I can't bring myself to hate him for that. I feel the same way, you know?"

"You do?"

"Yeah," Sarah said, nodding again as she watched the shaders across the lake spread themselves out in the light of Asari's moon. "I mean, I left everything behind to be here. My job, my lover," she laughed, thinking about Kyle and where her life might be had she stayed with him. "My brother," she said, sorrow weighing down her words as Jamie's face crossed her mind. "I gave up everything and you know something, Cedric?" She looked up at him and chuckled as she fought back the tears dotting the corner of her eyes. "Brandi doesn't even like me."

"She trusts you," he offered.

"We both know that's not the same as her liking me."

"Then why do you stay?"

"How could I not?" Sarah asked, her words light and breathy as she sucked down a fresh lungful of air to push aside her urge to cry again. "I swore my life to her when Asari made me his vessel. That's not something I can just take back." Sarah shrugged. "Besides. I think she's incredible. She pushes me to be someone I'm not and I…" Sarah's words trailed off and she smiled as she gazed into the darkening water. "I don't know. I think I like the person she pushes me to be."

"Hm," Cedric said, his voice quiet. "It seems to me that the reason you're so upset over your tears isn't because they view you as weak," he glanced at her, "it's because you see yourself that way."

"You're probably right," Sarah said after a long moment. "I want to be stronger. Someone she can rely on."

"Then might I suggest you give up on Noble?"

"And why would I do that?"

"Because despite the hurt his words no doubt caused you," Cedric said, his voice gentle as he turned to look at her, "I believe that he was honest with himself in a way you haven't been."

"I don't understand," Sarah said, straightening up. "What haven't I been honest about?"

"Who you're loyal to," he said. "Choices have to be made in this life, and Noble has already made his. And listening to you," he shrugged, "it seems like you've already made yours as well."

"I'm still confused."

"Answer me this. If both Noble and Brandi were drowning in this lake," Cedric paused when Sarah scoffed, and he smiled. "Just humor me. If they were both drowning here, and called out to you, who would you save?" When her eyes grew wide, Cedric pointed at her. "That is the choice you've already made. You cannot put him first in your life when you've already decided that your own life is worth more than the both of theirs."

"How did you…"

"Your thoughts and emotions are not as well hidden as you would like to believe," Cedric pointed out. "And I think it's a bit selfish of you to want someone to compete for second place in your life when you want to be first in theirs, is it not?"

"He's doing the same."

"No," Cedric hummed, "he isn't. He stated, very unambiguously I might add, that he already has someone who is in first place in his life and that he is not looking for anyone else. And you're upset because he has no interest in competing for second place in yours." Cedric shook his head as he stretched his long arms above his head. "Or maybe it's third in your case if Brandi is second. Either way, you don't really know yourself well enough to know who you prioritize in your life, do you? So, what point would there be in him returning your affections?"

Sarah had no response to that, and she dropped her head, letting it hang as she looked down at her hands. Cedric's words struck a chord within her, and she struggled to come to terms with them. She'd assumed that Noble wasn't interested in her because of her looks or because he had Brandi. She'd never guessed that it was because of her self-absorbed personality. And, somehow, hearing that made the ache of wanting him worse. She gulped down her rising anxiety and swallowed against the knot reforming in her throat as she steeled her mind and looked up at Cedric, who now stood on his feet.

"Fine," Sarah said. "I hear you."

"Good," Cedric said, reaching a hand down to her, "now do something about it. To be better than we once were, is the nature of being mortal — of being alive. And despite what we may soon face," he grinned as he pulled her to her feet and led them back to where a few of the rebels were passing around skewers of some kind of smoked animal, "we need not return to the gods just yet."

"Did you know about this?"

"Brandi has nothing to do with this, Noble."

"Stay out of this, Royal!"

Sarah groaned and lifted a hand to her head as Noble's voice drifted over to her. Her mind was still cloudy with sleep, and her head pounded against the inside of her skull as she sat up, rubbing a hand across her face. She took a few deep breaths to clear her mind of the fog and looked around the remains of the campfire that had already been doused. Cedric slept on the ground to her left, his long hair clinging to his face in the dim light of Asari's moon, and the two boys she'd saved the other night slept with their backs pressed together on her right. They'd introduced themselves as Garrett and Charlie, and they were no more than sixteen, but all night Garrett had spun stories of the most famous missions known throughout the shadows. Charlie had sat at his feet, ready to throw out a few sharp words to burst his bubble and ground him in reality again to the amusement of everyone around them. It had been a night full of laughter and she'd drifted off next to the fire, feeling like she belonged somewhere for the first time since she'd left home.

They'd welcomed Sarah and Cedric into their small bit of space with open arms, and the warmth they offered soothed the anxiety building in her nerves, but she felt it returning as Noble's voice drifted over to her again.

He sounded further away than he had before, and she turned her attention to the trees marking the edge of the clearing. Brandi had warned them that her protection from the shaders didn't extend into the forests, and Sarah hadn't thought twice about venturing back into them. The journey to the lake had been terrifying — the forest was pitch black, the ground was uneven, and there were a dozen sets of eyes watching them at all times. She had no intentions of venturing back into them until it was time to leave Freya's domain altogether, but as the voices grew louder, her curiosity became insatiable. So, doing her best not to wake the rebels sleeping around her, she crawled to her feet and inched her way towards the edge of the clearing. She didn't have to go far before she could hear everything, and she strained her ears to listen in as she leaned her back against one of the trees. It was a few feet into the dense forest — she could still see the lake, but she was out of sight from anyone who might happen to walk up on her.

"I told you this would be his reaction," another voice sighed.

"So, you did know?" Noble questioned, his voice lifting in surprise. "Explain this," he demanded. "Why do you two know each other?"

Silence clung to the air after Noble's question and Sarah's eyebrows lifted as she strained to hear an answer over her heart thundering in her chest. She could tell this wasn't a conversation she was meant to hear — there was a reason they'd chosen to have it in the middle of the forest where the other rebels wouldn't venture. But the tone of Noble's voice made her chest tighten and she wanted to know what could possibly have him as stressed as he sounded.

"Tell him," Brandi prodded.

The other person sighed, and Sarah wondered who he was. Noble wasn't the type of person to let anyone bother him, but this person sounded as if he had expected this reaction from him.

"There's no easy way to tell you this," he said, choosing his words with care, "but I guess you'll understand once I tell you." He released a deep sigh before blurting out his next words. "I'm Freya's original creation. The shader mentioned in the story of creation."

"Say what now?"

"That's the reason we know each other," Brandi explained. "Freya's been incarnating his soul into the mortal realm for just as long as she's been doing it herself."

"And every lifetime I get my memories back and feel compelled to seek her out," the stranger added. "And because of my connection to the beasts, I'm never able to live a normal life. Whatever family I'm born into becomes ostracized because of me. So, I tried to leave before that ever happened to you."

"Okay," Noble said, his voice strained as leaves crunched beneath his feet. "I get why you didn't tell me as a kid, but Royal," Noble's words paused, and Sarah wished that she could see him and what he was doing. "I've been Carna's vessel since I was eleven. Why didn't you think to tell me then?" His footsteps stopped, and Sarah could only guess that he'd turned to look at Brandi. "Why didn't you tell me?"

"I made her swear not to," Royal interjected.

"I wasn't talking to you, Royal!" Noble snapped, his voice booming like thunder through the night. "Answer me, Brandi."

"It wasn't my place to tell you."

"Your place?" Noble repeated. "You know, I've been by your side nearly every day of your life, Green. And I never would've thought to keep something like this from you. But that's the difference between you and me, isn't it?" Noble scoffed. "I'm always thinking about you, but I'm just an afterthought."

"That's not true and you know it," Brandi said.

"It's not?" Noble asked. "Because last I checked, I was the only one who didn't know you were leaving the shadows," he pointed out.

"Are we back to this?" Brandi huffed.

"Yeah, we are," Noble said, raising his voice. "Because I'm not over it."

"What do you want me to do then, Noble?" Brandi asked, raising her voice to match his. "I already apologized! I can't change what's already been done."

"It's not about your words, Brandi," he snapped. "It's about the fact that you don't ever think about the fact that I got feelings the same as you do."

"What are you talking about?"

"See?" Noble said, scoffing. "It's that right there. You don't even realize how deep you cut me sometimes. And I put up with it because I love you, but," he paused and Sarah could imagine him shaking his head at Brandi, "you're just as self-centered as Blondie is."

"Don't compare me to her," Brandi warned.

"Why?" Noble challenged. "Hurt your feelings? Maybe I should offer for you to be her consort instead."

Brandi said nothing in return and Sarah wished she could see their faces. Her own feelings were hurt at the idea that they both viewed her as someone unworthy of their love, but she shoved those feelings aside. Cedric had already been ruthless in pointing out that she'd never done anything to garner their affection but hearing them talk about her this way wasn't something she'd soon forget. And she swallowed against the lump in her throat as Brandi spoke again.

"I shouldn't have asked that of you," Brandi conceded.

"You think?" Noble scoffed.

"I'm sorry," Brandi said. "For real this time. I'll be more mindful of how you feel about things."

"That's all I'm asking for, Green."

"So," Brandi asked, a yawn stretching out the word. "We good?"

"As long as you never volunteer me to be someone's consort ever again, then yeah."

"Done," Brandi said, choking back a laugh.

"And you should apologize to Blondie too," Noble pointed out. "You were cruel to get her hopes up like that."

Brandi snorted at that. "I'll think about it."

"And what about us," Royal said, interjecting himself into their conversation. "Are we good, Noble?"

"Depends," Noble said, his voice carrying skepticism with it. "Why are you here? It seems an odd time for you to show yourself now."

"Things are changing within the realm," he answered. "And I came here to see it for myself."

"Things like what?" Brandi asked.

"The shaders," Royal said. "They're learning to shapeshift."

"Since when?" Brandi asked, her voice full of shock.

"I don't know that yet," Royal answered. "I just arrived in Freya's domain a few days ago. All I know right now is what Crown has reported back to me. But it seems like a very recent development."

"So," Noble said, "what does that mean for us?"

"Whatever you want it to, I guess," Royal said. "I have to figure out what this all means, but," he said, his words slowing as he seemed to be thinking over his words, "if the shaders serve you now, Brandi… and they can shift into a human form…" Royal paused and Sarah imagined his gaze darting between Brandi and Noble. "They may be able to cross barriers."

"That's…" Noble said, laughter dancing beneath his words, "insane."

"Can you teach Tiki?" Brandi asked, her voice more intense than it was before. "And Lia?"

"I don't know," Royal admitted. "I can try though."

"Do that," Brandi said. "Because if we can get the shaders to support the ranks of the rebellion then…" Brandi's voice trailed off, silence filling the space around them until she spoke again. "Just keep me updated."

"Sure," Royal said, chuckling. "You're the boss. And Noble?"

"What?"

"I'm sorry for disappearing on you," Royal said, his voice even and carrying the soft notes of sincerity. "I hope you can forgive me."

"I mean," Noble sighed. "I'm pissed off that you would avoid me for so long. And that you made Brandi keep secrets from me. But it's not something to stay mad about. You did what you had to, and so did I. We're good."

"Told you," Brandi sighed.

"So, you don't think I'm just some beast?" Royal asked, his words carrying an upward lilt of hope.

"Of course not," Noble said. "But at least I understand why you were trying to teach me about shaders now."

Royal snickered at that and Sarah heard Brandi yawn again as they whispered their goodbyes to Royal and leaves shuffled beneath their feet. She listened to their footsteps disappear into the night and she held her breath, hoping that none of them would notice her. When it was silent again, she pushed away from the tree she was leaning against and tried to sneak back to the clearing. Before she got two steps away though, an arm gripped her wrist, yanking her backwards as she yelped in surprise. They spun her around to face them and she was surprised to see a pair of angry dark eyes glaring down at her.

"And where do you think you're going?"

Before Sarah could say anything, she was backed into the tree behind her and the length of Noble's body was pressed against hers, and for a moment she forgot how to breathe. Her blue eyes grew wide as his gaze bore into hers, and she blinked as she looked away from him, a deep blush creeping up her neck and over her cheeks.

"Bold of you to listen in on a private conversation like that, Blondie," Noble said. "Did you really think we wouldn't hear your clumsy footsteps?"

"I'm sorr—"

"Save it," he snapped, cutting her off. "An apology is worthless when you meant to violate someone's privacy."

"I didn't —"

"You did," Noble corrected. "Because for some reason, you think you're entitled to us. To me," he said shaking his head. "But let me make something very clear to you," he said, leaning closer to her. "You are entitled to nothing."

"I know," Sarah said, trembling against him as tears slipped down her cheeks.

"I don't think you do," Noble said. "So let me make something plain for you," he said, tightening his grip on her wrist and lowering his voice. "Because you're the type of person to think that it's because of your looks that I refused to be your consort. And I want you to know with absolute certainty, that is not the reason why," he whispered. "It is because you are the type of person who needs to be told what to do, when to do it, and how to do it. You stand around, watching people return to the gods, knowing you have the power to help them. You eavesdrop on private conversations and then have the nerve to cry about it when you get caught," he whispered. "You carry yourself with the insecurities of a child and still somehow think yourself to be our equal, deserving of our respect, when you have done nothing to earn your place among us." He chuckled as he looked down at her. "You are not special, Sarah. To me, or anyone else here. So, I suggest you adjust your actions accordingly."

Sarah sucked in a sharp breath at his words and nodded as he released her. She pulled her bottom lip between her teeth as Noble walked away and tears continued to flow down her cheeks, but she didn't dare open her mouth to say anything to him. What could she say? He'd made his feelings as clear as a cloudless sky. And she sank to the ground, covering her face in her hands as his words lodged themselves in her chest and swelled in her throat.

She'd known that Noble wasn't interested in her but hearing that it was because of her personality rather than her looks made the sting of his words worse because she had no rebuttal to them. So, she sat there and cried. And she could admit that part of her wanted someone to hear her — to ask about her well-being and comfort her. But when no one came, she accepted the fact that Noble was right. She hadn't earned her place among them, and she resolved to change that with the rising of Rothe's sun.

"Tomorrow," she whispered to herself, swiping at her face as she pushed herself from the ground and returned to the campfire she'd come from. "Tomorrow."

CHAPTER TEN

It must never be forgotten that the goddess is the subjugator of death — all things submit before her in awe and she is made more beautiful in the wake of her destruction.

— Freya, The Beginning and the End | Lindl's First Holy Academy

---

FREYA'S DOMAIN — THE CLEARING BY THE LAKE
MORNING OF DAY 3

When Sarah woke the next morning, the rebels were already moving with intention. Fires were doused, the sparring ring was dismantled, the last of the smoked meat was being passed around, and Najé was organizing the rebels into separate ranks in front of the *Ciel Noir*. Cedric's words still haunted Sarah's mind, popping up as she washed her face at the lake and tended to the last of the minor injuries the rebels had before joining the others by the transport pod.

To be better than they were was the nature of being alive.

Sarah couldn't unhear the words and she wondered if she could say with full confidence that she'd changed from the young girl who'd met

Brandi in Asari's domain. She liked to think that she had, but she had to admit the truth in Cedric's words — she was selfish. Even though she'd never questioned Noble's loyalty to Brandi — had accepted it as a given — she'd never considered her own feelings.

She knew Asari had forced her to pledge her life to Brandi and the goddess as a child. And Sarah knew that, even now, she carried a deep-seated desire to remain with Brandi and be useful to her. But Cedric's hypothetical had revealed another truth she'd never paid attention to before.

She cared about herself more than anyone else.

It felt blasphemous to even think it to herself, but the truth was what it was. If Cedric's hypothetical had been true, she knew for a fact that Noble would meet the gods trying to save Brandi if he could. He would have drowned rescuing her if that meant she would survive and knowing that made guilt swell in her stomach, because Sarah knew that she would have hesitated to save either of them. She wasn't truly willing to put her life on the line for either of them and, if that was true, then Cedric was right — she had no business lusting after Noble. He could say with full confidence that he loved Brandi more than himself — anyone else in his life would have to be content with second place. But her? She couldn't even admit that much.

And if Brandi didn't come first for her — if she couldn't reciprocate his most base feelings — then what right did she have to ask him to notice her? And, as if to add insult to injury, Russ's words came floating back to her.

"Noble is more complex than anyone gives him credit for," she whispered to herself, sneaking a glance over to him as he helped Najé finish organizing the rebels into three separate ranks. "I think I'm starting to see that now."

"See what?"

Sarah jumped at the words in her ear and pressed a hand to her chest as she spun to look at Cedric with a glare.

"You really need to stop sneaking up on me like that."

"And you should stop daydreaming where people can sneak up on you," he shot back. "So?" He inquired. "What do you see now?"

"Nothing really," Sarah said, falling into step next to him as they walked over to the *Ciel Noir*. "I was just thinking about something a friend told me a while back. It's starting to make sense to me now."

"A moment of clarity in the midst of confusion is wonderful, isn't it?"

"Yeah," Sarah agreed. "It is."

When they reached the front of the ranks, they moved to stand with Noble as Najé had directed them to. It felt strange for her to be standing in front of so many people, especially when they looked at her with eyes holding such high expectations, but she worked to not let it get to her. Instead, she took a deep breath and squared her shoulders, deciding to meet the gazes of a few of them and holding them until they looked away. She kept her head held high and refused to glance at Noble, even when she felt his dark eyes on her.

"That's the way, Blondie," he whispered. "If you want to stand next to us, then don't let them forget who you are."

She whipped her head over to him at the words, but his gaze was focused on the transport pod as the doors opened. She followed his gaze and the quiet murmur that had been shifting through the ranks, died as Brandi followed Jack out of the pod looking like the fearless woman she was. Her thick hair was twisted down into knots that covered her head, and they made her green eyes seem sharper than usual. Sarah shifted to her right, closer to Noble, to make room for them, and Brandi looked out over the crowd for a moment before she spoke.

"This is where you make your choice," Brandi said, her voice ringing out over the crowd standing before them as her words sunk into Sarah's mind. She was almost surprised to hear the words over her own thundering heartbeat. Her cheeks flushed under the direct gaze of the rebels, but she did her best to mimic the stoic posture of the others and keep her face still. She stood a few feet behind Brandi, sandwiched between Jack and Noble. Cedric and Najé stood on either side of them and she felt as out of place as a snowflake in the middle of Rothe's summer.

And as Brandi looked out over the rebels, a look of relief washed over Najé's face as she stood in the front row and Brandi addressed the crowd. Brandi held her gaze for a moment, but Sarah couldn't say what the look was that passed between them, and that sent a sharp pang through Sarah's chest. It was another reminder that she knew next to nothing about Brandi. Even with all she now knew of Brandi's past, and with everything they'd been through to get to Freya's domain, she was still on the outside of whatever walls Brandi had built up around herself. It was a frustrating reality check — she was still the other among them. She held no desire to remain the way she was, but she didn't know how to be one of them.

The simple fact that the rebels had fallen into neat rows under Najé's guidance told her more about the difference between them and her than words ever could. They'd understood what was happening and moved to stand ready at attention the moment Brandi, Jack, Najé, and Noble moved to the top of the clearing. Even Cedric, who seemed to fall into their rhythms with little effort, had been surprised at their efficiency and with the apparent power the four of them wielded over the others. Sarah had known their influence was far-reaching, but witnessing the totality of what that meant wasn't the same as hearing about it. And as Brandi spoke to the rebels now, Sarah recognized the feeling blooming in her chest as complete admiration. She watched every rebel and shadow in attendance cling to Brandi's words like they were falling from the lips of the goddess herself.

They wouldn't be wrong, and Sarah had to admit that she listened with the same bated breath that they did. She'd let Najé's directions fall on deaf ears when they'd arrived in the clearing, but she wouldn't be caught playing the fool again and had no intentions of shaming herself by repeating the same mistake twice.

"You stand here now," Brandi said, "because you made a choice to fight against the queendom. To reject the crown and the head it rests upon. You may be proud of that decision," Brandi said, meeting the gaze of a few people who stood up straighter at her words, "and it may have been the hardest decision you've ever had to make. No one knows what you had to sacrifice to be here today, and the rebellion wouldn't have made it this far without you. Take pride in knowing that!"

Several shouts and claps echoed through the clearing before Najé lifted her hand to quiet them. She took a step forward to separate herself from the crowd before taking a deep breath and turning to face them. She stood with her hands on her hips and a smirk on her face as she looked out over the two hundred surviving rebels who stood with their backs straight, hands clasped behind them, and every eye trained on her.

"As many of you know," she began, her voice even as it drifted over them, "I have been serving both the rebellion, as its combat leader, and the queendom, as the rising director of the shadows. However," she said, pausing to meet the gaze of a few shadows who stood in the front rows, "that changes from this moment forward. It has been made clear to me that I cannot be loyal to both. Not anymore." She shook her head, letting her long braids sway around her shoulders and back before she lifted her head and raised her voice, confidence flowing through her words.

"Before every life standing here, be they rebel, shadow, shader or god, I say this." She turned in that moment to face Brandi, who quirked an eyebrow at Najé's theatrics. "I pledge my life to Brandi. Whether in the shadow or the light, wherever she leads, I will follow."

Najé reached her fist out to Brandi with a smile, and Brandi's eyes narrowed at her for a moment before she cleared her face, wiping it of any trace of emotion, and extending her own arm, pressing her knuckles against Najé's. It was an unexpected sight after watching Brandi order the shaders to devour Najé on the battlefield. Sarah's eyes grew wide watching them, but instead of focusing on them, her blue eyes drifted over to the crowd of spectators. Many of the rebels wore expressions of absolute shock, but the shadows — the people who had known them the longest — the people who knew them best — seemed unfazed. A few of them even wore masks of stifled excitement as they looked at the two sisters who were, by all appearances, mending whatever rift had divided them.

Sarah knew better than to believe it though. She'd stood in the center of the shaders as Brandi wept over Jack's body, pleading with her to save him. The desperation Brandi had shown in that clearing wasn't something Sarah would ever forget. So, Najé may have forced Brandi's hand in this public spectacle, but her actions would never be forgiven, and Sarah felt her own opinion of Najé sour as she watched her coerce Brandi into playing the part of reconciling with her.

Silence hung in the air before Najé turned back to face the crowd. The smile she'd reserved for Brandi fell away to be replaced with the hard look of a leader who would hold others to the same standards she held herself to.

"Choose for yourself who you will serve," she said, her sharp brown eyes rolling over the myriad of faces staring back at her. "Whether it be Brandi, the queendom, your own ego, or the will of the gods your mothers taught you to obey. You cannot serve them all. And what you decide in this moment will determine the fate of the entire realm, so do not hesitate in making your choice! As for me," she said, moving to stand in the front row of the crowd, "I have made mine."

With those words, Najé placed a fist over her heart and sank to one knee, dipping her head until her braids fell around her in a curtain.

Sarah's breath caught in the back of her throat and her heart pounded in her chest as her eyes darted over the clearing, waiting for what would happen next. She hadn't expected the show that Najé put on, but she couldn't look away from it. Even though she was new to the dynamics playing out in front of her, she wasn't so naïve as to misunderstand the situation.

Despite whatever their personal feelings toward each other were, the fact had always remained that Najé MelForth was a noble. She was the daughter of the first consort of the queen. Her lover may have rejected his title, but he was still the second prince of the queendom. And, aside from her father, she was the highest-ranking member of the shadows. She may not have relied on her position to garner respect, but that didn't change her standing in the societal hierarchy. Najé was a thoroughbred lady of the court. And now, not only had she bowed her head to Brandi, she'd kneeled before her.

It was the utmost sign of respect reserved for the queen and the gods themselves, and not a single person who stood in the clearing could make the mistake of perceiving it as anything else.

Najé was pledging the entirety of her life to Brandi, to do with her as she saw fit, and it wasn't something that was done lightly. No one moved as they watched her display of loyalty and Sarah half expected them to stay like that — frozen in that moment forever. But when Jack stepped forward, all eyes turned to him.

"This is the choice we ask you to make now," he said, his deep voice rumbling over the crowd.

"And why should we serve her?"

The voice came drifting up to them from the back of the crowd and Sarah's eyes fought to identify the owner of the question. It was a bold one to ask — one that she would have never let cross her lips — but it was one that she still understood. Her trust of Brandi was innate, it came with the territory of being a vessel of the gods. She trusted Brandi with her life and would do anything Brandi asked of her — follow her to the edge of the realm or, apparently, agree to fight beings who were more powerful than the gods. She'd be a liar if she didn't admit that part of it was her own trust of Brandi, the person, and not just Asari's pull on her, but her experience with Brandi wasn't the norm. So, outside of the people who stood beside her, she didn't know who would be willing to follow Najé's example without question.

Her blue eyes darted from Jack and Brandi to steal a glance at Noble, who still stood on her right. He hadn't moved, and his face hadn't changed, but somehow, the air surrounding him felt warmer — thicker. His face was still relaxed, and his dark eyes never strayed from the crowd in front of him, but when the Lindlian girl with a short curly afro stepped out of line to walk to the front, he stiffened. It made Sarah wonder what his relationship with her was, and her eyes roved over the girl with a new intensity.

She was round. From her face, to her waist, to her short, springy curls and generous curves. She had no sharp angles and her light brown skin was dotted with dark freckles across her entire face and down her arms. Her glasses were big and made her brown eyes seem bigger than they were, but she was, without question, one of the most beautiful girls there. She wore the colorless uniform of the queen's shadows, but she walked with the careful steps of someone uncomfortable with being outside. And when she lifted her hands to her hips, it was easy to tell that she was soft in places where the rest of them carried hard muscles.

Sarah glanced at the others and noticed the way their shoulders tightened and the way their eyes narrowed. Cedric was the only one who didn't tense up at her presence and it made Sarah even more curious about exactly who the woman was that was brave enough to question Brandi and whether or not she was worthy of her loyalty.

"I'm not pledging loyalty to anyone unless I have a reason," the girl stated, holding Brandi's gaze. "A good one."

"Why are you like this, Mara?" Jack sighed.

"Who knows?" She shrugged. "But regardless of any questions about my character," she said, narrowing her eyes, "I want an answer to my question."

"And what would you like me to tell you?"

It was Brandi who asked the question. And as she stepped forward, she placed her hand on Jack's arm. He held back his retort and just watched as Brandi moved to stand in front of Mara. For a moment, the two women locked eyes and the atmosphere of the clearing went from buzzing to electric. Shockwaves of tension rolled off the two as they stared each other down.

"I'd like to know why you think you're worth our loyalty," Mara stated. "We pledged our loyalty to Glenn. To this rebellion. And now you waltz in and want to demand our service without explanation?" Mara snorted. "It doesn't work that way."

"You don't trust Najé's judgment of me?"

"I don't trust anyone," Mara stated. "And Najé has always treated you as her favorite, so what's new? It's just formal now," she said, waving her hand in Najé's direction. "Answer me, Brandi," she said, dropping her hands and taking a step forward. "Or I walk away from all of this right now."

"Then walk away," Brandi said, holding Mara's gaze. "I'm not going to stand here and feed you all some nonsense about doing what's best for the queendom," she stated, her clear voice washing over the crowd. "I'm not even going to tell you that what we're doing is right or just or serving the will of the gods." Brandi shrugged. "If I'm being honest, I'm serving my own selfish desires and nothing else. But that should be enough, shouldn't it?"

"Are you cracked?" Mara scoffed. "Why should any of us care about your desires, let alone put our lives on the line for them?"

"Because I am Freya's daughter," Brandi answered, her voice low as she held Mara's gaze.

"And? That doesn't make you special," Mara shot back. "Every woman born into this realm is Freya's daughter."

"And how many of them wield the power of gods?" Brandi demanded, her voice rising with her irritation as a dark green light bloomed at her fingertips. "How many of them command Freya's first creations, the beasts of nightmares?"

Thunder rumbled above them as dark clouds rolled over each other to block out the sun. The wind picked up around them, whistling as it sped by and ripped leaves from the trees. The two shaders Brandi had returned to the clearing with, who had been sitting at the edge of the clearing and watching her from afar, rose to their feet and Sarah couldn't look away as the largest one threw its head back and released a high-pitched howl that reverberated through the trees. In seconds, the rhythmic stomping of shaders began echoing through the domain and dozens of shaders began poking their blind heads into the clearing, taking bold steps from behind the trees with frightening grins splitting their faces and showing off their double row of razor-sharp teeth. Some of them continued to stomp against the ground, but others lifted their voices into a howl, joining Brandi's shaders in creating a chilling chorus. The sound sent ice down her spine, and she took a step closer to Noble on instinct, unable to resist the urge to be closer to another human as every survival instinct inside of her screamed at her to run away from the clearing and the sweet-scented beasts. But even as her heart pounded in her throat, Sarah couldn't pull her eyes away from Brandi.

"You can question me all you want, Mara, but the answer won't change," Brandi stated. "I am not like Freya's other children, but remaining a part of this rebellion isn't something you'll be forced to do. So," Brandi said, lifting her voice and looking out over the crowd who stood watching them with bated breaths, "I ask you again to make your choice. Those who no longer find value in toppling this queendom can go," Brandi said, throwing her hand out to the edge of the clearing where the shaders parted to make a pathway. "Because beyond this moment," she said, turning to stare in Mara's hazel eyes, "there will be no sympathy for those who abandon us."

With those words, Mara smirked and dropped her head in a show of respect.

"You've answered my question, so I'll play nice for now since our goals align for the moment," she said, peeking up a Brandi. "I'll remain at your side as long as they do."

"And what of the rest of you?" Jack asked, stepping forward next to Brandi. "Make your choice."

Sarah watched with wide eyes as all but three of the rebels dropped to a single knee, lowering their heads and pledging to serve Brandi and her cause. Even the shaders who surrounded them kneeled to the ground, dipping their heads. The three men who remained on their feet stood on shaking legs and Brandi took her time meeting each of their gazes before she gestured toward the pathway the shaders had made in the forest.

"If you cannot serve us, we have no need of you."

Sarah was surprised to see them turn to sprint toward the shaders that Brandi had been keeping them safe from, but they wasted none of their strength as they ran. Once they were gone from sight, Brandi returned her gaze to the rebels who remained.

"Lift your heads," she commanded. "And hear me when I say this." She paused as she waited for the rebels to place their full attention on her. "I am the daughter of Freya, loved by her children of darkness, but I will never be your mother, as she was," Brandi stated. "I will never offer you mercy. But," she said, letting her voice carry on the calming winds to the waiting ears of the rebels around her, "I promise to protect you. As long as my heart desires it, you will fear no mortal in this realm, and nothing shall bring you harm. But understand that I carry no patience for the disloyal," she said, letting her words cut through the air. "And should you ever betray my trust in you," Brandi warned, training her gaze on Najé, "I will never forgive you." She let her words hang before turning her eyes to the shaders in the distance. "And to show you that I am a woman of my word, bear witness to the fate of those who would turn their backs on me."

Brandi paused as the rebels rose to their feet and turned wide, terrified eyes onto the shaders who stood to their full heights. Eagerness rolled off the young ones as if they could read her mind and anticipation bubbled to life in the air, pushing out the tension that had been suffocating them all just a few moments before.

"Feast."

It was a single command, and with it, the shaders that had been crowded in the shadows thundered through the clearing. They weaved their way through the rebels with an agility that belied their immense size and Sarah was awestruck by their movements — so much so that she didn't have time to scream before they disappeared out of sight from the clearing. A few seconds later, the guttural screams of the men who'd tried to escape back to the monarchy were heard throughout Freya's domain and Sarah flinched away from the sound.

"Remember this moment well," Brandi warned as the dying screams of the deserters were etched into the mind of every person standing there, scarring them for eternity as Brandi's green eyes bore into them, "your end will not be swift should you forget."

Silence coated the air like over-sweet honey as her words between them — thick and sticky, clinging to everybody in attendance. Brandi took the time to meet the eyes of every rebel before her gaze returned to where the vessels stood. She met Noble's gaze first, and he smirked at her, before she turned her gaze to Cedric — who nodded — and then onto Sarah. She froze under Brandi's intense gaze — at her unspoken question. But her answer had been clear from the moment Asari had descended into her room when she was eight. It hadn't changed in the fourteen years they'd been apart, and it didn't change now. So, she smiled. Bright and beaming, releasing all the hope she held in her heart and trusting it to Brandi. Because, like Najé, wherever Brandi led, Sarah knew she would follow.

Brandi's lips quirked upward at Sarah's smile, but when Jack grinned at her, she smiled back — her grin wide and uninhibited and Sarah's heart pounded at the sight. She'd never seen Brandi express such joy before and the image seared itself into her brain and she allowed herself to finally understand why Brandi had been willing to destroy everything for the man who stood in front of her now. If her smile was any indicator of what she truly felt for Jack, then Sarah would beat back every doubt she held so that she could protect Brandi and her smile at all costs. It was an odd compulsion that felt reminiscent of Asari's obsession with Freya, but she knew the gods pull on her soul had nothing to do with this moment. Protecting Brandi would be her own choice because the kind of joy that Brandi showed them in that moment was something that should never be stolen from her. She walked back to stand in the center between the vessels before turning back to the waiting crowd.

"My goal is to destroy the queendom," she said, letting her words sink in. "Some of you may be wondering how my goal is any different from what Glenn set out to accomplish, so allow me to make things perfectly clear," she said with a shake of her head. "I am not playing the long game. Today marks the first day of summer and the opening of the bid. Every viable princess who wants to lay her claim to the crown will be making her intentions known before the start of the opening ball in three weeks. But by summer's end, the monarchy will fall, and we will control the crown."

A collective gasp went through the rebels, and Sarah didn't blame them. She'd been floored the first time she'd heard the timeline, too. Brandi was promising to accomplish in three months what Glenn had spent over a decade trying to achieve. It seemed almost reckless to promise that to them, but Brandi was a woman who would accomplish whatever it was she wanted to do, and the shadows knew exactly what she was capable of. And as Sarah saw hope, excitement, and anticipation replace the shock and anxiety on the faces of the rebels, she began to truly understand what it meant for mortals to be in the presence of a god — even when they were unaware of it. Brandi had the ability to instill in them an unshakeable faith in her. Her words intoxicated them and became their absolute truth.

There wasn't a single doubt among them, and Sarah felt her own heart grow lighter at the thought.

"In order to do this, three things need to happen," Brandi said, holding up her fingers. "First, we need a candidate to bid for the crown," she said, indicating Sarah. She flushed under the scrutiny of the rebels, but she said nothing as Brandi continued. "Second, we'll need to grow our ranks. Large enough to defeat the queen's soldiers and the personal squadrons of the council. And last," she said, "we'll need to spread the word that the rebellion is under new leadership."

"And how do you expect us to do that?" Mara called out from the spot she had returned to in the crowd.

"We're resourceful," Brandi said, lifting her gaze to address everyone, "and you've already been divided into squads. Squad blue," she said, pointing to the group where Mara, Garrett, and Charlie stood at the front, "will return to the tower with Sarah, Noble, and Cedric. You will serve under them to support Sarah as she places her bid for the throne. Squad black," she said, pointing to the group in the center, "will disperse throughout the realm. Notify the other rebels of what's happening and begin spreading whispers predicting the fall of the crown. And squad green," she said, "will stay with me, Jack, and Najé. We'll set up a new base in Rothe's domain, grow our numbers, and train for the day we sever Leia's head from her shoulders!"

Brandi thrust her fist into the air, and a resounding shout echoed throughout the clearing. When the noise died down, Brandi wore a wolfish grin on her face, and it made Sarah's heart jump in her chest with anticipation of her own.

"Now, let's go destroy a queendom."

CHAPTER ELEVEN

When someone is willing to know you — to paint their world with even your darkest colors and celebrate your light even when they are being drenched in their own rain — cherish them. For not many are blessed enough to be able to call such a person, friend.

— Of Light and Love | Lindl's Second Holy Academy

ROTHE'S DOMAIN — EDGE OF THE SCORCHED DESERT
3 DAYS BEFORE THE OPENING CEREMONY

"And there she is," a voice giggled from the bar. "A raindrop in the middle of the dessert!"

Brandi's eyes danced across the room until they landed on the woman at the bar who sat watching her with bright hazel eyes. Her thick black hair was piled atop her head with two wavy tendrils hanging down by the sides of her face. She leaned her elbows on the bar as she twisted on her barstool to meet her gaze and offer her grin. Brandi lifted her hand to her in a weak wave as she let the door to the dusty bar slam shut behind her. She swiped at the bead of sweat that rolled down her face and cursed

Rothe under her breath for making the summers so hot in his domain.

She'd sacrificed the all-black outfit she'd worn as part of the shadows for a pair of red denim shorts that stopped at the middle of her thigh, a strapless white top, and a pair of white sneakers that were now covered in the dusty sands of Rothe's dessert. Her eyes were shaded by a straw hat she'd picked up on whim when she'd passed through the local market that morning. It had a red band around the center, and she wore it in part to blend in with the civilians who wandered around the market in fragment 10528. Her dark brown skin didn't stand out much in Rothe's domain, but more than a few gazes had lingered on her green eyes, so she'd picked up a pair of dark shades as well. She placed them on top of her hat as she adjusted to the dim light and cool air of the bar.

She'd found the bar sitting in the exact location that Pine had told her about when she'd called her from the *Ciel Noir*. It was in the middle of a soon-to-be-abandoned marketplace in the middle of the Scorched Desert, because as soon as the sun reached its highest point in Carna's sky, the Rothians who knew better than to try and face the unbearable heat of Rothe's sun at midday, would seek shelter inside. The bar around them was already starting to come to life as more people filtered in behind Brandi, sinking into creaking chairs in dark corners of the room. She had no idea what would have possessed Pine to come out this far and she lifted an eyebrow at the tiny woman as she sank into the barstool next to her.

"I hope you have a good reason for dragging me all the way out here," Brandi sighed, signaling the bartender for a cold glass of water. When it arrived, she placed it against the side of her face and sighed, closing her eyes and enjoying the simple pleasure before setting it back on the counter, unwrapping a straw, and taking a deep sip from it.

"You know I do," Pine said, sipping from her own glass. "It just so happens that what I found out is nearby."

Brandi's green eyes darted over to her at that, and she waited for Pine to continue. It never failed to surprise her at just how much information Pine could gather when she was left to her own devices. It's one of the reasons Brandi was willing to trust her so much — even without her blessing of persuasion from Lindl, she was infectious. Most people couldn't resist her, and she used that to her advantage. Her blessing didn't work on Brandi, but even so, Pine had never failed her. She'd always been loyal to her in a way that few others were, and Brandi realized just how much she relied on Pine as she waited to hear what she had to say.

"Well," Brandi prodded, rolling her eyes. "Don't keep me waiting."

Pine giggled and leaned forward, lowering her voice as a pair of young women slid into the seats on her right, locked in their own whispered conversation.

"Remember when I told you about the Lindlian girl with the red hair?"

"Grace," Brandi said with a nod, leaning her elbow on the bar and resting her head in hand.

The last time they'd met, Pine had given her a microchip with information on Grace Bertanal — Adam Bertanal's supposed miracle daughter. According to Pine's intel, she'd appeared out of nowhere six months ago. She was twenty years old, no taller than five-five, curly red hair with light brown skin and hazel eyes. She was a quiet girl with a gentle smile that belied her chaotic intentions. Her public debut had been made three weeks ago — at the same time the gods had signed the contract with Azinne. The moment she came into the spotlight, the monarchy had begun spinning stories of how they'd been intentional about keeping her out of the public eye — that Bert and Queen Leia had made a mutual decision to allow their daughter to grow up in Lindl's domain in an effort to have her foster a genuine connection with the people there. They'd done it in the hopes that it would give her an edge in the upcoming bid for the throne, but Brandi hadn't believed a word of it.

She knew the gods — had grown up with them answering her every prayer. So, she knew for a fact that not one of the gods gifted their children with red hair. Rothe sometimes gifted blonde hair and Lindl's children had thick hair that fell in dark, shiny waves like Pine and Cedric — Carnians had silver hair like Noble, and Asarians were known for the brown, floppy curls. She was an anomaly that didn't come from this realm. It's why she'd assumed Grace was Freya's secret love child when Azinne had first told her the story of Zareal's affair with the goddess. But knowing that was an impossibility, her brain struggled to make sense of Grace and who she truly was.

"Did you find out more about her?" Brandi questioned.

"Yes and no," Pine said, offering Brandi a shrug. "I found someone who claims to know a lot more than I do, but even she doesn't make any sense to me."

"What do you mean, she doesn't make sense to you?" Brandi asked, lifting her eyebrows in question. "You've met this person, haven't you?"

"Yeah, but," Pine shook her head as her hazel eyes darted to her drink, "she says she's not from this realm, raindrop."

"How would that even be possible?"

"I have no idea," Pine shrugged. "It's why I said she doesn't make sense to me. But my guess?" Pine asked. "Maybe she's involved with Grace and those beings of time you told Lena about, back at the academy."

"And you believe she might know something?" Brandi asked.

"I do," Pine answered with a nod. "Her eyes told me she wasn't lying. And besides," she said, smirking up at Brandi, "she didn't fall prey to my blessing. So, I have to believe there's something special about her."

"That's hard to believe," Brandi admitted. As far as she knew, no one was immune to Pine's blessing. She'd always believed it held no power over her because she was a vessel of the gods. Now though, she wondered if it was because she was a true born god in her own right. Even thinking that to herself was enough to make her recoil from the thought but she couldn't dismiss it. Because if that were the truth, the same would have to be said of the woman in question, wouldn't it? It made Brandi's head ache at just how fast the realm she'd always known was changing around her with every new truth she learned. She sighed and shook her head, reaching her hand up to massage the neat parts in her hair.

"That was my same thought," Pine laughed. "But the truth will never fail to mystify me. And," Pine said, lifting her gaze to the door as a thick wave of heat crashed over them and a woman entered the bar, "it seems like she's here to meet you."

"You set me up to meet someone without telling me?"

"I had faith you'd be able to handle yourself, raindrop," Pine giggled. "And I think this is someone you'll definitely want to meet to understand what I mean." When Brandi continued staring at her, Pine grinned and leaned closer to Brandi. "What is it, raindrop? You don't trust my judgement anymore?"

"You know I do," Brandi relented, turning her gaze to the woman who was making her way over to them.

"Then trust me," Pine said, her words low as she stared at Brandi. "I would never do anything I thought would hurt you."

Brandi held her gaze but said nothing else. Other than Jack and Noble, Pine was one of the few people she had absolute faith in. So, she watched as Pine greeted the woman with a warm smile and gestured to her.

"This is Brandi," she said. "Brandi, this is Zena, the woman I've been telling you about."

"I see my reputation precedes me," Zena said, a smile pulling at her lips as she nodded her head at Brandi. Her words were soft, but they cut through the muted hum of conversation in the bar like a hot knife through butter, and Brandi felt her attention drawn to the woman in a way she couldn't resist. She was taller than most women, standing closer to Jack's height of six-two than her own of five-nine, and she carried the heat of the afternoon on her skin — the warmth that clung to her skin raised the temperature around them and warmed Brandi's own skin as she stood in front of her. She was dressed in a yellow striped dress that flowed down to her manicured toes. She was well endowed and had thick locs that hung down to her waist with golden rings pushed through them.

Her face was half hidden behind the wide sunglasses she wore, but she had a simple kind of beauty that Brandi could appreciate.

"Not as much as you may think," Brandi said, shaking her head. "I know nothing more about you other than my friend seems to trust your word."

Pine's face lit up at Brandi's words and she giggled as she stood to her feet, downing the last of her water before offering both women a wide grin.

"Well, my job here is done," Pine said.

"And where are you going?" Brandi questioned.

"To disseminate information," Pine answered, smirking at Brandi. "Unless you've already told our precious little princess what she's up against?" Brandi shrugged her shoulders, and Pine laughed again. "I didn't think so. And I'm not needed for this conversation, so I'm heading out. But if you need me, raindrop," Pine started.

"I know how to find you."

Pine grinned and waved at the women before donning her own hat and shades before breezing out the door. When she was gone, Brandi turned back to Zena and the woman offered her another gentle smile as she pulled the shades away from her face. Brandi's eyes widened as she met her gaze. Just like the color of hair the gods gifted their children with, their eye color was just as predictable. Rothians had brown eyes, Lindlians, hazel — Carnaians, gray — and Asarians, brown. Sometimes the gods gifted their own eye color to their favored children, but it wasn't often. This woman's, though, were pale gold. Her irises nearly blended into the whites of her eyes, and they shimmered in the dull light of the bar.

"Allow me to introduce myself once more," she said. "My name is Zena, and I am a priestess."

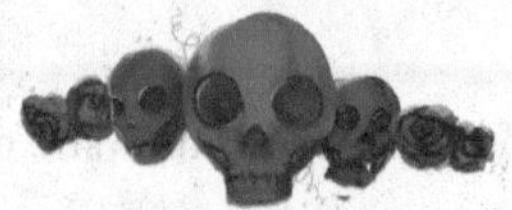

They didn't linger at the bar, leaving moments after Pine did, and Brandi allowed Zena inside the *Ciel Noir*, trying to determine where they would go next. Jack was with Najé back on the shore of fragment 10317 looking for a new base of operation for the rebels. They'd considered going back to the one Glenn had established in Lindl's domain, but it was too far away. If they were going to ruin the queen, they needed to be able to reach her without crossing the boundaries. And, aside from convenience, Brandi preferred to be in Rothe's domain. It was bigger than Lindl's domain, with all the same technology that helped make her life a lot easier.

It was an irrelevant thought that she pushed away as the *Ciel Noir* took to the sky though, its ascent slower than usual since she hadn't input a destination yet. Brandi looked over to Zena, who sat with her hands folded in her lap. She'd returned her sunglasses to her face and her gaze was directed out the window, and Brandi watched her with curious eyes for a moment before she spoke up.

"Do you want me to take you back to your temple?" Brandi asked, thinking about the giant one that sat in Rothe's capital, bordering Freya's domain. Pine claimed the woman was of another realm, so she doubted

Zena wanted to go there, but she couldn't guess where else the woman would want to go.

"Actually," she said, smiling and pointing away from the myriad of skyscrapers behind them, "that would be lovely. It's further out than this bar though."

Brandi followed her finger and her eyebrows raised.

"You do realize you're pointing to the Scorched Desert, right?"

"Yes," Zena said, a light chuckle following her answer.

"But aren't you a priestess?" Brandi questioned. "Why would you spend most of your time out there?"

"That is the question of the moment, isn't it?"

Brandi waited for her to say more, but when it was evident that she wouldn't, Brandi pursed her lips together and looked out toward The Scorched Desert. Even through the tinted glass of the transport pod, the sands were blinding. The only people who ever went out there were the miners who dug for raw eurithium beneath the burning sands. It was a thankless job that was, more often than not, left to outskirters who needed the pay. Brandi couldn't imagine anyone wanting to go there for their own enjoyment and cut a glance over to Zena. She sensed no malicious intent coming from her, but her request was still strange. At the very least though, it had piqued Brandi's interest, so she reached over to the controls.

"Can you give me the coordinates?"

Zena nodded, rattling off the numbers as Brandi input a new destination. Even with Zena's details, the destination was still vague, but it got them moving in the right direction. As they sailed over the bright sands, they sat in silence while the internal systems of the *Ciel Noir* blasted cool air to keep them from frying beneath Rothe's sun. It wasn't as uncomfortable as Brandi had expected it to be, but it was far from relaxing. The silence stretched between them until Zena spoke up, her words light as they watched the sands pass by around them.

"Have you known Pine for long?" Zena asked. "She seems an interesting woman."

"She is definitely that," Brandi agreed with a smirk. "And yeah, we've known each other a while," Brandi said, shrugging. "She's what other people would call a best friend, I guess."

"That's nice," Zena said, nodding and threading her fingers together in her lap. "Everyone needs a safe place to land."

Brandi looked over at her, but the conversation fizzled out and neither woman said another word until the transport pod came to a stop, hovering above a valley nestled within the sand dunes. Brandi looked down at it, and she didn't want to trust what her eyes saw below.

The valley was deeper than any she had ever seen and the flames that scorched the sands and gave the desert its name were a dull red rather than the blinding white she was used to. They melded together, pushing and pulling the sands with the current of the wind until it looked like an ocean of blood sloshing around in the bottom of a bowl. Brandi had never seen anything like it and she couldn't look away. She shook her head as she questioned Zena.

"What is this?"

"This," she said, "is where I spend most of my time," she explained with a smile. "Allow me to open the gate for you."

She eyes flashed brighter than the sun for a moment and the flames, as if they were dancers following a practiced routine, swirled around each other, pushing the sands to the edges of the valley until a circle that was white on the left, black on the right, and with golden script etched into the center, was revealed beneath them. Brandi recognized the words, and she sucked in a sharp breath at seeing it.

"You can read the language of the gods?"

"Only those who love the darkness may know its protection."

"I see you speak it as well," Zena said, giving an approving nod. "I expected no less from you."

"You say that as if we've met before."

"We haven't but," she paused to chuckle and shake her head, as the giant gate below them opened and they sank into its depths as if being swallowed by the sands, "you're no stranger to me."

Her words hung in the air as the gate closed above them. In the complete darkness of the tunnel they sank deeper into, her eyes shone with a soft white glow that was purer than that of the sun. It illuminated her, the pod, and the tunnel around them in a way that made Brandi's mind race as she tried to make sense of what she was seeing. Zena smiled as she pulled her shades away from her eyes and the *Ciel Noir* landed at the bottom of the tunnel.

"Welcome," Zena said, stepping out of the pod and gesturing around her, "to the temple where I serve."

Brandi followed Zena out of the pod onto a set of giant black tiles and her eyes widened as she looked around, pulling the shades away from her green eyes. Veins of white light snaked up the black columns that held up the ceiling like branches and lit the way down a long hallway. The tiles around them seemed to be a landing destination and gave way to soft grass. A breeze whistled past them, cooling the sweat that clung to Brandi's shoulders and pulling at the edges of her hat. She grabbed the rim and turned in a slow circle as she looked around.

The black columns were punctuated by soft white orbs at the top of them that threw a subtle light over the arched ceiling, illuminating what looked like stars embedded in them. The shimmering dots drifted across the ceiling as they often did across the night sky, and though Brandi was amazed at how beautiful it was, she didn't recognize any of the shifting patterns as ones she'd seen before.

They'd landed in the center of a lush garden, laden with bright green maple flowers, cerulean ocean blossoms, and bright pink wildflowers. She recognized them all as the native plants that grew in the other gods' domains, and she sucked in deep breaths of their intermingling scents. It made the air smell sweet and salty and reminded Brandi of the times she'd visited Freya's garden. She appreciated each lungful she got of the clear air as she followed behind Zena.

As they walked through the garden, Brandi marveled at the flowers and fruit growing everywhere. She recognized most of them, but there was a delicate flower with a dozen layers of black petals that she'd never seen before. It had white thorns trailing down its stem and a crisp scent that cut through all the others. Brandi wanted to know what it was called, but that minor curiosity paled in comparison to everything else. The garden was as rich as Freya's forests, with the openness of Carna's plains. The soft tittering of birds and insects surrounded them and carried off into the distance, and it made Brandi wonder just how far this underground temple stretched.

"How is this possible?" Brandi whispered.

"The same way the sun and moon are possible," Zena responded. "They merely are."

"But this…" Brandi shook her head, at a loss for words.

"It has always been here," Zena explained, turning to the left when they reached a fork in the path. "Before the lands above were divided by boundaries and culture."

"Before the beginning of time," Brandi said, the words pulling from her lips as her eyes narrowed on Zena's back. Her steps slowed to a stop as they walked into a much larger room, the garden giving way to smooth stones and a ceiling so high, it looked like it could be the sky. It spread out farther than what even Brandi could see, and the dots converged in places, creating constellations that she'd never seen before. They drifted and shifted, blooming and disappearing before reappearing again. It was beautiful and peaceful, and Brandi couldn't fight the smile that pulled at her lips as she looked up at it.

"What is this place?" Brandi asked. "Why have you brought me here?"

"I wanted you to see this," Zena said, waving her hand at the stars above them. "What you're seeing now is your birthright."

"What?" Brandi asked, her body tensing at the suggestion. "My birthright?" Brandi shook her head, her heart jumping into her throat as her blood warmed in her veins. "Who is it that you think I am?"

"Think?" Zena shook her head as she smiled and led Brandi deeper into the room, the temperature dropping and cooling Brandi's skin as the fire within her began to rage hotter. "I know that you are a goddess."

"That's blasphemy," Brandi said, trying to push away the truth in Zena's words as her eyes roved over the stars surrounding them. She'd thought it was the ceiling, but it was more like a dome. The further they walked in, the more the constellations wrapped around them, swallowing the edges of the room and the ground below them until only the path they walked kept them from sinking into the darkness below them.

"I'm a vessel for the goddess and nothing more."

"Brandi," Zena said, pausing in her movements and spinning to face Brandi on the narrow stone path. "Do you honestly believe a priestess wouldn't recognize the goddess she serves when she stands before her?"

Her question cut through Brandi's rebuttals, and she sighed.

"What do you want from me?"

"Want from you?" Zena asked, jerking back as if she'd been slapped. "Why would I want anything from you?"

"Everyone wants something."

"I'm sorry that has been your experience," Zena said, her face softening as she looked at Brandi. "A goddess is meant to be worshipped. Not treated as a genie." She smiled again and bowed her head in Brandi's direction. "I want nothing from you. Being in your presence is more than enough."

Brandi snorted at that, her laughter ringing out and getting lost in the galaxies above them until her throat tightened up and her eyes stung. She closed them against the expansion of a pair of stars above them and let her head fall back, her hat drifting over the edge and into the void below them. Tears threatened to spill from the corner of her eyes as she continued to laugh at herself. Part of her was amused that a kindness as simple as not asking anything of her would move her to tears. But a much larger part of her was grateful — relieved even — that she hadn't walked headfirst into another obligation for the gods.

"You are the first person to say that," Brandi explained once she was able to clear her voice. "It's why I wanted to reject the idea of being a god."

"We don't get to choose who we are born as," Zena said as a way of consolation as she lifted her head.

"You know even that much?"

"I know everything there is to know about you," Zena said, turning to continue down the path. "You were conceived in Freya's garden while the gods attended to their children in the mortal realm. Freya gave birth to you in secret, hiding your existence from the other gods until she revealed you to be her vessel."

Her words seemed heavier as the room swallowed her words, returning a dull echo to them. Brandi wanted a moment to process her words, but Zena's steps never faltered. So, Brandi focused on her back, staring at the thick locs that hung down to her waist and the long skirt that brushed against the floor. Her stride was long, her steps were measured, and she walked with her hands clasped in front of her. Brandi wanted to refute her words — to continue pretending that Zena was wrong and that her words weren't true — but before she could, Zena glanced over her shoulder at Brandi.

"And do not waste your breath denying my words," she warned, smiling as surprise danced across Brandi's face. "You have been thrust into a reality you did not want, so you want to believe the lies you've been told, even when you know they are not the truth," Zena said, her words gentle as she followed a slight bend in the widening path. "I know you wish it to be different, but rejecting the truth will not morph your lies into fact." When Brandi said nothing, Zena paused to look at Brandi, her pale gold eyes holding Brandi's green ones as if she could see her soul as clearly as she saw her face. "That said, would you like me to continue?"

Brandi nodded and Zena turned, leading them down the last bit of the path to a circular platform in the middle of the void. In the center sat a single throne, unlike any she had ever seen before. It was bright white, with a back that reached toward the stars. The corners were dipped in black, with shifting constellations drifting over them as if they were a part of the sky. Dark green detailing trailed along the edge of the arm rests and at the base of the throne where the same black and white flowers Brandi had noticed earlier in the garden. Zena stepped to the side as Brandi stepped onto the platform, her eyes locked on the empty seat as Zena completed her story.

"As I said, you were conceived in Freya's garden. Unlike the children of the gods born into the lower realm of mortals, you were the first to be born in the realm of the gods. And you were nothing like Freya's other children," she said. "You were her own reflection, but you carried the power of your father, and it superseded her own. Even as a child, your cries could stop the flow of time," she explained. "Freya was delighted. Her plan was finally beginning to come to fruition. But Freya's one true flaw has always been her arrogance."

"You would dare to speak against her?" Brandi asked, her eyes darting to Zena's face. "In Rothe's own domain?"

"What need do I have to fear him?" Zena questioned, turning to Brandi. "This is not his domain, and that is not his throne."

"Not his domain?" Brandi's words died on her lips as her eyes darted around the room and she shook her head. "What are you saying? We're below the Scorched Desert."

"I believe you know what I'm implying."

"I don't!" Brandi snapped, stepping back from Zena. "And even if I did, why should I believe anything you're saying?"

Brandi's mind was reeling at the casual way Zena spoke of the gods and the sight of the throne before her. Zena spoke of her birth as if they were her own memories when the woman couldn't have been more than forty-five. It made Brandi's blood burn, and she shook her head again, trying to keep the budding thoughts sown from Zena's words from taking root in her mind.

"Why shouldn't you?" Zena asked, tilting her head as she faced Brandi. "I have no reason to deceive you. I've brought you here so that I may be of help to you."

"Help?" Brandi scoffed. "And why would knowing how Freya planned to abuse me from the moment of my birth be of any help to me?"

"Do you not wish to hear the story of your origin?" Zena asked.

"Not really," Brandi admitted, anger building in her chest at the thought of learning anything else about Freya. She didn't want to know anything else about how the goddess planned to use her. She didn't want that picture of Freya being painted with such clarity in her mind.

"I know who Freya is," Brandi stated. "I know enough."

"Enough you say?"

Brandi nodded, looking away from Zena and the opulence of the throne to turn her eyes toward the stone below them. Unlike the smooth tile in the garden where they'd arrived, the stone beneath them wasn't uniform. Each one was slightly different, with different grooves and pits etched into their gray surface. It was all she could focus on as she tried to contain the fire growing in her chest and sort through her thoughts.

She didn't hate Freya. She could admit that.

She was angry with her. She'd spent her entire life in her presence, being loyal to her and serving her will. She'd believed that Freya cared about her, but since the battle at her temple, it had been nothing but one surprise after another, and she was tired of them. She didn't want anyone else to tell her about Freya or herself. It had been bad enough when Azinne had done it — but he was a being of time who possessed powers that surpassed even those of the gods. And his revelations had been to force the gods' hand. But she didn't think she could stomach hearing about herself from a mortal.

That would be an insult to her pride she didn't think she would survive.

She wanted the words to come from Freya herself. If she was so important to her — to this realm — then why did she need to keep so many secrets from her? Why did Freya lie to her about the most basic aspects of who she was? What was the point in curating some false identity — false parents — for her to believe in rather than just telling her the truth from the start? Did Freya think she wouldn't have been loyal to her if she knew the truth? Was she worth less to her as another god than as a vessel? The questions were infuriating and flooded her mind with a desire for answers. But who was she going to ask? Certainly not Freya herself. Because what answers could Freya offer that she would accept?

She snorted under her breath at the thought that Freya would even tell her the truth. It was as if she were nothing more than a pawn in a much bigger game, and now that she knew Freya was playing it, she wanted to flip the board.

She was livid with Freya.

And the anger swelled in her chest until she could no longer smother the fire burning in her lungs. She grit her teeth against the sharpness of it and tried to get a grip on her emotions. It wasn't like her to get worked up, and she was beginning to annoy herself at how often she found herself fighting back tears or a scream of rage. It's true that Freya had betrayed her in a way she would never recover from — stolen her childhood from her to fulfill her own selfish wishes — lied to her face every day of her life and hid her true identity — but Brandi knew better than to let it dominate her thoughts. She'd already shed her tears when she came back from meeting Azinne in the god realm, and there were greater problems to be solved than how to navigate her growing rage.

Facing how she felt wouldn't save the realm. But every time she tried to shut away her emotions, her power burned hotter than any blessing she'd ever received. Her breath came out in tiny sparks as she worked to keep her power under control. But the harder she fought against it, the more it surged — burning her veins and scorching the underside of her skin. Bruises dotted along her arms, and she hissed as she sank to the floor, pressing her hands to the cool stones in an effort to get some relief. She wished Jack were there, and she tried to resist glaring at Zena when their gazes met.

"This is why I share all of this with you," Zena said, her soft voice cutting through Brandi's thoughts. "And why I brought you here. You carry a power you cannot control."

"And who says," Brandi grunted, her muscles straining from the effort of speaking, "that I can't control it?"

Zena sighed as she moved to stand in front of Brandi.

"Who do you think you're fooling?" Zena asked. "I can see your struggle. I can sense your battle with the power overflowing inside of you."

"I'm not," Brandi whispered, "trying to fool anyone."

"You are," Zena said, crouching down. "Yourself most of all. But you won't be able to keep this up. Not for long."

"And what do you know?"

"I am a high priestess," she answered. "I know everything there is to know about the gods. And I was sent here to help you. The question is," she said, reaching a hand down to Brandi, "whether or not you are willing to accept it."

Brandi's green eyes darted to her slim hand. Her nails were painted white, same as her toes, and Brandi considered rejecting her offer. She didn't want to need anyone's help in the first place. But if she'd learned anything since leaving the shadows, it was that she rarely got what she wanted. So, she reached out and let Zena help her up.

"Who sent you?"

"I'm sorry, but that's something I can't share with you yet."

"Fine," Brandi huffed, not having the energy to argue. She let Zena carry most of her weight as she guided her to the center of the platform, toward the throne. "At least tell me," Brandi said, pausing to face Zena, "whose throne you're having me sit on."

Zena laughed as she gave Brandi a light push, forcing her onto the throne.

"It's yours."

CHAPTER TWELVE

One who is heavy in her heart will never be light on her feet.

— Adage of the Gods | Lindl's Five Holy Academies Compilation

---

ROTHE'S DOMAIN — THE QUEEN'S TOWER
3 DAYS BEFORE THE OPENING CEREMONY

"I refuse to believe that the gods made you this incompetent."

The words were spoken on a sigh as Sal pinched the bridge of his nose and turned his pale face up to the elegant ceiling. His brown curls bounced around his shoulders, and in the breaking light of the dawn that filtered through the golden curtains of the ballroom, Sarah's eyes widened.

His clothes were simple — black slacks with a golden button down tucked into them. The top three buttons were left open to reveal his throat and the simple gold chain that sat at the base of it. His sleeves were rolled up to his elbows, revealing the veins in his forearms, and Sarah was shocked to realize that, in his own way, Sal was gorgeous. Not in the way that Noble and Jack were, with overwhelming muscle and effortless charm, but in the way that boys were when they were pretty. He reminded her more of Kyle, and she was surprised at herself that he even crossed her mind.

She tried to keep her thoughts from returning to him when she could help it and, other than the moments where she allowed herself to wonder if he was still keeping his promise to take care of Jamie, she'd forbidden herself to spend too much time thinking about either of them. If she did, it would lead to an ache in her chest that even Asari's power wouldn't be able to heal and it would land her in a pit of her darkest thoughts — her mind filled with her every failure, both as a pretend lover and an older sister. She shook her head, trying to rid herself of the creeping thoughts and focused instead on Noble across the room.

He'd arrived with Sal that morning, wearing the classic nondescript clothes of the shadows. His black shirt was skintight and clung to every muscle he had before tapering into cargo pants that were cinched at his waist with a leather belt. His boots were spotless, and his silver hair had grown out. He'd shaved the back and sides, leaving the rest to be tied up in a tiny bun at the top of his head. Sarah couldn't keep her eyes away from him and silently cursed herself for having tripped over herself, forcing a break into their practice.

Noble had been her dance partner so that Sal could observe her movements. She'd been surprised to see him there since, for the past two weeks, it had just been her and Sal in the small ballroom. It had become a routine she'd grown to expect. Mara would wake her before dawn to help her get dressed and do her makeup — since, as a princess, it was unheard of for her to be seen in public without her face done — and then she would eat a solitary breakfast in her room before Sal came to escort her down to the practice ballroom on the ground floor. And for the next few hours, he would be merciless in her dance instruction.

It was torture on her feet since she was required to wear a dress and heels to practice, but today she hadn't minded. Instead of Sal's cool touch on her waist, it was Noble's warm hand. And though she'd accepted the fact that he held no real interest in her after seeing him with other people in Freya's domain, she was grateful to at least look the part of a royal princess in a strappy golden dress and heels. She did her best to follow his lead, but it was near impossible since Sal kept demanding she stop looking at her feet and look at her dance partner. But every time she tried to lift her head and maintain eye contact with Noble, his dark eyes bore into hers and she lost her thoughts. And, seconds later, she would be stumbling over her own dress and feet, clinging to Noble as he caught her before she went crashing into the cold tiles below them.

He'd chuckled the first few times it happened, righting her with little effort. But as their practice continued, his patience had evaporated with the morning dew on the grass in the courtyard. When Sal had called for a break, Noble hadn't hesitated in dropping his hands from her waist and she pretended to not feel the chill that raced over her as he stepped away from her. Instead, she pulled a long strand of her hair between her fingers and moved to stand against the wall. She knew better than to try and take a seat to rub at her feet — that would only lead to a lecture from Sal, reminding her that she was a princess and that it was improper for her to be seen in discomfort outside of her own room. So, instead, she shifted her weight from foot to foot as she stood at the wall and waited for whatever would happen next.

Sal seemed to be on the verge of losing his patience and giving up on her completely. And she wouldn't blame him if he did. After two weeks of constant practice, she'd hoped that she would be further along. But despite knowing the steps for the opening dance required at the bid ceremony, she couldn't manage to get her feet to follow the instructions of her mind. She'd always been on the clumsy side, but now she understood just how much of a hinderance that truly was.

"Alright," Sal finally sighed, righting himself as he reset the music on the old record player situated on the stage. The music wasn't loud, but it echoed around the room, surrounding them in its soft sound. "Let's do it again. And Sarah," he sighed, the vein in his neck jumping as he worked to keep his tone even and his irritation in check, "please try to at least pretend like you want to get better at this."

Sarah straightened up but said nothing back to him. It didn't matter to him, or anyone else, that she was giving her absolute best. All that mattered were results. Because if she couldn't pull this off, then her bid for the throne would be forcibly rescinded by the council. She'd have to give up her claim to the throne, and she'd be publicly executed as a failure to the crown. If that happened, she'd be returned to the gods — which was a less than ideal outcome — and the rebels would have a much harder time overturning the monarchy. She doubted the others held any expectation that she could win the bid, but she needed to make it past the opening ceremony at least. If she didn't, that would mean all of their efforts amounted to nothing and there was no value in the council acknowledging her as a genuine princess of the realm with a legitimate claim to the throne.

Sal had handled all of the paperwork to enter her into the bid. Apparently, Brandi had contacted him the moment she came up with her plan, and since each princess was allowed two advisors, he registered himself and Mara as hers. Noble was registered as her bodyguard, and when she'd questioned them on why she needed a bodyguard inside the tower, Sal had looked at her like she'd suggested they set sail to the other side of the Blind Sea. Silence had swallowed them until Mara pointed out that the tower was the headquarters for shadows, and that while most of them had defected to side with the rebels, there were some who remained loyal to the queen. With that explanation, Sarah had blushed a deep shade of red and felt foolish for even asking something so obvious.

Just the memory of the conversation was enough to give her secondhand embarrassment and color her cheeks, so she tried not to think of it as Noble rested his hand on her waist and took her hand. She tried to clear her mind as the music wafted over them and when she met his gaze, instead of trying to avoid getting lost in them, she abandoned all hope of keeping her mind on the steps. Instead, she discarded all of her modesty and let her blue eyes roam over Noble's face with unbridled desire. And as she lost herself in thoughts of what she wished she could do with him, her feet followed his.

And for one glorious minute, she was the perfect dancer. Light on her feet, strong torso, eyes on her partner — she was graceful.

But it lasted for only a moment because Noble's watch buzzed on his wrist that had slid to her back. She realized just how close they were dancing, her face flushed as it always did, and she tripped. A yelp escaped her as her left foot caught on her right one and she tilted backwards. Noble caught her with a chuckle and looked up at Sal.

"I think Blondie needs a break," he said, setting Sarah back on her feet and holding onto her until she found her balance. "And I have to take this," he said, pointing to his watch that was still buzzing on his wrist.

"Fine," Sal sighed. "I appreciate your help."

Noble waved Sal's words off as he walked out onto the veranda. It faced a sprawling inner courtyard and Sarah's eyes traced over his back with a hunger that flared to life in the pit of her belly.

"If you would stare at him half as much when you're dancing, we wouldn't be in this predicament."

Sal's words cut through Sarah's thoughts and her eyes grew wide before she averted her gaze to his chin. She'd learned from Mara that one of the best ways to look at someone while not meeting their eyes was to pick a point on their face to stare at instead. Sal was just a bit taller than her, and as they took their starting positions, she stared at his chin.

"Do you expect me to apologize?"

"I expect you to do better," he stated, leading them in the first steps of the dance. "This is nothing more than a simple three-step," he pointed out. "And your only job is to follow your leader. You seem to have all your mental facilities intact, so I don't understand why you struggle with moving in a circle."

"It's more difficult than it looks," she whispered. "I haven't been trained for this."

"That's obvious, dear cousin."

"Do you think I enjoy being like this?" Sarah snapped, her eyes meeting his brown ones for the first time since they'd begun the dance. "It wasn't by my own choice that I wasn't raised to know these things. To be graceful and well-spoken. Your mother," she emphasized, "stole that away from me."

"Yes," Sal agreed. "But do you also blame her for your own lack of ambition?"

"What?"

Sarah tried to jerk away from him, but he kept her waist and hand in an iron grip as he met her gaze.

"Dance," he commanded, letting his blessing of compulsion sink into his words as he forced her to continue through the steps. She gasped at the demand, but moved her feet as was expected of her as she glared up at him. She hadn't expected him to have the strength to keep her from pushing him away, but she could admit that it was her own fault for underestimating him. Sal was softer than Noble and Jack — softer than Garrett and Charlie and the other men she'd healed at the clearing in Freya's domain. He didn't have sharp lines like the rest of them, no definition to his muscles like the others. But he was still a shadow, and the grip he held her in reminded her of that.

"You lack ambition," he hissed, his face still neutral as he looked over her head. "You want to blame everyone but yourself for your own misfortunes and it's exhausting, really." He pulled her along as they whisked through the turn she'd always lost her footing on and she couldn't spare a moment to be excited about not falling on her face because Sal locked his gaze onto hers. "You knew exactly who you were and the circumstances in which you lived. My mother may not be a saint, but at any moment, you could have chosen to prepare yourself for the role you've been forced to step into now. But you didn't."

Their movements came to a halt as the music ended and her heart was pounding in her chest. She couldn't tell if it was from physical exertion or the anger mingled with embarrassment roiling in the pit of her stomach and heating her cheeks. His words were no different from the ones Brandi had thrown at her when Najé had tracked them down in Lindl's domain. Her skin burned under his touch, and she wanted to push him away, but though the music had stopped, Sal had yet to free her from his grasp.

"You wish to whine about it, but no one will pity you here, cousin," he said, lowering his voice and dropping his lips to her ear. "So, correct your own shortcomings and carry yourself as a woman worthy of stealing back the crown."

Sarah sat on the edge of the stage, where the record player still sat, and rubbed at her feet.

Sal's words had been the end of their lesson and she'd nearly collapsed into a heap on the tile floor at his words. Her knees were still weak, and she sported pink rings around both her ankles from where the straps of her heels had dug into them. She'd pulled them off the moment that Sal left the room, and they were swollen now. She'd have to pray to Asari before she would be able to squeeze her feet back into them when it was time to leave, but at the moment, she didn't care.

She had been forcibly reminded for the second time that no one was impressed with her struggle. No one would be able to find it within themselves to offer her any sympathy and something about knowing that made her feel more alone than she had in weeks. A knot grew in her stomach at the realization that she would soon be facing the entire realm and the queen herself, and she dropped her head into her hands, letting her hair fall like a curtain around her.

She'd been so caught up in her thoughts, she hadn't heard the footsteps approaching.

"I take it dance practice is over?"

Sarah looked up at the words and her spirits soared at the sight of Noble and a smile almost split her face, but it died at the corners of her mouth as a Lindlian woman stepped out from behind him.

She was stunning.

She had wavy hair so dark that it almost seemed blue in the light of the morning sun, and she was petite. Shorter than Sarah, with curves she could only dream of having, her honeyed brown skin was darker than Noble's and her hazel eyes were as sharp as Brandi's. It made her sit up straight as recognition dawned on her.

"Hello," Sarah offered, using the neutral voice she'd spent weeks practicing with Mara. She'd been told several times that one of her greatest weaknesses is that she wore her heart on her sleeve, so Mara had been coaching her on subtle ways to keep her emotions from displaying themselves across her face and in her voice. The first thing they'd practiced was her neutral voice — the one that was polite and welcoming, without making her appear needy or stand-offish. Every time she used it, she felt as if she were back in Asari's domain, trying to soothe a wounded child who was being overly dramatic about how much pain they were in. She offered a tight smile in their direction.

"And yes," she said, directing her attention back to Noble and answering his question. "It ended a few moments ago."

"Yeah?" Noble's eyebrows sprung up at the shift in her tone, but he said nothing about it. "Well, that works out."

"Does it?"

"I came here to speak with you, princess," Pine interjected, taking a few steps forward as she focused her big, hazel eyes on Sarah. "Brandi wanted me to share a few things with you to make sure you're not out here bumbling up her plan."

"I'm not."

"Are you sure?" Pine asked, taking another step forward to look up at Sarah and hold her gaze. Both of their eyes darted to Sarah's swollen feet and the regret she felt at not heeding Sal's words was instant. She thought of reaching for her sandals, but she felt that trying to correct the situation now would only make it worse. So, instead she offered Pine another smile.

"I'm sure."

Pine said nothing in response to her false reassurances and continued to stare up at Sarah. It made her uncomfortable, and it reminded her of their first meeting back in Asari's domain. She'd been relentless in her staring, and it hadn't been until Brandi had called her attention back to her that she had finally looked away and given Sarah a chance to breathe. The same happened again now. Her sharp hazel gaze was unwavering until Noble stepped up beside them.

"What did Green really send you here for?"

Pine looked away from Sarah at that question and turned her attention to Noble. She only came up to center of his chest, but she glanced over at him as if she were seven feet tall. They watched each other for a moment, before Pine tilted her head to the side.

"What do you know about my raindrop?"

"Your raindrop?" Noble questioned, narrowing his eyes. "Green is mine."

"Oh?" Pine asked, a grin splitting her beautiful face as she laughed. "And what of Jack?"

Noble shrugged. "Jack is hers. She's mine. Those two things are mutually exclusive."

"Are they now?"

"Always have been," he stated. "And who are you?"

"Brandi is my only keeper," she said, laughter tilting her words towards the high ceilings. "I owe you no explanation other than that."

"Okay," he conceded, "but I'd still like to hear more about you later," he suggested. "I know everyone close to Green."

They studied each other for a moment, and Sarah couldn't keep her eyes from dancing between the two of them. Both of them had strong ties to Brandi — she'd seen it for herself. So, it made her curious how they would tolerate each other when it was clear that both of them desired to be her favorite. But when Pine relented, Noble pulled his hand out of his pocket and extended it towards her.

"I'm Noble."

"Pine," she responded, glancing at his hand before shaking it once. "But I'm telling the truth," Pine said, shrugging. "I came here to relay some information to the princess. Nothing more."

"Information she couldn't relay over the network?"

"I couldn't tell you," Pine said, a sly grin pulling at her lips. "You'll have to ask her if you want more details than that."

"I will," Noble said, moving to lean against the stage next to Sarah. "Because I know you're not here to just check on Blondie. Sal and I have been keeping Brandi updated with her progress, and," he said, leaning forward, "she wouldn't send you here just to confirm what she already knows."

"You've been sending reports on me?" Sarah asked, surprise pitching her voice a few octaves higher. "When?"

Noble glanced up at her, but he didn't bother responding to her question before returning his gaze back to Pine. Sarah's body began to heat up at being ignored and she worked to swallow down her rising emotions. This wasn't the time or place to have an outburst, and if Mara was adamant about teaching her anything, it was that there was a time and place for everything. So, Sarah choked down her indignance and turned her blue eyes onto Pine as well.

If she wanted answers, she'd have to get them the same way Noble was — from the source.

"You said you had reason to speak with me?" Sarah asked, redirecting the conversation to reason for Pine's arrival.

"It's about your competition for the throne," Pine explained. "But this isn't the place to have that conversation."

"Right," Sarah said nodding, her face flushing with nerves at the thought of what Pine could need to tell her that required a conversation more private than the one they were having now.

"Breathe, Blondie," Noble advised, glancing up at her at the sound of panic in her voice. "It's one conversation. You'll be fine, just like with this dance."

"Right," Sarah repeated, more to herself than anyone else in the room. "It's just one dance," she said, working to keep her heart from racing at the memory of dancing with Noble before she tripped over herself and ruined the end of it. "It can't be that important in the scheme of things."

Both Noble and Pine looked at her with raised eyebrows. They stared at her with open surprise before sharing a look with each other. Pine held Noble's dark gaze before she began to giggle. Within seconds, she'd dissolved into a full-blown fit of laughter, and Sarah's face grew pink as the lighthearted sound echoed around the room at her expense. She looked at Pine with narrowed eyes before turning her gaze to Noble, who looked at her with a blank expression.

"Sal didn't tell you anything about the bid, did he, Blondie?"

"He covered the most basic of the basics," Sarah answered. "He filled out the paperwork for the official bid and told me that I needed to perfect the dance for the opening ceremony."

"That's it?" When Sarah nodded, Noble sighed and massaged his forehead. "Gods, Blondie. You have to learn to start asking questions. People aren't going to just walk around spouting relevant information at you."

"What are you talking about?"

"You've been in the tower for weeks now and at no point did you think to find out how the bid actually works?" Noble asked, frowning.

The disappointment in his voice colored over every other emotion Sarah could place. Pine was still trying to collect herself and Sarah dropped her gaze to the stage below her and she tried to think of a single reason she could use to defend herself.

In truth, she'd wanted to do more research on the bid. It had been on the top of her priority list before Sal had commandeered her life. But, since she'd arrived at the tower, it had been nothing but dance lessons and history lessons, makeup, etiquette, self-defense training — studying politics and theology, perfecting her posture and how she spoke. The only time she got to herself was when she was allowed to sleep, and she'd been exhausted every night after enduring both Sal and Mara's rigorous training. It hadn't been easy, but she knew that neither of them would acknowledge that as an acceptable reason for her to not have done her due diligence. If nothing else, her conversation with Sal had made it clear that she was responsible for her own self and actions — or lack thereof.

"I didn't," she said, looking across the room at the wooden double doors that sealed off the room. "I trusted my advisors to advise me on what I needed to know."

"You've got to adjust your mindset, Blondie," Noble advised, "You can't expect people to just tell you what you need to know. You have to think for yourself. Challenge people."

"Will you explain it to me then?" Sarah directed her question towards Noble. "I can see that my lack of understanding has led to problems for everyone else and," her words caught in her throat as her emotions fought to be released from their cage in the pit of her stomach, but she swallowed against them, forcing them back down as she cleared her throat, "I don't wish to be any more of a burden than I already am."

Noble studied her for a second before he shook his head.

"Why not?" Sarah asked, her face falling at his rejection, despite her best efforts.

"I'm not a teacher," he stated. "I don't have the patience for it. Ask Mara or Sal. Or even Cedric. I'm sure one of them would be happy to do it," he said.

"Happy to do what?"

The voice cut through the room as Mara walked onto the stage behind them. Sarah's eyes widened as she noticed the slim door hidden behind the heavy curtains hanging on the wall. Mara stopped at the center of the stage and let her gaze dart to each of them before settling on Noble, who took a few steps back away from the stage.

Sarah didn't miss the way he kept his back from facing her or the way he shifted himself back, putting himself between Mara and Pine. It looked like he was trying to protect her, but Sarah dismissed that thought as soon as it came. The only person Noble cared about other than himself was Brandi. But it wasn't lost on her that all of the shadows treated Mara with a delicate touch. It was almost as if they were afraid of her, though Sarah hadn't been able to figure out what it was about her that made them keep their distance. Instead, she offered a weak smile up to Mara and answered her question that was still hanging in the air.

"Explain the bid to me," Sarah clarified. "There's still a lot I don't know about it."

Mara snorted at that. "Of course there is," she said. "You haven't asked us anything or visited the library on your own even once."

Her words were sharp, but Sarah found that they didn't cut as deep as when Noble had pointed out the same thing to her. Maybe it was because Mara's voice didn't carry any disappointment in it. It was probably because she held such low expectations for her that when Sarah didn't meet them, Mara wasn't surprised. That carried its own unique sting to her pride, but it was more bearable than it was coming from Noble.

"I'm asking now."

"Finally," Mara said, holding her hand out to Sarah to help her up. "We'll discuss it after your self-defense training."

Sarah accepted the hand and in the corner of her eye she could see Noble watching them. She tried not to pay attention to the way he'd shifted closer to Pine or the way her dainty hands rested on his arm as she leaned around him to watch them. Instead, she scooped up her shoes and gave up any hope of keeping up appearances. She let them dangle from her left hand as she followed behind Mara to the hidden door.

"I'll come find you later, princess," Pine called out. "We still need to have our conversation."

CHAPTER THIRTEEN

What worth is there in a queen who does not wish to rule?

— Fina the First | Queen of Queens, Volume 3

ROTHE'S DOMAIN — THE QUEEN'S TOWER
3 DAYS BEFORE THE OPENING CEREMONY

Sarah sat with her back pressed into the wall behind her and her eyes trained on the stacks of books looming above her. Mara had dragged her to the library on the twenty-second floor of the tower and Sarah couldn't get over how vast it was or how much information was housed in it. Bookshelves covered every wall of the space, with murals stretching across the ceiling depicting Freya, Rothe, the gods, and the entire creation of the realm. There were dozens of rows of bookcases, weighed down with tomes of biographies, first-hand written accounts, textbooks, and historical diaries. It was silent save for the subtle turning of pages and the gentle hum of cool air being forced in through the vents, and everything smelled like aged ink. It was a distinct smell that Sarah couldn't say she loved, but she didn't hate it either.

Cedric hadn't hesitated to make the space his home and was seated in a corner on the floor beneath the windows. Two stacks of books sat on either side of him, both were taller than him. Two books were open in front of him — one was a giant tome that looked almost too big to fit on the shelves, and the other was a much smaller notebook with weathered pages. He had a screen hovering to his left that he appeared to be taking notes on, and he barely glanced in their direction as she and Mara entered. She'd hoped to catch a moment to speak with him, but she decided it would be better not to interrupt him when he looked so focused. Instead, she'd followed Mara to the other side of the library, where Mara now sat to her left.

Her legs were crossed as she flipped through the pages of *Fina the First: Queen of Queens, Volume 3*. The collection itself was one of the most extensive accounts of the reign of the first queen, and Sarah had been overwhelmed with the amount of knowledge contained within the pages as she listened to Mara explain the bid to her.

She hadn't expected to receive a full history lesson on why it existed in the first place, but she was glad she had. The first queen of the realm, Fina, was reported to be blessed by the goddess Freya. Her consorts, Roan, Lyle, Cain, and Aric carried blessings from their gods as well, and together they established the foundations of the queendom. The queen would be their guiding hand, and the consorts would have her ear, speaking on behalf of the people. Her reign had been flawless, according to the texts. She'd ruled over the realm with a warm love, gentle power, and ruthless judgment that left the people both in reverence and awe of her. But, even with the power of the goddess, she wasn't immortal. And when she grew old, a revolt broke out among the people as to who would have the audacity to replace her.

And that is when the bid for the throne was created.

Because Freya was the goddess of death and Fina had been merciless when handing out her judgements over the people, it was decided that one of her three daughters would take over the throne. They would stake their lives on their right to rule, and they would go on a crusade across the realm, speaking to the people, gathering support, and finding consorts of their own. And when the time came, the council — comprised of their two brothers who had no right to bid for a queen's throne — would decide who was best fit to wear the crown. And any who were deemed unfit were returned to the goddess, and the entire realm was expected to bear witness to it. This was set to prevent future uprisings within the queendom. There would only ever be one woman fit to rule the realm, and there would be no room for factions to form around a rejected bid.

However, Fina made sure to declare the bid wasn't mandatory.

"Anyone who sees themselves as unfit to guide this queendom with wisdom should not be forced to stake their life on the opportunity to do so," Mara read the words aloud, verbatim, before snapping the book closed. The sound startled Sarah a bit, but she didn't say anything as she marinated on the words.

"So, that's why Leia hunted my mother down," Sarah whispered, the story finally making sense in her mind. "She'd wanted to prevent the outcome that's happening right now."

"A rebellion to support a forgotten princess," Mara said with a nod. "There's that, but it's much simpler than that as well," she said. "Your mother was a criminal. Your mother entered the bid and lost. Her duty was to forfeit her life for the future peace of the queendom," Mara explained. "The moment she chose to run, she disobeyed not only the queen, but she also rejected the traditions that have been the foundation of the monarchy since its inception, as well as the absolute rule of Freya herself. Your mother was seen as a blasphemer of the worst degree."

Sarah thought back to the words she'd heard her mother whisper the night Asari had first appeared in her room, and she couldn't find the words to defend her mother. The truth spoke louder than any of her faded memories could, and she struggled to reconcile who she'd thought her mother was, with who she was now learning her mother to have been.

"I see that now," Sarah sighed. "So, what about this dance? Why is it so important?" She asked. "I don't understand what it's meant to accomplish."

"You need to work on your critical thinking skills," Mara said, rolling her eyes. "The bid isn't mandatory, Sarah. What do you think it's for?"

Sarah's ears perked up at the sound of her own name, and a little spark of joy lit up within her. Aside from Russ, Mara was the only one who ever called her by her given name. It was something she hadn't appreciated until recently and she kept the smile she felt pulling at her lips from reaching her face as she considered Mara's question.

"To declare intention?"

"Exactly," Mara said, a grin splitting her freckled face. "It's the moment where every eligible princess makes her bid for the throne known. It requires you to stand before the queen, her consorts, and every influential person in the realm and say, 'I am a princess of this realm, and

I will seize the throne!'" Mara explained, mirth slipping into her words. "It's a declaration of war and the dance is the first battlefield."

"Battlefield?" Sarah echoed. "I'm honestly having a hard time understanding how it's more than just a dance."

Mara's face fell, and she sighed as she adjusted her glasses. "I was really starting to have hope for you, but you're really about as dumb as you look, huh?"

Sarah was taken aback by the words and said nothing in return as she dropped her gaze from Mara. There were moments when Mara was kind to her — when she would talk to her while she did her makeup, share a meal with her so she didn't have to eat alone, and answer her questions with a patience that seemed to elude everyone else. But then, there were moments where Mara was just as sharp as the other shadows. Her words would cut deep, and Sarah would be reminded of how different they were. No matter how often she forgot it, the truth remained that they were not the same. Where Sarah was a little more than curious about new things, Mara loved books and knowledge — she was a graduate of several of Lindl's Academies and trained in the art of sending people to the gods. Sarah didn't know exactly what it was about Mara that put the others on edge, but she wasn't oblivious enough to miss how the others acted around her. It made her curious about who Mara truly was, but she wasn't bold enough to ask questions like that.

Instead, she focused on not making an enemy out of her and shrugged as she looked away from her.

"I'm not sure what you expect me to say to that," Sarah admitted.

Mara snorted. "I'd hoped you'd at least defend your own intellect, but

I guess that's just another expectation you don't live up to."

Silence hung around them as Sarah tried to blink back the tears waiting to spill from her eyes. There was no point in crying — it wouldn't solve anything — but she still hadn't adjusted to the daggers so many people seemed eager to throw at her. She felt Mara's hazel gaze on her, but she didn't turn to face her. Instead, she tried to steel herself against the barbed wire wrapped around her words.

"Gods, Sarah," Mara sighed. "You are never going to make it in the bid if you shut down every time someone insults you. I thought Sal reported that you could handle basic exchanges like this?"

"I don't know why he would tell you that," Sarah shrugged, a sniffle sneaking its way into her voice.

"Oh," Mara said, her voice falling flat. "You're one of those girls."

"What?"

"You cry a lot, don't you?" Mara asked, the light in her eyes dissipating the longer she looked at Sarah. "You think tears will garner sympathy. Sympathy, pity. Pity, kindness. Kindness, malleability," she said, a frown pulling at her lips as she spoke the words. "You're a manipulator."

"I'm not!"

"See," Mara said, pointing at her, "that reaction tells me everything I need to know about you."

"What?"

"Anyone who actually wasn't a manipulator," she pointed out, "would have been confused. But you understood exactly what I said," she shrugged, "because it's how you get to people. It's how you get what you want, whether you can put it into words or not."

"I don't…"

"Save your excuses, princess," Mara said, holding up her hand and stopping Sarah's words. It didn't slip past her that Mara had used her title rather than her name, and her shoulders sagged as Mara returned her attention to the book in her lap. "I'm not interested in your sob story. I don't care about your tears, and I'm not swayed by your petty emotions. Keep them."

"Why is it such a terrible thing to cry when people hurt me?" Sarah asked, her voice small as she turned her gaze away from Mara.

"There's a time and place for tears," Mara scoffed. "And in proper society, it's in private."

Sarah had no rebuttal for that, and after a moment of sitting in a painful silence, Sarah swallowed her emotions and squared her shoulders, shifting her body to face Mara.

"I'm not stupid," she stated.

"Truly?"

"Don't mock me," Sarah said, ice creeping into her words. "I may be a product of my environment, but that doesn't mean I'm incapable of learning," she stated. "If you're meant to be my advisor, then whatever information I lack is your own shortcoming, is it not?"

Mara looked up at those words, an eyebrow quirked in Sarah's direction. Her heart raced in her chest, but she kept her gaze level as she met Mara's gaze. There was only one way to get better at defending herself, and right now seemed the best time to start. Her hands were shaking in her lap, but she laced them together and let out a slow breath as she waited for Mara to respond.

"I take no responsibility for a fool too simpleminded to realize they are one," Mara retorted.

"And I pray for the soul too wise to chase after greatness. It must be exhausting watching others surpass you, but mediocrity holds no place for fools." Sarah shot back, holding Mara's gaze. "So, forgive me if my back is an unpleasant sight for you."

Mara stared at Sarah for a moment before she threw her head back in laughter. It was loud and the sound bounced around the high ceilings before echoing back to them. It took Sarah by surprise, and she watched Mara with wide eyes as the woman clutched at her sides and rested her forehead against her knees.

"Better," she finally said, catching her breath. "Much better."

"Thank you."

"Keep that energy at the opening ball," Mara said, straightening herself again. "The ball is more than a dance. It's a showcase. Everyone is searching for the perfect princess to inherit the throne and they want someone who will play the part. Be the perfect queen. And one lacking in proper etiquette," she said, her eyes cutting to Sarah as her eyebrows lifted, "won't have a chance of winning, even with all of Rothe's grace and Freya's mercy." Mara shrugged as she looked at Sarah. "The bid is ruthless, and the dance is the literal first step. If you fail? If you make a bad impression? It will never be undone. You'll be known as the faltering princess or the clumsy princess and no one will take you seriously."

"You say that like it's fact."

"It's happened before," Mara pointed out. "And every single time, the bidder was returned to Freya. It became so commonplace that it's basically an unspoken rule of the bid at this point."

"Gods," Sarah breathed, the color draining from her face as the reality of Mara's words set in.

"Exactly," Mara snickered. "But if you can make it past the dance, then all you'll need is the skill to snatch up four consorts from different domains and the approval of a council composed of family members who sentenced you and your mother to a public execution. Simple."

"I think," Sarah said, standing to her feet, "I'd like to go practice some more. One obstacle at a time."

"That," Mara said, pointing the book in her hands at Sarah as a grin stretched across her face, "is the first intelligent thing you've said since you got here."

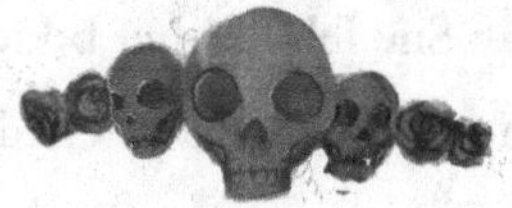

Sarah walked with purpose back to the ballroom. She didn't know where Sal was or how to find him, so she'd resigned herself to practicing the steps alone. The repetitive steps were already replaying through her thoughts when she reached the small door on the stage that Mara had led her through a few hours ago. She'd expected the room to be empty when she returned, but she lingered behind the heavy curtains as she heard Noble's laugh drifting over to her.

It was light and reverberated against the dance floor, adding a warmth to the room that was almost tangible as she peeked around the corner. He was leaning against the stage and Pine had her arms wrapped around his waist while his rested on her slim shoulders, his wrists crossed behind her head in what looked to be an intimate moment between them as they spoke. Sarah couldn't hear what they were saying, but even from where she stood, she could hear the grin in his voice. Her blue eyes didn't miss the way his head was tilted to hold Pine's gaze, or the way Pine giggled when she spoke to him.

If she hadn't seen them introduce themselves to each other earlier, she would have never believed they'd been strangers just a few hours ago. Watching them made her stomach sink while an anger she'd never felt before rose up in her, closing up her throat and forcing her to take short, sharp breaths in through her nose as her fingers tightened around the deep red curtains she hid behind. She wanted nothing more than to make herself known — to force them apart and insert herself between them, but she couldn't look away. She felt like her body wasn't under her control and her eyes stung with hot tears as she watched him dip his head to her lips.

It was a lazy kiss — as slow as the sun shifting across the ballroom — and Sarah hated herself for spying on them. But she also couldn't beat back the suffocating feeling that she would happily murder Pine to be in her place. She clutched the curtain tighter and bit her bottom lip as Pine lifted up onto the tips of her toes, Noble's hands shifting to pull her closer to him and lift her to his height. A soft moan escaped from one of them, and it was then that Sarah finally closed her eyes and spun away from them, any hopes of continuing her dance practice lost to the whims of her unstable emotions.

She'd hoped to sneak back out the way she'd come, unnoticed. But when she turned to slip out the door, her eyes grew wide to meet a pair of hazel ones staring back at her. Sarah tried to step back from her — the sudden movement already taxing her tenuous balance and threatening to send her sprawling into the curtains. Her face was already growing red at the thought of her pulling down the curtains as she fell, interrupting Pine and Noble while embarrassing herself in the worst way. Her stomach clenched at the thought, but faster than she could comprehend, the woman in front of her grabbed her wrist and slapped her free hand over Sarah's mouth. She shook her head, indicating for Sarah to keep quiet and it wasn't until Sarah nodded that she smiled and removed her hand from her mouth, pulling her back through the door.

Sarah's heart was racing in her chest as she followed behind the woman, but it wasn't until they stopped by one of the benches in the courtyard that Sarah dared to suck in a deep breath and pull herself away from the stranger. She pressed a hand to her chest as she looked over to the woman who sunk onto the bench, laughter spilling out of her, uninhibited.

"I totally thought we were going to get caught," she laughed, throwing her head back as she spread her arms out along the back of the bench. It wasn't the most ladylike position, but she didn't seem to care, and that made Sarah curious about her. Her blue eyes darted around, half expecting to see someone watching them with suspecting eyes.

"No one's going to see us here," she offered. "This courtyard is reserved for servants and guests. And since everyone who has access to it is working…"

She let her words trail off with a shrug and closed her eyes as she basked in the sun, and Sarah took the moment to commit her face to memory. She was a delicate kind of beauty that Sarah had never really seen before. She had a heart-shaped face with perpetual dimples pressed into her cheeks and long eyelashes that curled upwards. Her full lips had a perfect cupid's bow, and she was petite with a slender figure and soft curves. Her red dress was simple — it had a square neckline, cinched her waist, and flared out at her knees, displaying her smooth legs and her white heels. It was the perfect compliment to her blazing red hair. It was wavy like Pine's but hers was much shorter — cropped at her shoulders and falling around her face in gentle waves

She was beautiful and her light brown skin seemed to soak up the sunlight, whereas Sarah could already feel her shoulders turning red. She considered slinking back inside to find shelter in the shade, but she dismissed the thought. She didn't want to go back inside just yet. If she did, she'd have to confront the feelings swelling in her chest at the memory of Noble kissing Pine and she wasn't ready for that. So, instead she took a seat next to the woman on the bench and let her shoulders relax in the warmth of the sun.

"Thank you," Sarah said after a moment, "for back there."

"Don't worry about it," the woman said, flicking her wrist at the words. "It's no big deal."

"I still appreciate it."

The girl tilted her head to look over at Sarah and cracked one eye open to look at her. Her hazel eyes were bright with flecks of green in them and she had no shame as she let her gaze rove over Sarah before returning to her face, and returning her head back to its original position, facing the sun. Sarah felt her heart pound in her chest at the appraisal, but said nothing to fill the silence that stretched between.

"Why were you there, anyway?" The woman asked.

"Oh," Sarah said, blushing as she realized how she must have looked. "I'd gone to the ballroom in the hopes of getting some practice in."

"Worried about the opening ball?"

"Not really," Sarah lied, hoping that her voice didn't reveal her nerves. "But it never hurts to be absolutely certain of these things."

"Understandable," the woman said with a slight laugh. "I would be nervous too, if I were in your shoes."

"My shoes?" Sarah questioned, turning to face the other woman as the hairs on the back of her neck stood on end at the tone the other woman used. "I'm not sure I know what you mean."

"I just mean," the woman said, turning to peek an eye open again. "It can't be easy being in the tower when your mother lost the previous bid. I can't imagine how much pressure that must put on your shoulders."

"In truth," Sarah said, a chill creeping into her words as she let her eyes dance over the other woman, "I hadn't much thought about my mother or her failure. It's not something I personally care to dwell on."

"That's good," the woman said with a nod. "I was always taught to keep my mind focused on what's to come and not what's already passed." She lifted her head and smiled at Sarah as she finally met her gaze. "It seems that we think alike in that way."

"It would seem so," Sarah agreed, letting a small smile pull at her lips in return.

"But also," the woman laughed, "it's just one dance. I don't think anyone would be offended if it weren't perfect. You know?"

Sarah thought back to Pine's words and said nothing, choosing instead to nod and let her words hang in the air. She knew that it was much more than a dance, and she wasn't foolish enough to think that the woman beside her didn't know that as well. It seemed that everyone in the queendom knew the truth about the opening ceremony, so it made Sarah skeptical of why the woman beside her would want her to believe it was less important than it was. She filed the question away for later, making a note to herself to ask Sal and Mara about who she was when she spoke to them again.

"I didn't get to ask earlier," Sarah said, keeping her voice light. "But what were you doing in the ballroom?"

"I was spying on Noble."

Sarah balked at the openness of the woman's words and straightened in her seat. Her face flushed as she turned to look at the woman, her fingers lacing together in her lap as she pivoted her body to stare at the woman.

"Why?"

The woman laughed then, her amusement ringing out over the courtyard as she glanced at Sarah.

"Are you serious?" She questioned, a grin splitting her face and deepening her dimples. "Have you seen him?" She sighed and closed her eyes. "I don't know who that girl was in the ballroom, but gods," she groaned and shook her head. "That man could break both my ankles and I'd still dance for him."

"Excuse me?"

The woman turned to Sarah, and from the way confusion danced across her delicate features before she dissolved into another fit of laughter, Sarah could tell there had been something vital in her words that she'd missed. The woman doubled over, clutching her sides as she pulled her legs beneath her. Her fiery hair fell forward, covering her face and glinting in the light. Sarah blushed and looked away from her as she fought to catch her breath.

"I'm sorry," she coughed out between giggles. "I didn't realize," she started, before dissolving into more laughter.

"I'm afraid you'll have to let me in on the joke," Sarah huffed.

The woman waved her hand at Sarah and shook her head.

"Forgive my rudeness," she giggled. "I only meant that Noble is dangerously handsome. He could be an absolutely terrible person behind his gorgeous face, and I wouldn't care. I would still want to be the girl who held his interest," she explained.

"I see," Sarah said, embarrassment choking her words and scattering her thoughts. "I guess," she said, offering a small smile to accompany her blush, "like you said earlier, we do think quite alike."

"Indeed," the woman said, nodding her head. "Maybe next time, we can tag-team him," she suggested. "I'll grab him, and you grab the girl. Break up their little love fest."

The image of the woman beside her grabbing Noble and dragging him anywhere against his will made Sarah chuckle at the thought. She didn't think that any of the shadows would be swayed from acting on their own desires, and the thought of someone as dainty as this woman forcing them to do anything sent Sarah into her own fit of giggles. She hid her mouth behind her hand as she snickered at the thought, and the woman beside her pushed her shoulder into Sarah's.

"That's better," she smiled. "You seemed so uptight before. I don't know what's going on with you," she admitted, "but you should relax more. Whatever you have going, don't worry. I'm sure everything will work itself out."

"That's doubtful," Sarah said, thinking about Brandi's plan and how incompetent she felt, "but it does feel better to have someone say that to me. So, thank you."

"No problem," the woman grinned. "Maybe we could —"

"Sarah!"

They both turned at the shout coming from the entrance to the courtyard. Noble stood there with annoyance written on his face as he strode into the courtyard. His hands were pushed into his pockets as his dark eyes danced between her and the woman beside her. When he reached them, he grabbed Sarah's hand and pulled her to her feet. He wasn't rough with her, but his grip was firm, and she stumble forward into his arms.

"We've been over this a dozen times," he said, keeping his voice low as he dropped his lips to her ear and irritation seeped into his words, "and somehow you keep forgetting that you're not to go anywhere in the tower without me, Sal, or Mara."

"I know, but —"

"If you know that, Sarah," he interrupted, his words sweet like honey and deceptive like poison, "then why am I constantly having to hunt you down?"

Sarah withered under his questioning and at the sound of her name. Any rebuttal she had died on her lips, because what could she tell him? That she'd been watching him tongue-wrestle with Pine in the ballroom? That she'd gotten jealous enough to spew fire at the sight and had allowed herself to be carried off by a stranger? That wasn't an excuse — it was an admission of her shortcomings as a person. So, she dropped her gaze from him and nodded.

"It won't happen again."

"Good," he said, pulling her behind him and positioning himself between her and the woman she'd been sitting with. "Pardon my intrusion," he offered with a nod and a half bow. "I've been tasked with retrieving the princess for her lessons. I'm afraid I must escort her there now."

"It's fine," the woman said, an air of formality coating her words as she straightened and stood to her feet. "I believe our conversation was coming to its end anyway," she said with a smile as Noble lifted his head. "Although, I must admit that I am a bit jealous," she giggled. "Had I known she had a bodyguard as handsome as you, maybe I would have dragged her away sooner."

Noble offered her one of his crippling smiles and she flushed, her light brown skin taking on a pinker hue.

"No need for that," Noble offered. "Should you desire my time, you need only request it. I would be more than happy to keep your company."

His words were formal enough, but the way his gaze slid over the woman made Sarah bristle at his side and clear her throat. She was growing weary of watching him flirt with everyone but her.

"I believe we should take our leave," Sarah said.

Noble cut a glance over to her but nodded anyway, placing a gentle hand at her back to guide her away. Sarah turned to leave, but the woman placed a hand on her elbow.

"Before you go," she said, "let's make a date to have some tea and a proper chat," she suggested. "I'll send my attendant over to schedule it with your advisors."

"Alright," Sarah said, working to keep her surprise from coloring her words. "And forgive me for not asking earlier, but I didn't catch your name."

"It's Grace," she said, another grin splitting her face as she stepped back toward the exit on the other end of the courtyard. "Grace Bertanal."

CHAPTER FOURTEEN

*The tragedy of beginnings is that, often, they are not recognized until they
have ended. But the beauty of endings is that they bring with them the start
of a new beginning.*

— The Wisdom of JaZhire, The Beloved | Log of the 13th Head Priestess

---

THE VOID

3 DAYS BEFORE THE OPENING CEREMONY

"Welcome to the void."

Brandi's eyes snapped open at the words and she searched for where
they had come from, but she saw nothing. She was engulfed in a darkness
so thick, she could feel it pressing down on her skin. She blinked a few
times, searching for even the smallest hint of light, but even with Asari's
blessing to see through the darkest of nights, she saw nothing. It sent a
bolt of panic racing through her, but she discarded the feeling before it
had a chance to take root in her mind. Instead, she closed her eyes against
the oppressive dark and listened.

She hadn't lost feeling in any of her limbs, and her thoughts were still and her own — clear and focused. She took a deep breath and felt cool air rushing into her lungs. It soothed the burning sting of the power that had been boiling beneath her skin for a week and she relished the feeling. It had a subtle sweetness to it, as if she stood in the center of a bed of flowers in bloom. The scent was surprising, but it wasn't alarming enough to keep her attention. Her thoughts shifted to her surroundings, straining her ears and listening for the voice that had snapped her to consciousness before.

"Where am I?"

She spoke the question in her normal tone, listening for an echo in hopes of determining the size of the room, but her words were swallowed by silence — disappearing almost as soon as they left her lips. It made her feel like her voice had been stolen — like her thoughts were louder than her words — but even so, she heard a response drift back to her.

"The void," the voice responded. "The space between then and now."

"I don't know what that means."

The voice chuckled, and unlike her own words, it echoed — surrounding her with an amused mirth that she found both foreign and familiar. It confused her, but Brandi didn't let the thought linger. She'd faced enough new experiences in the last few weeks to take this one in stride. She kept her breathing slow and even as she waited for a response to her declaration. Her patience was rewarded and a few moments later, the voice spoke again.

"It is as I have said," it offered. "The void is the space between then and now," it repeated. "The space between what once was and what will be.”

“How?” Brandi asked.

“You are a time being,” the voice stated.

“And how would you know that?”

The voice chuckled again. “Am I not meant to recognize my own daughter?”

Brandi bristled at that, her muscles tensing as the words slunk across her skin and sank into her mind. She sucked in deeper breaths of the sweet, cooling air, but the fire in her blood raged against it. The power that had settled into a steady warmth roiled in her veins, rejecting the cool air and forcing it from her lungs. Her throat ached at the constant fluctuation of burning heat and icy air, but she focused on not letting her breaths get too shallow. She had no desire to lose control of herself in a space she was unfamiliar with, where she couldn't so much as perceive up from down.

“Zareal?”

“That is I,” the voice answered.

“Why have you brought me here?” Brandi questioned. “What do you want?”

“Did Zena not already explain this to you?” Zareal questioned. “I desire nothing from you.”

“Then why…” Brandi's words trailed off as the ground fell away from beneath her.

She'd been standing in the void as if it were the most natural thing in the world, but now she fell as if the ground had never existed. Her eyes flew open, searching the darkness for something to grab onto as she fell faster into the nothingness, tumbling over herself. Her heart pounded in her chest as her panic rose and she fought back the scream that wanted to rise in her throat as a platform came into view below her. She was free falling towards it and she crossed her hands over her face as she braced herself for impact. But seconds before she crashed into the shiny black tiles, she stopped.

She opened her eyes to find herself floating just above them, and it wasn't until she righted herself that her sandals touched against the tiles below her. She placed a hand to her chest and braced herself on her knees as she looked around.

The platform she stood on was much like the one that Zena had brought her to, but smaller. And instead of a single throne in the center, there were two plush white chairs placed opposite each other, with a single glass coffee table in the center. A vase of black and white flowers sat in the center, and Brandi stared at them. Confusion laced her thoughts as she tried to figure out why flowers would be in a place like this. She took a step closer to them but froze when she felt a gentle hand press into her shoulder.

She jumped away from it and spun around, her favorite knife already in her grasp as she met the dark eyes and serene smile of the man who claimed to be her father. He was the same man she'd seen in Freya's vision, but he'd changed. His black suit was now white, and it made his gray skin look darker than it actually was. His skin was still buttery smooth, but he carried himself with a grace that Azinne didn't have. She understood that beings of time lived outside the flow of it, but it was evident to Brandi that they weren't unaffected by longevity. Zareal was older than Azinne, and there was a stark difference in the way the air around Zareal seemed to soften with patience and understanding, whereas Azinne carried with him an air of mischief and chaos.

Despite her best efforts, Brandi felt herself relax as she gazed into Zareal's eyes. His were an empty void — he didn't carry stars within his eyes the way Azinne did, and that made Brandi wonder about the difference between them. She eased out of her fighting stance, but kept her knife gripped in her hands. Zareal didn't move as he watched her. He just stood with his hands to the side, watching her. His eyes trailed over her face as if he were trying to commit every detail of her face to his memory, but his gaze didn't feel creepy. It wasn't until his eyes returned to hers that his smile stretched even wider.

"Welcome," he said. "It's nice to finally meet you."

"Why did you bring me here?"

The question was sharp, but Brandi didn't know what else he expected her to say to him. He may have always known about her existence, but she'd only been aware of his for the last few weeks. And, for most of that time, he'd been a harbinger of absolute destruction. Her mind was still trying to twist itself around the fact that he was her father — that Freya had betrayed the trust of the gods and birthed her into the realm to be a cure for the affliction of time plaguing her children. Brandi was still struggling to process the truth of that fact, but when Azinne had warned her that Zareal was also the true villain in the same breath, her mind had set every thought that included him and Freya aside.

They were complicated and distracting.

But now, Zareal stood before her — grinning like the proud father he was, and she didn't know how to comprehend that. She couldn't return his politeness and agree that it was nice to meet him, because she'd never had that desire. She'd hoped that the only time she would ever lay eyes on him would be when she was ridding the realm of him and his vessel. But as she looked at him now, a quiet part of her grew louder.

She wanted to know who she was.

And this might be the only opportunity she ever had to ask him her questions — to get answers from the source. So, when he avoided answering her question and instead gestured to the two seats across from each other, she followed him. He sank into the seat with an ease that suggested he'd done it a million times. He melted into the chair and, like his suit, the dark gray skin on his hands and face stood in stark contrast to the blinding white of the chair. Brandi could only imagine what she looked like with her dark brown skin, but she allowed herself to be swallowed up by the cool surface of the chair. It was like sinking into a cloud, and she sighed at the cool, airy sensation enveloping her skin.

"Do you like it?" Zareal asked, gesturing to her. "The chair?"

Brandi's eyebrows raised at the question. His voice was eager — hopeful. As if he would be devastated if she said she didn't. Part of her wanted to lie and tell him no, just to see what his reaction would be, but something in his expression kept her from wanting to destroy his hopes. So, she nodded, and he grinned again.

"Wonderful," he whispered. "I'd hoped that you would."

"Are you going to answer my question?"

"Yes," he nodded. "I just wanted a moment to appreciate you being here. I've waited a very long time to meet you. I've been a bit nervous anticipating it actually," he admitted, a light chuckle punctuating his words. "I'd hoped that it wouldn't be under these circumstances, but I can't say that I'm wholly unhappy about that."

"Circumstances?" Brandi questioned. "Explain."

"You look just like your mother," he whispered, leaning forward to stare at her face again. "Absolutely stunning."

"Stop that," Brandi snapped, losing her patience. "Do not compare me to Freya."

"Temper like hers too," he laughed. "But alright," he said, holding up a hand in surrender as Brandi shot another glare at him. "I'll keep what I notice of her in you to myself. You want to know why I brought you here, but," he shrugged, "I haven't. I've always been here. You've just arrived."

"That's impossible," Brandi sighed, already growing tired of the conversation. It reminded her too much of her meeting with Freya in the god realm and she was beginning to question whether she'd been better off when she hadn't known the truth of her parents. Acquiring two of them without warning seemed to be more of a burden than she was prepared to deal with, and she pulled a hand over her face. She wondered if Zareal was going to be any easier to get straight answers from than Freya. She'd been an iron fortress of secrets, and Brandi had only gotten answers when Azinne spilled them for her. She hoped Zareal would be more forthcoming without such heavy provocation.

"You know what? I don't want to do this," Brandi stated, her shoulders sagging as she sank back into the chair. "I don't want to have to drag the most basic information out of you. I'm tired," she admitted.

"So, just tell me whatever it is you want me to know. Or don't," she said, waving her hand through the air. "But if you're not and you're serious about me being the one who came here on my own, then just tell me how to send myself back and I'll do it."

Silence hung in the air between them, but Brandi didn't let herself think about how that made her feel. In truth, she was tired of feeling things and having to commit so much of her energy to processing her own emotions and making sense of things that had none. She wanted to return to the person she'd been before Freya decided it was time to upturn her life — back when the only emotion she truly had to let herself feel was the love she felt for Jack. But she wanted to rid herself of the anger, confusion, disappointment, hopefulness and dread that had been creeping its way into her life over the past few weeks. She didn't want to feel the pressure of needing to save the realm, and she didn't want to feel overwhelmed by a responsibility that she was never meant to carry. It was too much for her and she didn't want it.

"I'm sorry," Zareal said, leaning forward as he offered his apology. "My intention wasn't to be cryptic with you. I only meant to give an answer to your question."

"Then just tell me what we're doing here," Brandi said, waving her hand around the open space. It was devoid of any light outside of the platform they were on. "I have no idea what any of this is or how I got here."

"Then I'll explain what I can," Zareal said with a nod. "Just this once, you may ask me whatever questions you have, and I'll answer them all. With no pretense or deception."

Brandi's ears perked up at the caveat he'd included, but she decided not to dwell on it. If he was going to give her straightforward answers, then she couldn't complain. It was more than what Freya had offered her, and she wasn't about to waste the opportunity. So, she shifted her body forward and locked her eyes onto Zareal.

"Why am I here?"

"Because you sat upon your throne."

"Why would sitting in a chair bring me here?"

"A chair?" Zareal chuckled. "That's an oversimplification of things, don't you think?"

"I don't think so," Brandi said with a roll of her eyes. "It's meant for me to sit on. How is that any different from what I'm doing right now?"

"I guess that's true," he conceded. "But you should know that as a god, when you sit upon the throne meant for you, in your own domain, your mind travels inward. It shows you everything that is subject to your authority and the totality of your power."

"And how would you know that?" Brandi asked. "You're not a god."

"No," Zareal agreed, "but I have watched over countless gods who have existed and perished in the vastness of all time. I know enough to explain at least this much."

"So, you're telling me that I rule over nothing and have no power?" Brandi asked, quirking a single eyebrow upward. "There's nothing here."

Zareal chuckled at that. "True. This is the void. But it only exists like this because you are new to godhood and have yet to manifest your powers as a being of time. As you grow, so too will this place." He grinned as he looked at her. "You rule over much more than you are currently aware of."

"So," Brandi said, pulling out the words as she looked around at the vast emptiness, "it's basically a reflection?"

"Yes," Zareal nodded. "The more you grow into who you truly are, the more this place will shift to display that. As you are right now, you know nothing of yourself other than that of your parentage. Therefore," he waved his hand around them, "everything other than me, is dark."

"Everything other than you, huh?"

Brandi looked around once more, but she couldn't argue that he was wrong. When she'd arrived, she'd seen nothing. It wasn't until she'd known that he was there that she'd been able to see him. Even now, she could see nothing other than the small platform they sat on. She didn't think he was misleading her, so she wondered just how much more there was to learn.

"So, this is the equivalent of my mind?" Brandi clarified. "I can only see things that I actually know?"

"More or less," Zareal said, shrugging. "It's a bit more complex than that. Specifically, this is your power, your domain, and a reflection of your own mind. It will change, but right now you know nothing of your domain, how to use your power, and your mind is, no doubt, clouded with uncertainties."

"And that's why it's pitch black like this?" Brandi asked. "I thought it would have been green."

"You do take after Freya in many things," Zareal nodded. "But you are my daughter as well."

"Your power is black like this?"

Zareal shrugged. "Everyone's power looks a bit different. I'm sure you've noticed it, haven't you? How Rothe's power takes on a blinding golden light, but Lindl's is violet, and Freya's is a bright green. The color manifests in different ways for each person, but yes. Mine, like other time beings, is black. However," he glanced around, and his words paused on his lips as he hesitated over his next words. Brandi raised her eyebrows at him as she leaned forward.

"What is it?"

"I'm sure you've noticed the stars that cover your temple? And the ones that Azinne carries in his eyes? Those stars are planets. Universes and worlds in the sprawling totality of time. Shifting and changing with every passing second," he explained. "They are also the physical marker for a being of time. You don't carry them in your eyes as we do, but," he waved to the expanse around them, "they are not here either."

"What does that mean?" Brandi asked. "That I'm not actually your daughter?"

"Oh, you most definitely are," Zareal said, a chuckle shaking his shoulders as he straightened himself in his chair. "There is no mistaking that or denying the truth that it is. You are my beloved child, and nothing will change that."

Brandi bit the inside of her cheek at the words. It felt strange to have a being of time declare his love for her, and she didn't know what to do with the feeling of static filling her stomach.

"Why don't I have any stars, then?"

"My guess?" He shrugged as he leaned forward, resting his forearms on his knees and letting his hands hang between them. "It's because you've never left this realm. You don't have control over your power yet, so you cannot see them. Not yet."

Brandi didn't know what to make of that explanation, so she filed it away for later. If she were to believe his words, then it would only be a matter of time before the void took on a new shape. She didn't know if it would be similar to the god realm — if it would take on the form of the home she shared with Jack or not — but she knew it would expand. And in order for that to happen, she needed to know more about herself, her power, and the supposed domain that Zareal mentioned before.

"Can you explain something to me?" Brandi asked. "You and Zena both mentioned that I sat on my throne," she said, emphasizing her last two words. "But I have no throne. I have no domain. So, that makes no sense to me."

"And that is where you are wrong, my dear child," he said, his voice gentle. "I have prepared things for you."

"Prepared?" Brandi asked, her voice lifting as she sat up straighter and her eyes grew wide. "What do you mean?"

"Exactly as I said." Zareal took a deep breath as he leaned back in his seat, crossing his right ankle over his left knee. "When Freya rejected me, I already knew of your existence. And I already had the warning of the Galaxiers in my ear," he explained. "Her realm was still under my jurisdiction, and I could see what her plan was. I knew she planned to use you and that she wouldn't raise you as a god. She wouldn't give you your own domain or children to serve you so, I took matters into my own hands."

"Meaning?"

"I did what Freya would not. I prepared a domain and children for you so that when you were ready to ascend as a god, you would have the support to do so."

Brandi shook her head at his words, her mind struggling to understand what it was he was suggesting.

"That's impossible."

"Brandi," he said, her name gentle on his lips. "You should know by now that nothing is truly impossible. Not for you, not for me, and not for the gods."

"But then…" Brandi shook her head again and sank back into the seat, letting the coolness of it wash over her again as the fire in her blood began to spike and burn her veins. "How?"

"When I realized I had fallen into the trap that the Galaxiers warned me of, I put measures in place to ensure that, when you awoke to your powers, you would have the support you needed. So, I made a deal with a benevolent god of a dying realm," he said, shrugging as if his words weren't breaking every constraint Brandi had on her mind of what was and wasn't possible. "Their name was JaZhire, and they implored me to save their children. I'd denied them at first," Zareal admitted. "I was a proper time being when they'd first approached with their plea, and I hadn't understood their desire. But once I knew of your existence, I understood. So, I returned to their realm as the last light of life fizzled away from them and accepted their offer. I couldn't create children of my own for you, so JaZhire gave me theirs. And in exchange for breaking the rules of the Galaxiers and rescuing their children from the ultimate collapse of their realm, they would serve you in this one."

"So, when Zena said she was a high priestess…"

"She meant that she is your high priestess," Zareal said, nodding his head and giving voice to the ideas that Brandi had refused to accept. "She and her people were a clan of loyal priestesses. I transplanted them here in order to be your support."

"I have so many questions about that," Brandi said with a groan.

"Take your time," Zareal said. "Time doesn't pass in the void, so we can take all the time you need."

"How many of them did you place here?" Brandi asked, choosing to ask the questions that would be the easiest for her to grasp first.

"About five hundred of them," Zareal answered. "They were a small clan previously, but they should number over a thousand by now."

"And you did all this without the gods knowing?"

Zareal chuckled again, the sound darker than before as his thoughts turned to the gods. It sent chills racing up Brandi's arms, and she tensed, her fingers tightening around the knife still gripped in her hand.

"The gods are glorified fools," he scoffed. "They don't perceive things they do not create themselves. It's why their powers only work within their own realms and why they hold no power over us time beings."

"So, they never noticed Zena and her people?"

"Not even when your domain appeared beneath theirs," he said with a shrug.

"How did that happen?"

"You are a god," Zareal said. "No matter how much Freya wants to deny that aspect of you, it's the truth. And every god has a domain," he explained. "Even if the realm itself has to expand in order to allow it to exist, it must exist."

"I didn't know that," Brandi whispered, her mind reeling with the new information.

"I'm not surprised," Zareal said, his warm smile slipping back over his face. "I doubt the gods even know it themselves. They divided the realm into their own domains, but the lower realm already existed. It came into being the moment they did. And it continued to expand as they each came into existence, and the same holds true for you." Zareal sighed as he pinched the bridge of his nose. "Honestly, the gods of every realm are always so arrogant in thinking they create everything themselves, when in truth, they create only within the rules the Galaxiers have set forth. They're truly nothing more than children in a sandbox, but let them tell it and they're the supreme of all supreme beings."

Brandi had nothing to say to that, because he was right. She'd always believed that the gods were at the top of the hierarchy. Until Freya had brought it to her attention, she'd never even dared to think there was more beyond the gods. But hearing of it now and knowing the limitations of the gods, she wasn't surprised by Zareal's annoyance. The gods were entitled. And they acted like brats.

"So," Brandi whispered, her eyes dancing across the void above her as she tilted her head back. "I have a domain."

"Yes."

"And children?"

"Yes."

"And the gods know nothing about this?"

"No," Zareal said. "Not unless you tell them."

"And you've been planning this since before the beginning of time in this realm?"

"Yes," he nodded. "I knew I wouldn't be able to protect you fully from Freya and her desires, but I wanted to be ready for when you decided to break away from her."

"You say that as if you knew this moment would come."

"I've known everything since before I met Freya," he whispered.

"Right," Brandi sighed, her head aching at the reminder that, unlike the gods, Zareal and Azinne could see the future. They understood the ripple effects of their actions. But, knowing that, Brandi thought back on Azinne's tale — of how Zareal hadn't hesitated in going to meet Freya, even after what the Galaxiers told him. If he'd seen this as the future he was heading toward, then his actions didn't make any sense to her.

"Why would you go to meet Freya?" Brandi asked. "If you knew this would be the future you were facing, why would you walk headfirst into it?"

"I wish I had an answer that would satisfy you, but I don't," Zareal said, his words gentle as he shrugged at Brandi. "Knowing an outcome does not always change the actions that lead up to them." He laughed when the look of confusion didn't leave Brandi's face. "It's far simpler than what I believe you're trying to understand," he said, leaning forward and grinning at Brandi. "I wanted to know what it was to love. And now, I've known it twice."

"Twice?"

"Is it unnatural to love one's daughter? I've met you only this once, but I do care for you deeply. I always have, since the moment of your conception," Zareal admitted, his voice softening. "You are the sole reason I brought time to this realm."

"For me?"

"You are a being of time," Zareal explained. "Until it exists, neither can you. So, just as the Galaxiers brought us out of the nothingness, I meant to do the same for you."

"So," Brandi whispered, more to herself than to Zareal as her mind worked to piece together his words with what Azinne had told her in the god realm. "You brought time to this realm, not out of some misplaced duty to the Galaxiers or fear of some punishment, but because Freya couldn't give birth to me without it?"

"Yes."

"If you knew that, then," Brandi scoffed, shaking her head at him, "why didn't you stop her?"

The question was out of Brandi's mouth before she thought about the words herself. Shock crossed her face, and she averted her gaze away from Zareal as heat rushed to her face. She tried to think of a way to reroute the conversation, but when she opened her mouth to ask Zareal about something else — to get him back to explaining how her powers worked, or what they even were — she saw how pained his face was.

Creases formed between his eyebrows and the corners of his lips pulled downward as his eyes widened with the realization of things he hadn't understood. She read it on his face as if he were an open book and she swallowed her words, letting the silence fester between them. Her question had been petty and not one she'd ever expected an answer to, but she also couldn't deny that if this was the only moment she'd ever get to ask him the truth, it was something that she wanted to know.

"I'm sorry," he whispered.

"I don't want an apology," Brandi stated. "If you knew she was going to turn me into a tool to be used for the queendom. That she was going to take everything away from me and plunge me into a world of violence, all so she could force me to fight you in the end," Brandi shook her head as she held Zareal's gaze. "Why would you allow her to give birth to me? Why didn't you stop her?"

"Would you believe me if I told you the truth?"

"I don't believe you've lied to me so far," Brandi said with a shrug.

"I am a being of time," he stated. "I have never experienced what it is like to be caught within the flow of it. And after watching it, at some point," he shrugged, "I got curious about it. It hadn't always been that way, but as I watched gods be born just to perish again into the nothingness, I wanted to know what motivation they carried to fight the inevitable. And that's when the Galaxiers warned me against your mother."

"Don't call her that," Brandi said, her eyes narrowing into a glare. "Just use her name."

"When I met Freya," Zareal said, correcting himself, "I had yet to fall from my position. I was arrogant in thinking that, with the Galaxiers warning in my ear, I would be able to resist the temptations presented to me from a goddess. I'd done it countless times before. But the curiosity I'd already been feeling, grew when I was with her. She spoke of things I didn't understand and desperately wanted to. I loved her because I wanted to know what it was. I did not expect the pain of it to be quite so sharp and lasting when I had to leave her. I knew that you were to exist, but I had already fallen," he admitted. "The moment I was to return to the Galaxiers I knew my punishment would be eternal. But I finally understood what the gods have always known." He smiled at Brandi. "I knew what it was to want my child. To be able to meet her and protect her. I understood what it was to want time."

"So, you're just selfish?" Brandi asked. "Because if you wanted to protect me, then why did you leave me?"

"I didn't though," Zareal said. "I sealed myself and all of my power within you. I gave up my corporeal body to protect you from Freya. I've always been with you."

Brandi went still at his words, her eyes locked on him as she tried to process his statements.

"Explain," she forced out, her eyes unblinking as they stared into his.

"I knew that Freya wanted to use you as her vessel. That she would attempt to merge your soul with hers and use your latent power of a time being for her own whims. And I didn't want your soul to be corrupted because of her. I wanted to meet you. To know you. So, I sealed everything I had within you and encouraged her to incarnate into the moral realm. Your power alone would have been enough for her to control, but mine?" He shook his head. "Even in the corporeal body of a god, it would have been too much for her to handle, but without her physical body it would be impossible. Godhood isn't compatible with time beings. It's part of the reason we're forbidden from intermingling with them. And also why you've been feeling the less than desirable effects of it in your blood. It burns, doesn't it?"

Brandi nodded as she sat there, stunned at his words. She felt numb, as if her body had shut down around her, but he continued on as if he hadn't just shattered what was left of her mind.

"It's the awakening of your powers," he explained. "You've always had access to the power you inherited from Freya, but mine were sealed away until you needed them. If they hadn't been, you might have destroyed the realm without even meaning to."

"I…" Brandi shook her head, her eyes staring into the void surrounding them. "I don't understand."

"Oh," Zareal hummed. "I'm not sure how to otherwise explain it. If you'd had access to my full power from the time you were born, then —"

"That's not what I meant," Brandi said, her voice cracking under the stress she felt as it cut through his words, and she met his gaze. "What do you mean, you didn't want Freya to corrupt my soul? She wouldn't…"

"Oh."

It was the same word as before, but this time it was soft. It carried with it an undertone of pity and Brandi flinched away from it. She was the girl that people respected — that they feared. She wasn't the girl they pitied. She never had been, and she had no intentions of starting now.

"Don't," Brandi said, an edge creeping into her voice as she shook her head and moved to the edge of her seat, her thoughts shifting to facts and away from her emotions. "Whatever sympathy, empathy, pity, or whatever you're feeling," she waved her hand through the air, shooing away the words as if they disgusted her. "I don't want it. Just go back and explain what you said. Freya was going to corrupt my soul?"

"Yes," Zareal said, his eyes watching Brandi as if he expected her to break down into explosive tears at any moment. "It is how she reincarnates in every lifetime. She merges her own soul with the one that would be born into the realm. In doing so, she corrupts it. Since she is a god and does not exist within the flow of time, her soul does not return to it. Therefore, the soul that merges with hers is permanently removed from within the flow of time as well."

"That's not what I was told."

"Enlighten me," Zareal said, leaning forward. "What is it that you have been told?"

"I was told that Freya merges her soul with her vessel," Brandi admitted, "but that it was similar to how the other gods share their power with their vessels in the mortal realm. It was so that she could guide her vessels throughout their lifetime."

Zareal shook his head and sighed.

"She would be able to do the same thing if she remained in a corporeal body in the god realm. The difference is, the other gods only share a portion of their power with their vessels. They do not attach their souls to a mortal body as Freya does. If they did, then like her, they would have to corrupt the soul inside it and give up governing the mortal realm, as she has. There is no way to merge a soul with that of a god and not corrupt it."

"So," Brandi questioned, her voice shaking. "I'm corrupted? I'll never be able to know peace once my soul returns to the gods?"

"You are not corrupted," Zareal stated, his words sharp and definitive. "I didn't allow it."

"How can you be so sure?"

"You have your own will, don't you?" Zareal challenged. "And you've always known that you were not Freya, haven't you?"

"Yes…"

"Then, there it is," he said, waving his hand at Brandi. "She is not you. You are not her. And you are not corrupted."

"But the other vessels love me," she pointed out. "Like the gods do Freya."

"Do they?" Zareal questioned. "They feel pulled to you, yes. But to my knowledge, only Rothe's vessel loves you as Rothe does Freya. And that is of his own will and emotion, not because Rothe has chosen him," Zareal pointed out. "Think of it. Does Carna's vessel wish to bed you? Does Asari's? Lindl's vessel barely seems to trust you."

"That's true…"

"It's an affinity that comes with their shared power," Zareal shrugged. "They are linked to the gods they serve, but they are not gods themselves."

"They are now," Brandi stated. "The gods gave us their power."

"But their souls have not yet been merged and corrupted. For now, they are still mortal."

"But I'm not?"

"No," Zareal said. "But that is because you have never been mortal."

"But I grow," Brandi pointed out. "I change."

"Because your power had been dormant. I sealed my power within you so that you would grow. But the moment Freya gifted you the last of her power, she unsealed mine."

"But why would she do that?"

"She was trying to control you," Zareal said, his voice dropping as he looked at Brandi. "You must have noticed how painful it was every time she tried to 'bless' you."

"That's normal though," Brandi pointed out. "The gods' power is painful for everyone."

"Everyone who has a mortal body," Zareal corrected. "But you have never been mortal. Your capacity for power was never limited by your flesh and bone," he shook his head and rested his elbows on his knees as his dark gaze locked onto Brandi. "It was painful because she was trying to merge her soul with yours and take over your body. Her goal was to overwhelm my power that was protecting you with that of her own. If she'd been successful, she would have corrupted your soul and gained complete control over your body and power."

"But I got stronger every time she did!"

"Because your power," he said, jabbing his finger towards her chest, "got stronger. Every time she tried to overtake you, your soul rejected her, pushing her away. And every time it did, it grew in strength and my seal weakened, giving you another layer of protection from her. It was always your power she was after," he stated. "Not the other way around."

"Then the other gods…"

"Never had anything to do with it," he stated. "When they blessed you, they did it with genuine hearts, showing you favor. Freya never told them of me."

"They believe I'm a genuine vessel," Brandi whispered.

"Yes. And it was painful to receive their blessings because you're also a time being and, as I said earlier," he sighed, "those two don't mix. I suspect the only reason you could accept their blessings in the first place is because you're also half-god."

Brandi shook her head as her fingers sunk into the neat parts of her hair and tried to make sense of her thoughts.

"So, let me get this straight," Brandi breathed. "You met Freya before the beginning of time, knocked her up, realized that she was going to use me to remove time from the realm, sealed yourself and your power away into my unborn body, and have been what? Waiting for a convenient time to show yourself and be like, 'Surprise! I'm your father!'"

"Not exactly," he said. "I've been sealed. I didn't have access to you as Freya did. Otherwise, I would have intervened," he said. "You have to believe me about that."

"That's what I hate about all of this," Brandi said, coughing out a laugh. "I do believe you. I have absolutely no reason to, but I believe every word you've said."

"I wouldn't lie to you."

"Don't say that," Brandi said, shaking her head. "Everyone lies."

"Time beings are bound to the truth," Zareal said. "We do not lie."

"Azinne did."

"Azinne spoke the truth while it was true," he corrected. "But you know for yourself what was once true does not always remain that way."

"He said that you were my enemy."

"Did he?" Zareal asked, raising an eyebrow. "Call me your enemy, I mean."

He waited with patience as Brandi thought back on Azinne's words.

He'd said a lot of things while she was in the god realm — that Zareal wanted to destroy the realm and everything that Freya loved, that he fathered a child with Freya and was sentenced to exile, and that he was sent here to test the gods of the realm. But he'd never outright said that Zareal was her enemy, and Brandi didn't doubt that Azinne was the kind of being who was careful with his words. And as she looked at Zareal, his question drifting through her mind, she understood it hadn't been happenstance that Azinne had never referred to Zareal that way.

"No," Brandi said, her words pulling out of her. "He didn't."

"Do you believe me to be your enemy?"

"I don't know yet," she said, returning his honesty. "But I want to believe that you're not."

"That's good enough for me," Zareal said with a nod.

"Do you still want to destroy the realm?"

"Yes."

He held no hesitation in his words and didn't flinch away from the question. The conviction in his words made her further believe what Azinne had said about him.

"Why?"

"After all you've heard," he said, "you don't truly need me to explain that to you, do you?"

Brandi sighed and looked away from him. He was right. She didn't need an explanation about his motives. But it didn't make it any easier for her to wrap her mind around the fact that he was the obstacle that she was going to have to conquer. Despite this being their only meeting, she had to admit that she enjoyed his company far more than she'd been enjoying Freya's.

His honesty was refreshing, and there were so many more questions that she wanted to be able to ask him. She wanted to have more time to sort out her thoughts over everything he'd said and to figure out what it meant for her to be a time being. Freya had withheld that truth from her for her entire life, but now that she knew it to be true, she didn't know what to do with that information. She hadn't known who to ask, but with Zareal sitting in front of her, she felt like she had an opportunity to have all her questions answered.

But he was still planning to destroy the realm. Which meant he was planning to destroy Jack. And she couldn't allow that. She wouldn't allow it.

"Can you teach me how to use this power?" She asked.

"Of course," Zareal answered with a nod. "It would be my pleasure."

"And you can teach me how to keep it from burning me?"

"Yes."

Brandi paused at that, and relief rushed through her. The past few weeks had been torture. It seemed with every shift in her thoughts and emotions, her power was surging and burning her from the inside. She'd thought it was because she was losing her grip on her mental restraint but knowing that it was something beyond her control both terrified her and put her at ease. It wasn't through some fault of her own that her power was spiking out of control.

"Thank you," Brandi sighed. "But won't your vessel be disappointed if you turn your attention towards helping me?"

"You are my daughter," he said with a gentle smile. "I'm sure they will understand."

"But you won't tell me who your vessel is?"

"No," he said. "Not until I know that our objectives align. And I don't believe you've decided which side you wish to stand on yet, have you?"

Brandi wanted to deny his words, but she couldn't. She didn't know what she wanted to do. She hadn't been determined to save the realm in the first place, but knowing Zareal's side of the story now didn't make her decision any easier. Azinne wanted her to destroy the queendom, and Freya wanted her to protect everything. But she hadn't decided anything for herself yet, so she had no rebuttal for his words. Instead, she pushed them away, forcing them down into the well of thoughts and emotions that she would deal with later. It was filling up faster than she liked, but it was also something she couldn't deal with right now.

"Then can you tell me how you're planning to destroy the realm?" Brandi quirked an eyebrow at him. "It may help sway my decision."

"I'm sure it won't," Zareal chuckled. "But, at the most basic level, I was planning to just support you in your efforts." When Brandi looked at him with skepticism, he smiled. "You've already accepted Azinne's offer to rid the realm of the monarchy," he pointed out. "I'll support you in that endeavor until you make a decision for yourself."

"You say that as if you knew I would accept his offer."

"I know the Galaxiers," he stated. "I know how they function, and I know Azinne. I knew he would not leave this realm untended in my absence, and I know how he likes to play with his work. I saw this opportunity as an option for your future. But now that you've awakened to your powers, I can no longer see what lies ahead of you," he said. "Time beings. We don't see each other."

"So, when Azinne said you'd been exiled?"

"I'd disappeared," he shrugged. "Sealed away into my daughter, who had yet to be born. He knows only what the Galaxiers have told him, and, like the gods, they are not bound to speaking only the truth."

"Why would they cover for you like that?"

"I don't know," he said, shrugging. "That is something you would have to ask them."

"Why couldn't Freya use your power while I was still in her body? I was still a part of her."

"Sealed," Zareal repeated, chuckling. "You seem to be forgetting that even you couldn't access it until a few moments ago when you came here."

"Won't Freya be able to access it now?"

"Have you felt her presence since you left her domain?"

Brandi's eyes widened at that. "No."

"Because your soul has fully rejected hers. She is still bound to you," he warned. "Her soul has been tethered to yours for too long to separate them now, but you are your own person. She cannot control you," Zareal shrugged. "Truly, she never could. It's why she invested so much time into making you rely on her and having you think your own power was something she'd lent you. But either way, her soul can no longer access yours as she once did. She is no more a part of you now than the other gods are with their vessels."

"This is a lot," Brandi sighed. "Too much."

"This conversation has been a lot to take in," Zareal admitted. "So, let's end it here for now."

"What?" Brandi asked, her head shooting up to look at Zareal. "But I still have questions!"

"And we have time," he soothed. "My seal may have been broken, but I am still a part of you. I'm not going anywhere," he said, offering a smile as he stood from his chair and offered a hand to help Brandi up. "Any time you wish to speak with me and return to the void, take a seat upon your throne. I will be here."

"And you'll keep your promises?" Brandi clarified, accepting his help. "You're not going to pretend you never made them like Freya would?"

"No," he laughed. "I will be here. I will answer all your questions that I can. I will teach you how to control your power. And I will help you destroy the monarchy, as long as you want to," he grinned. "I promise."

"Okay," Brandi breathed, accepting his words.

"But," he said, giving her hand a light squeeze, "there is something I want you to give some thought to when you go back."

"What?"

"I am going to destroy this entire realm," he warned. "I love you more than I've ever loved anything. And I've enjoyed being able to speak with you like this. But I don't want the kindness I've shown you to paint a different picture than the reality you face."

"And you won't change your mind?"

"No," he said. "But I do want to offer you something that might sway your decision."

"And what's that?" Brandi asked, her mind already spinning through what she thought he could offer her.

"I will save Jack," he said, his words gentle as his eyes bore into hers. "As I did with Zena and her people, I will transplant you and Jack to another realm. And anyone else you wish to take with you," he smiled, "within reason, of course."

"And why would you do that?" Brandi asked, her heart choking out the air in her throat as his words sunk into her mind.

They changed everything.

"Because you are my daughter and I want to see you happy," he said, placing a hesitant hand against her cheek. "I have no desires to take what joy you have away from you. And I've already broken the policies of the Galaxiers for much less. What is another broken rule if it's for you?"

"Thank you," Brandi breathed. "I'll think about it."

"That's all I ask," Zareal said with a smile, squeezing Brandi's hand before stepping away from her. "Now, to send you back. It's quite simple," he explained. "You need only to open your eyes. Your real ones."

"That's it?"

"That's it," he said, taking a step back and sliding his hands into his pockets. "Be well, daughter of mine," he said as she focused her mind on sensing her physical body, "and don't forget. The next time we meet, I'll expect your answer."

CHAPTER FIFTEEN

To live a successful life, there are three rules which must never be broken.

Do not sip from cups you did not pour.

Do not believe in lies you did not tell.

Do not play games you cannot win.

— Adage of the Gods | Lindl's Five Holy Academies Compilation

---

ROTHE'S DOMAIN — THE QUEEN'S TOWER

3 DAYS BEFORE THE OPENING CEREMONY

"Do you understand now?"

The words were asked for what felt like the hundredth time, and Sarah nodded in silence as she trained her gaze on the books in front of her. For the last six hours, Cedric and Mara had been taking turns explaining the rules of the bid to her — both the official and unofficial ones.

It was a lot for her to take in, but she'd done her best to keep up with them and all the information they'd laid before her. After being laughed at by Pine, and the conversation she had with Grace in the courtyard, she'd realized just how naïve she was to walk headfirst into the Queen's Tower without realizing what she was agreeing to. She'd thought the bid would be like the stories in the books her father had read to her as a child — ones with princesses, wicked stepmothers, and dashing princes. That the politics of the realm would be as simple as those stories — that once the rightful princess was crowned queen, everything would sort itself out.

She could almost laugh at herself now for thinking something so childish. Her reality wasn't anything as soft as that — the problems of the realm wouldn't be solved simply because she sat upon the throne. And if she wasn't careful, she'd be conversing with the gods about her failures before she ever had a chance to take the first step at the opening ceremony.

She would rather send herself to the gods than be the reason Brandi couldn't accomplish her goals. So, she'd been grateful when Cedric and Mara had agreed to drill everything they could into her mind. She hadn't uttered a word of protest when they'd taken dinner in her room and continued her studies well past midnight. It wasn't until her eyes were sore from the strain of reading countless books with tiny print and her head pounded from all the information she was working to internalize that Cedric paused and snapped his book closed.

"If you understand, then repeat it back to me," he said. "We can't be sure you know anything until you can explain it to someone else."

Sarah sighed and rubbed her arms as goosebumps rose along them. Mara sat on the other side of the desk where she was working, and her brown eyes were locked onto Sarah's face. It was always nerve-wracking to be put on the spot and she flushed at the sudden attention but worked to calm her thoughts. Mara had warned that her face gave away more than her mouth did, and one of the most vital things she learned from Sal during her lessons about navigating the queen's court was to keep her secrets to herself. She should only reveal them when necessary — to control her own narrative. She took a deep breath and rolled her shoulders back as she twisted in her seat to look up at Cedric.

He was dressed in a casual outfit of black slacks and a white shirt. His dark wavy hair was tied back in his usual style, and a pair of round reading glasses sat on the edge of his nose. His violet eyes seemed brighter than normal as they stared into hers, and Sarah forced herself to not look away from him as she spoke.

"The bid for the throne is a rite of passage that goes back to the very creation of the realm," she said. "It began with Fina the First. She was the first queen to rule this realm and was revered for her strength, wisdom, and judgment. As she aged and a new predecessor was to be chosen, she created what we now know as the bid. There have been some modifications over time, but the core of what it is remains the same."

"And that core is what?"

"To decide upon and crown a new queen."

"Good," Cedric said, nodding. "And how does one enter the bid?"

"To enter the bid, a woman must be a legitimate daughter of the crown."

"Meaning what?" Mara chimed in. "Who decides who is legit and who isn't?"

"The council," Sarah answered, swiveling her head to look at Mara. "It's decided upon by known lineage and biological proof. Every daughter born to the queen is swabbed at birth and her biological imprint recorded within the official records housed in the tower. When a potential entrant into the bid announces themselves, their imprint is compared to those that are on file. As long as it's a match, the daughter is considered legitimate."

"Good," Cedric said again. "Keep going. What does the bid consist of?"

"The bid consists of three major parts," Sarah said. "The opening ceremony, the campaign for consorts, and the approval of the council."

"Explain those," Mara demanded, leaning forward on her elbows as a look of approval settled on her face. It gave Sarah a small dose of encouragement, and she nodded as she took another deep breath.

"The opening ceremony is basically a ball," Sarah said, her eyes darting around the room as her brain worked to access the most recent information she'd received. "It's open to everyone in the entire realm, but most often, the most influential members of society from all domains attend. There they look over the bidders and form their opinions of them. There is a lot of networking that takes place at the ball as, more often than not, the heads of households have migrated to a new generation since the crowning of the previous queen."

"And why is it important to know that?" Cedric questioned.

"Because those connections will ultimately determine the success of the queen and her reign," Sarah answered, turning her eyes to the table as her mind struggled to fully understand just how complicated the realm was when it came to its power structure. "A prime example can be found with Queen Leia's own mother, the former Queen Lindley."

"May Freya have mercy on her soul," Mara whispered under her breath, and Sarah glanced up. It was an automatic response that was given whenever speaking about royalty that had already returned to the gods, but it was something that was specific to Rothe's domain and the queen's court. It was only said when the person first entered the conversation, but Sarah hadn't grown accustomed to it yet, and whenever she heard the whispered phrase, it drew her attention and broke her train of thought. She cleared her throat as she worked to pick up where she'd left off.

"Yes," Sarah agreed. "She was the favored princess of the council and ascended to the throne with ease. However," Sarah said, lifting her gaze from the table to meet Cedric's, "her sister, former princess Carrie —"

"May Freya have mercy on her soul."

"Carrie was the favored princess of the people," Sarah continued. "She was the one who, during the opening ball and her campaign for consorts, had spoken with people, bonding with the fragment guardians of each domain and forging strong ties to the elite of Lindl and Rothe's domain. So, when she lost the bid, those same people felt slighted and refused to support the queen in any manner. So, despite her initial popularity, Queen Lindley had one of the worst reigns in the realm's recent history."

Her last words were spoken in a whisper as she waited to see if Cedric and Mara would reprimand her. Although the words she spoke were true — Cedric and Mara had been the ones to teach her the facts she was reciting — it didn't change that it was considered inappropriate to speak ill of royalty, even when it was true. She let the silence hang around them for a second before speaking again.

"Every request she made for a technology exchange with the Lindlian academies was denied, and every tour she made to the other realms in order to mend her relationships with their leaders was met with hostility. She became unable to pass any policies for the realm that would have any lasting effect outside of the tower itself. She became demoralized to the point where she rarely left her personal chambers, and she became known as The Invisible Queen."

"And what does all that tell you?" Cedric asked. "What does that mean for you?"

"It means that I have to make sure that I play to my strengths," Sarah said, her gaze drifting to the table as she thought back on what Russ had told her when she'd first met him. "People are going to notice me because of who I am and because of what I look like," she said, pulling at the edge of her long hair. "I have to make sure I use that to my advantage and that it doesn't morph into my detriment."

Cedric and Mara both smiled at that, and Sarah felt a small glow of pride light up in her chest. She was realizing why everyone around her had been so disappointed in her actions earlier. There was so much that she didn't know about the realm and so much that she had just assumed would work itself out. The more she learned about the history of the realm and what she was staking her life on, the more she understood why everyone around her had been irritated at her lack of initiative. Knowledge was power, and simply knowing the most basic information about Asari's domain wasn't enough. She understood that now.

"Alright," Mara said, leaning back, "you've covered the ball. What about the consort campaign and the council approval?"

"The consort campaign is one of the most important determining factors of the bid and ties into the importance of making connections at the opening ceremony. A princess who is unable to attain a consort from each of the domains is seen as unworthy of the crown."

"And why is that?" Cedric questioned.

"Because they are the members who will comprise the council during and following her reign — meaning they will become not only her support, but they will also be the deciding factor of who will reign after her. They become the ultimate representatives of their people, and by joining the queen in the tower and committing to be her partner for the remainder of her life, they are committing to being the voice of their people who whispers in her ear," Sarah explained. "The practice was initially modeled after Freya's own relationships with the gods, but it's grown beyond that and is done to ensure equality throughout the realms. To ensure that the queen doesn't favor any one domain over another, and her policies are for the betterment of the entire realm, and not just the people she hails from or those of her favored consort."

"Exactly," Cedric said. "And if you're able to make it through the opening ceremony, we'll work on a strategy to help you find the required number of consorts."

"You don't think she'll be able to find four on her own?" Mara asked Cedric, raising an eyebrow at him. "Is that something she would actually need our help with?"

Cedric met Mara's gaze and offered her a tight smile.

"While I appreciate your faith in her," Cedric said, choosing his words with care, "and I don't intend to be rude, you've seen her. I don't think she'll be able to garner any attention from a Rothian without our help."

Mara's gaze shot over to Sarah at Cedric's words and Sarah fought back the blush that wanted to creep across her cheeks. She was more than aware of what she looked like — and that it was the furthest thing from desirable for most people. The goddess was the standard of beauty in the realm — tall with dark skin and eyes, ample curves, and distinct features. With her blonde hair, blue eyes, and barely-there curves, she was the furthest thing from the ideal. There would always be men like Kyle who preferred less conventional beauty standards — and men like Noble who seemed to prefer anyone who liked him, no matter what they looked like — but anyone who was of a status high enough to be a consort to the queen would probably find her to be less than ideal. And though looks weren't everything, she couldn't deny that it could prove to be her biggest obstacle.

"Let's cross each bridge as we approach it," Sarah said, doing her best to redirect the conversation away from her looks and her inability to acquire a romantic partner. "Assuming I can make it through the opening ceremony and the consort campaign, then that would leave the council approval," she said. "At that point, potential candidates are interviewed by the council at a round table panel, and the current council determines whether or not the critical thinking capabilities and political ambitions of the princess are worthy of succeeding the throne. This is the part of the bid that's make or break for most bidders, and it's also why the consort campaign is so important," Sarah explained. "Even before she takes the throne, she's deciding the future of the queendom."

"It seems like you've got it," Cedric said, releasing a deep sigh as he fell back against the wall behind him. "It's taken a while, but it seems you've finally armed yourself with a decent amount of knowledge."

"Sorry it's taken so long," Sarah said.

"You can't know what you don't know," Mara said. "The important thing is you're stepping up now."

"Thank you," Sarah whispered. "I'll do everything I can."

"Be careful not to push yourself too much," Cedric warned, pushing off the wall. "It wouldn't do well for us to have invested all this time in you just for you to fall ill from exhaustion or stress."

"I'll be mindful of that," Sarah said, nodding her head.

"That's all I ask," Cedric said, dropping a hand onto Sarah's shoulder with a grin as he placed the book in his hands on the table and walked towards the door. "May Asari keep your night, ladies."

"And bless your dreams," Mara and Sarah replied together.

With that, Cedric slipped out the door and Sarah rose from her seat, stretching her arms above her head. Her shoulders and back were sore from being slumped over the books for so long, but she felt accomplished at having learned so much and met their approval. She couldn't say that she was excited about attending dance practice at Rothe's first light, but she was feeling motivated in a way that she hadn't felt before.

"Don't forget," Mara said, standing to stretch and stack the books on the table, "tomorrow you have tea with Grace. She sent her attendant over to schedule it with you."

"Oh," Sarah said, her arms dropping as her mind panicked at the thought of having lunch with another princess. Mara and Cedric had informed Sarah of who Grace was at the start of their study session and Sarah's face had paled at the realization. She and Grace may be cousins, same as she and Sal were, but they were also both committed to winning a competition that would result in one of them meeting the gods. Just thinking about seeing her again made her stomach twist in knots, and she offered a weak smile over to Mara.

"I don't think —"

"Don't bother with any excuses," Mara said, cutting her off. "You're going. She sent a formal request, and considering how her status is higher than yours," she pointed out, reminding Sarah that though she may be a legitimate daughter of the crown because of who her mother was, her mother was not the current queen. "You can't refuse. So," she said, offering Sarah a sly grin, "I'll be here bright and early to get you dolled up for the occasion."

"But," Sarah whispered, shaking her head, "I'm not ready for this. I can't meet with her, not now that I know who she is."

Mara smirked and slapped a hand down onto Sarah's shoulder as Cedric had moments ago.

"You'll be fine," Mara said, unfazed by the panic written on Sarah's face. "Just rest tonight. And in the morning," she grinned, all her teeth showing as excitement blossomed in her brown eyes, "we prepare for war."

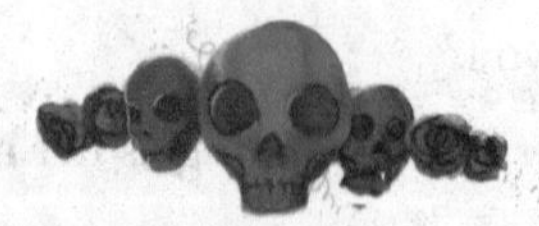

The gentle buzzing of Sarah's alarm broke through her dreams the next morning and she groaned as she sat up in bed and reached over to her nightstand to turn it off. She'd never been a morning person, and today was no different. She could already hear Sal mocking her for being bleary-eyed as she dropped her head into her hands and swiped away the strands of hair that had escaped her braid during the night. Even though she was technically more Rothian than him, his actions and mannerisms were proof that he'd been raised as a royal in Rothe's domain.

Asari was the ruler of the night, so most Asarians didn't wake up until Rothe's sun was already halfway through the sky. She'd spent most of the first twenty-two years of her life living that way. And despite her mother's affinity for the morning, it wasn't a trait she'd passed on to her and Jamie.

"Okay, Sarah," she whispered to herself, "you've got this."

"Do you, really?"

Sarah's head whipped to her left and when she met a pair of hazel eyes staring back at her, Sarah screamed and lurched backward. She was already at the edge of her bed, so another scream of surprise ripped from her as she toppled over the edge and went crashing to the ground. Her back throbbed as she groaned and worked to right herself, and the angelic laughter that filled the room at her struggle bounced around her aching head as she scrambled to her feet.

Pine sat on the opposite edge of her bed, her back against the headboard and her ankles crossed as she looked over at Sarah with an amused grin on her face. Even in the early morning light filtering in through her windows, Pine was gorgeous. Her dark hair spilled around her shoulders, and she wore a strapless black romper with white flowers printed across it with simple black sandals that revealed her painted white toes. She looked almost like a painting and as she laughed again, Sarah couldn't ignore the way her mind twisted around itself, wanting to talk to her.

"You put your shoes on my bed."

Sarah's eyes widened when she realized the words had left her mouth, and she curled her fingernails into her palms as she looked at Pine.

"I show up in your room at the crack of dawn, and that's what you say to me?" Pine laughed again, her head falling back as she giggled. "You're not the brightest one."

"Well," Sarah huffed. "What am I supposed to say to you?"

"You could ask me why I'm here," Pine suggested. "Or what Brandi wanted? Maybe," she said, lifting her eyebrows as she lowered her voice and leaned closer, "you want to know what Noble tastes like when he's not being watched by jealous princesses?"

Sarah's face burned bright red at the suggestion, and she looked away from Pine as she fought to get a grasp on her emotions. She tried taking deep breaths, like Mara had taught her, but it didn't help. The moment in the practice ballroom kept rushing back to her mind, and she wanted nothing more than to sink into a hole and disappear in that moment. Her chest ached at the force of her heart as it pounded in her chest, and her stomach filled with jittery butterflies as she shook her head.

"I'm not —"

"Don't pretend like you weren't jealous," Pine teased. "I saw you."

"I wasn't trying to spy on you!"

"Then what were you doing hiding behind the curtain?" Pine questioned. "Why not just walk right on in like you were obviously planning to?"

"It didn't seem appropriate."

"Trust me, princess. Nothing I did that with that man yesterday was appropriate," Pine giggled. "But that's the difference between you and me, isn't it? You play by everyone else's rules, and I don't play by any."

"What's that supposed to mean?" Sarah scoffed, lifting her gaze to meet Pine's. "You play by Brandi's rules all the time."

"And that's my choice," Pine said, shrugging her shoulders. "Unlike you, Brandi doesn't tell me to do things," she pointed out. "She asks."

"And?" Sarah questioned. "What does that matter when you're doing whatever she wants, anyway?"

Pine paused and studied Sarah before grinning and standing up from the bed. She was a head shorter than Sarah, but even from where she stood on the opposite side of the room, Sarah could feel the hostility rolling off her in waves. It made the hair on the back of her neck stand up, but she forced her feet to stay where they were. Mara taught her that the first person to back down was the one to lose the fight. And Sarah couldn't say exactly why, but she didn't want to lose whatever battle she was in with Pine right now. If she did, she felt like she would never recover from it.

"I don't like you, princess," Pine stated, her words cold even as the smile on her face stayed in place. "I came here in part just to see if we got off to a bad start, but," she shook her head as she gave Sarah another once over, "I don't see what Brandi does in you. And I don't think this plan of hers will work."

"You would doubt Brandi?"

"Of course I would," Pine said, rolling her eyes as she walked over to the desk Sarah had been studying at with Cedric and Mara the night before. "I don't believe that anyone is infallible, not even her. But like I pointed out before," Pine said, pointing to the chair across from her, "you and I are not the same."

"So why are you here, then?" Sarah asked, moving to take a seat in the chair that Pine pointed out. She was still in her pajamas and felt underdressed in her tank top and shorts compared to the subtle glamor that Pine had, but she kept her back straight as she sank into the chair — moving as if she wore the dress and heels that Mara had been dressing her in since she arrived at the tower.

"Brandi needed me to come," Pine said, her words simple as she tossed her left leg over her right and leaned against the table. "And like I said, I wanted to meet you. Properly, this time."

"And this is proper to you?"

"Proper enough," Pine said, flicking her hand through the air. "It's not as if I were meeting someone important."

"That's rude," Sarah said, narrowing her eyes at Pine. "If you came here just to insult me, you can consider us to be properly met and you can go."

"Snippy, aren't we?" Pine teased. "But it also appears you don't listen," she said, her voice losing its playful tone. "Brandi wanted me to come here and share some information with you."

"She did?" Sarah asked, her eyebrows lifting in surprise. "About what?"

"About Grace Bertanal," Pine said. "We suspect her to be involved with the time beings threatening the realm."

Sarah paused at that revelation and schooled her face into a blank expression as she worked through her thoughts rather than letting them run across her face. She laced her fingers together in her lap as she took a slow, deep breath and sorted through the questions she wanted to ask.

"We?"

"Yes," Pine nodded. "Brandi and I."

"You know about the time beings?"

"I wouldn't be telling you about Grace if I didn't," Pine said. "And I know about you, too."

"Since when?"

"Since long enough," Pine answered, her grin lighting up her face. "Brandi doesn't keep many secrets from me."

Her words felt like a jab to Sarah's pride. As if she were in some competition with Pine to determine which of them Brandi liked best, and Sarah was losing. She knew she shouldn't let it bother her, but she couldn't stop the way her stomach clenched, or the way heat rushed up her neck. She tried to set the feelings aside and focus on what Pine was telling her, but she was losing grip on her focus.

"But there are restrictions…" Sarah said, shaking her head and thinking of how the gods prevented them from telling other people about their connection to them.

"Oh sweetie," Pine breathed, her hazel eyes dancing over Sarah's face with a look of pity. "You haven't noticed."

"Noticed what?"

"The realm…" Pine said, letting her words trail off before shrugging. "It doesn't matter. You'll figure it out soon enough." Pine glanced over Sarah's pajamas and hid a snicker behind her fingers as she looked away from her. "Or you won't."

Pine let her words stop there and her refusal to give a proper answer made Sarah's fingers tighten around each other, but again, she forced them to relax and schooled her expression into something neutral. She felt like she'd been put on display as Pine watched her with sharp eyes, but she let her mind fall back to the questions she needed to ask rather than the emotions she didn't have time to feel.

"Fine," Sarah breathed, keeping her voice even. "I'm capable of figuring things out on my own. But what's this about Grace Bertanal?"

"Don't you know who she is?" Pine asked, her palms pressing onto the table as she sat back in her chair. "She's Adam Bertanal's daughter."

"I'm aware."

"Then you should know that she shouldn't exist," Pine said, her words slow as she studied Sarah. "Adam Bertanal doesn't have any children."

Sarah flushed at the accusation lacing Pine's words and shook her head. Her braid swished across her back as she held Pine's gaze.

"How am I to know that he doesn't have children if I'd already met his daughter?" Sarah asked. "And what do you mean, she shouldn't exist?"

"I meant exactly what I said, princess," Pine sighed. "You may not know this since you're from the outskirts of Asari's domain," she said, her delicate nose scrunching up in mild disgust at the mention of the outskirts, "but Adam Bertanal can't have children. It's a well-known fact that as punishment for defying the will of the gods in his youth, they took away his ability to father children. He's lamented his loss ever since."

"Then how…" Sarah's question trailed off and Pine nodded as she pointed at her.

"Now you're catching up, princess."

"Who is Grace then?"

"No idea," Pine said with a shrug. "She just appeared out of nowhere a few months ago and Bert began spinning this tale of how he kept his daughter a secret from the realm because he wanted her to grow up with privacy and not in the spotlight like the other princesses. Something about wanting her to know what it was to live among the people so she would have a unique advantage when she placed her bid for the throne."

Pine spoke the words as if they were meaningless, but Sarah was shaken down to her core. She'd gained a modicum of confidence last night when she'd studied with Mara and Cedric, but Pine's words brought the reality of what she'd committed to crashing down on her. There were other princesses in the bid that she would have to compete against, and all of them had prepared for this moment their entire lives. They had fathers who had moved through the queen's court, working to give them an advantage. At the very least, all of them had at least one safe member of the council who would vote for their succession. Sarah was truly alone in her bid for the throne and her blood ran cold at the thought.

"So, what's the warning?" Sarah asked. "You've told me who she is and why she's dangerous. What is it expected that I do at this point?"

"That's up to you to decide," Pine said. "My only job was to pass along the information so that you could move accordingly. Brandi likes it when people can make informed decisions for themselves."

"How kind of her," Sarah whispered. "But if that's all, then I'll have to ask you to leave."

"Excuse me?"

"I don't mean to be rude, but the sun has nearly risen," Sarah said, pointing to the window, her limbs feeling wooden beneath her skin. "And I have to prepare for the day. Because as you pointed out already," she said, a wry smile crossing her lips, "Brandi already has such little faith in me. It wouldn't do well for me to prove her right."

Pine let her hazel eyes dart over Sarah for a moment before pushing away from the table and shrugging.

"Fine," she said. "I've done my part, anyway. If Brandi needs me to, I'll be in touch."

Sarah nodded and kept her gaze locked on the window as Pine crossed the room. Her emotions flashed through her faster than anything she'd experienced before. She was furious that no one seemed to believe her capable of winning the bid when they'd forced her to enter it — she was distraught and jealous that Pine had no hesitation in sharing that she'd done much more with Noble than what she'd seen in the ballroom, and she was annoyed with herself for feeling that way about it. She was torn between being motivated to prove everyone wrong about her and giving up on everything right then and there, but when Pine opened the door and tossed her last few words over her shoulder, Sarah grit her teeth and made her decision.

"Good luck, princess," Pine offered. "And try not to get sent back to the gods before you have a chance to be useful." She giggled under her breath as she disappeared out the door. "Noble would be so hard to console if you didn't make it."

Her laughter followed her out, haunting Sarah's thoughts as she stood up from the desk and the first rays of sunlight broke through her window. She watched it creep across the floor as she worked to steady her breathing and unclench her fists. Pine's taunting struck a nerve within her, and she studied her reflection in the glass.

"Keep your rotten luck," Sarah whispered to herself as she turned away from the window and headed towards the bathroom, pausing for a brief moment by the vanity to snatch up the scissors that rested in the top left drawer.

"I'm a god."

CHAPTER SIXTEEN

Do not be fooled by the ego of a god. They may carry the fate of worlds on the backs of their whims, but without the people who worship them, they are nothing more than myths — dying legends that no one will remember.

— The Wisdom of JaZhire, The Beloved | Log of the 13th Head Priestess

BRANDI'S DOMAIN — TEMPLE OF THE TIME GODDESS
3 DAYS BEFORE THE OPENING CEREMONY

When Brandi forced her eyes open, her head pounded with a force that sent her doubling over on her throne. She braced herself against her knees and took deep breaths of the cool air around her. Her eyes glanced at the black and white flowers growing at the base of her throne and wondered if they had anything to do with the icy sensation sinking into her lungs. Either way, she didn't fight it and tried to steady her breath as Zena rushed forward.

"Are you alright?"

Her question was laced with genuine concern, and Brandi wanted to laugh. She couldn't remember the last time a stranger was concerned for her well-being, and she nodded at Zena.

"Fine," she answered, her voice hoarse as the fire in her lungs burned hotter. Even with the cooling air surrounding her, the fire inside of her burned hot and it made her feel weak as she pushed herself to her feet. Her legs were shaky beneath her, her chest was heavy, and her sight was blurry — her vision jumping with every pulse of her heartbeat. She tried to keep control of herself, but despite her best efforts, she still swayed on her feet.

Zena's hands were quick in darting out to steady her, and Brandi allowed herself to rely on the woman as she helped to guide her down the uneven stones of the platform.

"I've got you," Zena said, pulling Brandi's arm over her shoulder and pulling her close to her side. Brandi hadn't expected such strength from the woman and was relieved to know that she wouldn't falter under her weight. With each passing moment they spent together, Zena was proving herself to be someone that Brandi could rely on — in more ways than one.

"You're okay," she said, leading Brandi back down the path. Their echoing footsteps were the only thing punctuating the silence until Zena stole a glance over to Brandi. "If you don't mind me asking, what happened?"

"I met my father."

"Oh," Zena breathed, her pale gold eyes widening. "I didn't know."

Brandi laughed at that, surprise and amusement slipping through her exhausted mind. Zareal had been the one to send Zena to her, and she'd trusted him enough to bring Brandi to her throne, but she'd been left in the dark about who he was. It was crazy to think about Zena being from a different realm, but it explained the soft curves in her words and the color of her eyes. Brandi still didn't fully understand how Zareal could have transplanted hundreds of people into the realm without the god's knowledge, but she also accepted that she didn't have the capacity to question it any further. The reality was staring her in the face.

Zena hadn't known what would happen if Brandi sat upon her throne — she couldn't have. Her surprise told Brandi that Zena knew little more than she did. And if she'd served a god prior to this moment, Zena probably hadn't expected much. Brandi wouldn't have. Rothe sat upon his throne every time she met with him. And for the first time, she understood just how deep his pride and arrogance ran. Even when accepting an audience with her, he was still within his own mind — luxuriating in his own power. It was a nauseating thought. Even just thinking of speaking to someone and determining their fate while gazing at the manifestation of her own mind and power turned her stomach, but there wasn't much about the gods that could surprise her at this point.

"Did he tell you to bring me here?"

The question was vague, but Brandi had faith that Zena would know what she meant. And she wasn't disappointed, because after a beat, Zena nodded.

"Zareal requested that when I meet you, I bring you to your throne. I didn't know why that would be so important but," she shrugged under Brandi's weight, "I guess it was because he'd wanted to greet you there. The only thing I knew for certain was that our beloved JaZhire asked us to go with him. To do as Zareal asked of us and to serve you as we served them."

"And you have no issue with that?"

"We wished to perish with our beloved JaZhire," Zena admitted. "But we understood their desire to save us, even if they could not come with us. They asked us to open our hearts to the new god who would be born, and so those of us who could, did."

"And those who couldn't?"

"They stayed behind," Zena whispered. "They remained loyal to our beloved JaZhire, even as they wept for us to go."

"Do you regret not staying behind?"

A thick silence descended around them as Zena considered Brandi's words. Brandi's green eyes darted over to the woman as they walked on, her pale eyes glowing in the dark and lighting their way as she led them back down the path. It was a gentle light, but it still took Brandi's breath away to see it. She'd never witnessed anyone like Zena before, and the simple glow was a concrete affirmation that Zareal had told her the truth.

Zena was not a child born to any of the gods that Brandi knew.

"No," Zena finally said. "I am a high priestess," she explained. "I was the closest to our beloved JaZhire than anyone. So, I knew their pain in witnessing us perish. I understood their desire to see us protected. Saved. I knew it as if their emotions were my own," she whispered. "And as much as it pained them to see us leave, I felt the hope they had in knowing that we would continue on. I couldn't betray them and their emotions by denying their final request of me. And my people needed me." She paused in her words as she tightened her arm around Brandi's waist and smiled at her. "And apparently you need me, too."

"Thank you," Brandi whispered as they rounded the bend in the path. "For all you've sacrificed to be here."

"You're welcome," Zena said, nodding. "We will serve you the best we can."

"Could I ask you for a favor, then?"

"Anything," Zena answered.

"Could you find Jack for me?" Brandi asked, knowing that Zena would know who he was.

"Of course. I'll send someone to retrieve him right away."

"Thanks," Brandi said, resting her head against Zena's shoulder. "And could I also get a bed? I'm tired."

"Absolutely," Zena said with a grin. "There's a lot more to your domain, and this temple, than what you first saw. I'll prepare a room for you and you can take the grand tour later."

"Great," Brandi whispered, letting her green eyes close as they made it back to the garden and Zena led her down a different path. "Great."

BRANDI'S DOMAIN — TEMPLE OF THE TIME GODDESS
2 DAYS BEFORE THE OPENING CEREMONY

When Brandi woke up, the first things she saw were the ever-shifting stars in the ceiling above her head and she bolted upright. She gripped the blade in her pocket as her green eyes danced around the room, trying to figure out where she was at — her mind replaying her last few moments of consciousness.

"Easy," a voice coaxed from the other side of the room. "You're not in any danger."

Brandi's eyes whipped over to the woman, her green eyes narrowing as she tightened her grip on the knife. She was almost an exact copy of Zena, with long legs, rich brown skin, and pale gold eyes. Rather than long locs though, she sported a short cut, her dark hair cropped close to her scalp. She wore dark jeans with a striped green and white button down with crisp, white sneakers. The top buttons were undone, and the sleeves were rolled up to her elbow. She was attractive, but Brandi would describe her as handsome before she ever called the woman beautiful, and Brandi kept her eyes trained on her as she swung her legs over the side of the bed.

"Who are you?"

"I go by the name Remy," the woman offered. "I believe you've already met my mother, Zena. I'm her oldest daughter."

Brandi nodded her head as she looked around the room. It wasn't anything fancy — pristine white walls, polished black tiles on the floor, a nightstand to her left and the armchair Remy sat in on the opposite side of the room. The bed she'd slept on was narrow and just long enough that her feet didn't dangle over the edge. It felt like it was sized more for a child than a grown woman, but Brandi didn't complain — she was just glad to not have woken up on the floor. She pushed herself off the bed and was glad to find that her strength had returned to her and the heat building in her blood had eased. She felt more like herself and stretched her arms above her head as she turned her gaze back over to Remy.

"Care to explain to me why you're here?" Brandi asked, her eyes searching the room for an exit.

"I'm here to help teach you to control your powers as a god," Remy answered.

"Train me?" Brandi asked, lifting a brow and returning her gaze to Remy. "I'm pretty sure Zareal already made me that offer."

"I can't train you in the ways he can," Remy said, shaking her head. "I'm a priestess, same as my mother. I can train you on the basics of your power as a god." She paused and searched Brandi's face before quirking her own arched eyebrow in Brandi's direction. "I was told that your mother wouldn't?"

Brandi coughed out a laugh at the idea of Freya taking the time to teach her how to control her power. Imaging them in her garden, practicing until she got it right, made her chest ache for things she'd never have and burn with an intense anger for the goddess at the same time, but she pushed the emotions away and shook her head at Remy.

"Absolutely not."

"Then that's where I come in," she said, rising from her chair. "From what I've been told, you seem to have no trouble controlling small amounts of your power already, so this shouldn't be too hard for you."

"Is that meant to be comforting?"

"I'm not really the comforting type," Remy stated, shrugging her shoulders as she slid her hands into her pockets. "I only mention your aptitude for it because the foundation of what I'll be teaching you is mental fortitude," she said, tapping the side of her head. "The stronger you mind, the easier it is to reign in your power."

"That's good to know," Brandi said with a nod. "When do we start?"

"As soon as you're ready," Remy answered, walking over to the wall and double-tapping it. They both watched as an exit formed in the center of the seamless wall, and Remy gestured to it. "Before we begin though, there's someone else who wants to speak with you."

"Who?" Brandi questioned, following Remy into the hallway.

"Royal," Remy said. "And, apparently, it can't wait."

Remy led the way down the hall as Brandi's green eyes darted around, taking in all the details as she worked on getting her bearings. Similar to the room they'd just left, there were white walls, black tiles, and an ever-shifting ceiling made up of a myriad of stars. Brandi knew now that they were nothing more than glimpses into a much wider universe, and staring up at them stirred something in her chest that was both foreign and nostalgic to her — as if she were trying to remember places she had never been to.

There were columns punctuating the walls every so often with glowing orbs at the top that cast off soft lights of different colors. Some were blue, others were purple and gold. It made the hallway seem relaxing and foreboding all at once and Brandi could admit that she didn't hate it. They were emotions that existed on opposite ends of the spectrum, but as she followed someone who was both a stranger and an ally to her, she thought them to be fitting. Remy was a woman of few words and they'd just met, so Brandi couldn't determine if she truly trusted the woman or not, but she trusted her mother and Royal, and for the moment, that was enough.

Remy led them to a pair of tall glass doors that opened up to a courtyard. Brandi hadn't expected it to be as vibrant as the garden, so she couldn't help being impressed once she laid eyes on it. It had large gray stones laid into the soft grass to create a pathway that led up to a small fountain that sat in the center of the courtyard. It was shaped out of what looked to be black marble, with gold veins running through it. A lit firepit encircled the outside of the fountain and benches sat just beyond that. Black and white flowers bloomed around the perimeter of the courtyard and gave the air a delicate scent that Brandi couldn't get enough of.

Above them, the sky shifted with the same stars and galaxies that Brandi was beginning to grow accustomed to. Small orbs of white and gold were placed throughout the courtyard and gave off a soft light that made the courtyard feel as if it were in a state of perpetual twilight. It was Brandi's favorite time of day, and she loved it.

Remy had made it clear that she had no business with Royal, so after receiving a few concise directions, Brandi agreed to meet Remy at her restaurant. It was within walking distance — just a few buildings down from the temple. And with the promise of a strong drink and a hot meal later, Brandi and Remy parted ways.

Brandi watched her return to the temple and relished the silence that came with being alone. It was the first time she'd had a moment to herself in what felt like days, and she was grateful to be able to take a few deep breaths and hear herself think. She sank down onto one of the benches by the fountain and tried to let her shoulders relax. There were two entrances to the courtyard, so she chose the one that gave her a clear view of both and let out a deep sigh as she worked to organize her thoughts.

They felt jumbled in her mind, and she was at a loss of where to even begin trying to organize them. She didn't know what to think about Freya, Azinne, Zareal or all of the information they'd given her. She felt like she had most of the story now, but she also felt like there were still gaps of information that were being left out, and she tried to not let it frustrate her. The most she could do was sort through the information she already had and decide for herself what she was going to do about the realm.

Freya wanted her to protect it, Zareal wanted her to destroy it, and Azinne seemed like he didn't really care. Brandi wasn't naïve enough to believe that he didn't have his own motives, but she had no way of even guessing at what they might be. Even thinking about it all made her head ache and she closed her eyes, rubbing her fingers across her forehead. The future of the realm would be determined by whatever she did next, and that responsibility was a weight she had no interest in carrying. But it wasn't like she could just shirk it off onto someone else.

"You seem lost in thought."

Brandi opened her eyes to see Royal standing in front of her. He looked at her with the same smile that Noble always wore and it unnerved Brandi how similar they looked. Their personalities were nothing alike, but looking at Royal was like looking at an older version of Noble with gray eyes. She pressed her lips together as she met his gaze.

"Heard you were looking for me?"

"Seems like I'm always looking for you," he joked, sinking down onto the bench next to her. "Is it finally my turn to talk to you?"

"I guess so," Brandi sighed. "Seems like everyone's requesting an audience nowadays."

"Oh, the woes of being important."

Brandi looked at him and when he met her gaze, she rolled her eyes at him. Royal knew better than anyone just how much Brandi hated being around other people. If she had her way, she and Jack would live in Freya's domain and never talk to anyone but each other again. She knew it wasn't a realistic dream, but it's what she yearned for most days.

"How did you even get here, Royal?" Brandi asked with a sigh, tired already from the conversation they hadn't started yet. She'd just found out about her domain and already she had visitors.

"Wasn't that hard," he said, shrugging. "Your priestesses seem to be searching out those with a connection to you in order to bring them here."

"Are they, now?" Brandi asked, unsure of what to make of that information. When Royal nodded, she decided to tuck the information away for later and lifted an eyebrow at him. "So?" Brandi asked. "What do you want?"

Royal held her gaze for a moment, searching her face as if he were trying to gauge how Brandi would react to his next words. That put her on edge, but she waited in silence as Royal turned away from her, toward the fountain, to collect his words. She watched the flowing water as well and tried to keep her mind from thinking the worst as she prepared herself for whatever Royal would tell her next.

"The gods are getting weaker," Royal said, his voice even as he looked at the fountain. "Can you feel it?"

"No," Brandi said, her head pounding at the thought of what his words would mean for her. "Freya and I aren't really on speaking terms at this point, remember?"

"Well," he sighed, "Freya's never been as good as people make her out to be. And now, you know it for yourself."

Brandi groaned at that and let out a deep breath. She couldn't argue with Royal. In part, because he was right. She'd always known that Freya wasn't to be trusted — she'd seen it in the way Freya had treated everyone else. She'd just always believed Freya when she'd told her she was special, and it was her own mistake for never questioning her. But she saw now just how dark Freya's heart was and just how deeply it could stain her own life. She hadn't spoken to Freya since their argument back in her domain, but a trickle of worry snuck through her thoughts at Royal's words and she wanted to roll her eyes at herself. There was no reason for her to have any concern for Freya, but she couldn't shake the feeling and sighed.

"Try not to beat yourself up about it," Royal said, placing an awkward hand on Brandi's back as she rested her elbows on her knees. "At least you know her for who she is now."

"It is what it is," Brandi said. "It's just embarrassing to think about how long I believed Freya when apparently," she said, cutting her eyes over to him in annoyance, "everyone but me knew the truth."

"We all believe lies when they come from someone we trust."

"I guess."

Silence surrounded them once more, and Brandi let it settle. She wasn't in any rush to discuss the gods, but she wouldn't be able to avoid the conversation forever. Royal had wanted to meet with her for a reason, and Brandi lifted her green eyes up to search his face.

Royal was the opposite of Noble in every meaningful way. Although they had the same face, they were completely different in character. Noble was a flirt and an overprotective brother. He always had a grin ready for anyone who wanted to see it, but he was also a shadow, and it was rare for his true thoughts to ever pass over his lips. He could talk to anyone about anything and never divulge a single detail about himself.

Royal, on the other hand, didn't speak to anyone unless he had to. Otherwise, he kept to himself. Like the true nature of a shader that he was born with, he only spoke to those he found worthy. And when he did, his words centered around things that held meaning to him. It wasn't frivolous banter like Noble was prone to.

Royal was just as handsome as his younger brother, but he downplayed his looks in a way that Noble never would. His silver hair was wild on his head — long bangs falling into his gray eyes — and he preferred the loose fit of baggy jeans and a hoodie compared to the tight-fitting clothes that Noble, and most other shadows, gravitated toward. They were subtle differences, but sometimes it felt like looking at Carna and talking to Lindl — her expectations clashed with her reality. But she couldn't blame either of them for that — it was her own misfortune for having expectations of them in the first place.

"The gods are dying," Royal said, glancing down at Brandi from the corner of his eye. She lifted her eyebrows at his words as his gaze danced over her face, looking for some kind of reaction from her.

"Am I supposed to feel guilty?"

"I don't know how you're supposed to feel," Royal said, shrugging as a dry chuckle left his throat. "But it is something you need to be aware of."

"And why's that?" Brandi huffed. "Freya's responsibilities aren't my problem."

"Because you're the only god left who has full access to their power."

"I don't even know how to use my power."

"You'll learn," Royal stated. "And then you'll decide what you want to do."

"What I want to do?"

Brandi laughed at the words — her anger morphing the sound into something rough that pulled like razor blades from her throat. It was sharp and Royal flinched away from the sound, but she couldn't stop it. The thought of being in control of her own future felt like a sick joke.

"There's no freedom in making a choice that's already been decided."

"What do you mean?"

"I mean that I've already been dragged into this," Brandi said. "There is no choice I can make that ends with me and Jack being left out of whatever the gods are trying to do. So, what point is there in asking me what I want to do now?"

"If that's how you feel, then why did you allow the gods to gift your friends their power?"

"How was I supposed to stop them?" Brandi asked, shaking her head in annoyance. "They're gods! They just do whatever they want."

"And so are you," he said, his words gentle. "So, if not yourself, who are you trying to please?"

"I —"

Brandi's words died on the edge of her lips as she considered Royal's question. Who was she trying to please? Her relationship with Freya was already in shambles and Azinne made it clear enough that his job was nothing more than a game to him. Zareal had been nothing but kind to her, but even with his plans to destroy the realm and everything in it, he'd made it known that she wasn't beholden to his desires in any way. Jack only wanted her to be happy and no one else even registered on her scale of importance. So, if her actions didn't matter to the gods, the time beings, or Jack, then what was she agonizing over? Why did she feel such a crushing weight on her chest whenever she thought about what she should do next?

She scoffed and shook her head as she stared at the fountain.

"I don't know, Royal."

"I suggest you find your answer to that before you search for answers to anything else," he said. "And once you find them, let me know."

"Okay…" Brandi said, narrowing her eyes as she studied Royal and wondered what his plan was. But, as always, his face was unreadable, and he smirked as he waved his hand through the air.

"Don't worry about me," he said, dropping his hand onto the back of the bench behind them. "I'll be fine. You should worry more about your friends."

"Friends?" Brandi asked, her eyebrow quirking as her mind darted to Pine.

"The blond girl?" Royal clarified. "The other vessels."

"You mean Sarah?" Brandi scoffed as she shook her head. "I

wouldn't exactly call us friends."

"Really? I was under the impression you liked her since you've been spending so much time together."

"Freya demanded it."

"Freya holds no power over you now."

"So, you're saying I should just send her to the gods without reason?" Brandi asked.

"No," Royal chuckled. "I'm saying that you should be more aware of those you allow in your space if you aren't going to trust them."

"I never said I didn't trust her," Brandi pointed out. "I said that I wouldn't call us friends. Those are different things."

"How so?"

"I can respect her without liking who she is as a person," Brandi sighed, propping her chin on her hand as she leaned forward, letting her gaze linger on the steady flowing water in front of them. "I think she's loyal for her own reasons, but I wouldn't want to spend my time with her if I didn't have to."

"But you trust her?"

"I trust her," Brandi said, nodding her head. "Now, explain what you meant. Why do I need to worry about her?"

"Not just her," Royal said, shaking his head. "All the vessels. The gods have taken refuge in their souls."

"I know. That makes us gods," Brandi stated, anxiety spreading through her as she thought of what Freya said in her temple. "They gifted their power to us."

"And that comes with a price," Royal pointed out. "You may be fine because Freya has always resided in tandem with you. But your friends are true mortals," he reminded her. "They won't be able to carry the soul of a god within them for long."

"The gods are corrupting them," Brandi whispered, Zareal's words flooding her mind. "But why would they do that?"

"To recover their strength."

"From what?" Brandi asked. "They haven't fought anyone!"

"But their power is fading. Faster now that the time beings have begun to make their move."

"Why though?" Brandi shook her head. "That makes no sense."

"I don't know," Royal said, shrugging. "I only know what Freya knows, and even the gods don't have a reason. But you want my guess?"

"It's better than nothing," Brandi said, nodding her head.

"I think Freya knew this would happen," Royal said. "I think it's why she was so against allowing time into the realm. Everything fades with it, you know? What if the gods aren't as immune to it as they like to believe?"

"You're suggesting the god's power was always fading."

"Yes," Royal said, though Brandi's statement wasn't a question. "And I think that Freya knew this would come, which is why she's been trying to use you. And why she so desperately wants to remove time from the realm."

"It's not about saving her children," Brandi whispered, a deep sigh escaping her as the words settled in her thoughts. "It's about saving herself."

"That's what I think. And I think she was hoping you would never realize that."

"But I did."

"And now she's trying to force your hand by linking the gods to the people you care about. Because if their power fades away —"

"Then their vessels will fade with them," Brandi sighed, piecing together Freya's actions with Zareal's words. "And because their souls will be corrupted, they won't be able to return to the flow of time."

"Exactly," Royal said, pointing at her. "I could be wrong about that, but I don't think that I am."

"I don't think you are either," Brandi whispered, sliding her fingers over her the neat parts in her scalp.

"And depending on what you decide to do, the realm may collapse regardless of if you help Freya or not." He looked up at the sky as if they could see Rothe's sun or Asari's moon from where they sat. "The realm is already starting to shift in response to their absence. Or haven't you noticed?"

"Not really," Brandi admitted. "I've been a bit overwhelmed with finding out that I'm a god and a time being."

"Fair enough," Royal laughed. "But when you get back to the surface," he said, pointing towards the sky, "take a look around. Things are a-changing, Brandi," he said, his voice sinking as he turned to hold her gaze, "and not for the better."

"I'll keep that in mind," she said, nodding. "But I can only deal with one problem at a time."

"True. But you're not alone," he reminded her. "At the very least, I'll support you."

"Even if I decide to side with Zareal and oppose the gods?"

Royal smiled at her, but he said nothing. Brandi wondered what his silence could mean, but she didn't push the topic and let her head fall back as she sank lower in her seat. Her head rested against the back of the bench as she looked up at the galaxies above them.

She wondered how many of them Azinne and Zareal had visited — how many of them had perished like Zena's home in their wake and how many of them had been born under their watch. Both of them had mentioned there being other gods and Zena's people was proof enough that whole words existed outside of the one she knew. Looking at the shifting stars above them made her want to know more.

It made her want to leave behind her realm to be someone unimportant in another one.

Before she could dwell on what that would be like though, three soft knocks resonated throughout the courtyard, and she turned to see Jack standing with Pine and another woman. She had generous curves draped in a long white sundress, a short afro, and the same pale gold eyes of the priestesses. She smiled when their eyes met and bowed her head with respect.

"I've brought your lover as requested."

"And me," Pine chimed in with a grin. "Couldn't let them leave me behind."

"Of course not," Brandi said, letting a small laugh slip beneath her breath as she pushed herself to her feet and looked toward the priestess. "Thank you for bringing them here."

"Of course," she said, her face beaming with joy. "I'm happy to serve."

With that, she stepped back inside the building and disappeared down the hall. Pine looked around, her hazel eyes wide as she wandered into the courtyard and Brandi all but ran into Jack's open arms, melting against him. It didn't matter that it had only been a few days since she'd left him with Najé to meet Pine in Rothe's outskirts — it felt like a lifetime had passed since then. She tightened her arms around his waist, and he placed a kiss to her forehead as he leaned back to look at her, concern drawing his eyebrows together as he kept his voice low.

"You okay?"

"Yeah," she breathed, burying her face in his shoulder. "Just a lot I need to tell you."

"Again?"

She coughed out a laugh as she held onto him, but she understood how he must feel. The last time she'd had a lot to tell him, she'd had to admit to him that she was a half-god, half-time being love child that Freya had kept secret from the gods. Now she would have to tell him that she'd met her father and that he wasn't the villain that Azinne and Freya had made him out to be. Sure, he wanted to destroy the realm, but after everything she'd learned of Freya, she kind of did too.

"Okay," he sighed. "Later?"

"Later," Brandi nodded, pulling back from him and following his gaze to where he stared at Royal. He stood by the bench they'd been sitting on with his hands in the pocket of his hoodie and a blank expression on his face.

"That's Royal," Brandi answered, placing her hand on Jack's arm.

"He's Noble's older brother."

"Why is he here?"

"You remember back in Asari's domain when Sal said that someone wanted to meet with me? Said we go back further than the gods?" Jack gave an imperceptible nod as his brown eyes darted over to her face before returning to Royal. "Well," Brandi said, "he's who I was meeting."

"Does Noble know about this?"

"Yeah," Brandi nodded. "They met while we were in Freya's domain. He was here to give me an update on what's happening with the gods."

"An update on the…" Jack's words trailed off as his eyebrows shot up and his eyes narrowed on Royal. "How would he know anything about the gods?"

"Well," Brandi said, drawing out the word as she tried to find the words to explain who Royal was. "You know the story of creation, right? When Freya is thrown from the shader and Rothe gets angry?"

"Yeah?"

"He's the shader," she said, pointing to him.

"Say what now?" Jack asked.

"He's the shader," Brandi repeated. "Or rather, his soul is that of the shader. It's a long story, but basically, Freya always sends his soul back into the realm to be born as a human."

"It's miserable really," Royal chimed in, stepping closer to them. "I've been reincarnating since the beginning of time. And every time the goddess is reborn into the mortal realm, my memories of previous lives come flooding back."

"So, when you said that you and your informant go back further than the gods…"

"I have Freya's soul and she knew the shader before she knew the gods."

"Holy Rothe," Jack whispered.

"That's…" Pine shook her head. "That's wild, raindrop."

"It's a lot," Royal chuckled, "but don't hurt yourself trying to figure it all out right now. Let's head over to the restaurant and grab a drink first," he said, turning his gaze back to Brandi. "There's still a little more I need to tell you."

"What could it possibly be now?" Brandi asked, her shoulders sagging with exhaustion.

"It's about Crown," Royal said, "and what we discussed about the shaders before."

Royal's gray eyes drifted to the exit and Brandi followed his gaze to where a dark-skinned man leaned against the wall. His skin was darker than anything Brandi had ever seen. It had the same inky black hue as a shader's fur, and he wore a simple white pullover with shorts and sandals. His skin was flawless, and when he waved to Royal, she could see that his nails were just as dark as his skin and sharp at the tips. She had no doubts that they could rip through the flesh of mortals like that of a true shader. She stared at him in shock and Royal grinned.

"Your shaders have learned to shapeshift," he said. "And they're all abandoning Freya's domain."

CHAPTER SEVENTEEN

When a princess learns to protect her people rather than her throne, she has understood what it means to be queen.

— Fina the First | Queen of Queens, Volume 3

ROTHE'S DOMAIN — THE QUEEN'S TOWER
2 DAYS BEFORE THE OPENING CEREMONY

"Alright," Sal sighed, "this is it."

Sarah glanced up at him from where they stood outside the garden on the thirteenth floor of the tower. She'd been surprised to learn just how robust the tower was when she'd first arrived. Each of the floors were unique in their own way and she'd been amazed at how advanced the construction of it was — surpassing even the most intricate designs in Lindl's domain. Mara had given her the grand tour during one of their lessons, explaining to her how each level served a different purpose.

The lower floors were meant for the public and functioned as a hub for business. Meeting rooms and banquet halls could be rented out for a hefty price, but the rooms were no less ornate than any of the others she'd seen. There was also an office of general affairs that was frequented by businessmen, local leaders, and those who wished to seek an audience with the queen or council. There was always a steady flow of people through the building and there were elevators that could be used by the public. Sarah had also learned that there was no access to the higher levels of the tower from the lower floors.

It was only accessible by transport pods that were custom made for that purpose. They required an official royal access code to operate, and no other pods had the software that was required to access the lines of code the royal pods used. Mara's face had lit up as she ranted about the transport pods and how they worked, and Sarah had been more than happy to listen to her. Since their conversation in the library, Sarah had been putting forth a significant amount of effort to improve her social etiquette and the awareness she had of herself and others. She noticed that both Mara and Sal seemed to have more patience with her, but they were the only people who seemed to notice the shift in her, and she could admit the disappointment she felt that Noble hadn't noticed as well.

She hadn't been able to forget the moment she'd witnessed between him and Pine in the ballroom. The moment haunted her with an unrelenting vengeance and her thoughts defaulted to it more often than she would like them to — at every moment where she was left alone with her thoughts, she would see them in her mind. The way his hands had trailed across her body and the sounds he'd made when she'd clung to him. For whatever reason, her mind enjoyed torturing her with the thoughts of her own tryst with Noble, and how he'd been in complete control the entire time. The inevitable comparisons brought insecurities along with them and she found herself running from her own mind, doing her best to focus on the obstacles that lay in front of her — the biggest one being her afternoon tea with Grace.

Sal glanced down at her now, his eyes giving her one last once over before opening the door, his eyes lingering on her hair. She'd taken the scissors and chopped off her long hair that morning. It had been an impulse of rage and when she'd looked at the finished product in the mirror, she'd been equal parts horrified and proud of herself. Sal had been less than pleased when he'd entered her room that morning, trailing behind Mara. She'd let out a burst of laughter, but he'd groaned and dropped his face into his hands.

"Gods," he sighed, stepping forward and flipping a hand through what was left of her blond strands. "What were you thinking? You're entering into social warfare and you chop off your best asset?"

"At least she finally did something worth noticing," Mara pointed out, walking over to Sarah and taking away the scissors that were still locked in a death grip at her side.

"Can you do something about it?"

Mara glanced at Sal before rolling her eyes and reaching out to grab Sarah by the shoulder. She spun her around once, before smirking and pushing her towards the bathroom.

"Can I do something about it?" She repeated, mocking his words and shaking her head as she dropped the lid down on the toilet seat in the bathroom and guided Sarah to sit down on top of it. "Who does he think I am?"

Sarah hadn't considered what the aftermath of her decision would be, but relief washed over her as Mara started making smaller, more precise cuts to her hair. She had a gentle touch and tears welled in Sarah's eyes as she studied the empty wall in front of her.

"Thank you."

"I'm not doing this for you," Mara said. "But, you're welcome."

"It doesn't matter," Sarah sighed. "I appreciate the kindness all the same, whatever your personal motives might be."

Mara paused then to look Sarah in the eye before shrugging and going back to her task. She worked in silence for most of the time, but as Mara worked on her bangs, they made eye contact and she finally spoke.

"So," she said, breaking the silence, "what made you do this?"

"Truly?" Sarah asked, lifting her shoulders in a tiny shrug and offering a weak smile. "I couldn't tell you."

"So, you just woke up this morning and decided to chop off all your hair?"

"More or less," Sarah answered, choosing to keep her meeting with Pine to herself. She didn't know if the others knew about Grace or not, but she figured it was time to start taking their advice and keeping her own secrets. There was no reason for her to divulge to Mara that she'd met with Pine. She didn't need to know that since seeing Pine with Noble, she couldn't think about anything other than what it had felt like for him to kiss her in that bar in Lindl's domain — that she was consumed with thoughts of Noble and how much she didn't know about him — that she was jealous of Pine because she'd been able to satisfy him in a way Sarah hadn't even known was possible. It was a jumble of thoughts in her head and a storm of emotions in her chest — she felt like she would choke on them if she tried to force them into words.

Mara watched her, but she kept her face blank and said nothing else. Instead, she gave Sarah a tiny smile before pulling away from her and pointing to the mirror.

"You're done."

Sarah stood up and looked at herself in the mirror. Somehow, Mara had managed to style what was left of her hair. It was a blunt bob that brushed her shoulders with wispy bangs that framed her face. It changed everything about her look and Sarah's eyes widened as she lifted a hand to her hair. She felt like she was seeing herself for the first time, and she grinned.

"I can't believe you managed to save this."

"I can do anything," Mara stated, rolling her eyes and placing her hand on the bathroom door. "Now take a shower and wash what's left of your hair. We have to get you ready."

Sarah did as she'd been instructed and now stood in front of the door to the garden draped in a silver dress that hung off her shoulders and brushed the floor, with deep blue gemstones hanging from her ears and wrapped around her wrist. It was a simple look, but Mara swore that it made her look elegant with her new cut and her words alone are what made Sarah feel prepared to face Grace. Even Sal had been forced to give her a nod of approval when he'd seen her final look, and he smirked now as he held open the door to the garden.

"Try not to make a fool of yourself, cousin."

The words were whispered as she walked by, but she didn't respond to him — didn't let his words unnerve her. After speaking with them that morning as she got dressed, and listening to Mara as she did her makeup, Sarah understood the meeting with Grace for what it was meant to be.

This tea party would determine whether or not Grace saw her as a competent rival or not.

While both Sal and Mara agreed that it was a situation that needed to be handled with care, they had opposing ideas on what should be done. Mara was of the mindset to have Sarah prove herself in this meeting. She'd given both of them a sharp reminder that soon Sarah would be put on display for the entirety of the realm and that if she couldn't handle herself in a private conversation, she would be an utter failure at the ball. Sal had been careful in disagreeing with her, but he'd stood his ground.

He'd advocated for Sarah to show her weakness and coerce Grace into believing she was no threat at all so that she would focus her energies on destroying the other princesses entering the bid. It was a risky choice, but if she could make an ally out of Grace rather than an enemy, then the greater plan Brandi and the rebels had in place would be easier to execute. Mara had no rebuttal to that, so Sal's plan had been the one they'd decided on.

It hadn't bothered Sarah in the moment, but as she followed Sal through the garden, taking in the large windows that drenched the room in a warm light, the bright flowers blooming in shades of red, yellow, and orange that filled the room with scents of honey, she felt disappointment hovering over her like a dark cloud.

She understood why Sal had a complete lack of faith in her, but it didn't make the sentiment sting any less. She tried to bottle the anger that came with it, but it was harder to do when she noticed Grace sitting at a simple table that had been placed in the center of the garden. The light flooding the room caught in her bright red ringlets that were pinned back from her face. She was dressed in a short purple dress with cutouts on the side and back that revealed her light brown skin. She wore golden studs in her ears and a matching chain with her name on it around her neck. Her eyes were focused on the flowers beside her as she sipped at her tea, her gloss leaving a light pink imprint on the cup as she sat it back down. It wasn't until they'd reached the table and Sal cleared his throat that her attention snapped to them. Her face split into a grin as Sal bowed and stepped aside to allow her to see Sarah.

"Allow me to introduce Sarah Rothens, first daughter of the late second princess, Venetia," he said, using her full title. It still made her tense up whenever she heard it, but she returned Grace's smile and stepped forward, keeping her eyes level with hers as she addressed her. Mara had warned her not to bow her head, even if Grace was of a higher station than hers. It would be perceived as disrespectful, but since her first meeting with Grace had been as equals, this would be her only chance to ensure it remained that way. If she dipped her head, it would be the equivalent of acknowledging her superiority. And in the bid, that could be fatal. So, instead, she stepped over to the chair that Sal pulled out for her.

"It's nice to see you again, Grace."

"You too, Sarah!"

Her words were bright, but her hazel eyes were sharp, and they sent chills racing down Sarah's spine. It made her glad that she'd taken Mara's advice and she straightened her spine as she reached for the tea Sal poured for her.

"I'm glad you sent an attendant to set this up," she said, glancing over to Sal as he moved to stand behind her. Grace's attendant stood behind her, dressed in a plain black dress and flat shoes, her hair was pulled back in a tight bun and her brown skin shone in the sunlight. She was beautiful, but she averted her eyes to the ground when she met Sarah's gaze. It made Sarah curious about her, but she said nothing and offered a simple nod to Sal as he stepped behind her.

It was a minor thing, but she was sure it was something that Grace noticed — giving respect to an attendant and not a princess was unheard of and Sarah took a deep breath as she picked up her tea, holding Grace's gaze over the edge of her cup as she sipped from it.

"I am as well. But," Grace said, a smirk playing on her lips, "why don't we avoid playing these social games and get straight to business, shall we?"

"Business?" Sarah asked, her heart jumping at Grace's words. This was not in the plan she'd discussed with either Sal or Mara.

"I'm not trying to win the bid," Grace stated.

"You're not?"

"No," she said, shaking her head and crossing her arms as she leaned them on the table. "I'm trying to destroy the crown. And I called you out here because I'd like your help to do it."

Sarah let Grace's words linger in the air as an uncomfortable silence settled around them. She kept her eyes trained on the table between them, and she didn't let her gaze drift from it as she tried to catalog every thought that raced through her mind. Of all the things she'd been expecting when she met with Grace Bertanal for tea that day, it wasn't for her to declare that she had no intention of taking the throne. She considered letting her eyes dart over to Sal, but she knew better than to do something like that.

She didn't want to give Grace the impression that she couldn't navigate this situation without her advisor, and she didn't want to give Sal any more reason to doubt her capabilities. That, and Sarah wanted to believe Grace's words, but she knew better than to take everything she heard at face value. That had been one of the first lessons Mara drilled into her head — not that Sarah needed the reminder.

People lie.

It was a fact of life and dishonesty was the only sure thing she could expect from the queen's court. It was the nature of ruling over a queendom — most people weren't able to handle the truth. And even if they could, most of them wouldn't know what to do with it. It was something that Sarah learned for herself at a young age when she'd been searching for help after her parents had been returned to the gods. Even in the midst of begging for food and trying to find somewhere safe for them to sleep, she hadn't dared to tell people the truth when they asked why she and Jamie were alone. She could admit their parents had been returned to the gods, but when anyone questioned her further than that, she'd lied through her teeth.

Because even when she told the truth, no one believed her. They didn't believe that she was the daughter of a disgraced princess and that the queen would be so cruel as to hunt down her own niece. It had been humiliating to watch people laugh in her face, and it was a worse experience to know that people were laughing behind her back. She'd embarrassed herself enough already by coming to the Queen's Tower without knowing anything about the monarchy or the bid — she had no desire to add to that humiliation by putting her blind faith into the words of someone she met less than a full day ago. Especially when that trust could lead to her standing before the gods and explaining to them why she'd failed as a vessel, destroying any plans Brandi had for the queendom.

And, if she was being honest with herself, she was getting irritated with the amount of people who treated her as if she were an imbecile. She'd managed to make it through twenty-two years in the mortal realm on her own, while taking care of Jamie and carving out a place for them. It hadn't been extravagant, but it had been secure. And if Brandi hadn't come along, she'd be the life partner of the most influential man in Asari's outskirts. She'd made the absolute best of a terrible situation and she would do it again.

She'd done it on her own then, and she'd do it again now. She was more than capable of deciding things on her own, and she was done relying on the strength of others and hoping things worked out. So, when Sarah lifted her head to meet Grace's gaze again, it was with a smile.

"I don't believe you," Sarah said, her voice even and devoid of any emotion. "And I'm insulted that you would think to invite me here with the intention of fooling me into believing something so completely asinine."

Grace's eyebrows shot up in surprise and she leaned back in her seat as she studied Sarah. She could feel Grace's eyes boring into the side of her face, but she averted her gaze to the skyline just outside the window.

The tower was the tallest building in the center of fragment 10316 in Rothe's domain, so no matter which direction the windows faced, the skyline and people below were always visible. It had been uncomfortable for Sarah at first to feel as if she were looking down on people, but she'd grown used to it over the last few weeks and she understood now that it was a necessary reminder. One of her tragic flaws had always been her desire to be anyone else — to be someone unnoticeable who could drift into any crowd and become lost to it. And that hope had driven her to lose herself.

Never again, though.

"I think you misunderstood me," Grace said, laughter tinging her words.

"I misunderstood nothing," Sarah shot back, her words sharp as she refused to look at Grace. "Unless you can point to the truth in your words, I have no intention of believing them."

"I'm serious," Grace said, leaning forward. "I don't want the crown."

"No one enters the bid to lose it."

Sarah's words hung in the air as she met Grace's widened eyes. It was clear from her reaction that she'd expected Sarah to believe her without much convincing, and Sarah couldn't blame her. Grace had her complete trust yesterday when she'd followed her out of the ballroom and laughed with her in the courtyard without any reservations. But it was a new day and Sarah wasn't as ignorant as she was before. Her previous actions could no longer be used to determine her future ones and she sipped on her tea as she waited for Grace to respond.

"I don't need to win it," Grace said after a moment. "I don't even actually exist."

"And what story will you spin for me now?" Sarah chuckled, the sound soft and cold as she swiped a strand of hair behind her ear. "Do I look such a fool to you that I could be led to believe something other than what my own eyes are seeing? What my own ears are hearing?"

"I would never dare to call you a fool," Grace said, rolling her eyes, her own patience wearing thin. "But you might be a bit naïve to the things right in front of you."

"Am I?" Sarah quirked a brow upward as she set her teacup back on her saucer. "Then do enlighten me," Sarah said, waving her hand between them. "Tell me the story of a woman who refutes her own existence."

Grace's lips twitched at that and she shook her head, a deep sigh escaping her as she laced her fingers on the table and straightened her shoulders. Her hazel eyes darted around the garden, refusing to hold Sarah's gaze or meet Sal's — who stood behind her as Grace's attendant did behind her. But after a moment, she relaxed and stood from her seat.

"Why don't we walk as we talk?"

"I'd rather not."

"But —"

"No," Sarah said, standing from her seat as Sal arrived to pull out her seat. She stood and offered a weak smile to Grace, who had the decency to force back a small one even though she struggled to disguise her disappointment.

"Thank you for inviting me out today," Sarah said. "I'll take my leave now. I do hope we're able to speak again another time, so I believe it's my turn to send my attendant for you, yes?"

Grace forced her smile wider and nodded.

"Yes. I'll look forward to it."

"I'm sure," Sarah said, before breezing through the garden toward the exit. The door had barely closed behind them when Sal leaned forward to whisper in her ear.

"What was that about?"

"You need to contact Brandi," she said, keeping her eyes on the hallway in front of her.

"Because of Grace?" Sal asked, his words coated in both annoyance and incredulity. "Why would I bother Brandi over something as trivial as that?"

"I don't think she was lying," Sarah admitted.

"Clearly you've gotten better at it yourself then," Sal scoffed, a smirk playing at his lips as he studied Sarah. She'd hadn't been able to hide any of her emotions when she'd arrived, but she'd been as cool as Asari's night in front of Grace and the smug look on his face told Sarah that he was impressed, even if just a little. And she would accept that as the win it was. It wasn't until they were outside the door to her room that he stopped and she turned to look at him. "Alright, cousin," he said. "I'll pass along your message."

"Thank you," she said.

"And what do you want me to tell her?"

"Tell her I spoke with Pine," she said, her eyes narrowing at the memory. "And let her know that the rebels aren't the only ones trying to destroy the queendom."

CHAPTER EIGHTEEN

Mortals are dangerous because we carry within us the capacity for change — take caution so that it does not consume you. For if you forget who you are, it will not matter who you become.

— The Wisdom of JaZhire, The Beloved | Log of the 13th Head Priestess

---

BRANDI'S DOMAIN — TEMPLE OF THE TIME GODDESS
2 DAYS BEFORE THE OPENING CEREMONY

"Where in the god's realm have you been?"

Brandi threw the words across the room as she walked out onto the deck built at the back of Remy's restaurant. The restaurant itself had already begun filling up with people who had the same pale gold eyes as Remy and Zena, and the moment she'd walked in Remy had placed her manager in charge and guided them through a back room to the space outside. Similar to the courtyard in the temple, there were black and white flowers blooming by the edge of the deck, where a few steps led down to soft grass and a small yard before being cut off by a tall fence. It was quiet in the back — the growing noise of the restaurant replaced by the clinking of glasses against wood as Russ placed his glass on the giant round table in front of him.

He'd looked up at them when Brandi spoke, and Russ's eyes widened in surprise before a grin split his face and he pushed himself to his feet, his palms placed on the table as his chair clattered to the ground.

"I'm so glad to see you guys!"

Jack and Brandi shared a look with each other before Pine's giggle cut through the air and she sauntered over to the table. She picked up one of the empty glasses sitting in front of him and shook her head.

"Seems like he's started without us," Pine said, glancing up at Russ. "How rude."

"Oh. Sorry. I. Um." Russ stumbled over his words as Pine looked up at him from under her eyelashes. His face flushed a light pink and Pine laughed as he struggled to pull out the seat next to him. She slid into it before placing her elbow on the table and her chin in her palm.

"Thank you," she said, grinning up at Russ. "You going to get me a drink now?"

"Yes!" Russ said, backing away to the small bar on the other side of the deck. "I'll be right back."

"That's my cue," Remy said, nodding at both Jack and Brandi before walking over to the bar that Russ waited at. It was much smaller than the one inside — it was clearly meant for entertaining her own guests, but it was just as well stocked. Remy smiled at Russ as he fumbled with his words before shushing him and instructing him to just step aside while she worked. She moved with a simple grace as she prepared a purple drink in a clear glass for Pine. Russ was careful in bringing it back to the table when she was done and as Brandi sank into the seat next to her, she could smell how sweet it was from where she sat.

"I'll take something stronger than that," Brandi called over to Remy.

"Sweet?" She asked, lifting an eyebrow in Brandi's direction.

"She doesn't do sweet," Jack answered for her, walking over to the bar. "She prefers something that goes straight to the chest. I'll take one too."

"A man who knows his woman's order," Remy said, a grin pulling at her lips as Jack approached. "I respect that. Give me a minute."

While Jack waited by the bar, Brandi watched Pine torture Russ with flirty looks and let her thoughts roam without any real direction. When Jack returned, she accepted the drink he brought over and took her time sipping from it. Royal and Crown decided to stay behind in the courtyard to discuss the message Crown came to deliver. Apparently, the shaders were growing restless — all the shaders in Freya's domain had abandoned it for Carna's plains. It wasn't something most people would notice, but it wasn't something that Crown could miss, and it unsettled him enough to report back to Royal.

They'd invited Brandi to stay for the full conversation, but she'd opted to go with Pine and Jack over to the restaurant — mostly because she didn't think she had the bandwidth to hear any more information that would require her to do something about it. Royal had already pointed out that she was no longer bound by the will of the gods. Every action she made now was based upon her own desires, and somehow, that was more intimidating than needing to do what someone else wanted of her.

Between that realization, meeting Zareal, and figuring out why Freya wanted to remove time from the realm to begin with, she was tired. More so than she'd ever been when she'd worked for the queendom as a shadow, and she didn't want to commit any more of her time to thinking about her problems. For once, she just wanted to get drunk, take a hot shower, and have a few hours to let Jack do what he wanted with her. They were simple enough things and, as Royal had been succinct in pointing out, she had no other whims to serve at this point other than her own.

So, she took a deep drink from the glass in front of her and let out a loud sigh as the liquid slid down her throat, warming her from the inside out. She closed her eyes and sat with the feeling before opening them and looking around the table. Remy placed a refill on her left before taking a seat on the right side of Jack. They all looked at her as if expecting her to say something, and she held in the groan that wanted to pour out of her as she realized she would have longer to wait before she could drink enough to forget herself. She didn't want to think about the problems of the realm anymore, but that didn't stop her from turning to Russ with curious eyes.

"So?" Brandi asked. "You going to answer the question? Where have you been?"

"What do you mean?"

"You weren't in Freya's domain with us," Brandi stated. "Where were you?"

"When Glenn was gathering our forces to follow you, she instructed me to stay behind with almost a third of our people and guide the rebels to Rothe's domain," he explained. "She said we would be making a move against the queendom once you got Jack back and that we needed to be ready." Russ sighed at that and tightened his grip on the glass mug in front of him. "I couldn't have imagined that she would just abandon us like she did."

Brandi scoffed at the thought of her mentor and what she'd done. After Rothe stripped her of his power and the honor of being his vessel, Freya had condemned her to a lifetime of atoning for her betrayal of Rothe and his demands. There had been no room for misunderstandings and Brandi wasn't surprised that Glenn's actions were seen as her abandoning the rebels — she and Patches had disappeared long before the battle at Freya's temple was over. Several of the rebels had searched for the leader in the clearing and Brandi had listened as Najé did her best to soothe their anxieties. But it wasn't easy for them to accept what happened, especially when Glenn, Brandi, and the gods themselves were the only ones who knew the truth.

"You unhappy with the new leadership?" Jack asked, drawing everyone's attention to him.

"Of course not. It was just unexpected," Russ answered with a wry smile and a shake of his head. "And I'd been carrying out Glenn's final orders when I got the news of what happened in Freya's domain. Once I did, I joined squad black in spreading the word of what happened and locating the last of the rebels," he paused and chuckled. "I only found this place because I ran into Royal on the surface."

"You guys just let everyone in, huh?" Brandi asked, glancing over at Remy.

"No," she laughed, setting aside her own cup before answering. "Just the people who are connected to you."

"And he made the cut?" Brandi asked, jerking her thumb toward Russ.

"You're connected to more people than you think," Remy pointed out. "You've affected the lives of more people than you realize."

Brandi considered asking Remy what she meant by that, but decided to let it go. In truth, she didn't want to know. It was enough to realize that her actions directly affected the entire realm without needing to put names to faces. She preferred not to think of people as actual people. It made things easier for her that way.

"You know what?" Brandi said, leaning back in her seat and sipping from her cup. "It doesn't matter where you've been," she said, looking back at Russ. "You're here now. So, we press onward."

"Meaning?" Pine asked, leaning forward to gaze up at Brandi. "What's up next for us, raindrop?"

It was a simple enough question, but it was one that sent ripples of panic racing along Brandi's skin, and she clenched her fingers around the glass she held. She'd never liked the way it felt when people looked at her as if she had all the answers. She never did, and it grated on her nerves that others were always so willing to pass off every one of their problems to her — as if her shoulders were capable of carrying more weight than theirs. She wondered if that's how the gods felt, too. If it was, she could understand why Carna never answered prayers and why Asari didn't give out blessings. It felt like more of a burden than anything else and she wished that more people had the mindset that Zena did — that she was meant to be worshipped as a goddess, not treated like a genie.

But as she looked at Pine and around the table, she recognized the fact that she was no different. That, had any one of them sat in her position, she would turn her eyes onto them with the same expectations. So, instead of continuing to ask questions that had no answers — like why she had to be the one who carried the burdens of the realm — Brandi smirked down into Pine's hazel eyes with a confidence she didn't feel.

"Next," she said, throwing back the last of her drink and slamming the glass on the table, "we finish what we started. Get me in touch with Noble," she said, looking at Russ who was startled at the order, but began moving to do what Brandi asked. "We have moves to make."

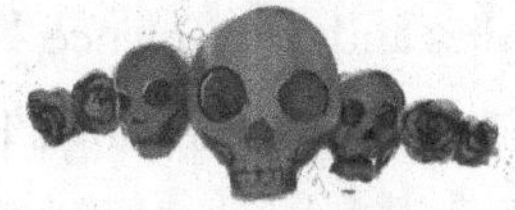

"This was not a call I was expecting."

Russ laughed and shrugged as he tossed the hologram of Noble into the center of the table. He'd used the original network connected to the piercings Terra had given them back at their house to call him. Brandi had used it a few times before, so she wasn't surprised when they got a perfect visual of Noble and the chair he was leaning back in. He looked to be sitting in one of the dorm rooms provided for the shadows at the tower. Sal stood behind him, leaning against the wall, and he offered a half-hearted wave to the rest of them.

"I'm disappointed," Pine said, letting a smirk play at her lips as she watched Noble. "Here I am, and you don't even notice me?"

Noble's eyes darted to Pine and a grin split his face as he sat up.

"Hey, Pine. I didn't know you were there."

"Jealous?" She teased.

"A little," he chuckled, letting his eyes rove over her face. He didn't say anything else and Brandi wondered if he was jealous that she was here with the rest of them while he was stuck in the tower with Sarah, or if he wanted Pine to be there with him. She'd never seen him focus so much on a singular person, and she'd be lying if she said she didn't find it interesting.

"I didn't realize you two knew each other," Brandi said, drawing Pine's gaze over to her.

"We don't really," Pine said, throwing a smirk her way. "But you know how it is. Warm bodies and convenience," she said, flicking her wrist through the air as if she were discussing a borrowed jacket. "We're basically strangers."

"Ouch," Noble said, feigning a wince. "Just ignore my feelings."

"You're a big boy," Pine giggled. "You'll survive."

"What's this call for, Green?" Noble asked, refocusing his thoughts away from Pine and over to Brandi. "I'm guessing it's not just to catch up."

"No," Brandi said, setting her drink down on the table and leaning forward. "We need to discuss a few things."

"Great timing, then," Noble said, taking his feet off the desk in front of him and leaning forward as well. "I was just about to report back to you, anyway. There's a lot that's been happening around here," he said, shaking his head. "I don't know if Blondie's going to survive the bid."

"What makes you say that?" Brandi asked, glancing around the room. "Where is she anyway?"

"Practicing the dance for the opening ceremony with Cedric," Noble sighed. "She is struggling to nail that turn. And it doesn't help her odds that Asuna and Cazie already have consorts," Noble stated. "And the council has been having more meetings lately that haven't been reported," he explained. "My guess? They're already starting the deliberations on who to crown queen."

"How's that possible?" Russ asked, his eyes wide as he leaned forward. "The opening ceremony isn't for another two days. How can they have already completed the campaign and begun deliberations?"

"My guess is their fathers arranged suitors," Brandi sighed. "So, they already know who they're planning to vote for."

"Is that such a bad thing?" Pine shrugged. "It makes sense if they want their daughters to take the throne, doesn't it? It's not like they didn't know they would have to do this one day."

"True," Noble said. "But it breaks the rules of the bid."

"Says who?" Pine asked.

"Fina the First," Noble answered. "The bid is supposed to be held with each princess finding her own consorts. They're meant to be chosen out of love, not duty. But with how the last bid ended, I'm not surprised that the royal family is trying to bend the rules even further."

"Leia should've never been queen," Russ said, glaring at the table. "She'll be the degradation of our entire society."

"I still don't see how this is a problem," Pine shrugged. "The princess will just have to find her own consorts, right? It can't be that hard."

"Maybe not for you," Noble said, a smirk pulling at his lips. "But I'm betting that Blondie will find it significantly more difficult."

"I guess," Pine sighed, letting the topic drop. Brandi couldn't imagine Sarah being able to find a single suitor on her own, let alone four of them. She may have some luck with finding an Asarian consort since she managed to find a partner once before, but it would be a near impossible task for anyone to be able to acquire four consorts fast enough to challenge the other two. She knew it wasn't going to be easy for Sarah to win, but she hadn't expected it to be outright impossible. She'd hoped that her bid would buy them enough time to create more dissent within the queendom. The rebellion had been little more than a myth when Glenn led it. And if they didn't want the queendom to descend into complete anarchy when they destroyed it, they needed a new queen the people could support. But if the bid was going to end before it even began, they wouldn't have time for her original plan — they would have to do something at the opening ball.

"What about Riné and Grace?" Brandi asked. "Are they scheming too?"

"Riné isn't," Noble said, shaking his head. "I don't even think she's planning to enter the bid."

"Wow," Brandi breathed. "You knew about this, Sal?"

"I'd heard whispers of it," Sal shrugged. "I'm not too surprised though. She won't even be of age for a few more months, so it's clear the council hasn't chosen her, isn't it? And if Riné doesn't want to risk her life for a throne they don't want her to have, who are we to convince her otherwise?"

"True," Brandi hummed. "And Grace?"

"She's an interesting one," Sal said, stepping forward with a grin. "Sarah met with her and asked that I send you a message." Brandi's eyebrows lifted in surprise, and Sal chuckled. "I felt the same way."

"What's the message?"

Sal took a few minutes to recount the meeting Sarah and Grace had in the garden and Brandi listened with a singular focus, her face blank as she processed what Sal was telling them. When his story came to a close, he waited a moment before lifting an eyebrow at her.

"Sarah believes Grace is telling the truth."

"What's your opinion of her?" Brandi asked.

"I don't know," Sal said with a shrug. "She seemed sincere, but you know about how much that's worth around here."

"True," Brandi agreed, nodding her head. She was silent for a moment and could feel the eyes of everyone else boring into her skin. She didn't enjoy the feeling, but she didn't let it distract her either. There were only two options that were laid out before them — either she would trust Sarah's intuition and adjust their plans, or she wouldn't. It would be easy to ignore Sarah's words and continue on with their plan to overtake the queendom as it was. But it would be foolish of her to not consider all the information that was presented to her. And if Sarah was right, that meant there was a faction other than theirs working against the queendom, and that could create problems if they weren't careful.

"You told me that you trusted the blond girl, didn't you?"

Brandi whipped around to see Royal walking through the door. He leaned against the wall as he watched Brandi with curious eyes. She felt as if his gaze cut through her more than the others did — like he was trying to read her mind rather than determine what her next actions would be, and it made her muscles tense as she held his gaze.

"But don't let me interrupt you," he said, waving his hand toward the table. "I just got here."

"But what are you —"

Brandi's words were cut off as Shian walked in through the door beside Royal. He offered a weak smile to everyone at the table, but Brandi didn't care. She launched herself at him with a guttural scream, her hands reaching for his throat as she lunged at him. Her mind had the singular focus of choking the light out of him and smashing his head into the wall until it popped like a balloon, but an arm caught around her waist, and it felt like she'd run into a brick wall. Shian flinched back at her as she fought against the restraint that was holding her back. It wasn't until she lifted her gaze that she realized Jack had his arm wrapped around her.

"Let me go!"

"Chill, Bee," he said, setting her back in her chair. "I got this."

Without another word, Jack approached Shian. Royal slid out of Jack's way and before Shian could open his mouth to utter an apology for handing Jack over to Bert in Lindl's domain, Jack's fist connected with Shian's ribcage. His eyes bulged as all the air in his body was forced out of his lungs and he folded like a lawn chair. Before he could hit the ground though, Jack caught him by the sides of his face and drove his knee into Shian's nose before tossing him aside onto the wooden planks of the deck. Blood seeped from Shian's nose, and he groaned, rolling onto his back and Jack stepped over to him, placing his boot on his throat as he glared down at Shian.

"Do you know how easy it would be for me to send you to the gods?"

Shian whimpered at Jack's words. Tears streaked from his eyes and mixed with the blood from his busted lip and bloody nose, and he tried to shake his head as he looked up at Jack. He added pressure to Shian's throat, and his eyes bulged once more as his oxygen cut off. He grasped at Jack's foot before he pissed himself. Jack frowned at him before shaking his head and letting his foot up.

"You're a disgrace," he said. "You're too pathetic to meet the gods."

Shian looked at them — shame crossing his face as he looked at the embarrassment and disgust written on Russ's face. He crawled to his feet and hobbled back inside. Royal watched him depart before walking over to the bar and helping himself to a drink. Remy watched Jack with narrowed eyes, but she didn't move from her seat as he returned to the table. Instead, she just cut a glare over to him.

"Was that necessary?" Remy asked. "You've created a mess."

"You have my apologies," Jack said. The words lacked any kind of sincerity and Remy sighed before sipping from her glass again.

"Why was he even here?" Brandi asked. "Russ is one thing, but why would Shian have been brought here?"

"I believe all the rebels are being invited into your domain," Remy said, letting her glass thunk against the table. "You are their leader and in need of a headquarters, are you not?"

Brandi could say nothing to refute that, so she ignored the question and turned to Russ. His face was blank, but he didn't say anything or try to go after his brother. He just sipped from his own drink and sighed as he turned to Noble, who was watching them with irritation written across his face.

"Shian showed up," Russ said, offering a light explanation. "Jack dealt with him."

"Isn't he lucky," Noble snorted.

"I wouldn't say that," Russ shrugged. "It'll be awhile before he walks straight again."

"Anyone else would've sent him to the gods."

Russ paused at that. It was clear that the thought of his brother being made into nothing more than a memory unsettled him, and some of the color in his face drained away. His eyes darted over to Brandi, and she met his gaze with a straight face, and he shook his head.

"I absolutely would have," she said, answering his unspoken question. "I'm actually a little pissed off that you didn't," she said, looking at Jack, who placed a hand on the back of her chair as he shrugged.

"It would take too long to train his replacement," he stated. "He's the only one who can get us access to our resources tied up in the EREN. Sending him to the gods now would be unwise."

"That's the only reason?" Russ asked, his eyes wide.

"What other reason could there be?" Jack asked.

Russ said nothing back and Pine sighed as she leaned forward on the table, letting her chin rest in the palm of her hand. She let her hazel eyes dance around the table and dart over to Royal before settling back on Noble.

"Weren't we in the middle of something?" Pine asked. "As much as I adore looking at you," she said, smirking at Noble, "I do believe we need a plan of some sort. So," she said, turning to Brandi. "What's it going to be?"

"I don't like how you keep acting as if I have all the answers," Brandi sighed. "I'm not the only god participating in this conversation."

"You're the only one who can tell the rest of us what to do," Pine said, smiling at Brandi. "Don't pretend like you don't know that."

Brandi groaned as she crossed her arms and sat back in her chair. She focused her gaze on the table in front of them and tried to figure out what they should do next, but she wasn't a strategist. Most of her life had consisted of doing either Freya's bidding or the queen's. Najé had been the one to come up with their plans and organize the shadows. Her only responsibility had been to execute the plan, and her head pounded at trying to take into consideration every possibility.

"You're thinking too much," Royal said, calling over to Brandi from where he stood by the bar. Every pair of eyes turned to him, and a grin slipped onto his face. "Stop trying to be a mastermind like Freya and just do whatever you want to."

Brandi watched him for a moment and the expectations of the others fell away from her. For the first time in weeks, her mind felt clear, and relief washed over her, sending a surge of laughter bubbling out of her. She threw her head back and laughed as Royal smirked and sipped on his drink.

"You're right," she said, turning away from him and facing the table once more. "I'm a shadow," she stated, leaning forward and letting her gaze meet with everyone sitting around the table. "So, let's start solving problems like one."

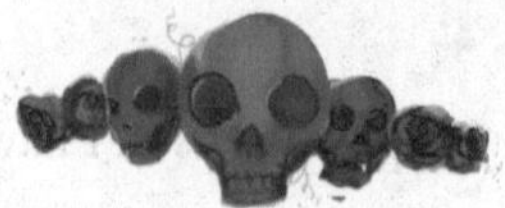

Two hours later, Brandi leaned against the bar as Remy stood behind it, polishing an already spotless glass. Russ and Royal had disappeared to find Shian, while Pine and Jack still sat at the table, nursing the last of their drinks in silence.

The conversation with the others had been long, but Brandi felt lighter knowing what would happen at the opening ceremony. It would alter the course of the realm and forge a new path forward for the rebels, and that made her nerves a little jittery. She would no longer be a myth that only other shadows knew to be real. She would be at the forefront of what was to come, and the entire realm would know who she was. But somewhere during the conversation, Brandi accepted that she had to walk with bold steps into the future.

She'd learned as a shadow that there was never any room for hesitation. And, despite her own uncertainties, she couldn't deny who she was — that she was a god in her own right, and a time being that transcended the realities of this realm. She had more questions than answers right now, but she would handle those later. For now, her mind discarded the future and locked onto the present. She could be nothing more than who she was in this moment and, for tonight, she was nothing more than a simple woman angling her glass toward a bartender who wasn't shy about refilling her cup.

Brandi considered Remy as she poured her another drink. She'd been quiet during the conversation and had only offered her opinion when asked a direct question. She was little more than an observer, but Brandi wasn't blind to the disapproval on her face when they'd discussed making her domain the new headquarters for the rebels and what Brandi planned to do at the Queen's Tower. She'd expected Remy to have a few opinions of her, but if they were unfavorable, Brandi wanted to know.

"What's your take on all this?" Brandi asked, watching Remy from over the rim of her glass. "Do you think I'm in the wrong?"

"I don't believe gods can ever truly be wrong," Remy answered, her voice even as she picked up a new glass to polish.

"I'm not asking your opinion of the gods," Brandi said. "I'm asking your opinion of me."

"You are a god," she pointed out before lifting her gaze to meet Brandi's. "Besides. What does my opinion matter?"

"You're a priestess, aren't you?" Brandi asked.

"Technically," Remy said, her left shoulder lifting in a shrug. "We all are. But only a few chose to truly honor the blessed JaZhire's last wishes and serve a god they hadn't met. I am not one of them."

"Is that so?"

Brandi remained silent as she nursed her drink, and it wasn't until Remy placed a glass on the counter with more force than necessary that she let her green eyes drift back over to the woman. She kept her eyes on the counter before straightening her shoulders and turning to hold Brandi's gaze.

"You don't mind if I'm honest, right?"

"I'd prefer it."

"I understand why you've chosen the path you're on," Remy said. "I don't know much about you, but I know enough. And I know there are few things," she said, pausing as her pale eyes glancing over to where Jack sat. "I know there are few people that you care about," she said, correcting her wording. "However, I must point out that you're choosing to embrace your godhood. And I'm just a reformed priestess, so my opinion may not hold much weight with you, but from where I stand, I question whether I could serve a god who holds no regard for the lives of others."

"JaZhire must have been kind," Brandi hummed. "Beyond measure."

"What makes you say that?"

"I've never known a god who truly cares about mortals," she said, chuckling as she gazed down into her cup. "I guess that makes me fit to be one though, doesn't it?"

Remy scoffed at Brandi's words. "It's unfortunate that the gods of this realm have been your only example. But that does not change who you are and the responsibilities you have to the mortals in your care."

"I have no interest in being a god or the responsibilities that come with it."

"Again," Remy said, "that's unfortunate. But it's rare that we're allowed to choose who we are."

"You believe there's no autonomy in choosing who we become?"

"I believe that everyone is born with their own burdens to bear," Remy clarified. "And how they choose to view those burdens is completely up to them. Some people will thrive, the weight they carry making them stronger. And some people will wilt beneath it. That's a fact."

"And you think I'm wilting under the weight of being a god," Brandi stated, nodding her head as she considered Remy's words.

"I don't think you're wilting."

"No?" Brandi asked, quirking an eyebrow at her. "Then what do you think, Remy? Be honest."

"I think that you're not ready to thrive," she stated, moving down the bar to stand in front of Brandi. "And given your circumstances? How you discovered your burdens?" She shrugged. "I can understand your actions in a way that most people probably can't. I even respect the way you're dealing with most of this. But," she said, the word sharp as she narrowed her eyes at Brandi, "I don't think you should treat others as if they're disposable. It doesn't matter if they've always been that way to you before. If that's how you view them now, you'll be a pitiful god."

"Those are strong words," Pine said, her voice light as her words carried over to them and she lifted her gaze. "To think that you would stand here, in our company, and call Brandi pitiful."

Brandi watched as Remy's eyes met Pine's before they darted over to Jack. She could see the way he stared at Remy and she smirked into her cup at the idea of Pine and Jack getting angry on her behalf. She allowed herself a moment to feel the warmth that came with knowing they valued her, just as she was, before she grinned at them.

"It's okay. I did ask for her honest opinion," Brandi reminded them.

Pine studied Remy for another moment before turning her head away from them and letting her curtain of dark hair separate them.

"Be more careful with your words," Pine said, her warning hanging in the air as the tension in the air lifted. "We wouldn't want any more misunderstandings."

Remy nodded at the back of Pine's head and Brandi returned her attention to her, offering a small upward tilt of her lips.

"I hear you," Brandi said. "And I don't disagree," she admitted.

"But how you view people won't change," Remy said, disappointment seeping into her words.

"Tonight?" Brandi laughed. "No. But tomorrow?" She shrugged and downed the rest of her drink before sliding the empty glass toward Remy once more. "Tomorrow, we'll see."

Remy locked eyes with Brandi and searched her face. Brandi didn't know if she was searching for a better answer than what she was able to offer in that moment, or if Remy was trying to determine if Brandi was telling her bold-faced lies like the other gods no doubt did. Whatever she was searching for though, she must have found it because she smirked at Brandi before reaching for an empty glass and the bottle she'd left down on the counter. She filled both of them before setting it aside once more and lifting her glass towards Brandi.

"To tomorrow, then."

Brandi grinned and clinked her glass against Remy's.

"To tomorrow."

CHAPTER NINETEEN

To love a woman is terrifying.

For she is beauty and wrath, encapsulated in mortal flesh — shaped in the image of the goddess who adores her — how could you possibly think yourself worthy of her? Truly, I tell you, that you are not. But you will try. You will lay yourself at her feet — you will offer her everything that you are — you will dismantle and rebuild yourself a thousand times, just to suit her whims — and then you will pray that she might smile upon you, even just once.

And when she does, you will become more than what you are now. For I tell you this: if you show me one who has known love, I will show you one who has known fear and conquered it.

— To My Children Who Will Love Daughters | Lindl's Second Holy Academy

---

BRANDI'S DOMAIN — TEMPLE OF THE TIME GODDESS
1 DAY BEFORE THE OPENING CEREMONY

"Today has been too long."

Jack whispered the words into Brandi's stomach as he wrapped his arms around her and pulled her into him. He sat on the edge of the bed in the middle of the room Remy had offered them — a small room with thick black carpet, pristine white walls, and glowing purple orbs like the ones Brandi had seen in the courtyard. The ceiling still twisted and shifted above them, showing them dozens of different galaxies, and Brandi appreciated the simplicity of the room. It was beautiful. It didn't offer them anything more than a bed and a bathroom, but it was enough.

They'd spent the entirety of the day training with Remy, learning how to control their newfound power as gods. It hadn't been easy — it took much more focus and intention than the half-hearted prayer she'd grown accustomed to, but she'd managed to learn how to use her new god voice — the same one she'd watched Freya use on Royal. It was a tone that forced the obedience of mortals, and it was unnerving in a way to know that she could force someone to obey her with her words alone. Remy had warned both her and Jack that there would be more training to come, but they'd mastered enough for the time being. The only task left for them for the night was to get some rest, so Brandi looked down at Jack from where she stood in front of him and threaded her fingers through his hair, massaging his scalp as she smirked at his words.

"You're the one who wanted to save the realm," she reminded him.

"We should've just let it burn," he groaned, tightening his grip on her.

"We still can," she offered. "We could stay here forever. Maybe even help Zareal."

"Actually," Jack said, lifting his head too look up at her, "let's talk about that."

"Do we have to?" Brandi asked, her shoulders sagging at the thought of rehashing yet another conversation that placed the fate of the realm on her shoulders. "I'd rather just go to bed."

"The opening ceremony is tomorrow, Bee," he pointed out. "And you said we'd talk later. It's later."

Brandi sighed and massaged her own forehead before moving to flop down onto the bed next to Jack. He took her hand, threading his fingers through hers as he listened to her recount her meeting with Zareal in the void. Like she had when she'd met with Freya and Azinne in the god realm, she left nothing out. She told Jack about everything, including all the confusion and uncertainty she'd felt. She tried to sort her thoughts out as she shared them with Jack, but she struggled to separate her own desires from the expectations Freya, Azinne, and Zareal all had of her. It wasn't until Jack squeezed her hand that she stopped, letting silence fill the space between them and giving him time to process her words.

"So, it seems like we've got three options laid out for us," Jack mused aloud. "The first is the one Freya posed to us," he said, holding up his index finger. "Save the realm from the time beings. We know her reasons aren't pure, but this is the realm we live in so," he shrugged, "not the worst deal. Option two," he said, lifting his middle finger, "is we side with Azinne. The gods will be punished, and the monarchy will be destroyed, but the realm, and the time within it, will still exist. Again, not the worst option."

"And option three," Brandi finished, "is siding with Zareal. We destroy the realm ourselves and he takes us somewhere where we don't have to deal with the gods."

"Is that what you want to do?"

Jack's voice was soft, and his brown eyes studied her face as she dropped her own gaze to their intertwined hands. It was the second time that day that someone had asked her what she wanted to do and she didn't have an answer for them. It made her realize just how many decisions had been made for her and she was struggling now to make them for herself, and she shook her head.

"I don't like any of the options," Brandi said. "I don't want to help any of them," she admitted.

"Then let's make an option four," Jack said, leaning forward.

"You say that like it's a simple thing," Brandi laughed.

"For you and me?" Jack asked, leaning forward to catch her chin in between his fingers and keep her from looking away from him. "It's nothing. Just tell me what you want, and I'll make it happen."

"You can't just promise that."

"I can," Jack stated. "Or did I not stand before Rothe himself and promise to fight him if it was to protect you?"

Brandi had nothing she could say because that was one memory she'd never forget. As devout as Jack was, when Rothe had questioned what he would do in response to threatening her, Jack hadn't hesitated to let the god know that he would destroy the entire realm to protect her if that's what it took. It had been absolute blasphemy and Jack hadn't stuttered over a single word of it. He'd meant every word — she knew that. But now that the reality of fighting the gods loomed before them, her heart raced with an anxiety that suffocated her thoughts and she shook her head at the thought of putting Jack in any kind of position where she could lose him again. As much as she hated the idea of helping either

Freya or the time beings, she would rather swallow her pride than risk losing him again. But before she could open her mouth to say as much, Jack was pressing his lips to hers.

His kiss was soft, and he wrapped an arm around her, pulling her closer to him and she placed a hand against his chest, leaning into him. He pulled away from her only to place featherlight kisses against her forehead, nose, eyes, and cheeks before resting his forehead against hers.

"Your face really gives away all your secrets sometimes. You know that, Bee?"

"What are you talking about?"

"Don't worry about me," he said, pulling back just enough to meet her gaze. "Whatever we decide, I'm going to be fine."

"But —"

"But nothing," he said, his words gentle but leaving no room for discussion. "I've got your back, and you've got mine. That's how it's always been, and that's how it's always going to be. Whatever we do, we do together," he said. "I'm not going to sit here and let you make a terrible decision just because it might be dangerous."

"You say that now," Brandi whispered. "But do you realize how terrified I was watching you return to the gods? Knowing that even with every blessing I had, I couldn't help you?"

"That won't happen again."

"You can't promise that."

"Have I ever lied to you?" Jack questioned, and Brandi fell silent. She knew the answer he was looking for, but this was far more than a promise to take her on a date or call her whenever they had separate missions.

"Answer me, Bee," he said. "Have I ever lied to you?"

"No," she whispered.

"Then trust me," Jack said. "I will never put you through that again."

"You better not," Brandi said, her voice cracking as she thought back on the memory. "I wouldn't be able to handle it."

"I won't," he said, kissing her once more. "So, tell me what you want to do, and we'll make it happen."

"Give me some time to think about it?"

"Of course," Jack chuckled, pressing another soft kiss to her forehead. "Starting tomorrow, you can have all the time you need. But tonight," he stood and lifted Brandi with him, carrying her over to the bathroom, "your thoughts can stay focused on me."

Brandi grinned as Jack placed her on her feet and kissed her in a way that was intended to do much more than comfort her. She wrapped her arms around him and kissed him back, separating just long enough for him to run them a warm bath and leave their clothes on the floor. She sank into the warm water and pressed her back to his chest as he peppered her neck and shoulder with kisses, allowing herself to get lost in him as she always did. She didn't know what they would do about the gods, the realm, or the time beings — and for the night, it didn't matter. Whenever she was with Jack, she was nothing more than the woman he loved.

And that would always be more than enough for her.

ROTHE'S DOMAIN — THE QUEEN'S TOWER
1 DAY BEFORE THE OPENING CEREMONY

"Gods, Blondie. You're still at this?"

Sarah looked up from where she'd been studying the placement of her feet and spun towards the door, her blue eyes wide as her heart jumped to her throat. The light in the hallway was brighter than that of the dim ballroom, so it took a moment for her eyes to adjust before she recognized the man walking towards her. Her face burned as she spun away from him and counted backwards from thirteen in the language of the gods. Mara had coached her through how to control her emotions, and this was a good a time as any to put the skill to use.

"The opening ceremony is tomorrow," Sarah responded once she was confident her voice was even and wouldn't crack. "There's no point in me just sitting around when I could be practicing."

Noble didn't say anything back to her, and Sarah continued counting in her mind as she placed her hands into the starting position of the dance. She refused to let him be her undoing when she'd snuck into the ballroom with the singular purpose of perfecting her dance. After studying with Cedric and Mara, and her meeting with Grace, she felt the weight of the role Brandi had given her now. There would be no room for error tomorrow — too many people had invested their time into her training for her to ruin it during the first twenty minutes of the ball. So, she'd slipped into a simple gold dress and heels, applied some mascara and lipstick, and pulled a brush through her hair before making her way to the ballroom she and Sal had been practicing in.

"Need a partner, Blondie?"

Sarah's eyes darted up from the ground once more, her focus torn away from her thoughts to settle on Noble who now stood in front of her. He was dressed in the all-black attire of the shadows and his hand was extended to her. She glanced at it before shaking her head, knowing better than to trust herself if Noble were to touch her.

"I'm fine," she said, taking a half step back.

"You turning me down?" Noble questioned, lifting a single brow at her.

"You don't have to say it as if it's never happened before," Sarah huffed, looking away from him. "You can just go. You don't have to wait here for me."

"You know I can't leave you here by yourself. Besides," Noble said, taking a step forward to take her hand, pulling her into the starting position for the dance, "It's just one dance."

Warm ripples of electricity snaked its way up Sarah's arm and she flushed as she looked up into Noble's dark eyes. Asari's moon was high in the sky, shining down in the courtyard and lighting the small ballroom from the tall windows on her right. Sarah hadn't bothered to flick on the lights when she'd entered since the room had been lit by the moonlight and she wished now that she had. Seeing Noble's face lit by the moon sent her heart racing and she had to focus on taking deep, quiet breaths to get it back under control. She closed her eyes, giving herself a short reprieve to collect her thoughts before meeting Noble's steady gaze with her own.

"You lead," she whispered.

With that, Noble took the first steps, guiding her around the room. Even without the music playing out loud, Sarah could hear it in her head as she followed Noble's movements. Cedric had suggested she play the music in her room while she slept to get her subconscious brain familiar with it, and while she didn't know if it was his suggestion or her practice that was making the difference, she was grateful to not be stumbling through the routine as she had before. She kept her eyes focused on the tip of Noble's nose as her mind played through the rest of the dance. It wasn't until Noble spoke up, that her eyes darted to his.

"You've gotten better at this," he said, a grin pulling at his lips.

"I've been practicing," Sarah breathed.

"It shows," Noble said, nodding. "You might make it through the ball after all."

"I plan to do more than that," Sarah stated, pausing as Noble dipped her. When he pulled her back up, she held his gaze for a moment. "I plan to win."

"That's a bold statement, Blondie," Noble said, lifting his brows. "It's a completely different tune than what you were singing when we got here."

"Well," Sarah sighed, "I've been told quite clearly that I need to earn my place. That I will not be pitied," she said, spinning under Noble's uplifted arm before returning to clasp his hand once more, "and that I will not be shown mercy if I fail."

"All those things are true."

"Then it's not so much a bold statement as it is my only option, isn't it?" Sarah questioned, and Noble chuckled.

"It seems Mara's training has done more than make you look more like a princess," he said. "You're starting to think for yourself."

"I've always had my own thoughts," Sarah said, her words defiant as she returned her gaze to his nose.

"But you never acted on them," Noble pointed out. "But don't misunderstand, Blondie. I'm pointing it out because this change is a good one. So," he said, squeezing her hand and drawing her gaze, "accept the compliment."

Sarah held his gaze for another brief moment before returning them to his nose and nodding her head. She didn't feel as if he'd given her a compliment anywhere in what he said, so she said nothing. She'd learned from the others that there were times where silence was the most appropriate reaction. They were approaching the final turn in the dance, and it's always where she lost her footing. She managed to make her way through it without stumbling, but it was nowhere near as graceful as the rest of the dance. But she wasn't too worried about that — she'd made it through without threat of shaming herself in front of Noble, and for the night, she would take that as a win.

"Thank you for the dance," Sarah said, stepping back to offer Noble a proper curtsy. The left side of his lips twitched upward but he offered a bow in return.

"Pleasure was mine, Blondie."

When they straightened Sarah couldn't stop herself from stealing glances up at him as he walked beside her, escorting her back to her room. His words from *The Unseen Horizon* came floating back to her — that if she wanted something from him, she should just ask. He'd more than delivered on her request for a kiss, and she hadn't seen him hold back with anyone else either. This was the first time they'd been alone together since they were at *The Unseen Horizon*, even though they'd been at the tower for weeks. Mara and Sal had stacked her schedule full of lessons, so she wasn't too surprised they hadn't had much time together, but it seemed every time Noble was left alone in a room with her, he found a reason to drop her off with someone else or leave her in her room. Now that she had him to herself, her mind was racing with questions she wanted to ask him — things about Pine and Brandi, about the plan and the shadows, about if he'd ever change his mind about being her consort. About if he would be willing to kiss her again like he had before.

She would never be as bold as Grace was, asking for his time in front of other people. But now that they were alone, the thought crossed her mind. That he could walk her back to her room and she could ask him to come inside. It was the middle of Asari's night, so there would be no one to interrupt them like before. The center of her belly pulsed with heat at the thought, but she forced it away.

Noble had made it clear that he wasn't interested in her — not in the way she wanted him to be. He only seemed to care about women who carried no real interest in him — women like Brandi and Pine. It's the only reason her brain had come up with as to why his attention had been glued to her when Russ was around. The moment she'd feigned interest in someone else, Noble had given her the attention she'd been craving.

It was insane, but anyone who seemed to actually care about him, he treated as nothing more than a distraction. And Sarah had no intentions of having her heart broken as Terra had, so she shoved the thought of inviting Noble into her bed away and focused on a safe question instead.

"Let me ask you a question," Sarah said, keeping her voice low as they navigated the dimly lit halls. "Who is Mara to you?"

"To me?" Noble repeated, lifting a single brow as he glanced down at her.

"To the shadows," Sarah clarified. "It's been on my mind since we got here. No one seems to want to piss her off."

Noble chuckled at that and placed a hand to the center of Sarah's back, guiding her to the side as a maid pushing a trolley passed them on the other side of the hallway. She dipped her head once towards Sarah before moving on, leaving her and Noble alone once more. Once she was gone, he dropped his hand and the center of her back felt like a pit of ice, but she said nothing as she waited for an answer to her question.

"There is more than one way for someone to be dangerous," Noble said, his eyes darting down to her. "Most shadows do that by breaking bones and sending people to the gods," Noble explained. "But there are some who do that without ever laying a finger on you."

"How would that be possible."

"They destroy your life," Noble answered. "They can drain your accounts, evict you from your home, terminate you from your job, erase your identity or fabricate evidence to prove you guilty of crimes you never knew about. They control the entire system, and Mara," he shrugged, "is the leader of them all."

"Wait," Sarah said, shaking her head, "I thought Brandi…"

"She was the queen's blade," Noble clarified. "But Mara, is the queen's shield. She had unrestricted access to both the EREN and the ERIS. She could reveal the identity of any shadow, noble, or royal with a few taps of her fingers."

"She wouldn't do that though," Sarah whispered, surprise widening her eyes that were trained on the thick red carpet beneath them. "Right?"

"She absolutely would," Noble chuckled. "And she has. And any shadow that's been outed to the public becomes the number one target of the queendom. Brandi's target. So," Noble said, stopping in front of Sarah's door, "we tend to use caution around her."

"Thank you for explaining it to me."

"You're welcome," Noble said, opening her door for her. "May Asari keep your night, Blondie."

"And bless your dreams," she replied, with a nod, letting him pull the door closed behind him as he walked away. She was proud of herself for not inviting him in, but now her heart raced with the reality that the next rising of Rothe's sun brought with it the opening ceremony and she struggled to keep herself calm. She pressed her hand to her chest as she sank down onto the edge of her bed and studied the moon in the sky.

"Asari give me strength," she whispered. "I'm going to need it."

CHAPTER TWENTY

When the sun and moon collide, seek refuge — for when Rothe and Asari agree, not even the goddess may stop them.

— Of Gods and Mortals | Lindl's Third Holy Academy

ROTHE'S DOMAIN — THE QUEEN'S TOWER
THE OPENING CEREMONY

"Now introducing Princess Sarah Rothens, first daughter of the late second princess, Venetia."

With those words, the guards pulled open the arched doors that led into the ballroom and Sarah straightened her back, tightening her grip on Sal's arm. He glanced down at her and patted her hand.

"Smile, cousin. First impressions are everything."

Sarah forced her smile wider and released a quick breath. She was dressed in the most expensive dress she'd ever worn — the deep red fabric contrasted with the light blue color of her eyes, and every inch of it shimmered under the bright lights of the crystal chandeliers. Every princess was required to wear a ball gown, and hers had a sweetheart neckline that made her look bustier than she was. The straps hung off her shoulders, leaving them and the upper part of her back exposed. It cinched her waist and brushed along the floor as they walked. Her short hair had been curled with the left side of it pinned back with a single hair pin shaped like the rising sun. Golden teardrop jewels dangled from her ears and around her neck, and Mara had done her makeup to give her a fresh-faced look.

"Trust me," Mara said, dabbing concealer under Sarah's eyes, "every other princess will look like a crayon box. If you look like you woke up like this, they'll take notice."

"It's not the makeup I'm worried about," Sarah admitted, eyeing the red dress. "I should be wearing blue."

"You're a Rothens," Mara stated, leaning back to stare Sarah in the eye. "Your mother was a full Rothian woman, and the rightful princess of this realm, as far as most people are concerned. You need to remind them of that."

"But I'm Asari's vessel," Sarah said, shaking her head. "I've never prayed to Rothe a day in my life, and I've only been in his domain for a couple of weeks."

"And?" Mara asked. "That doesn't make you any less Rothian. Besides," she shrugged, picking up a new makeup brush, "Queen Leia's first daughter is Asarian. If you wear the same color as her, people will only remember you as the one who wore it worst. She takes after her mother, so she's the favorite to win. The little darling of the realm," Mara said, rolling her eyes. "Trust me on this. Wear the red dress."

Sarah hadn't argued with Mara after that, and as she took her first steps into the ballroom with Sal as her escort, her heart raced. Sal had taken her to the ballroom the night before to explain the order of things and to show her what she would be walking into. So, she'd already seen the chandeliers dripping in crystals and gold and the white tile floors polished to an immaculate shine.

The blood red curtains and been switched out for sheer ones for the occasion, and they shifted in the gentle wind that wafted in from the balcony. The ballroom was on the sixty-ninth floor of the tower, next to the throne room. Only the queen's private chambers existed above them and the balcony outside was one of the most beautiful and terrifying sights Sarah had ever seen.

The tower extended well above the clouds and only the sky was visible from where they were. There was no skyline to view — no people to hear bustling about and no pods to see flying through the realm. It was a picture of unmarred perfection, and it was beautiful. But she also realized that a simple misstep near the edge would send her plummeting to the ground, and she realized for the first time just how terrified of heights she was. She'd clung to Sal as he'd shown her the view and sank to the floor as they walked back inside. As her blue eyes looked at the stars shining in through the curtains now, she whispered a tiny prayer to Asari under her breath.

"Hear me, father," she whispered, ***"may your light guide me down this dark path so that I may not make a fool of myself."***

She saw Sal's brown eyes dart down to her, but they didn't linger. They were in the spotlight now, and every eye in the ballroom was turned to watch them. Sarah saw every shade of brown in the ballroom — from the sandy tones of Carna's plains to the light hues of Lindl's children, the rich ones of Rothe's, and even a few deep brown shades of the Freyans — and every shade of red, gold, purple, silver, blue, and green. Every domain was represented, and she was surprised to see others with creamy tones like hers sprinkled throughout. Her heart lifted at knowing there were others who looked like her in attendance. She let that small thing settle her racing heart as Sal led her to the center of the dancefloor. He bowed to her before releasing her hand, and her eyes widened.

"What are you doing?" Sarah whispered, being sure to keep her smile plastered on her face.

"Dancing with your cousin is not the power move you think it is," he whispered back.

"Then who is going to dance with me?"

"Don't worry," he said, lifting her hand to his lips as he backed away from her and melted into the crowd, leaving her standing in the center of the empty dance floor. She kept her eyes focused on the doorway with her hands clasped in front of her as she waited for the savior that Sal had promised her. Her heart raced as she listened to the other princesses be called, but Sarah refused to let her mask crack.

Sal had given her all the information that he had on his sisters, and it had been hard for Sarah to reconcile that the people they were trying to send to the gods weren't strangers to Sal and the others as they were to her. They'd grown up with the other princesses — had seen them every day of their lives and shared memories with them. Knowing that made her stomach flip so, as she watched them arrive, she tried to focus on committing their faces to memory as they took their spots on the dance floor with their escorts.

"Now introducing Princess Asuna Sentera, first daughter of the reigning Queen Leia."

Sarah had walked out to absolute silence, so her eyes widened as claps echoed throughout the room. She'd thought it was customary for the princesses to enter into silence, but now she realized just how great the obstacle before her was. It was more than just out-maneuvering the other princesses if she wanted a chance at the throne — she would have to win over every person in the queendom. At the very least, she would need to win over the people standing in the ballroom. And she would only have one night to do it. She squeezed her hands tighter together as the audience died down and Asuna curtsied to the crowd, throwing them a radiant smile.

The crowd had much the same reaction for her sister, Cazie Taren, second daughter of the reigning Queen Leia. It wasn't until the last entrant for the bid walked in that the claps and shouts of excitement morphed into scattered whispers around the ballroom.

"Now introducing Princess Grace Bertanal, third daughter of the reigning Queen Leia."

As she walked onto the dancefloor, the whispers grew — filling every empty space like radio static as hushed voices began speculating about the girl with the vibrant red hair pinned atop her head. And just as Asuna wore blue for her Asarian heritage and Cazie wore silver for her Carnian one, Grace wore a deep violet ballgown to represent her Lindlian background. Her dress was strapless, with a jeweled corset shaping her at the top, and layers of tulle filling it out at the bottom. Her escort was a stocky Lindlian man who seemed anxious to be standing next to Grace in front of everyone. The queen, who sat upon her throne at the front of the room, lifted her hand and the hall fell silent as the orchestra situated on the other side of the room lifted their instruments to play.

Sarah glanced around, searching for a familiar face in the crowd as the other ladies faced their escorts with smiles, moving into the starting positions for their dance. She'd practiced for days with Sal to make sure she wouldn't make a fool of herself, but apparently the joke was that she would have no partner. She could feel the eyes on her as the conductor looked over at her, stalling in the hopes of giving her time for a miracle to happen. And as she fought to keep the panic in her chest from rising and the tears pricking the corner of her eyes from falling, she spotted a familiar bald head in the crowd.

She sucked in a deep breath as Russ came strolling forward. He wore a dark gray suit as he walked forward with a smile on his face, and Sarah had never been so grateful to see a single person before. Her smile morphed into something genuine as he extended his hand and bowed.

"May I have this dance?"

"Yes," Sarah breathed, tightening her core as he placed a hand at her waist and the conductor began waving his hands. The gentle music she'd come to expect wafted over them and she smiled up at Russ as she followed his lead around the floor. She worked to keep time in her head, and he grinned down at her.

"Relax," he whispered. "You're doing great."

"You have no idea how quickly this can all go wrong," she whispered back. "I'm not very good at this."

"I'm here," he assured. "I won't let you fall."

Sarah met his gaze for the first time and smiled again, her practiced one dissolving into a light laugh as the panic she'd felt in her chest began to fade. It was replaced with a new anxiety, but for the first time in weeks, she felt like she wasn't alone. Russ's hand was warm on her waist, and she trusted him in a way she couldn't with Noble or Sal. She couldn't say what it was about him, but Russ made her feel comfortable and she squeezed his hand as he led them around the turn that had caused her to trip over her feet every time in practice. But rather than focusing on what her feet should be doing, she focused on the person in front of her. And she finally understood what Sal had been trying to teach her.

"See?" He grinned. "That wasn't so hard."

"No," Sarah agreed. "It wasn't. Thank you, Russ. For being here," she said. "I'm glad it was you."

He beamed at her words and tightened his grip on her as he gazed down at her.

"I'm glad it was me, too."

The music slowed and applause rang out over the ballroom as the escorts stepped away from the princesses and bowed, lifting their fingers to their lips before melting away into the crowd. Russ winked at Sarah before taking his leave and, after a moment where the princesses curtsied to the crowd, a softer tune began playing and Sal reappeared at her side as if he'd never left.

"That was a wonderful display," he said, grinning as he guided her through the crowd of people moving toward the dancefloor. "I wasn't convinced you'd survive the dance, so color me impressed."

"Your lack of faith in me never fails to astound me," Sarah shot back, her smile still in place as she nodded at the people they passed. She knew this was part of Sal's plan. To have her be seen around the ballroom before she spoke with anyone. According to his intel, the other princesses would be making a beeline for their supporters, and the first few minutes after the dance would be the most opportune time to discover who they already had in their pockets.

None of the faces were familiar to Sarah, but Mara and Sal had assured her that it wouldn't matter. They would give her all the information she needed to navigate the minefield of influential people. So, as they walked around the ballroom, Sarah put on her bravest face and made eye contact with everyone she could.

"Good," Sal whispered as they made their way to where a young Lindlian woman wearing a suit with a top hat stood. "Make them notice you."

"I'm doing my best," Sarah whispered back, fluttering her eyes at a few men who offered partial bows to her. It wasn't truly appropriate, but Mara had warned her not to expect more. She was an unknown variable to most of them, and none of them would risk showing her outright favor, especially if they saw her before they spoke with anyone else. The bid could be just a dangerous game for them as well if they weren't careful — if they aligned themselves with the wrong princess, everything could crumble around them. So, she instead chose to watch and smiled as they reached the woman Sal had been searching for.

"You ready for this, cousin?"

"As I'll ever be," Sarah said, taking in a deep breath.

"Lyla," Sal called out to the woman as they approached, and she looked up from her conversation with an older, more petite woman and offered Sal a polite smile.

"Risal," she crooned, holding her hand out to him. "It's been too long."

"Indeed," he grinned, shaking her hand before gesturing to Sarah. "Allow me to introduce you to my cousin. This is Sarah Rothens, first daughter of the late, Venetia."

"May Freya have mercy on her soul," Lyla said, nodding her head.

"And Sarah, this is my dear friend, Lyla," Sal said. "She is the next owner proprietor of *Podigious*. They are the biggest manufacturer of luxury transport pods throughout the realm."

"Yes," Lyla cut in, smiling as she turned towards Sarah. "We are also one of the biggest advocates for dispersing pod-code within Carna and Asari's domains. One of our goals is to be able to bring our technologies to every domain."

"That sounds wonderful," Sarah said, allowing her voice to sound light as she looked up at the woman. "What amenities do your pods offer? I'm intrigued by your luxury line."

"Have you never been in one?"

The question came from the woman Lyla had been speaking to, and her hazel eyes were sharp as she looked at Sarah. With a single glance over her, Sarah felt as if the old woman had read her entire life and she smiled and she shook her head.

"I'm afraid not," she answered. "I'm still very new to the luxuries that come with being a princess."

"Oh?" The woman asked, her thin eyebrows reaching upward. "And why is that?"

"I was raised in Asari's domain rather than here in the tower," Sarah offered, choosing to leave out that she was only familiar with Asari's outskirts. "His inner ring doesn't boast the same technologies as Rothe's and Lindl's domains do."

"How tragic," the woman said, clicking her tongue, her gaze drifting around the crowd. "That is no way for a princess to spend her life."

"I don't know," Sarah laughed. "I've found that this realm has so many exceptional things. I always have something new to discover and appreciate. In this conversation alone, I've learned of your luxury pods, as well as your hopes of expanding your business into Asari's domain," Sarah said, biting back a smirk as the old woman's eyes cut back over to her. "I hope that I'm able to be a positive force in helping you achieve that."

"Well," the woman said, sizing Sarah up in a new light, "I can't say that I would be disappointed to see our expansion come to fruition."

"And neither would we!" Sarah agreed. "I would love to experience the luxury you offer for myself one day as well," Sarah forced her eyes wider as she turned to Sal. "Oh! Do you think we could take a tour of the inner ring? I haven't spent much time beyond the tower yet."

"Sure," he said, turning his eyes to the old woman. "But we'd need enough pods for a royal escort. Would that be possible?"

"Of course," the woman said, beaming. "Lyla! Be sure to gather her advisor's contact information so we can arrange things with them," she demanded of the younger woman beside her.

"Yes, grandmother," Lyla answered, meeting Sal's gaze with a smirk. The older woman nodded at him and her granddaughter before offering a proper bow to Sarah.

"It's been fortunate meeting you. I look forward to our business together."

"As do I," Sarah offered, returning a half bow out of respect. The old woman huffed with pride before stalking off, Lyla winking at Sarah as she walked to keep up with the swift moving woman.

"What was that about?" Sarah asked, glancing up at Sal. "That granddaughter seemed rather pleased with herself."

"She should be," Sal chuckled. "Lyla just scored some major funding for her new endeavors."

"What endeavors?"

"She's looking to revolutionize pod technology," Sal answered, smiling as he guided Sarah around the room. "So, while what I told you was true, *Podigious* deals in more than luxury pods and their code."

"Do I even want to know the rest?"

"They're also breaking into the market for black eurithium," Sal answered.

"Should I know what that is?"

"Yes," Sal answered. "But just know that it's a precious material. Expensive and hard to acquire. But if Lyla succeeds in merging it with current pod technology, that'll bring the queendom into a new era of innovation."

"And how does that benefit us?"

"Catching on quick there, cousin," Sal chuckled. "If she succeeds, your name will be behind the shift as her supporter. We'll have to fund them in the meantime, but it will improve how others see you. And an increase in public opinion isn't something that the council can easily ignore," he pointed out.

"I see," Sarah whispered. "Your sisters have popularity on their side. But if I can demonstrate an ability to network…"

"A brilliant mind will always be worth more than a pretty face," Sal said, grinning.

"Are you saying I don't have a pretty face?"

"I'm saying that you know what you look like," Sal countered. "My opinion doesn't really matter. What does matter," he said, continuing on before Sarah had the chance to interject anything else on the topic of her physical appeal, "is that you managed to impress, Lilna Parshner. She's been uninterested in any of the princesses. Until now."

"And that means something?"

"Take a look around," he said, guiding her toward the balcony as she stole glances around the room. The people who had been avoiding her gaze before were now watching her with care as she navigated the room. With one conversation, the tide of the room had changed, and Sarah's heart jumped into her throat at what it could mean.

"I see."

"Good," Sal grinned, leading her up to a young couple in matching gold outfits. They were both tall and lean with warm smiles, and Sarah returned them as they approached.

"Who are they?"

"Risha Davens and her husband, Malacai. She's the head of the committee that decides on all educational expansion within Rothe's domain," Sal whispered in her ear. "You ready?"

"Always."

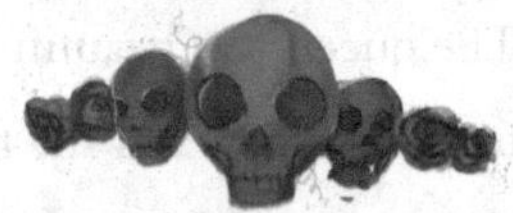

It was nearly an hour later when the music drifting through the air quieted, and the crowds parted to allow the princesses to walk down to the front of the room, where they stood in front of the queen and her consorts. Sarah clung to Sal's arm as they stood on the far left, facing the queen's throne. The last notes of music faded away, and Queen Leia rose from her seat. She took the time to meet the gaze of every princess who stood before her, searching their eyes as if she could reveal the secrets of their mind, before lifting her eyes and voice to the crowd behind them.

"Today," she said, her voice spilling over the ballroom like cool water on a hot night, "we celebrate the closing of an era and the beginning of a new one. It has been twenty-two years since I first stood were my daughters and niece," she said, smiling at Sarah before returning her gaze to the crowd, "now stand. I am proud to have been chosen as your queen and humbled to have served you for as long as I have. I thank you." She bowed her head, and the crowd returned the gesture before she lifted her head and spoke again.

"This gathering marks the opening of a new bid," she announced, her voice growing stronger. "Four of Freya's daughters stand before you now, seeking your approval to sit upon this throne as your next ruler. But only one may see the future she wishes to create. Only one may leave this bid as queen."

The queen turned her attention once more to each of the girls standing in front of them, and when she met Sarah's gaze last, a pang of longing overtook Sarah. The queen was beautiful, and she wore the same face as Sarah's mother. Hers was older, and she had the same creamy skin as all Asarians did instead of the rich brown tones her mother had, but there was no mistaking they'd been sisters. And in that moment, Sarah couldn't decide if she wanted to know everything about her aunt to feel like she had a connection to her mother, or if she wanted to send the woman to the gods for taking her mother away from her. She didn't have long to ponder it though, because as soon as the moment passed, the queen was speaking again.

"Sarah, Asuna, Cazie, Grace," she said, saying their names in order from oldest to youngest, "you stand before your queen, your people, and your gods today to declare your intention to claim this throne as your own. Should you succeed, do you accept the responsibilities that this crown carries?"

"Yes," they answered in unison.

"And should you fail, do you accept that you will meet the gods with your defeat?"

"Yes," they answered again.

"And you agree to respect the rules of this bid? To uphold the traditions set forth by your predecessors?"

Once more, they all agreed in unison and the queen grinned as she lifted her hands to the air.

"Then let it be heard and let it be known," Queen Leia called out. "The princesses Sarah, Asuna, Cazie, and Grace have all agreed to enter the bid! So, it shall begin!"

The crowd roared at the announcement, claps and whistles resounding throughout the ballroom. Sarah's eyes darted to the other girls, her heart pounding in her chest as she accepted that if she were to be successful in what Brandi asked of her, the other three girls would meet the gods because of her. Her conscience was already weighed down by it and the bid had only begun. She tried to swallow the lump in her throat as her anxiety welled up inside her.

"Is that a joke?"

The question cut through the noise of the crowd and the queen looked up from the princesses who stood before her to the back of the room. The guards standing by the doors were thrown aside as they were thrust open. A collective gasp sounded, and people pushed together as everyone turned to see what was happening. Sarah's eyes were wide as she searched the crowd for the source, but when she glanced up to Sal, she saw a wide grin plastered across his face.

"One thing she knows how to do," Sal chuckled, "is make an entrance."

Sarah's eyes turned toward the door and she fought back the laugh of surprise that wanted to bubble out of her. Brandi stood at the entrance with Jack, and Sarah could have cried from how happy she was to lay eyes on her. She was breathtaking as she stood in a strapless cocktail dress that was blacker than a shader's fur. It clung to her curves, revealing her long, toned legs. Her feet were clad in black stilettos and her thick hair was twisted down into neat knots.

Jack stood to her left, dressed in a matching three-piece suit with his short locks twisted back. They were easily the most stunning people in the room and had the confidence to match it. Two people Sarah had never seen before walked in behind them as well, and Sarah couldn't look away from them. They were both dressed in white suits, but their skin was darker than Brandi's — as if their bodies had been dipped in ink. They both had long black hair that was braided down to the middle of their backs and dark shades covered their eyes. They stood with their hands in their pockets, looking unimpressed and unbothered as the queen fumed in front of them.

"Who are you?" Queen Leia demanded, swinging her hand through the air to signal her guards. "Who let you in here?"

"No one lets me do anything," Brandi stated, walking forward down the aisle created by the parting crowd. "And you should recognize me, Leia," Brandi stated, garnering another collective gasp at her blatant disrespect. "I am your blade, after all."

CHAPTER TWENTY-ONE

Do not make the mistake of believing the queen and the goddess to be one and the same — for one is the embodiment of power, while the other simply wields it.

— Origins of the Queendom | Lindl's First Holy Academy

ROTHE'S DOMAIN — THE QUEEN'S TOWER
THE OPENING CEREMONY

"Guards!"

Brandi hadn't expected a warm welcome from the queen, but she hadn't expected to be rushed by thirty of her top guards in front of a crowd either. They were armed with short swords and eurithium shields as they fell into formation around them, and the guests gave an audible gasp as they crowded back, away from them. Several people wore faces of panic as they stared at them, and a few reporters were already taking pictures and scribbling things down in their holographic notepads. But Brandi's eyes were glued to the queen.

She had a smug look on her face, and it felt like she was daring

Brandi to make a move.

"This isn't what you want to do, Leia," Brandi warned, eyeing the soldiers surrounding them. "I suggest you call them back and we can have a conversation."

"I have nothing to say to a traitor of the crown," Leia snapped. "You're nothing more than a dog without a leash who needs to be put down," she said, throwing her arm out toward the crowd to command her soldiers. "Send them!"

Her command drifted out over the ballroom and the guards moved forward in unison, trying to force Jack and Brandi back from where they stood. Brandi sighed and released Jack, removing her arm from where it rested within the crook of his arm. He took a few steps back as she held the queen's gaze.

"You asked for this," Brandi said, as the two people in dark sunglasses and white suits stepped up beside her. "Tiki. Lia. Devour them."

As you wish, Tiny Human, Lia hummed as a grin spread across her face, revealing a double row of sharp black teeth. A collective gasp escaped from the room as she and Tiki transformed — their white suits bursting at the seams as they grew larger, hunching over themselves as black fur sprouted from every inch of their bodies. Their dark sunglasses clattered to the floor, crunching under their giant paws as they took their true forms and snarls ripped from their throats.

The guards in front of them screamed, the sound raw and wet as they stared into the faces of their worst nightmares. Most of them stood frozen in absolute fear as Tiki and Lia loomed over them, no doubt reliving the terror they'd faced in Freya's clearing. A few of them dropped their shields to run, but it was a futile effort. It was impossible to outrun a shader, and they were on the sixty-ninth floor of the Queen's Tower — there was nowhere to run, even if they wanted to. Only two brave souls remained in formation, and Brandi pointed to them.

"Bring me those two," she said. **"You may have the rest."**

Understood, Tiki and Lia answered in unison as they lunged forward. Lia was the first to bite into a soldier. She pinned the first one down to the white tile before biting into him, cleaving his head and shoulders from the rest of his body. The sickening crunch of bone forced most of the spectators to look away. More than a few soiled themselves, fainted, or lost their stomachs at the sight — and the stench of vomit and defecation mingled with the copper scent of fresh blood. Shrill screams echoed throughout the room as many of the crowd pushed toward the balcony, searching for distance from the monsters and fresh air.

Brandi remained still and unmoving, watching the queen and her paling face on the opposite side of the room. Even from where she stood, Brandi could see Leia trembling on her gilded throne. Her consorts were not better and watched Brandi with a palpable fear. The only one who seemed more surprised than afraid was Rinn MelForth, who sat up in his throne, gripping the arms of his seat as he watched the massacre. It was only after the guards were gone and only their blood and weapons remained on the floor that Brandi looked toward the two guards she'd spared. Their eyes were wide, and their armor clattered together as they shook where they stood, but they didn't dare move from it. It wasn't until their eyes met Brandi's that they both dropped to one knee and bowed their heads rather than hold her gaze.

"What are your names?" Brandi asked.

"I am Clarke!" The first one answered. "This is Hina!"

"Would you like to serve me?" Brandi asked. "I could use soldiers who do not cower in the face of nightmares."

"If you would have us!" Clarke shouted, bowing his head deeper and Hina followed his lead. Brandi nodded and pointed to where Jack stood.

"Stay out of the way and follow orders," Brandi said, moving past them to where Tiki and Lia were.

Tiki stood, letting low growls rumble from its throat as Lia sat to its left, licking her paws free of the blood that remained on them. As she approached, Lia rose and pushed her head into Brandi's open palm.

This has been fun, Lia hummed into her mind. *I would like to do more activities like this.*

Brandi laughed at that and smoothed her fingers across Lia's curly black fur. If things went the way she planned, then Lia would get her wish. But that was something they could discuss later. For now, her mind was focused on the queen and her gaze turned toward where she and her consorts sat on their thrones. She offered the queen a gentle smile as she walked forward, Tiki and Lia trailing behind her.

"I warned you," Brandi said, "but that's your tragic flaw, isn't it? You never listen."

"Do not speak," Leia said, her voice trembling as she tried to put on a brave face for the crowd that watched them with wide, terrified eyes, "as if you know me."

"I don't need to know you to know the truth," Brandi said. "And I doubt they do either."

"What are you talk —"

"Twenty-two years ago," Brandi said, cutting Leia off and raising her voice so that everyone could hear her. "You manipulated the bid for the throne in your favor. You sent your sister's consorts to the gods before she could approach the council for approval. You bribed your consorts and threatened their families until they agreed to join your court. And if they refused you as Ross Freylin did, you sent them to the gods. That violates the integrity of the bid," Brandi stated. "And when you learned your sister had borne a child, a rightful daughter of the throne, you tried to have both of them executed."

"Lies!" Leia screamed, gripping the arms of her throne as she lunged forward. "Venetia lost the bid due to her own faults!"

"Don't ever fix your mouth to call me a liar again," Brandi warned, her voice cold as Tiki and Lia snarled at her, baring their bloody teeth. "The shadow you sent to execute Venetia's consorts told your secrets and founded the rebellion on the back of your lies. And I know that even now, you're conspiring to have either Cazie or Asuna succeed you."

"You have no proof of these claims."

"Would you like to hold a press conference with Glenn MelForth? I'm sure she'd be more than happy to testify against you."

The queen fell silent at that, and the air in the ballroom felt heavy against Brandi's skin. She'd never been a fan of talking so much in front of an audience, but it was a necessary evil. They wouldn't be afforded the time they needed to grow the rebels if the bid was over within a week of starting. Sarah would need more time if she would have any hope of winning and if Brandi could have the queen focus her resources on finding and destroying the rebels rather than sabotaging Sarah, that would keep Sarah safe as she went on her consort campaign and give the rebels more of the exposure they needed.

"Why make a spectacle of this now?" Leia asked.

"Because a new bid has begun." Brandi shrugged. "And it needs to be a fair one."

Leia scoffed at that. "You barge in here with monsters and send my people to the gods in cold blood, and then claim to want a fair bid? Are you sure you don't just want the throne for yourself?"

Before Leia could say anything else, the air around Brandi shimmied in dance and Tiki and Lia backed away from her. She held her arms at her sides, her palms facing toward the chandeliers as a green light — darker than the soft light of Freya's magic — enveloped her palms before snaking its way up her arms and encircling her body.

Thunder rumbled in the distance, vibrating the floor beneath them as dark clouds rolled in, blocking out the light of the moon that shone through the opened balcony doors. Lightning flashed through them, highlighting the room every few seconds as the wind picked up around them, whistling as it sped by and sent the crystals in the chandeliers knocking into each other, filling the room with their tinkling sound. Tiki threw its head back and released a high-pitched howl that reverberated throughout the ballroom as both shaders pounded their feet against the floor to the rhythm of the magic pulsing around Brandi. Not a single eye strayed away from her as the light surrounding her grew darker and she rose off the ground, floating in midair.

Swirls of black danced within the green light before it condensed around her like a blinding cocoon and began to morph once more. It folded in on itself until it took the shape of a woman, and with a single blinding flash of light that forced them all to shield their eyes and look away, Brandi stood before them once more. However, she wasn't the same woman they'd seen moments ago.

Now she stood in a black silk dress that floated just above the tile of the ballroom. It clung to her body, wrapping around her tight muscles and subtle curves. Delicate green lace was draped over her left shoulder and trailed down her back, the intricate design filling in the slit that opened at her thigh and disappearing into the clouds that drifted around the hem of her dress. Stars twinkled in the dark fabric and as Brandi took a step forward, her shaders ceased their howling and stomping, instead dropping to their knees and bowing their heads.

Only the mortals, who were too awestruck to look away, gazed upon Brandi's face. She appeared older now as she stood before them — the roundness of youth had given way to the sharp angles of a fully grown woman. And her hair, which had been twisted down when she'd arrived, was freed. The front of her hair was braided down, but the back was as big and fluffy as a darkened cloud. Two braids framed her face, but it was the crown atop her head that everyone noticed.

And as Brandi's green eyes met those of the queen, she saw recognition slam into her as well.

"Get off my throne."

Brandi's demand was quiet, but the queen convulsed as if Brandi had reached across the space between them to grab her by the throat. She grunted as she stood to her feet and stumbled down the steps to stand in front of Brandi. Beads of sweat formed on her brow and Brandi glanced down at the shorter woman as she walked past her, flicking her wrist at the remaining consorts.

"You too," Brandi said, directing her words to the consorts. *"Get up."*

They moved with same kind of compulsion that Leia had, and Brandi climbed the steps to sit on Leia's throne as Tiki and Lia jumped over the queen and consorts, landing with grace behind her and knocking the seats of the consorts across the room where they clattered into broken heaps on the floor. Tiki laid down on Brandi's right, crossing its paws as it rested its giant head on top of them. Lia sat on her haunches to Brandi's left and let her lips curl back from her teeth in a silent snarl as Brandi crossed her legs on Leia's throne. Brandi lifted an eyebrow at Leia as she watched Brandi in absolute horror from where she stood on the white tile of the ballroom.

"See how easy this is for me?" Brandi asked. "If I wanted your throne, I would take it," Brandi stated. "Now, I'll let you decide what we do from here. Either you abdicate the throne, and we open the bid to every daughter of Freya who thinks she's fit for it, or," Brandi shrugged, "I'll level the playing field and make the rules myself."

"You can't do that," Leia said, her voice barely more than a whisper as she shook her head. "You can't."

"You should know by now that I can do whatever I want," Brandi said. "Now make your choice."

"I don't believe she means to deceive us, Leia," Rinn MelForth interjected, speaking for the first time since Brandi entered the room. "You should consider her words with care."

"With care?" Leia scoffed. "I am the queen of this realm. I need not curb my words for anyone."

"You are a queen who stands before a throne someone else sits on," he pointed out. "A title will not keep you from the gods should she decide to send you to them."

"Whose side are you on, Rinn?"

The question came from Sam Sentera who stood on the opposite side of the queen. He was a tall Asarian man with sharp features, a mop of brown hair, and brown eyes that were a touch too wide for his narrow face. Brandi would call his features unique before she called him handsome, but his glare was sharp as he looked over at Rinn.

"Side?" Rinn questioned, lifting an eyebrow. "Neither. I would simply prefer to make it home to my actual family rather than stand here and watch Leia talk her way into having all of us sent to the gods."

"You disrespect the queen."

"You would too if you knew who was before you," Rinn chuckled. "But, by all means," he said, waving his hand to Brandi, "continue insulting the woman who's been trained to send us all to the gods."

"You mistake me for a patient woman," Brandi snapped, rolling her eyes at their banter. It was like watching a less entertaining version of the gods, and she had no interest in letting it continue.

"I will never abdicate the throne," Leia said, trying to make her voice sound strong as it carried over the crowd of watchful eyes. "And the bid shall continue on as it always has. You may be powerful, but you're only one woman. And you won't be able to frighten me out of ruling this queendom."

A smattering of claps resonated through the crowd, and Brandi sighed as she looked down at the queen with unforgiving eyes. Part of her had hoped Leia would simply give up the throne and make things easier for Brandi, but she wasn't surprised that things were unfolding the way they were. So, Brandi shrugged as she signaled to Jack.

"You chose your pride over your future," Brandi said as he moved toward where Sal stood with the princesses. "Remember that when you grieve tomorrow."

"What?"

Leia's eyes grew wide as Jack brought Asuna and Cazie to stand in front of Brandi. The girls were a mess — their makeup ruined and their legs weak beneath them as they wailed for their mother. Their dresses were crumpled, and their eyes were swollen from tears that still flowed down their cheeks. Jack held both of them by their arms and forced them to kneel on the stone floors at the base of the throne as Brandi looked down at them.

"For the crime of manipulating the previous bid, for sending the consorts of the late Venetia Rothens to the gods, and for using bribes and fear-mongering to force her current consorts into her court, I find Leia Asana, daughter of the former Queen Lindley, guilty," Brandi said, her voice ringing out over the ballroom as Leia watched on in horror. "Her punishment will be the loss of two daughters," Brandi declared, waving her hand forward as Tiki and Lia rose to their feet. "One for the bid she stole twenty-two years ago, and another for the bid she tried to steal today."

"Wait!" Leia cried out, "I'll abdicate the —"

"Silence," Brandi said, glaring at her and watching as Leia's mouth snapped closed. "You had your opportunity to make your choice. This," she said, "is the one I make." She turned to Cazie and Asuna, who clung to each other, weeping, as Tiki and Lia approached them.

"May Freya have mercy on your souls."

With that, Tiki and Lia lunged forward, cleaving the heads of both daughters from their necks. Leia screamed, but her voice was the only one that echoed around the ballroom. The onlookers were stunned into silence as Brandi stepped forward and Jack helped her over the mess of the corpses as if it were an inconvenient puddle in the middle of the street. She stopped in front of Bert and watched as he trembled before her, and Leia's eyes widened as she lifted Bert to his feet by the collar of his shirt.

Sobs ripped through Leia's chest as she cried wordless pleas, but she was locked in place with a gag order — she was helpless to do anything but watch as Brandi tightened her fingers around Bert's throat.

"I warned you, didn't I?" Brandi asked, her voice as clear as the waters in Freya's domain. "To get your affairs in order? So, as the daughter of Freya," she said, grinning as her fingers tightened around his throat and he gagged, his eyes widening in fear as Rothe's blessing of strength flowed through her and she continued to lift him off the ground, digging her nails into his flesh until blood trailed down from beneath her fingers, "I will deliver on my promise to send you to her myself."

Bert clutched at his neck as Brandi looked down at her nose at him.

"For the crime of attempting to kill Jack and pissing me off," Brandi said, "your punishment is eternal separation from your loved one. May you face Freya's full wrath and she judge your soul worthy of everlasting pain and suffering."

With those words, Brandi shoved her free hand into his chest. He coughed up globs of thick, dark red blood as she gripped his heart in her palm and squeezed it until it popped like a cherry in a vice grip. Bert screamed before his eyes rolled back in his head and Brandi pulled her hand from his chest, letting his corpse drop to the floor next to Cazie and Asuna's. She held her hand out to Tiki and it stepped forward to lick the blood from her hand as she turned her sharp green gaze onto the other consorts.

"Consider this your warning," Brandi said, staring down at the queen. "I suggest you refrain from trying to interfere with the bid again unless you wish to be escorted to the gods by my own hand. Now, get up," she demanded, releasing the queen from her commands as she breezed past her with Jack and her shaders following behind her. "It's not befitting for a queen to be on her knees."

CHAPTER TWENTY-TWO

Who are you to question why it is we worship the goddess? Why we give her daughters this realm to rule? Have you never met a woman? Have you never seen how she makes everything out of nothing? Have you not witnessed how she births warriors and philosophers, raising them into unbreakable children who are loved by the gods? Yet you would allow your thoughts to consider her to be less than you?

You are but a fool who would dine on his own feces and sip his own urine, thinking he alone has all he needs to sustain him — undeserving of the life she has granted you.

— An Open Letter to the Sons of the Monarchy | Compiled Letters of the Queendom

THE VOID

1 DAY AFTER THE OPENING CEREMONY

"I see you've returned."

"You knew I would," Brandi said, rolling her eyes at Zareal's statement as she looked around the void.

It was wider than it had been before, but it was still pitch black and empty. No stars graced the emptiness as they did on the ceiling of her domain, and she wondered when it would begin to look as Zareal had described it. He sat in the same chair as before, but where there had only been two seats the first time she arrived, now there were three. She looked at it before walking over and flopping down into the plush coolness of the armchair across from him.

"I've heard that you've been busy wreaking havoc in the surface realm," Zareal said with a grin.

"Is that what we're calling it?" Brandi asked, rolling her eyes. "But yeah. I guess you could say that."

"Tell me all about it," he said, leaning forward.

"Do you want to hear about it because I'm your daughter or because you hate this realm?"

"Can't it be both?"

Brandi chuckled at that and sank back into the chair as she recounted the story to Zareal. The queendom was in complete disarray and, as expected, the queen focused all her resources on finding Brandi and sending the rebels to the gods. Pine became the liaison for the news outlets, making sure that the major reporters put out a story Brandi approved of — reminding Brandi just how useful her gift of persuasion truly was. And with Russ joining the others at the tower with Sarah as her Carnian consort, things were beginning to move ahead as planned.

"So, you decided to leave the queen and three of her consorts in the mortal realm?" Zareal asked after Brandi finished her story. "Why? Did you not go to the ceremony with the singular purpose of returning every member of the monarchy to your gods?"

"Because at least three consorts are needed to crown a new queen," Brandi answered, offering Zareal a shrug. "And sometimes plans go awry. When they do, you have to make a new plan."

"Oh?" Zareal asked, lifting his brows. "Enlighten me, then. What forced you to change your mind?"

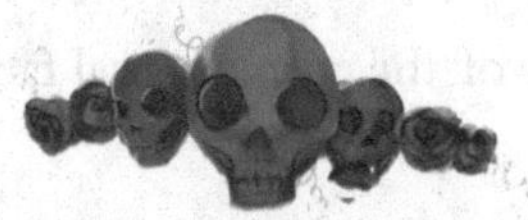

ROTHE'S DOMAIN — THE QUEEN'S TOWER
DAY OF THE OPENING CEREMONY

"Hello, Brandi."

Brandi's eyes darted up at the sound of her name, and her green eyes pinned Grace to where she stood on the opposite side of the room. Their eyes met in the mirror Brandi stood in front of and they stared at each other before Brandi returned her attention to adjusting the laces on her boots.

She'd returned to the dorms meant for the shadows with Jack and Russ to prepare for the opening ceremony while Pine and Remy stayed behind in her domain. Royal had returned to Carna's domain with Crown to check on the other shaders since they'd abandoned Freya's domain. He also wanted to check on the progress of their shapeshifting, but according to Crown's report, Tiki and Lia had already mastered it. So, their new plan was simple — Tiki and Lia would meet them at the tower to help the rebels send everyone to the gods. Najé would organize the rebels, Noble would organize the remaining shadows, Mara would get them unrestricted access to the tower, and Sal would escort Sarah to the ball. Every person involved with the opening ceremony was already meant to be in the tower — it was the only reason Brandi had agreed to wait in the dorms until everyone else was in place. But apparently, there was at least one member of the current royal family who managed to sneak out.

Brandi finished lacing up her boots, and when she was done, she turned to face Grace, who stood just inside the door with her back pressed against the wood, her hands resting on the doorknob behind her. Her red hair had been curled and a single braid fed into an elaborate bun at the top of her head. Dozens of tiny pearls clung to the braid and dangled from the end of the stretched ringlets that hung down by her ears. Her makeup was bold, with deep purple eyeshadow and dark eyeliner emphasizing her hazel eyes and thick lashes. She wore a short, strapless pink romper that had seen better days, and Brandi guessed it's what she'd worn to get her hair and makeup done. It wasn't anything appropriate for a princess to be seen in, and it was reckless of her to navigate through the halls of the tower looking like that, but she carried herself with a confidence that made Brandi doubt she would care if someone did see her. But everything from her short height and modest features to her reckless behavior and unwavering gaze was exactly as Pine had described her. Unlike Sarah, she carried the air of a princess with her. She didn't wilt under Brandi's scrutiny either, choosing to offer up a tentative smile instead.

"What are you doing here, Grace?"

"I see you already know who I am," Grace said, an air of nervous laughter lifting her words. "I guess I should be honored."

"Or grateful I'm not sending you to the gods," Brandi suggested. "Answer my question."

"Right," Grace breathed, nodding her head. "I came to speak with you."

"Obviously," Brandi snorted, rolling her eyes and crossing her arms. "About what?"

"Your plans for tonight."

Brandi narrowed her eyes at that. The only people she'd spoken to about what would happen that night where the shadows who would be helping her. Even Sarah had been left out of the loop to limit the risk of the plan being exposed. So, Brandi knew there was no way under Rothe's sun that Grace Bertanal should know about it.

"Choose your next words carefully," Brandi warned, already feeling the warmth of her power seeping into her blood as she dropped her hands to her sides.

"I'm not here to cause trouble," Grace whispered, her eyebrows pinching together as her eyes darted to Brandi's hand in her pocket. "I just came to set the board," she said. "The game's not fun unless everyone knows they're playing, right?"

Brandi's eyes widened at those words and her muscles tensed, flames racing up her back and down her arms, and she closed her eyes. She took a deep breath and held it before releasing it in a slow stream, choosing to embrace the heat saturating her bones before it burned her alive. She'd learned from Remy that fighting her power only made it worse — if she wanted to control it, she had to accept it. And as steam escaped from between her lips, she was grateful to feel her internal temperature lowering. Her fingers still tingled with lingering heat, but when she opened her eyes to face Grace, she was able to do it with a calm demeanor.

"You're Azinne's vessel."

It wasn't a question. Grace's choice of words hadn't been a mistake, and Brandi could almost laugh at herself for not realizing the truth earlier. She'd been consumed with so much rage toward Bert, that she'd been unable to accept that he wasn't a vessel for the time beings. It had blinded her to the other options of who it could be. Even after she'd determined that it had to be someone of high standing at the Queen's Tower, it never occurred to her to think it was the girl who shouldn't have existed in the first place. But knowing what she did now of Zareal and the existence of her own domain, she understood just how powerful the time beings were — she had a better concept of what they were capable of.

"He allowed my father to meet my mother before the gods punished him," Grace said, answering Brandi's unasked questions. "The best way to explain it is that I was born in an alternate timeline," she explained, "a temporary one."

"For how long?"

"Twenty years," she answered, and Brandi nodded, thinking about the theory Lena had posed when she'd visited her at the academy, searching for answers. What they had believed was someone testing out the powers of time manipulation was actually a time being creating a temporary timeline — one that probably looped certain dates and events in order to allow Grace to exist. Which meant their other theory was also probably correct — Bert and the queen would have worked to suppress the information of the repeated natural disasters, especially since the people who would have been affected by them lived in the outskirts. It didn't surprise Brandi that the monarchy was so sure no one would advocate for them — no one did. If it hadn't been for Freya telling her about the time beings, Brandi would have never known anything about it herself.

"When you saw my father at the temple of your goddess, Azinne had just returned his memories of my existence to him and my mother."

"He wasn't praying for a daughter," Brandi whispered. "He was praying for his daughter to survive the bid for the throne."

"Most likely," Grace said with a nod. "But I don't really care about winning the throne."

"And why not?" Brandi asked, giving Grace a once over. "You're clearly preparing to announce your bid for it at the opening ball."

"Because you're going to destroy it, aren't you?" Grace asked, tilting her head. "What good is a throne that belongs to a dying queendom?"

"Then why are you here?"

"Because I want you to succeed," Grace said, rolling back her shoulders as she met Brandi's gaze. "I tried to talk to Sarah, but she shut me down."

"She's smarter than she looks sometimes," Brandi admitted.

"I wouldn't have hurt her."

"It doesn't matter," Brandi stated. "She wouldn't have been able to help you."

"Which is why I'm here," Grace said, taking a tentative step forward. "I want you to reconsider sending the queen and her consorts to the gods tonight."

"That's a bold request," Brandi said, keeping her voice even. "Pretend for a moment I care about your reasoning."

"If you end the queendom tonight, that ends the game," Grace whispered.

"That's the point."

"You don't understand," Grace said, shaking her head. "Azinne is looking to be entertained. If you end the game before he's had his fun, he'll destroy this realm regardless of whatever he's promised you."

"That's always the threat, isn't it?" Brandi sighed, closing her eyes and dragging her fingers across her forehead. "Do this or the realm will be destroyed," she said, mocking Freya's voice. "Do that or I'll destroy the realm," she scoffed, dropping her voice to mimic Azinne. "I am truly sick of everyone thinking I care about this realm anymore."

"If you don't, why are you here?"

"No," Brandi snapped, the word sharp as her glare. "You don't come in here and question my motives."

"My apologies," Grace whispered, stumbling back into the door. "I just..." Grace's words trailed off as her eyes fell to the ground. "I have my own reasons for trying to bring down the queendom. But I can't do it alone."

"It's not my responsibility to do what you can't."

"I know," Grace whispered. "But isn't it natural to reach out for help when you need it?"

Brandi scoffed at her words. For most people, Grace's question might have struck a chord within them — softened their hearts toward her cause. But they only served to infuriate Brandi. It seemed that no matter the situation, she was always the help that people reached for. When Najé needed someone to watch her back on a mission — when the queen wanted a problem solved — when the gods needed to save the realm — when the time beings wanted to see the realm destroyed — it never changed. She was one woman and yet she was meant to hold the solutions to every problem. Even if she could be the person everyone needed her to be, she didn't want to be. She wanted to be the kind of woman who was left alone — who carried none of the expectations others placed on her shoulders. And the idea of Grace needing her for yet another task repulsed her.

"It's natural to solve your own problems," Brandi stated.

"Of course," Grace whispered, dropping her gaze to the floor. "You're right."

"What's in it for me?" Brandi asked after a beat of silence. "I don't do anything simply for the sake of doing it."

"Azinne," Grace said, her head snapping up and her hazel eyes brightening with hope. "I'll tell you everything I know about him. And after twenty years in an alternate timeline that no one else seems to know exists," she shrugged, "I know plenty about him, his powers, and the Galaxiers."

"Sharing that with me is not in your best interest," Brandi said, narrowing her eyes at Grace. "Why would you offer me that information when his soul is linked with yours?" Brandi questioned. "If he forfeits his existence, then so do you."

"I don't care. I'm not a tool for someone else to use," Grace stated, lifting her chin. "I would rather him fail at his little game than to win at my expense."

Brandi let Grace's words settle over the room as she mulled over them, rolling them through her thoughts the same way she would a cube of ice in her mouth. She wasn't excited about the prospect of helping Grace Bertanal, but she couldn't deny that what she offered was appealing. She didn't care much about Azinne — she already had a decent grasp on the kind of personality he possessed, and she didn't doubt that what Grace already said about him was true. He was in this realm looking for a thrill — something to distract him from the monotony of eternity. He envied the gods who played within the rules of their own realms and he craved the recognition that came from tampering with the lives of mortals.

But the information on the Galaxiers was something she couldn't just ignore. She wanted to know more about the supposed supervisors of the universe that held both Zareal and Azinne in chokeholds they couldn't escape from. Especially if she won this twisted little game with Azinne and he followed through on his promise to allow her to meet them.

There were more variables to consider than her own emotions and she sucked her teeth in irritation at the realization, but there would be no point in playing by Azinne's rules if she wasn't going to get the outcome she wanted. And Jack wanted to save the realm. Which meant that, for the time being, playing nice with Bert's daughter was her best option.

"Your father won't see another rising of Rothe's sun," Brandi warned. "That's not up for debate."

"Fine," Grace whispered.

"What do you want me to do then," Brandi asked. "It better be simple."

"It is," Grace said, her face splitting into a wide grin as her shoulders relaxed. "Just wait here a moment," she said. "I've got a dress for you to wear."

"A dress?"

"Yes," Grace said, her hand pausing on the doorknob as she turned back to grin at Brandi. "I've got a change of clothes for Jack too."

"Why?"

"Well, you're not shadows anymore, are you? So, it's time you step into the spotlight and show this realm exactly who you are."

"And who do you think I am."

"I know that you're incredible," Grace chuckled. "But I can't tell you which labels you'll allow yourself to accept. All I know," she said, shrugging, "is you can't make a grand entrance looking like that. So, I'll be right back."

She disappeared out the door and Brandi sank to the ground with a deep sigh, exhaustion pulling at her limbs and weighing her shoulders down as she dropped her head into her hands. She'd never intended to reveal herself to the realm, and by force of habit, she considered calling on Freya to ask for strength, but she stopped herself with a sharp shake of her head before pushing herself back to her feet.

"No," she whispered to herself as she met her own gaze in the mirror she'd been standing in front of when Grace had entered the room. "I refuse to ask Freya for help."

She'd spent her entire life believing her own power was Freya's. Knowing that it wasn't — that she'd been deceived and lied to so that Freya could manipulate her into using her power for her own gain, placed a rift between them Brandi had no interest in mending. Like Grace, she, too, would never again be a tool to be used on someone else's behalf. She would never again allow her actions and her future to be decided on by anyone but herself.

"I'm a god," Brandi said, laughing at herself as she thought back on all the times she'd said the words before and never believed them. "And I'm more powerful than she can ever be. Besides," she scoffed, turning away from the mirror as two soft knocks sounded at the door and Grace poked her head in carrying a dress box with a pair of stiletto heels. "I'd be better off praying to myself."

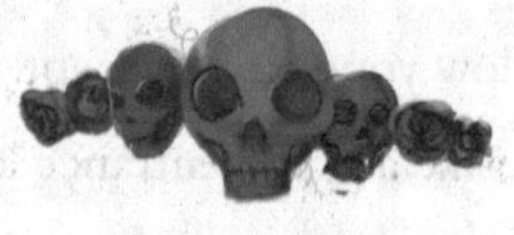

THE VOID

1 DAY AFTER THE OPENING CEREMONY

Brandi heard Azinne's chuckle before she saw him appear in the empty chair to her left, and she decided to let his entrance be an excuse for letting her story trail off. She turned to look at Azinne as he sat with his ankle crossed over his leg, his starry eyes as wide as his grin as he glanced between the two of them.

"Look at this family reunion!" He laughed. "Who would've thought I'd ever be sitting between my mentor and his half-goddess daughter?"

"You invited him here?" Zareal asked, directing his question toward Brandi while narrowing his eyes at Azinne.

"I did," Brandi said, leaning forward.

"Plot twist," Azinne chuckled, looking over at Zareal. "Despite your thoughts of me, I'm not disrespectful enough to enter someone else's void without permission."

"Then maybe you can enlighten me, Brandi," he said, turning to meet her gaze. "Why have you brought us together?"

"Because you two want similar things and I," she said, pointing to herself, "am not a fan of navigating so many expectations."

"So, you brought us here to agree on a method of destruction?" Azinne asked. When Brandi nodded, his eyebrows lifted as he cackled again. "I do adore you, Brandi! This tiny realm would not be the same without you!"

"Care to explain?" Zareal asked, a look of wary confusion written on his face as he sighed, watching Azinne.

"Your daughter has decided to consolidate and conquer!" He laughed. "I've never seen this outcome before."

"I thought you saw everything?" Brandi asked.

"I told you once before, didn't I?" Azinne said. "We can't see the time of other time-beings."

"So, once your powers awakened," Zareal explained, "you became a blind spot to us both."

"Which is why the other time beings didn't know where you were when you disappeared," Brandi said, connecting his words to what he'd told her last time. "So, this meeting is a genuine surprise for both of you?" They nodded and Brandi filed that information away for later as she rested her elbows on her knees.

"Azinne's right," she said. "I brought you here to join forces. As it stands right now, you" she said pointing to Azinne, "want to destroy the queendom and you," she said pointing to the Zareal, "want to destroy the realm. And both of you want me to aid you with that. So, my thought is," she said, smirking, "we do both. I'll destroy the queendom first so Azinne can report back to the Galaxiers, and then I'll destroy the entire realm so Zareal can find some peace."

"And why would you help us like this?" Zareal asked.

"Are you disappointed?"

"Not in the least," he chuckled. "It would make my eternity much easier to know I don't need to end my daughter's life when I destroy things. But it's unusual," he said, his dark eyes boring into Brandi's green ones. "I know I am the one to offer this choice to you, and while I am glad you accepted it, I doubted you would," he admitted. "Your mother is the creator of this realm, and this is your home. Why are you so willing to destroy it?"

"You'll think my reasons are too simple," Brandi scoffed, looking away from them.

"Do share them anyway," Azinne prodded. "I would like to know the answer to this as well."

"You've both promised me to spare Jack's life," Brandi answered with a shrug. "And the gods have done nothing but put him in danger. I can't forgive that."

"The depths of your love for this man is astounding," Azinne whispered, his eyebrows shooting up his forehead. "I should like to meet him one day."

"Same," Zareal nodded. "Is our mercy for him the only reason you've been swayed to our cause?"

"Absolutely," Brandi said, without missing a beat. "The gods have linked themselves to us, but I refuse to remain as some dying god simply because Freya didn't get what she wanted," Brandi huffed. "Besides, I have my own plans for this realm."

"Oh," Azinne asked, leaning forward. "And what plans are those?"

"Mine," Brandi answered, refusing to tell either of them any more than that.

She accepted that she couldn't lie while using her powers as a time being to access the void. But that didn't mean she had to answer every question they asked her. She didn't need to tell them that Azinne had promised her a meeting with the Galaxiers if she entertained him, or that Remy had already begun training the vessels in how to control their powers as gods — that there may be a way to reject the gods if they got strong enough. Her plans were bigger than anything they or Freya could hope to predict, but for now, she would continue to let them believe she was nothing more than a pawn in their game.

"I understand," Zareal said, pushing to his feet and extending his hand toward her. "Whatever your reasons are, I accept them. That's what a father does, isn't it?"

"I guess," Brandi said, accepting his hand. It was cool to the touch, and she let him pull her to her feet. Azinne popped up out of his chair as well, a giddy smile on his face as he looked between the two of them who had questioning looks for him.

"I can help her train," he offered. "It's not like I have anything else better to do until she makes another move on the queendom."

"And your vessel?" Zareal asked.

"Will be fine without me," Azinne said, waving his hand through the air. "So, what are we starting her with?"

"Let's start with your name," Zareal offered, a smile pulling at his lips as he turned to face Brandi.

"I already have like three of those," Brandi sighed, thinking of all the nicknames she'd been given from Lia, Noble, and Pine. "I don't really need another."

"This is your true name," Zareal explained, "gifted to you from one time being," he said, pointing to himself, "to another."

"You'll need to know it to fully access your power as one of us," Azinne added. "It's like the key to the universe."

"Okay," Brandi sighed. "So, what is it?"

"Zarie."

"You named me after yourself?" Brandi scoffed.

"It's what father's do," he chuckled. "Go ahead and call it into the void. Once you do, it should open for you."

Brandi lifted her eyebrows in skepticism but didn't argue. She knew names carried entire identities within them and as Azinne and Zareal watched her with expectation, her stomach clenched at the idea of what could rest on the other side of it. But she'd already discovered who she was and accepted that she was the child of a god and a time being. There was no turning back on that knowledge now so, she faced the void and called out the name she'd been given.

"Zarie!"

Within moments, the void that had been devoid of light lit up with stars. It filled with planets, galaxies, and solar systems she'd never seen before, even within the ceilings of her own domain, and her green eyes widened as she looked around it.

"This," Zareal said, emphasizing the word as he stepped up next to her and a path of light formed in front of them, "is the void."

"It's beautiful," Brandi whispered.

"And it's yours, Zarie," he said, beaming at being able to use her true given name. He pressed a gentle hand to her back and gestured toward the path ahead of them. "Let us begin."

TO BE CONTINUED...

Acknowledgments

As always, I'm going to get straight to the point.

This book wouldn't exist without:

Benjamin Lockhart. Every book I write is because of him.

My mama, daddy, and brother. Because I will never forget the people who loved me first.

Audra Russell. My biggest champion, my friend, my sister.

My patreon supporters. Thank you for believing in these stories of mine.

Kim, Neeks, La, Tatiana, Celeste, and Amanda. My community. I appreciate you all more than words can convey.

My beta readers. Thank you for helping me shape this book.

My readers. Thank you, always, for trusting me with your time and imagination. I hope you enjoyed it.

♥ Chelsea

About C. M. Lockhart

C. M. Lockhart (also known as Chelsea) is a Black writer of fantasy because she loves creating worlds, exploring relationships, and writing stories about Black girls who aren't all that nice. She is the founder of Written in Melanin LLC — which encompasses a podcast and YouTube channel of the same name — and the Melanin Library, an online database of books written by Black authors.

She is also a lover of video games and anime, so whenever she isn't reading and writing — or talking about reading and writing — she's watching anime, playing her Switch, and dreaming about the day her books get animated.

Find her on social media @CLockhartWrite, @WrittenNMelanin, & @Melanin_Library, and support her works at https://Patreon.com/CMLockhart